For Such a Time

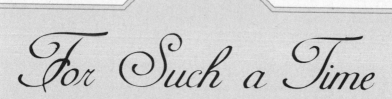

For Such a Time

KATE BRESLIN

BETHANYHOUSE
a division of Baker Publishing Group
Minneapolis, Minnesota

Published by Bethany House Publishers
11400 Hampshire Avenue South
Bloomington, Minnesota 55438
www.bethanyhouse.com

Bethany House Publishers is a division of
Baker Publishing Group, Grand Rapids, Michigan

Printed in the United States of America

Library of Congress Cataloging-in-Publication Data

Breslin, Kate.
For such a time / Kate Breslin.
    pages cm.
    Summary: "A powerful retelling of the biblical story of Esther set during WWII: Blond
and blue-eyed Jewess Hadassah Benjamin must save her people—even if she cannot save herself"— Provided by publisher.
    ISBN 978-0-7642-1160-7 (pbk.)
    1. Jewish girls—Fiction. 2. World War, 1939-1945—Jews—Fiction 3. World War, 1939-
1945—Jewish resistance—Fiction. I. Title.
    PS3602.R4575F67 2014
    813′.6—dc23   2013039563

Scripture quotation in chapter 5, Esther 2:11, is from the King James Version of the Bible.

Scripture quotation in chapter 37, Hebrews 10:39, is from the Holy Bible, New International Version®.
NIV®. Copyright © 1973, 1978, 1984, 2011 by Biblica, Inc.™ Used by permission of Zondervan. All
rights reserved worldwide. www.zondervan.com

Scripture quotation at the close of the author's acknowledgments is from the New Revised Standard
Version of the Bible, copyright © 1989, by the Division of Christian Education of the National Council
of the Churches of Christ in the United States of America. Used by permission. All rights reserved.

Unless otherwise indicated, Scripture quotations are from the Holy Bible, New International Ver-
sion®. NIV®. Copyright © 1973, 1978, 1984 by Biblica, Inc.™ Used by permission of Zondervan. All
rights reserved worldwide. www.zondervan.com

This is a work of historical reconstruction; the appearances of certain historical figures are therefore
inevitable. All other characters, however, are products of the author's imagination, and any resem-
blance to actual persons, living or dead, is coincidental.

Cover design by Kathleen Lynch/Black Kat Design

Front cover photograph of woman © Daniel Murtagh / Millennium Images, UK
Front cover photograph of European Jews © Getty Images

Author is represented by Hartline Literary Agency

14   15   16   17   18   19   20   7   6   5   4   3   2   1

For John, my beloved

When Esther's words were reported to Mordecai, he sent back this answer . . . "And who knows but that you have come to your royal position for such a time as this?"

Esther 4:12–14

1

Esther also was taken to the king's palace. . . .

Esther 2:8

MONDAY, FEBRUARY 14, 1944

The stench was unmistakable.

Seeping through the walls of the two-story chalet, turning pungent from the warmth of an oil furnace, the insidious odor drifted upstairs to where Stella lay asleep on a window seat. It filled her nostrils and roused her with a jerk; she struggled upright, shielding her eyes against the bright light penetrating the glass.

Dawn. The burning had begun.

Beyond the chilled pane lay the Ceaseless White. Stella gazed out at the endless mantle of snow punctuated by clusters of bare-limbed trees, a handful of farmhouses, and St. Jakob's onion-shaped cupola in the distance. To the west, the nebulous sky grew dark as the stacks of Dachau's *Krematorium* belched gritty smoke against a colorless sun, permeating the air with a sickening-sweet odor.

She imagined the tiny charred flakes, soaring high, borne off to God Forsaken . . .

Despair struck like an angry fist; she grabbed at the sill, feeling dizzy and out of breath as she pressed her bruised forehead against the cold glass. How was it that she still felt anything?

The nausea soon passed, and she turned from the window—away from death—to stare at the austere whitewashed walls that hemmed her in. Not the train, not the Block at Dachau where she'd been held for months, but a room. Her makeshift prison for untold days.

Why was she here . . . and why had *she* been singled out? The repetitive questions preyed on her anxiety as she began the day's ritual of scouring her surroundings for clues.

Uncle Morty once said that a person's possessions spoke much about them. Stella believed their lack often revealed more. This room, for instance, like her dignity, was stripped bare except for a low-slung cot and a nightstand disguised as a battered fruit crate. Nothing else—least of all any frivolous female comforts that might capture her interest. No vanity with ruffled seat, no perfume bottles, lipstick cassettes, or cosmetics to clutter its top. Even the windowpane had felt brittle against her skin, bereft of any delicate lace curtains. With the war in full swing, no silk stockings hung idly over the back of a chair (had there been one) or tumbled from an open dresser drawer (had there been one). Not even a shard of mirrored glass hung on the stark walls. She'd simply been locked away upstairs in an empty room, the fabled Rapunzel in her tower. Except for the hair . . .

Hardly a princess, Stella thought bitterly, smoothing blistered fingertips over the new growth at her scalp. She surveyed her spindly extremities—barely discernible arms and legs that protruded from the capped sleeves and knee-length hem of her blue cotton dress. She looked more like the room: an empty husk, lifeless, genderless. Temporary . . .

The faint purr of a car's engine drew her attention back to the window. A black Mercedes approached the chalet, cutting a path through the snow that concealed the road. The disjointed white cross of the *Hakenkreuz* emblazoned its door.

Jew Killers. Stella froze as the Nazi staff car pulled up beside the house. Fragments of memory collided with her mounting apprehension. The gritty-faced *Kapo*—a Jew trusted by the Nazis to guard their Block of prisoners at Dachau—had stuffed her into the blue dress. The feel of warm wool against her skin as she was wrapped in a blanket and carried. The dark trunk of a car . . .

The driver wore the black uniform of the *Schutzstaffel* and exited first before rushing around to open the passenger door. The man who emerged next stood tall and broad-shouldered in a heavy greatcoat. His presence evoked every aspect of authority. Dominance. Even the cane he gripped in his right hand failed to diminish his aura of power.

He looked up at her window. Stella's heart pounded. Did some intuitive force reveal to him her hiding place, or had he already known? She pulled back from the sill, then quickly changed her mind, meeting his stare.

His face was a canvas of strength—rock-hard features fortified with asperity, amplified by the grim line at his mouth and the tautness of his squared jaw. Features much accustomed to pain. More in giving it than receiving it, she decided.

Beneath his black officer's cap with its skull-and-bones death's-head insignia, eyes of an indiscernible color watched her a long moment. Without looking away, he raised his free hand and snapped his fingers, bringing his driver to heel like a trained beast. He passed his cane to the underling without comment and then strode to the front door.

The bell sounded below, and every nerve in Stella's body screamed. She heard the frantic voice of the housekeeper—her jailer—greet the Nazi.

Pressing chapped palms against her thighs, she was vaguely aware of the dampness of sweat seeping through the thin cotton dress. Her pulse hammered in her throat as the first wooden step leading upstairs groaned beneath his weight. She'd heard about medical experiments performed on prisoners. Was he a doctor? Was that why she'd been brought here?

A key turned in the lock. Stella's body bucked in reaction, launching her to her feet. She became aware of a winded sound, a shallow, rapid rushing of air—and realized it was her own breath.

"*Gut*, you're awake."

The stout, ruddy-cheeked *Hausfrau* stood on the threshold. Not the Jew Killer.

Stella's knees nearly buckled.

"You have an important visitor. Follow me downstairs."

Stella didn't immediately grasp the command. Fear rooted her to a spot by the window, a sapling anchored to earth. She could only blink at the sour-faced woman standing at the door.

"Are you deaf, *Jude*? I said come with me!"

The sharp words freed Stella's invisible fetters and she shuffled forward, swallowing the bubble of terror in her throat. *In deference lay my survival, in deference lay my survival . . .*

"Your kind brings nothing but trouble," the housekeeper hissed before turning to leave.

Stella ground her teeth to keep silent. She wasn't surprised at the woman's hostility. Even the word *Jew* had become dangerous to utter. Deadly.

Following the Hausfrau downstairs, Stella felt panic escalate with each step. She fought it the only way she knew how: by lulling herself into a languid state that had so often shielded her sanity. She became oblivious to the gold-gilt lithographs framed along the stairwell and the moan of warped wood beneath her bare feet. Dust particles swirling in a shaft of winter sunlight from an upstairs window went unnoticed.

When pain from a protruding nail on the step finally jarred her benumbed state, Stella blinked and stared down at the blood oozing from her torn flesh. Her chest tightened with flashes of memory. *Bloody hands . . . gunshot . . .*

"Move!"

Like an ill-wakened sleeper, she raised her head to glare at the housekeeper. What was the point in deference? She was already dead inside. Did it matter what they did with her body?

Fear and disgust flashed across the other woman's face before she hastily resumed her descent. Stella followed, determined to buoy her defiance with each step—

Until she came face-to-face with *him*.

Terror sank its claws in deep. As the housekeeper fled to the safety of the kitchen, Stella clung to her last shred of newfound courage and focused on the man before her. He swiftly removed his hat, the brim pitching flecks of snow against her cheek.

From the window above, she'd imagined him much older. Stella was surprised to see that, up close, he was nearer in age to her own twenty-three years. His thick russet hair, shot through with gold, lay close-cropped against his head, while eyes—a vibrant shade of green—studied her with open curiosity. "Good morning, *Fräulein*."

Startled by his deep voice, Stella teetered backward on the step. He caught her bony wrist to steady her. When she tried to wrench free, the gloved fingers held firm. His dark brows rose in challenge. "I trust you're feeling better?"

The ice from his brim numbed her cheek. Stella fought for calm as she glanced from his arrogant face to the imposing grip on her wrist. She could smell him—new leather and pine, the dampness of snow.

"I can assure you that you're quite safe here."

Safe? Her free hand fisted at her side. How often had that word been used, that promise given and broken at Dachau?

The snowflakes melted against her skin. Stella raised her fist to wipe at the wetness; his hand was faster, and she flinched at the contact of soft leather against her cheek. Would he beat her now for being weak, mistaking the water for tears? Or maybe criticize her first?

But the Jew Killer did nothing, said nothing. Even his touch felt surprisingly gentle. She watched his gaze drop to the hand still in his grasp. In that he took care as well, as one by one he uncurled her clenched fingers. Turning her hand over, he assessed the bruises on her knuckles and joints.

Stella's fear battled against his oddly comforting touch. The heat she could feel through his leather glove made him seem almost . . . human.

The raw fury in his eyes shattered the illusion. "You have my word," he said mildly. "While you are here, no one can harm you."

Clicking his heels together, he offered a curt nod. "Allow me to introduce myself. Colonel Aric von Schmidt, SS *Kommandant* to the transit camp at Theresienstadt in Czechoslovakia."

When she made no response, he added, "Lucky for you, on my way to Munich I stopped at Dachau to see my cousin Frau Gertz. I also chose to visit the camp while I was here and oversee the first transfer of laborers into my command."

An effort to smile died on his lips. "You see, I'm relatively new to my post, so I can hardly afford mistakes. Nor am I a man who tolerates them. When my sergeant informed me that one body from the train's manifest was unaccounted for, I decided to track it down myself. Care to guess who it was?"

Stella shook her head, too afraid to speak.

"No? Well, here you are—proof of my good deed. And if you're wondering why I didn't put you on that train, it was due to an inconsistency on your papers. They state you are Aryan, Fräulein Muller. So you will explain to me now why they have been stamped JUDE."

Stella lowered her head to hide her resentment. The false identification papers Uncle Morty had purchased for her in secret from Berlin had done nothing to save her. She'd spent the past several months living in quarters unfit for livestock. She'd worked outside in the cold, wearing thin rags and wooden clogs several sizes too big. Not even stockings to protect her feet from chafing or frostbite. And hunger—the Nazis had tried to starve them all.

"Answer me!" he snapped at her, all pretense at politeness gone.

Stella's head shot up as she choked on her fear. "*Gestapo* . . . at the checkpoint . . ."

"Gestapo did this? Why?"

His eyes narrowed on her. Stella's panic exploded. "He wanted to . . . tried to . . . I wouldn't let him . . ." She struggled against his grasp. "Please . . . not my fault . . . !"

"Enough!" His grip was like iron. "I told you that you are safe here. Why do you think I brought you to my cousin's house?"

Stella quit her struggle. The fact that he'd gone to such lengths to save her came on the heels of realizing he wasn't a doctor. Instead of feeling relief, a cold shiver crept up her spine. What did he want? She tried to recall further details from that night, but could remember nothing prior to her awakening days before on the cot upstairs.

It seemed her life had changed in the span of an instant, and this man, this Jew Killer, took credit for the act. Yet Stella had no recollection of him. Nor did she feel gratitude. "I don't understand. Why did you bring me here?"

High on the foyer wall, a Black Forest clock ticked the seconds. Stella held her breath, every nerve attuned to the man's response.

This time his smile reached its destination. Dazzling white, its unexpected warmth surprised and unsettled her. Only his somber green eyes dampened the effect. "Do I need a reason, Fräulein?" A pause. "Very well, I wanted an explanation and you've given it—more or less. I know the Gestapo's breed of men, so I can fill in the blanks." He eyed her a long moment. "Trust me when I tell you that you are not the first to fall victim to their pranks."

Stella's throat tightened with anger. Her experience at the hands of the Gestapo had hardly been a mere joke. She swallowed her ire and said, "And now . . . what will you do with me, Herr Kommandant?"

"Fatten you up like a Christmas *Gänsebraten*, for a start." He glanced at her spare limbs. "Soon you'll return to the pretty dove I imagine you once were."

Stella looked away. Was he toying with her? Morty once told her that her beauty would save her—a "changeling," he'd called his young niece, Stella's blond hair and blue eyes a rarity among their people.

Her uncle had been wrong. Beauty was dangerous, a liability for someone desperate to remain obscure in a crowd, inconspicuous to the eyes of soldiers.

She turned to him, this time her bitterness unchecked. "Christmas goose or fatted calf, both meet the same end, do they not, Herr Kommandant?"

The muscle at his jaw clenched. Too late, Stella realized her foolish outburst. Horrified and amazed at her own audacity, she braced against the expected Consequence. Surely he would beat her, or worse—

"Frau Gertz!"

The force of his bellow nearly knocked Stella back. He continued to hold her in his grip until his cousin appeared cautiously from the kitchen.

"Get her a coat. We're leaving."

Frau Gertz bobbed her head like some peasant to a feudal lord before she rushed toward the closet. Stella could only watch, frozen in place. The colonel promised she would be safe . . . *here.* And now they were leaving.

The Hausfrau returned with a coat disguised as a frayed white shawl.

"Have you any shoes, Fräulein?"

He sounded impatient. Stella gaped at her bloodied feet, her mind seized by more forgotten memories. Someone at Dachau had taken her shoes, her clothes . . .

She knelt naked in the snow, her soul seared with humiliation, her body numbed by cold. Faces streaked with dirt and

14

pity surrounded her as though she were some freak in a carnival. Soon guards dragged her away. Her flesh burned with pain, then fear. Fear for the little hands shoving a bundle in her direction. A blouse . . . little hands in danger . . . crying hands . . . struggle with the guards . . . the crack of a rifle . . .

Images ripped through Stella like shards of glass. She hunched forward, dizzy with pain, her eyes shut against the brutal past.

"I will not ask you again!"

The colonel's frighteningly cold voice sounded a thousand kilometers away. She clawed her way up through the terrifying haze and struggled to recall his question. *Shoes . . .*

"Gone," Stella managed to say before her knees buckled. She collapsed toward the floor just as he caught her and hauled her against him. She made a puny attempt to push away, but his strength clearly outmatched hers. Exhausted, she slumped against him, only vaguely aware of the shawl being placed across her shoulders.

She cried out in protest as he lifted her into his arms. That seemed to fuel his anger. "You fed her while I was away, didn't you?"

"Oh, she ate." Frau Gertz's blunt fingers bunched in the folds of her white apron. "She ate food enough for three people! Then she threw it up on my floor. Now she refuses anything but broth."

The Hausfrau shot an accusing look at Stella, as if demanding corroboration. Stella's face heated. She'd been so hungry. Afterward, she'd sworn that no one, especially this nasty woman, would ever again witness her humiliation. So far, the broth seemed safe enough.

"What about clothing, cousin?" The colonel's tone held an edge. "I had assumed that for the week I left her in your care, my money would more than compensate you for your trouble."

"But you said to use discretion," the Hausfrau whined. "How could I go to town and buy new clothes without the tradesmen asking questions? She is so much smaller than me—"

"I'm done with excuses! Now give her *your* coat, and shoes for her feet. *Schnell!*"

His bark sent her running back to the closet. She returned with a voluminous black wool coat and a pair of dirty pink house slippers. "My other shoes are still at the cobbler's. . . ."

Her voice trailed off. The colonel was staring at the boots on her feet. The Hausfrau looked alarmed. Stella felt a spurt of vindication. "Please, cousin."

Before she could utter another plea, he swore and snatched up the clothing. He wheeled around and departed with Stella, leaving a startled Frau Gertz in his wake.

Outside, his driver held the car door open. Once the colonel deposited Stella against the seat, he offered her the coat and slippers. She took them before scooting to the far end of the car. His hulk-like frame followed her inside.

The engine of the Mercedes roared to life while heat blasted from vents in the car's dashboard. Stella bit back a blissful sigh as she hugged the borrowed coat to her chest. Casting a surreptitious glance at the colonel, she found herself caught in his steady, impenetrable gaze.

A brief moment passed before the line at his mouth thinned and his features hardened, as though he'd reached some distasteful conclusion. Alarms began going off in Stella's head as he reached a gloved hand deep inside his coat . . .

A gun! He was going to shoot her! She grabbed the door's handle and pulled. Locked! A scream lodged in her throat as she shut her eyes, pressing her body hard into the leather seat—

"Put this on."

Her eyes flew open. She swallowed her cry when she saw he held not a pistol but a woman's red hairpiece. He offered it to her. "As you've discovered, papers mean little at this stage of the war. We don't want you looking too conspicuous."

With unsteady hands, she fitted the wig so that the strands fell about her shoulders.

"You'll get across the Czech border safely enough," he said when she finished. "But the color doesn't suit you, Fräulein."

Ignoring the petty insult, Stella turned toward the window and struggled to regain her composure.

Outside, emerald fir and barren poplars rushed past the car as it sped along the winding ribbon of road into Germany's lower wine country. The war hadn't yet touched this pristine countryside; instead of burned-out buildings and cratered fields, she saw only arbors, barren of fruit, cast against a backdrop of snowy white. In summer their latticed bowers would again be laden with plump grapes, peacefully unaware of the suffering only a few kilometers away.

Freiheit. Freedom. Stella gazed out at the forested hills and felt a stab of yearning like physical pain. She embraced it, ridding herself of fear as fury from the past several months replaced it. Fury at the old God for abandoning her. Fury at this new one, the uniformed monster beside her who now controlled her life.

Silence stretched with the miles, and though she burned with questions, Stella was grateful for the respite. She had no use for small talk with this Nazi, and having to answer more of his questions could only become a dangerous undertaking.

At Regensburg, a town near the western bank of the Danube River, the colonel ordered a halt at a local *Gasthaus*. He dispatched his driver, Sergeant Grossman, to go inside and procure three lunches. He then turned his attention to her.

"Your papers state you are from Innsbruck. I too am Austrian, from the little town of Thaur, not far from there." His penetrating eyes looked at odds with his smile. "I once knew a man by the name of Muller: Tag Muller. He and his family lived in the town of Innsbruck, where I ventured often as a boy. Are you any relation? I'm sure I would not have forgotten you."

Stella shook her head, glancing at the bruised hands in her lap. Mentally she cursed her false papers. In all of Europe to conjure a birthplace, Morty happened to choose this man's backyard and the name of a family friend!

"Well?"

She moistened her dry lips. "Muller is a common name."

"True. Is your family still there?"

Again she shook her head, refusing to look at him. Stella desperately hoped he would mistake her silence for grief and stop asking questions. Her ploy failed.

"Speak!" He grabbed her chin and turned her face until their eyes locked. "I trust, since you have the ability to make rash remarks, that you can also make intelligent conversation."

Trembling beneath his touch, Stella did not look away. "My parents died when I was five." That much was true, anyway. "I had no other family, so I was taken in and raised by their closest friends." A spurt of defiance made her add, "They were Jews."

Expecting a violent reaction, Stella was surprised when his grip on her eased. In fact, he looked only mildly curious. "Your papers also state you have performed clerical work. Did you attend school at Innsbruck?"

"Yes." It was another lie, though Stella *had* received instruction, but not in any school—not past the age of thirteen when Nuremberg law forbade Jews to receive an education. Instead, Mrs. Bernstein, a retired schoolteacher living upstairs from their old apartment in Mannheim, had tutored her in the basics of bookkeeping and clerical skills.

"How well can you type?"

Stella straightened in her seat. Did he have need of her abilities? "Very well, Herr Kommandant," she said. "I also know shorthand and general accounting." She tried to repress her optimism, painfully aware of the Nazis' verbal traps.

He seemed genuinely pleased. "I'd hoped as much, Stella."

The sound of her name on his lips disturbed her, as though linking them together in some intimate way. Stella wanted nothing personal between them. She'd much rather hate him.

Sergeant Grossman returned with their packages of food. As he began passing them through the open car window, Stella noticed his left wrist bore no hand; the steel hook in its place both frightened and moved her as she watched him struggle with his burden.

The colonel offered her a boxed lunch. Stella vehemently shook her head.

"You will eat," he growled. "Not only did your bones cut into me while I carried you, but you weigh less than a pair of my boots. And if you starve yourself, well . . ." He shot her a calculated look. "We won't be able to plan out your future, will we?"

An artful strategist. She took the box, hating that he'd correctly guessed that her curiosity at his statement would outweigh any risk of nausea. She concentrated on taking small bites of the cheese sandwich and apple slices packed inside while her attention strayed back toward the miles they had crossed.

"Relax." The colonel read her thoughts. "Dachau is only a speck in the distance."

She paused with a dried apple slice halfway to her lips. *What of those who still suffered?* There was no hope for them. Unlike her, they wouldn't be rescued.

But was she safe? Stella stared at the man beside her, this Jew Killer who had taken possession of her. With or without false papers, her life might only stretch as far as the next hour. What did he really want with her? Why had he taken her from Dachau?

Would he ever let her go free?

Her throat ached at the unbearable uncertainty. *Lord, please let me know my fate.*

Silence. Had she expected otherwise? "What is my future, Herr Kommandant?" she managed to whisper.

"That depends on you, Fräulein." His smile was enigmatic. "Can you act as well as you type?"

2

Esther had not revealed her nationality and family background, because Mordecai had forbidden her to do so.

Esther 2:10

H alt!"

The Mercedes rolled to a stop in front of a manned gate at the border blockade into Czechoslovakia. A soldier in the brown uniform of the *Sturmabteilung* marched to their car.

Stella cast a nervous glance at the colonel.

"Stop looking guilty," he whispered, but his smile held a perceptible tightness.

Stella's anxiety intensified. Her safety depended on the colonel. He was the enemy, true, but whatever his motives, he'd so far shown her considerable concern.

The border guard standing outside her car window was a different matter. If their ruse failed, not even the colonel could save her. The Brownshirts would shoot her dead.

The soldier pinned her with a glare as he barked an order at Sergeant Grossman to produce their identification papers. Stella's nostrils flared with the sharp tang of fear. She began fidgeting with the red strands of her hair until the colonel caught her hand in his and gave it a gentle squeeze. Whether a silent reprimand or a token of encouragement, the small gesture helped her regain a measure of control.

"Herr Colonel!"

The car door on Stella's side flew open.

"Where are the woman's papers?" The Brownshirt waved their documents in his hand.

"The Fräulein needs no papers. She's with me."

The young guard's face reddened. "But this is highly irregular, Herr Colonel. She must have papers!"

"I'm running late, Corporal." Now the colonel sounded bored. "Do you purposely delay my urgent business for *der Führer*?"

"*Nein*, of course not." The Brownshirt glanced behind the car. Relief swept across his features. "Please, you will wait here a moment, Herr Colonel."

Sergeant Grossman stared into the rearview mirror. "Gestapo."

Stella followed the colonel's backward glance to a black unmarked car pulling up directly behind them.

The colonel muttered an expletive, then said, "That's all I need—those sniffing dogs." He gripped Stella's shoulder. "It was necessary to bend a few rules in order to get you out of Dachau. No matter what happens, say nothing to them. *Verstehen?*"

Hair prickled at her nape. She nodded, ignoring the pain as his fingers dug into her skin.

A fleshy-faced, stocky man in black leather appeared at the open door. Stella had the fleeting thought that this Gestapo pig actually looked like one. His snout nose was wedged between a pair of rounded spectacles, while his eyes shone like black, wet beads behind the frames. They scrutinized the colonel and then stared at her. "Get out of the car, Fräulein."

Pig-nose uttered the toneless command from lips too red and thick to be considered masculine. Stella couldn't rouse herself. She froze, unable to look away.

His beady eyes narrowed while his nostrils shot twin streams of billowing steam into the cold afternoon. He unholstered his pistol, drew back the slide, and took aim. "Get out, now."

Instinct pushed Stella back against the solid wall of the colonel. She turned to him, knowing her bloodless face conveyed panic.

The muscle at his jaw compressed with fury as he gave her a flicker of a nod.

Pig-nose stepped back while Stella clambered out of the car.

Air froze in her lungs as icy slush pooled inside the slippers; she felt her joints ache all the way up to her teeth. Drawing in several shallow breaths, Stella raised her gaze to him.

Pig-nose stared at her ridiculously shod feet. "Give me your papers, Fräulein."

Two uniformed men approached to stand on either side of him. Pig-nose glared at her. Stella struggled against gravity, tilting her chin to meet his scowl. Cold moisture trickled down her back as the silence ticked off in seconds, palpable sounds like the pulse pounding in her ears.

She didn't hear the car door open. Nor was she more than vaguely aware when the colonel moved to stand beside her.

"Here's what you're looking for, Captain." He thrust her identification papers into the outstretched palm.

Pig-nose scanned the documents. "These have been marked JUDE, Herr Colonel."

His gloved hand whipped out and tore away the red wig. Cold pierced Stella's exposed scalp, stinging her ears. "So, it seems, has she."

The murky eyes behind the glasses barely registered surprise. "Take off the coat."

With jerking motions, Stella removed the warm garment. Pig-nose then grabbed her left wrist, exposing the numbered tattoo near her elbow. "She has all the attributes."

He cast another mocking smile at her dirty, water-soaked slippers before he crumpled her papers and tossed them to the ground. Stella watched the remnants of her life grow damp and soiled in the dirty snow like so much refuse.

He signaled the guard on his right toward the colonel's car. "We will need more details on this matter, Herr Colonel. You and your party will accompany us back to the Gestapo office in Regensburg. My man will escort you."

More courteous words; their ominous weight buried Stella like an avalanche. She struggled to breathe, tasting the danger in them, the promise of death.

"That won't be necessary, Captain."

The colonel's congenial tone was welcome relief. Stella's exhausted limbs, numbed with cold, wavered beneath her.

"I requested Fräulein Muller months ago from Austria," the colonel continued smoothly. She glanced at him as he gave her arm a warning squeeze. "She was my brother's secretary in Linz—he generously allowed me the use of her services at Theresienstadt, where I've been assigned as Kommandant by the *Reichsführer*. Unfortunately she was arrested on her way to Munich, where we were to meet. If you'll check her papers closely, you'll see the mistake."

He smiled a cold smile. "Himmler himself admitted it was great luck that I happened to find her at Dachau, though he was perturbed that the Gestapo's error delayed me in reaching my new post."

The colonel was a better liar than she was! Stella watched as his implied intimacy with the same powerful man who also controlled the Gestapo had its desired effect. Pig-nose's red smirk faded. He straightened and holstered his pistol.

His speculative expression darted between Stella and the colonel. Then he snapped his fingers at the man beside him and pointed to the crumpled, water-stained wad on the ground. The orderly retrieved Stella's papers, and Pig-nose made a great show of rereading them before he thrust them back at the colonel, along with Stella's red wig.

"I trust you will inform Herr Reichsführer that Captain Otto Meinz, of Gestapo Regensburg, gave you no cause for further delay, Herr Colonel?"

"I will, of course, report your expediency in the matter, Captain."

Pig-nose thrust out his arm. "*Heil* Hitler!"

The colonel returned the salute as he lifted Stella by the waist and stuffed her back inside the car. Tossing the wig in after her, he slammed the door and got in on the other side.

Pig-nose signaled the guard to open the gate. Glancing back in at Stella, he offered her a curt nod. She could hear his bootheels snap together. "My apologies, Fräulein."

Inclining her head slightly, she shrugged back into the coat and stifled her giddy relief as the Mercedes rolled forward.

Plowing eastward, they gradually ascended along the base of the Sumava Mountains into the Bohemian Forest. Steel sky vanished, replaced by a thick canopy of pine and fir merging along either side of the road. Shadows inside the car danced with occasional breaks in the trees as the Mercedes sped along a road largely cleared of snow. No doubt German *Panzers* and the tank troops had been through recently.

"Give me your feet."

Stella shot him a startled look.

"Now, before they become completely useless." The colonel reached for her legs, swiveling her around in the seat to settle them against his lap. Tearing away the water-soaked slippers, he removed the muffler from around his neck and wrapped her bare feet, briskly massaging her heels, soles, and toes. Stella winced at the pain of blood flowing back into the nerves.

"You did well back there." His grim expression belied the compliment. "I trust I've now sufficiently answered your question?"

Rattled by her confrontation with the Gestapo and distracted by the needles pricking her sore feet, Stella nodded in reflexive obedience. "What question, Herr Kommandant?" she asked.

24

Heat bullied its way up her cheeks at his amusement. Disgusted at her own bottomless well of humiliation, she added the obvious. "I'm to be your secretary then."

The car's shadows disappeared along with the deepest part of the forest. Stella caught the colonel's silent assent and relief flowed like honey through her limbs. It seemed she would live . . . at least for a time.

"Actually, one of my reasons for traveling to Munich was to obtain an assistant. But then I found you at the camp and saw that your papers listed clerical skills." In the dimness she glimpsed the slight shrug of his broad shoulders.

"I am taking a chance on you, Fräulein Muller." His brusqueness stifled her newfound assurance. "That does not mean I tolerate marginal work. I'm a demanding employer, so your best had better be good enough.

"Nor will I permit deceit. There's enough political intrigue stalking my back within the *Reich* without adding your name to the list. Your loyalty belongs to me"—he leaned close so that his warm breath grazed her cheek—"and no one else."

His nearness, as well as her vulnerable position, with her legs pinioned across his lap, amplified the tremor along Stella's spine. She'd already lied to him; her whole life had become one big falsehood. "I won't deceive you," she said, unable to look him in the eye.

"Excellent. Because as easily as I netted you from that cesspool Dachau, I can toss you back."

"I understand perfectly, Herr Kommandant."

"I believe you do." He rested back against the seat and continued massaging her feet. Humor touched his voice. "I suspect your intelligence is only matched by your beauty."

Stella set her chin as she glanced at her battered hands and bony wrists. She turned to stare out the back window, refusing to let him see how his insults affected her.

He paused in his ministrations. "You doubt my sincerity?"

She pretended not to hear him, but the pressure of his hand on her cheek brought her around to face him. "Beneath hollowed cheeks and bruises, beauty sleeps."

He spoke aloud as though to himself; his somber green eyes darkened to the depths of the forest they had just passed. Stella refused to fathom the reason it disturbed her.

"Wounds to the flesh eventually heal, Fräulein," he said, releasing her. "Your beauty will return soon enough."

"What about wounds to the soul, Herr Kommandant?"

She instantly regretted the question. Yet he didn't seem angry; his features registered only mild surprise, then resettled into their matrix of hard angles and planes. "A much more complex injury," he said. "One for which I have yet to find a cure."

His dispirited tone made her wonder at its cause. From the moment she'd first spied him through the window of the chalet, he'd worn a furrowed brow and a hard line at his mouth, as though another, more intimate battle raged.

Stella shunned any further consideration. He wasn't worth it—he'd already made it clear he would send her back to Dachau without a second thought. She'd learned enough of the SS ways to know he meant every word. This reprieve she'd been granted could all change in an instant.

Disquieted, she removed her legs from his lap. "Thank you, Herr Kommandant. I'm much better now." She unwrapped her feet and offered the scarf back to him.

"Keep it."

Of course he wouldn't want it back—it was stained with her blood, her filth. Stella blushed as she wadded the cloth into her lap.

She darted another glance at him. The colonel's sizable frame took up most of the seat. His head rested back against the leather, a briefcase near his feet. The same brass-topped cane she'd noticed earlier lay propped against the door. She wondered at the nature of his injury. He had managed to carry her with such ease.

26

He seemed preoccupied staring out the window. His head bobbed slightly with the car's motion. Perhaps he planned the first execution of Jews at his new concentration camp. Or decided on Consequences with which to abuse her people first, like the SS guards at Dachau.

Her tormentors had invented many such Consequences. One particularly sadistic sport, which Stella had likened to a game of *Katz und Maus*, involved the guards acting like sly felines as they waited for a prisoner to cross the assembly grounds. After sufficiently torturing their "Maus," what remained was carted off to the Krematorium—sometimes dead, sometimes not.

Stella knotted the scarf in her hands. What would her Consequence be if she didn't type fast enough or she misconstrued one of the colonel's dictated letters? Mrs. Bernstein had reprimanded her often enough about her shorthand—

"The worst is over, Fräulein. Relax." The colonel studied her as he nudged her back against the seat. "Are you warm enough?"

Stella nodded. Another lie, but he would hardly care that her months of shoveling snow trenches at Dachau had left a chill that refused to go away.

"Get some rest. We'll be home in a few hours."

Home . . . Leaving behind the lofty slopes to descend the mountains into Czechoslovakia, Stella looked out at the patchwork swells of white amidst evergreens that swept past the car. She was reminded of the quilt she'd made, a surprise birthday gift for her uncle. That was before the Nazis destroyed it along with the rest of their possessions—before they took Morty away.

Lord, why don't you hear me? Why have you taken away my joy?

Anger battled her exhaustion with the drowsing lull of the car's motion. Home was a place that, even if she lived, would never be the same.

"Wake up, *Meine Süsse*."

A deep voice beckoned her toward consciousness. *My sweet* . . .

Stella's lashes fluttered open. Moonlight flooded the back seat of the car. She blinked and turned her head to stare out the window.

Nightfall replaced the day's dingy sun; the sky now seemed as dark and unfathomable as her future. Only the moon animated the Ceaseless White, bringing into sharp focus the barbed wire and searchlights of Dachau. . . .

"Nein!" she screamed and launched forward in the seat. Blood pounded in her ears as dark spots crowded her vision. It had all been a cruel trick—

"Breathe!"

Rough hands forced her head down between her knees. Voices buzzed against the roaring pulse in her brain.

". . . do you understand? You're safe!" The colonel's words finally penetrated her fear. "We've arrived at Theresienstadt."

Not Dachau. Stella's breathing slowed. The pain in her chest eased. She tried to raise her head, but he held her still. "Did you hear me? You will not be afraid. This is your new home."

She moved her neck in an effort to nod. "*Ja,*" she gasped.

He released her. She eased back against the seat, feeling light-headed and vulnerable. She instinctively drew away from him.

"You act as if I would bite." His voice held a trace of mockery. "Anyway, I prefer a meatier dish. Perhaps once you've been properly fed?"

Stella hugged herself while his tasteless attempt at humor hung in the air.

Sergeant Grossman opened their door.

"Enough. Come." The colonel got out first, then gestured to her. Before she could reach for the soggy slippers, he pulled her from the car into his arms.

She stared back toward the barbed wire and glaring search-lights that had frightened her. Beyond the cordoned-off section rose a fortress, high and formidable. Were the prisoners inside? The stronghold didn't look like a concentration camp; no sentries marching, no barking dogs. The place seemed deserted.

"Well, Fräulein, will it suit you?"

Stella tensed before she realized the colonel wasn't looking at the fortress but at a lovely two-story brick house directly ahead. Pointed tips like sharp teeth rose from the picket fence surrounding the yard. "I'm to live . . . here?"

"Would you rather live over there?" He angled his chin toward the fortress.

"Nein!" She had an inkling of what lay beyond those walls: deprivation and incarceration, two conditions she'd gladly forgo to live in this charming house.

"Then I trust you'll behave yourself." But his tone held no threat as he carried her toward the house.

They had reached the latticed gate to the yard when a man's crisp voice sounded behind them, "Heil Hitler, Herr Kommandant."

The colonel swung around to confront two soldiers garbed in the black uniform of the SS. Like a pair of stout oaks laid bare to the cold, they stood dark and rigid before their commandant.

"Ah, Captain Hermann. I trust my camp is still in one piece?"

"*Jawohl*, Herr Kommandant," said the officer who had spoken. "Only a few troublemakers." The captain's expression remained cold, impassive. "Sergeant Koch and I handled the situation."

Beside him, the sergeant grinned, his gold-capped front tooth gleaming in the moonlight.

Hermann turned his icy stare on Stella. A chill grazed her nape as she realized she'd left the red wig in the car. "You've captured a runaway Jew, Herr Kommandant?" he asked with a smirk.

"Nein, Captain." The strong arms that held her tensed. "A secretary."

"With all due respect, she looks like a J—"

"She's not, Captain." The colonel's tone held an edge. "Merely a victim of circumstance. You must trust me on this . . . or do you doubt my loyalty to the Reich?"

"Of course not, Herr Kommandant!"

"*Gut*." He kicked open the latticed gate with a polished boot. "If there's nothing else . . . ?"

"Nein, Herr Kommandant," the captain said, and he and the sergeant saluted.

The colonel turned and continued with Stella along the shoveled walk toward the front door. She glanced over his shoulder at the pair still at the gate. Even in the moonlight she could see their contempt. Every female instinct in her recoiled as she watched Hermann's harsh expression turn deliberate, covetous—

"Are you afraid I'll drop you, or do you try to strangle me?"

Her gaze turned back to collide with the colonel's amused look, and she realized her arms were wrapped tightly around his neck. Blushing, she loosened her grip. "Herr Kommandant, I . . ."

The front door burst open, spilling golden light onto the porch. A scrawny boy stood at the threshold, a yellow *Mogen Dovid* star sewn to his blue jacket. He couldn't be more than seven or eight years old.

Anna's age. Stella sucked in a breath and shoved away the memory.

The boy eyed her curiously as he doffed his overlarge brown tweed cap and stepped back to let them enter. "*Guten Abend*, Herr Kommandant."

"Good evening, Joseph."

The colonel's tone held genuine warmth, which surprised Stella. He crossed the threshold into the foyer before releasing her to stand beside him. Her toes sank into a thick Aubusson carpet, the luxuriant fibers soothing her raw feet.

"Come, stand by the fire."

Loath to move from the spot, Stella nonetheless followed him into the main living room. A blaze crackled in the hearth, and its welcome heat raised gooseflesh along her skin. The smell of fresh-baked bread wafted into the room, and she felt a sudden, ravenous hunger. Cramps seized her belly all the way to her throat, saliva flooding her mouth with such force she had to swallow. She took a deep breath to stifle her anxiety. Would she disgrace herself at his table?

"Joseph, ask Helen to prepare an extra plate for supper."

The boy, having taken the colonel's cane and briefcase from Sergeant Grossman at the door, set them near the hearth and disappeared into the kitchen.

"I'll get you a chair." With only a few long strides, the colonel crossed the living room to pluck a heavy leather armchair from the foyer and carry it back to the hearth. "Sit."

She complied and again wondered at his need for the cane. He seemed fit enough.

The colonel shed his greatcoat, then assumed an imposing stance beside her. He stared into the fire, their communal silence broken only by the pop and crackle of orange flames licking over fresh logs.

Stella turned to look up at him openly. Without the heavy coat he was still a broad-shouldered man. Decorations littered his tailored black uniform; among the rows of medals and ribbons covering the area over his heart, he also wore the highly distinguished Knight's Cross.

She quickly shifted her focus back to the fireplace. The rare commendation was given only to officers with exceptional valor in battle. Morty too had received a Knight's Cross—the most coveted of all, the Grand Cross. He'd earned the prestigious medal during the first Great War when he'd fought for Germany. The same country that now turned its back on him because of his Jewish blood.

Fear and resentment flooded her. Had the colonel received his commendations for true valor . . . or for killing Jews? A man of his size and strength could easily kill someone like her.

"There is a study that adjoins the library, which serves as my workplace."

Stella schooled her thoughts as he pointed to a set of double doors off the living room. "You should find everything you need at the desk I've installed there. If you require anything else, let me know. Breakfast is at seven each morning. Work will commence at eight." He gave her a sharp look. "Miss either one and you'll discover the limits of my good nature.

"Weekends are your free days. You will of course be restricted to the immediate house. With an armed escort you may visit the woods at the back of the property."

He reached to trail a finger across the blond stubble at her scalp. "Only until you put on weight and your hair grows out a bit more. It's for your protection. We can't risk a mistake."

No hint of cruelty colored his voice, which made the danger he spoke of even more real. She hugged her waist and nodded.

"Joseph will show you to your room upstairs." He signaled the boy returning from the kitchen. "I'm sure you'd like to . . . freshen up before supper."

Stella glanced around at the colonel's beautiful home before staring down at her bloodied feet. She'd soiled his expensive carpet. "Of course, Herr Kommandant," she whispered.

"Schnell, Fräulein. Supper is ready and I am starved."

She refused to look at him as she struggled out of the comfortable chair and walked to where Joseph waited by the stairs.

"Fifteen minutes, Fräulein Muller. Any longer and I'll come after you myself, because you *will* eat. I need an important letter sent to Berlin in the morning and I won't have you fainting from hunger in the middle of my dictation."

Stella turned at the colonel's good-natured threat. His humor and consideration threw her off-balance. It also bothered her that when his features relaxed, he was a handsome man. She preferred to maintain her view of him as the grim-faced killer whose presence alone sent armies running in the opposite direction.

She finally followed the boy up the carpeted steps, assailed by new emotions she wasn't prepared to deal with. Except guilt—that heavy weight threatened to smother her. A warm house, delicious-smelling food, and a place to sleep while others died in the cold.

The colonel had told her his reason for rescuing her—that he needed a secretary. But once she no longer resembled a prisoner, would he allow her to leave?

And in the meantime, could she forget who he was? What his kind had done to her?

Never.

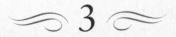

3

He assigned to her . . . the best place in the harem.

Esther 2:9

It was the loveliest room she'd ever seen.

Stella leaned against the doorjamb and marveled at the profusion of ivory lace curtains draped across an elongated window above the single bed. Matching ivory pillows sprawled against a blue chenille coverlet, while beside the bed sat a mahogany nightstand; a lavish Girandole crystal lamp rested against its polished surface, along with a small book and an exquisite clock of inlaid pearl. An armoire in the same honey-toned wood stood along the opposite wall.

Crossing the threshold, she tossed her borrowed coat onto the bed. A framed watercolor beside the armoire caught her attention: A young girl in a red, beribboned straw hat lay in the tall grass of a sunny meadow. Yellow pansies, vibrant against a blue stream, surrounded her.

The picture seemed quiet and peaceful, blissfully silent. Unlike the noisy, crowded Block at Dachau where Stella and other female prisoners had been crammed together like a tin of sardines. She breathed a wistful sigh. Solitude was a luxury she'd once taken for granted.

Moving deeper into the room, Stella spied a narrow door off the bedroom—her own personal bath! She rushed inside and stood in the middle of the small, tiled room. How long had it been since she'd bathed in a real tub? Or slept in a feathery bed?

Was it a trick? Why would God now tempt her with hope . . . after all she'd been through? Yet she couldn't deny the feeling, as alien and vague as her freedom.

Stella returned to the bedroom. The boy still hovered at the door. "You're Joseph?"

He stared at her, then dropped his gaze and nodded.

"How old are you?"

His face shot up. Long brown lashes lowered slightly. "Ten."

Older than Anna. Stella blocked the memory as swiftly as it came. The boy's clothes were clean but worn and hung loosely on his small frame. He seemed so fragile; no wonder she'd thought him younger at first.

She'd also failed to note his missing right ear.

"How old are you, Fräulein?"

Stella found a smile, despite her cracked lips. "You should never ask a lady that question."

His olive cheeks bloomed with color.

"Twenty-three," she relented. "How long have you lived here, Joseph?"

"A year—in the ghetto, anyway. I only been with Herr Kommandant about a month."

"Does he treat you well?" Stella tried not to stare at the bloody scab where his ear had been. If the colonel did this to him, then her own fate would surely be worse.

"I like it here. The work's easy and I get to eat all the *Käsespätzle* I want. I even got my own bed."

Maybe the colonel hadn't hurt the child. Stella thought of the two soldiers she'd just seen outside. Her heart raced as she struggled to recall their names . . . a captain . . . Hermann?

Yes—and Sergeant Koch. Easing out a breath, she asked the boy, "What about the other Nazis?"

His features tensed, and she closed the distance between them. "Listen to me, Joseph," she said as she crouched to his level. "I know the cruelty they can inflict. I give you my word I won't repeat what you tell me. But I must know . . . what to expect here."

His intelligent brown eyes studied her with an intensity beyond his tender years. "You're Jewish, aren't you, Fräulein?"

"Nein!" She reared back, her reaction automatic, borne of fear, rehearsed a thousand times as Morty had taught her. And they hadn't even asked . . .

She stood with others at the Mannheim checkpoint, regretting her decision to leave the safety of Marta's Heidelberg apartment and return to search for her uncle. The place was crawling with Nazis. A fat Gestapo man moved up close behind her in line, his comrades shouting encouragement. Stella gasped when his filthy wet mouth grazed her neck, the rankness of stale beer and tobacco on his breath. When he began to touch her, she lost control. Like a feral cat unleashed, she turned and attacked him before several pairs of hands dragged her away. Her satisfaction at the bloody welts she'd raked along his face exploded into pain with the first blow; the second knocked her flat against the ground.

Afterward he'd grabbed up her scattered papers and marched with them to the checkpoint table, stamping them in red with the damning word that bought her passage on the next train to Hell . . .

"I'm no Jew," she told the boy. "Please don't say that again."

Hurt flashed in his eyes. Stella felt shamed by her defection, as though she'd left him alone to the fate of their race. Yet there was no choice but to lie; she wouldn't burden him with that kind of secret. She couldn't risk another . . .

She offered him a contrite smile. "I'd still like to be your friend, Joseph. I'll need one in this place."

His features brightened with a child's ready acceptance. "I'll have to teach you the rules," he said. "The first is, stay away from Captain Hermann. He hits the prisoners with his fists." The boy cocked his head. "And you look like a prisoner, Fräulein."

Stella flushed. "Anything else I should know?"

"There's Sergeant Koch and Lieutenant Brucker. They just like to hurt people." His gaze skittered to the floor. "Especially the older ones who can't defend themselves."

"And the children, Joseph?" she whispered, glancing at his angry scab.

He wouldn't look at her. "Children too."

Stella swayed as she crouched against the floor; images exploded in her mind. *Anna's sweet face . . . brightest, most beautiful star at Dachau's makeshift school . . . Anna . . . her own precious child after Bella Horowitz died . . . Anna . . . small, trembling hands . . . holding up a piece of cloth, a blouse to cover Stella's nakedness as the guards dragged her toward the shooting pit . . . Anna . . . those little hands dragged behind Stella . . . an explosion of gunfire . . .*

"Noooo!" she cried, pulling the surprised boy into her arms. Grief overwhelmed her as she held him close, the way she would never again hold Anna; offering comfort and needing to be comforted . . .

His small body stiffened an instant, then clung to her with unspoken ferocity. The two were strangers, yet in that moment they were more closely linked in their desire for human touch than any bond of blood.

Stella pressed her cheek to the unruly brown curls at the side of his head, so baby soft against her skin. "Where are your parents?" she finally managed to ask.

"Dead," he whispered. "Mama and Papa got real sick while we were at Neuengamme."

Cold crept along her spine. "Neuengamme?"

"A work camp. Near Hamburg, I think."

"How did you get here?"

"Herr Van dee Moss said I could be his assistant. He was a famous painter in Amsterdam, so they let us both come to Theresienstadt. He died last summer."

The child's words trailed off against her shoulder. Stella could only hug him again.

He finally raised his face to her. "Will you pray for my mama and papa . . . even though they were Jews?"

How could she tell him God had abandoned their people? "I'll pray," she lied, holding back her bitterness.

"On my honor, I'll look out for you while you are here."

Stella's eyes burned at his earnest expression. Suddenly he seemed much older than ten. "Thank you, Joseph. I'm proud to know a man who still values honor."

He flushed at her praise. "Please, we must go. Herr Kommandant is waiting."

Stella rose from the bed, nauseated at the prospect of returning downstairs. "Give me a minute." She then went to the bathroom to wash most of the dirt and dried blood from her body.

Downstairs, glassware and silver clinked as they arrived at the archway connecting the kitchen and dining areas. A silver-haired woman wearing a bright green neckerchief with her black-and-white service uniform bustled back and forth between the two rooms.

She halted before Stella and then raised a questioning brow at the boy.

"Helen," Joseph explained, "meet Fräulein Muller." To Stella, he said, "She doesn't speak, but she hears real good."

"Helen." Stella forced a smile and offered a hand in greeting. The other woman made no move to reciprocate and merely eyed her with derision.

A water kettle on the stove whistled. Smells of sauerkraut, fried onions, and something rancid seized Stella's nostrils as she waited with mounting humiliation. Only when she started to withdraw her hand did the stout woman brusquely wipe her own on the apron and thrust it at her. Helen didn't smile but merely jerked her head in acknowledgment and returned to her tasks.

Stella's face burned. She raised a self-conscious hand to the stubble at her scalp.

"Don't worry." Joseph squeezed her arm. "She's like that with everyone."

Stella eyed him dubiously. She'd bet money the woman didn't treat the colonel that way.

Helen swept back by them long enough to tug at a lock of Joseph's hair. She pointed to the dining room.

"Come, Fräulein. Supper is ready. I'll fetch Herr Kommandant." He pulled Stella through the archway into the dining room before disappearing around the corner.

Helen might not be personable, but she set a beautiful table. Stella eyed the snowy linen tablecloth. Two complete settings of silver-rimmed china were placed at either end, while a milk-glass vase of holly, ripe with crimson berries, stood in the center. A pair of beeswax candles burned along either side, dancing light off polished brass holders.

A basket of fresh bread sat alongside the centerpiece. Stella touched the rim of the basket, willfully resisting temptation as she gazed into the flames. Similar candles once gleamed in her own home on the eve of *Shabbat*. She recalled the reverent anticipation as her uncle made *Kiddush* over their wine, declaring holiness to God's day of rest. Afterward he would uncover and bless the *Challah*, bread that God had provided them in the desert—

"Fräulein, you will sit here."

The colonel called to her from the opposite end of the table. Stella snatched her hand away. This wasn't Challah or Shabbat. Not in the Jew Killer's house.

Overwhelmed by a sudden avalanche of anger, she marched toward the chair he held for her. Nazis were the worst kind of thieves. They took everything, from the rabbi's *Tallit*—his prayer shawl—to the last *matzo* wrapper, until nothing of Jewishness remained. They had destroyed synagogues, families, lives. *Faith* . . .

"Have you met Helen?"

The colonel leaned to push in her chair. Stella stiffened, assailed by his nearness, the spiced scent of his cologne. She glanced at the aproned woman carrying in a water pitcher and glasses. "Ja, Herr Kommandant," she whispered.

The colonel took his place at the head of the table. "Helen is not only my housekeeper, but she is also my best-kept secret."

His remark drew both women's attention. "She's the finest cook in all of Europe. I've considered sending her to the Front, armed with her baked *Apfelstrudel*. The smell alone would entice a legion of soldiers to follow her into battle."

Helen's cheeks flushed as she served them drinks.

"She won't be leading battalions, however." He turned to Stella. "You will be her newest target, Fräulein—pastries, pies, dumplings, whatever it takes. We'll start you out with smaller portions, but I want you healthy as soon as possible."

Why? Stella wanted to ask. Even Helen looked surprised. Yet the housekeeper merely met his glance and nodded before leaving the room.

"You do understand your part in this arrangement?"

Stella took great pains to smooth her napkin over her lap. "Eating."

"And . . . ?"

She felt heat crawl up her neck. "Keeping it down."

"Ah, your honesty, if not your enthusiasm, is refreshing."

An amused gleam lit his eyes, and she didn't know what to make of it. Helen reappeared with a platter of steaming food. Taking the colonel's words to heart, she served Stella a small helping of fried onions, sauerkraut, and a meat-stuffed bell pepper. Stella's insides cramped with hunger, before she detected the peculiar odor she'd smelled earlier in the kitchen. Not beef . . .

"Helen prepared this *Gefüllte Paprika* the Austrian way," he said from his place at the table. "You should find it quite delicious."

Pork. Stella stared at her plate, her stomach raging between hunger and a sudden queasiness. She picked up her fork and pushed aside the pepper before nibbling at her onions and sauerkraut.

"You will sample *everything*, Fräulein."

She glanced up at the colonel's mutinous expression. "I . . . I cannot."

"Cannot? Or will not? Helen has gone to much trouble to prepare this meal. And considering what you've had to eat in the past, I would expect you to be grateful."

She lowered her gaze. "I am, it's . . . it's just the bell pepper. I get hives," she lied. "Besides, I'm not very hungry."

"I don't care if you're hungry or not," he said, ignoring her statement. "You may leave the pepper, but eat the filling."

She poked at the stuffed pepper and eyed the rest of her meal wistfully. She'd been starved at Dachau; the Nazis used hunger as a weapon, making the weak fall victim to disease and death, while the strong grew feeble enough to be easily managed.

Shame pricked her. Any of those still suffering in that place would gladly eat dog were it roasted on a spit and served up to them. *"And the meek shall inherit the land . . ."*

Only the strong survived in it. Stella took a bite of the pork and resisted an urge to gag. Three more and her stomach roiled. "I'm sorry." Her fork clattered onto the plate. "No more—"

"That wasn't so terrible, was it?" he cajoled. "Soon you'll regain your strength."

Despair swept through her like an icy wind. He'd made her defile herself before God.

"You'll need new clothing for your position as my secretary. Helen will find you a suitable wardrobe."

She barely heard him. It was *she* who had remained faithful; now she'd failed.

"You're exhausted." He rose from his place at the table and moved around behind her. "Upstairs with you. Get some sleep. Morning will arrive soon enough."

Helen had returned with a tray of cheese and dried fruit. "Helen, please help Fräulein Muller to her room," he ordered.

"I can manage." Yet as Stella started to rise, her knees gave out. She grabbed at his arm to keep from falling.

"You're so thin, and much too weak," he said gruffly. "Helen will help until you're stronger. Meanwhile, I won't have you falling down and cracking your skull."

"Please, I'm fine." She hated being treated like a child, or worse, like an invalid. She pulled away and walked carefully toward the stairs.

On the wall at the foot of the landing she spied a painting she hadn't noticed before. Larger than the watercolor in her room, the oil-on-canvas scene was also quite different. Snowcapped peaks—the Bavarian Alps, she guessed—rose behind a castle of gray rock and mortar that lay nestled in a green meadow. Hazy clouds drifted in a blue sky, and beyond the meadow stood a monastery, its bell tower visible in the distance.

Oddly she found the image comforting. Stella imagined the rich, loamy smell of grass as the cry of a solitary bell chimed the hour. Her home in Mannheim's bustling city had differed greatly from this pastoral scene.

Again she felt a violent longing for what she'd lost: her uncle and their cheery apartment above his shop on the *Roonstrasse*; her clerk's job at the printing press manufacturer, *Schnellpressen AG*, in neighboring Heidelberg; her best friend, Marta Kurtz. Parties. Music. They were all gone, as if her former life had never existed except in dreams.

Only uncertainty remained. Tangible, oppressive, it weighed her down like a shackle, knowing that someday she would be caught in a lie or cause some slight. Or perhaps there would be no reason at all, simply that this new monster would grow tired of her.

When that happened, not even God could save her. She reached for the banister, pulling her exhausted body up the stairs.

Maybe it would have been better to die.

4

"If I have found favor with you, O king, and if it
pleases your majesty, grant me my life."

Esther 7:3

*S*tella *shivered in line on the* Appellplatz *during roll call as
the horse-drawn* Moorexpress *paused to collect another
body. Corpses, piled at contorted angles, glistened in the gray
light, clothed in the crystalline gauze of half rain, half snow.*

At the top sprawled a dead child.

*Stella shoved a fist in her mouth. The ground shifted beneath
her. Please, God, no!*

*Then a tiny breath rose like mist from the heap; she caught the
imperceptible flutter of baby-soft lashes. Stella tried to scream,
though no sound emerged. She broke from the line, but strong
hands pulled her back. She turned to meet Greatcoat's gaze. His
green eyes were cold, his grip painful.*

The Moorexpress *had reached the* Krematorium. *A loud wail
echoed from inside the ovens. A child's cry of terror . . .*

*Anna! Stella fought to free herself from Greatcoat's arms.
Biting, kicking, she exhausted every ounce of strength to try
and save her little girl—*

"Wake up!" Stella's eyes flew open to the sound of her own screams. She spied the black SS uniform and fought harder.

"Look at me!"

The colonel shook her. Stella froze. Perspiration pooled at her back as she obeyed him.

Concern, not cruelty, etched his features. Her panic slowly abated, washing away the last traces of sleep. Her own cries had filled the nightmare; her desperate flailing had been against the bed, not the monster in her dreams.

Anna was still dead.

She emitted a choked gasp and turned her head away.

"Easy." The colonel drew her into his arms, rubbing her back as if she were a child. "Bad dream? I'm not surprised, considering what you've been through."

Grief, humiliation, and more disquieting emotions seized her. Stella became acutely aware of her nakedness under the robe, having fallen asleep on top of the coverlet after her bath.

She pushed away from him and scooted toward the head of the bed. An awkward silence passed.

"I'll get you another blanket," he said at last.

She watched him rise from the bed and go to the armoire. Imposing in his sinister black uniform, he seemed to limp more than he had earlier.

What did he really want from her? Secretarial skills . . . or something else?

He returned to the bed with a standard military-issue wool blanket. Loosening the black tie at his neck, he said, "Take off that robe and lie down."

She gaped at him, unable to move as old nightmares paralyzed her. Did she have the strength to fight him off? Pressed up against the headboard, she tugged on the hem of her robe. "I won't," she whispered.

He tossed the blanket at her, clearly exasperated. "I only thought you'd be more comfortable."

She quickly covered herself in the wool and averted her eyes.

"I was on my way to bed when I heard your screams," he continued. "If you like, I'll stay until you fall back to sleep."

She shook her head, still uneasy.

"I bid you good night, then."

Yet he didn't move, as though he wanted to say more. Finally he turned and strode to the door, switching off the light. A wash of moonlight flooded in through the lace curtains, casting a pattern of shadows across the floor.

"The child . . . was she yours?"

His question pierced the darkness between them like an unseen blade. Stella huddled beneath the blanket, hardly breathing. Only when typhus had finally taken Anna's mother did the little girl leave her cooling flesh to crawl into Stella's warm bunk, and into her heart. "She meant more to me than my life."

The colonel's silhouette shone in the dim light from the hall. "I wish . . ." he began, but his voice trailed off. "Good night."

"Herr Kommandant?" Stella used the shadows to cloak her anxiety while she voiced her most burning question. "When will I be able to leave?"

The figure in the doorway grew still. "Are you so eager to go?"

"I . . . I want to return home."

"But you have no family, and I doubt the Jews who raised you are still living there."

The truth of his remark stung; she'd returned home on the train after work one day to discover their apartment boarded up, the streets empty, and not a trace of her uncle or her friends.

"Besides, Innsbruck is many miles from here, Stella," he added. "How far do you think you could travel in your condition?"

She didn't intend to travel to Innsbruck, but he was right about that, too. She'd barely made it up the stairs to her room after dinner. "But when I'm strong enough, Herr Kommandant . . . ?"

"Once you're completely rested and have eaten plenty of Helen's good cooking, we can discuss it." Light from the hall danced as he shifted against the jamb. "But it wounds me that you choose to abandon me, especially when we are marooned out here in miles of hip-deep snow and I'm in desperate need of a competent assistant. Is this the thanks I get for saving your life?"

"Of course not, Herr Kommandant. Thank you." She swallowed her misery, grasping his real meaning. For now, anyway, she would remain his prisoner.

"You're most welcome." His darkened profile relaxed. "I wish you pleasant dreams."

After he left, she settled back in bed and tried to sleep, but memories of Anna kept her awake—and her anxiety over the colonel's motives.

He'd told her of his plan to obtain a secretary from Munich, a place with doubtless hundreds more qualified for the post. And yet he'd made up his mind to hire Stella, even before knowing her explanation for the red JUDE stamped on her papers.

Why had he chosen her? She had no wealth, no affluence. And who could possibly desire a bald, bruised scarecrow of a woman? He would have raped her tonight in this room, otherwise.

Stella watched as shadows danced across the ceiling. Aric von Schmidt frightened her. She also found herself drawn to him—a more terrifying prospect than the fat Nazi who accosted her in Mannheim or the guards at Dachau who bruised her with their clubs.

This man, for whatever reason, toyed with that place inside her long buried beneath degradation, despair, and mistrust . . . a place as deep as her soul.

The part of her that yearned for human love.

Stella blinked against the early morning's achromatic brightness and rolled onto her back.

"*Guten Morgen,*" a voice whispered from the doorway.

She jerked her head around, then groaned in relief. "Good morning yourself, mischief."

Joseph's brown eyes lit with amusement. He obviously felt safe with her. That was something.

"Where's Helen?"

"She's making breakfast," Joseph answered. "Herr Kommandant says you can eat in your room this morning. And you don't have to work today." He paused. "Did you have a nightmare?"

Stella sat up in bed. "What time is it?" she asked, ignoring his question.

"Six fifteen."

"I'm getting dressed and going downstairs." She didn't doubt the boy's words, but she wasn't falling for another Nazi trap, either. The thought of returning to Dachau made her shiver.

Joseph looked glum. "I'm supposed to . . . help you, if you need me to."

Stella hid a smile at his obvious discomfort. "You can help me find my underthings."

His mouth dropped, and a furious blush stained his cheeks.

"I suppose I can manage on my own," she relented, taking pity on him. His relief was comical. "Give me thirty minutes to get ready, all right?"

He nodded before turning to swagger from the room. Stella tried not to think of Anna. *Later*, she promised herself, *when it won't hurt so much.*

She eased out of bed, stretching sore limbs as she stumbled toward the window. The fortress stood against the pewter sky like a secret island rising above a sea of white. Stella could only glimpse the tallest spires inside the stronghold. The place seemed impenetrable.

She shivered once more at the sight of barbed wire and searchlights staking off ground to the right of the entrance. Theresienstadt was no haven. Its walls didn't protect; they trapped their victims, just like the gates at Dachau.

Did the people inside suffer as much . . . or worse?

Stella spun away. She didn't want to think about it. She couldn't help them, anyway.

Inside the bathroom, she avoided her reflection in the mirror. The red wig had found its way in from the car to a wire stand beside the sink. Doubtless the colonel's unspoken command was that she wear it.

Stella turned on the shower, again feeling a need to wash despite her bath the previous night. The clove-scented soap she'd been given reminded her of *Havdalah*, when the closing of each Sabbath was blessed with spices like cloves, nutmeg, and cinnamon—an offering for sweetness and peace in the coming week.

She tried to focus on that memory as she welcomed the hot, clean water against her skin. Stella ignored the pang of guilt she felt at such luxury. Suffering had become a way of life. Would she be a fool and deny Pleasure's offering?

Back in her room, she found the armoire filled with colorful sweaters, pants, scarves, and socks. One drawer held a profusion of lace; as she rummaged through panties, bras, garter belts, and real silk stockings, she marveled at Helen's generosity.

Once she'd located a white cotton slip that wouldn't slide off her hips, Stella perused the dozen tailored suits crammed inside the cabinet. Mildly curious over the varying sizes, she chose the smallest of the lot: a houndstooth jacket and matching skirt.

Donning the outfit, she had to double the jacket's belt around her waist. Afterward she bit back a cry as she stuffed her tender feet into a tight pair of high-heeled pumps; she hadn't worn real shoes in months. Sucking in a painful breath, she tottered back to the bathroom and put on the hairpiece.

Stella forced herself to look in the mirror. Hadassah Benjamin, a *Mischling*, half Jew, bursting with a young woman's exuberance, had ceased to exist. In her place stood Stella Muller, subdued Austrian bookkeeper and suitable stock for the Third Reich. A frail disguise comprised of no more than a scrap of official-looking paper, a red wig, and beneath her bruises the inherent fair features of a Dutch grandmother.

Staring back at the stranger with beggar's eyes and hollowed cheeks, Stella wondered for the thousandth time how something as insignificant as a Nazi's pride had turned her world upside down. Loaded into a cattle car reeking of unwashed bodies and excrement, she'd spent endless hours standing between sweaty strangers and suffocating from the lack of fresh air. Her parched throat had warred with the mounting pressure in her bladder as the beast that trapped them all in its maw plundered steadily along the tracks toward Dachau. *To God Forsaken . . .*

She leaned against the sink, overcome by a sudden wave of exhaustion. The colonel was right. How could she leave when the simple act of getting dressed depleted her strength? How far would she make it, trapped in a body still so weak?

Frustrated, Stella stumbled back to her bedroom. She sat on the edge of the bed to wait for Joseph and again noticed the small black book on the nightstand. A Bible. She'd seen it the previous night but was too tired to take much notice.

She picked up the leather tome, feeling its weight. Her co-worker, Marta, had possessed such a book; many times her best friend had tried in her earnest, gentle way to convert Hadassah to Christ.

Perhaps that was why they *were* best friends, she thought with a wistful sigh. Marta's efforts hadn't borne fruit, but Hadassah was always touched by the genuine concern for her soul.

She let the Bible fall open to a random page and immediately recognized the words of Psalm twenty-two from her own Jewish *Tanakh*:

> My God, my God, why have you forsaken me?
> Why are you so far from saving me,
> so far from the words of my groaning?
> O my God, I cry out by day, but you do not answer.

Snapping the book shut, Stella shoved the Bible inside the nightstand drawer. The rest she knew by heart—King David spoke of hope and his complete faith in God for deliverance.

Her only deliverance lay in tatters. The ruins of her home in Mannheim, the haunted, glassy-eyed faces of those dead and dying at Dachau. Anna's face . . .

A sharp knock sounded at the door. Stella's mouth felt dry as she made herself move to answer it. Would her clerical skills satisfy the colonel's expectations, or would he send her back to that place?

Joseph leaned against the jamb and quickly straightened when he saw her. A shy smile touched his lips. "You look pretty, Fräulein."

His compliment had the power to bolster her confidence. Stella's shoulders eased, and she offered an affectionate smile. "Now that's something a lady always likes to hear, Joseph. *Danke.*"

He ducked his head shyly, then turned toward the stairs. Stella took a deep breath before she followed him down to face her new employer.

The colonel sat at the breakfast table, a sheaf of papers in one hand, while the other held a steaming cup of *Kaffee.* Perched on the end of his nose—a slightly crooked one, she noticed—were a pair of gold-rimmed spectacles. The glasses lent him a disarming air of intelligence, and it struck her with the disconcerting notion that in different clothes he might pass for any other average man at breakfast.

He seemed preoccupied with whatever he was reading. When he finally glanced at her, he paused, the cup of Kaffee hovering near his mouth. Slowly he lowered it to the table and then removed his glasses. "Did Joseph fail to relay my message?"

"He did as you requested, Herr Kommandant. But I chose to come downstairs."

"Turn around," he said quietly.

Self-consciousness wrestled with her hunger as she inhaled

the tantalizing smells of real Kaffee and fried potatoes. Obeying his order, she bit the inside of her lip against the pain of her too-tight shoes and spun in place slowly.

He rose from his chair. "Come, you'll sit here." He spoke gruffly as he indicated the place next to his own. "Any more nightmares?"

A solicitous question. Intimate. Heat assaulted her cheeks. "No, Herr Kommandant." Deciding she owed him at least a minimal courtesy, she added, "Thank you for . . . last night."

"You're welcome."

Stella thought she glimpsed a smile before he returned to his seat. Her attention moved to the sideboard, anxious to see what she'd be forced to eat this morning. To her relief, she spied a tureen of steaming oatmeal, slices of buttered rye toast—and no pork. Once she served herself, she sat down and began eating the warm, thick cereal with enthusiasm.

"You want nothing on it, Fräulein? Personally I find it tastes like paste unless it's buried under a mound of sugar."

She glanced up with a mouthful of oatmeal.

"But I'm pleased to see you taking my orders seriously."

His eyes lit with amusement, and Stella almost choked in her haste to swallow the food.

"It's been a long time since I've eaten so well," she said. "At Dachau we had gruel—"

The sudden fury in his expression stopped her. Had she angered him? Would he change his mind and take away the food? She tightened her grip on the spoon she held. "I'm sorry, Herr Kommandant, I meant no disrespect."

"Eat," he growled. Then with a sigh, added, "Please, Fräulein. Enjoy your breakfast."

Stella's hand shook as she reached for the silver tureen of cream, then the jar of golden honey. After heaping liberal amounts of each into her bowl, she held the spoon halfway to her lips before stealing another glance at the colonel.

He'd returned to studying his papers. She relaxed and ate more slowly, enjoying the forgotten delicacy. *Mmmm . . . oatmeal, land of milk and honey.* Her eyes drifted shut as she lost herself to the creamy sweetness. She couldn't remember when she'd savored such a treat, and surely it had never tasted so good.

When she opened her eyes, she found the colonel watching her, his features sharp. Like a hungry wolf . . . and she, the lamb?

Unnerved by his scrutiny, she picked up a slice of toast and cast a purposeful glance around her. In daylight, the soft beige walls of the dining room seemed more cozy than elegant. In addition to the sideboard stood a traditional German *Schrank* honed from walnut. Overhead, a spindled wood shelf ran along the room's perimeter, exhibiting an array of porcelain plates hand-painted with exquisite flowers. Six pictures decorated the walls, pastoral scenes much like the painting near the stairs.

"They belonged to my mother." He had followed the direction of her gaze. "I was fortunate to be able to bring them from Austria."

"As well as the castle painting by the landing?" She was unable to get the comforting scene out of her mind.

"The picture of my father's house? Yes. Baron von Schmidt commissioned a local artist in Thaur to paint it. I was born there—grew up there, in fact. I stayed until I left to go to university in Bonn." His expression turned pensive. "Of course, being from Innsbruck, you undoubtedly recognized it."

"Of course," Stella lied, relieved that she had guessed correctly. "Did you ever return?"

"Once. Long enough to bury my father."

He didn't elaborate, yet Stella sensed his bitterness. He'd also said his "father's house," not his own. Was this another piece to the puzzle of his character?

"Enough chatter." He glanced at her half-eaten bowl of oatmeal. "Finish your food, then back to bed."

"Bed? But I thought . . . what about your urgent letter to Berlin?"

"See, you're already proving to be a good secretary! Keeping the boss out of trouble with the boss, eh?" He grinned, and the hard lines disappeared from his face. Stella was again taken aback by his attractiveness; the slightly crooked nose merely enhanced his rugged features.

"I'll take care of Berlin," he said and patted her hand in an oddly affectionate gesture. "Actually, my giving you the day off is not as chivalrous as you might think. I must leave for a few days—meetings in Prague. You can rest while I'm gone. Now eat." Retrieving his glasses, he took up the sheaf of papers he'd been perusing.

———————

Aric glanced at Stella over the top of his report, noting how the dark half circles beneath her eyes emphasized her drawn features. Only her enthusiasm over breakfast tempered his anger each time he looked at her bruised face or the way her clothes hung loosely on her frame. He was amazed that he'd stumbled on to her in the first place; the *Lagerführer* should have caught the error on her papers when she first arrived at Dachau. Of course that meant believing the uniformed thugs in charge actually had the capacity to think.

The sight of her standing in front of a Dachau firing squad would haunt him the rest of his days. Half naked, with only a soiled shirt to cover her long-limbed frame, she'd leaned against a blood-spattered wall, gripping the hand of a child.

Aric shifted in his chair. He'd arrived at the precise moment a shot was fired—and the small girl crumpled like a rag doll. Stella's face was taut, her blue eyes blazing, yet she'd refused to let go. The small corpse dangled in her grasp, a sight made more grotesque for its sheer desperation.

He may have originally gone in search of her because of his attention to detail, or the inconsistency of her papers, or even because he'd once known a Muller family in Innsbruck—but everything changed for him in that instant. He'd plowed through the armed squad and bullied the guards for her release, then kept her off the train and instead bribed a Kapo to clothe her before stashing her inside the trunk of his car. Grossman drove with the speed of an all-out retreat to the nearby house of Aric's cousin, Hilde Gertz.

Aric couldn't understand why she mattered so much to him. The war had inured him to so much death and brutality; Stella was a stranger, who because of Gestapo malice had become merely another warm-blooded obstacle in the Reich's path.

Yet, having returned yesterday to retrieve Stella from his cousin's house after his business in Munich, he'd lifted her into his arms and felt jarred by his own fury. It was the first time in a long while something—someone—had moved him.

She was so thin he'd felt the protruding ribs beneath her thin cotton dress. Even this morning she seemed weak, enough so that he was glad he'd changed his plans.

Aric hadn't intended to leave her alone, but Eichmann's early phone call had changed all that. The SS-*Obersturmbannführer* was in Prague for a week's summit before continuing on to Berlin. When he'd suggested driving up to Theresienstadt to meet, Aric convinced him the city would be a better venue.

Aric didn't fool himself over his motives; he meant to protect her. *His wounded dove . . .*

His jaded humor left him as he watched her eat. Last night she'd asked to leave. He'd all but refused her, telling her that he needed a secretary. Aric knew that wasn't the whole truth of why he'd saved her. Still, whatever his real motives, he felt compelled to finish the task, to feed her until the hollows disappeared from her cheeks, dress her in fine clothes—blue to match the shade of her eyes—and pearls to encase her slender neck. She would smell of fragrant cloves and fine cigarettes, not body odor and fear.

He willed her to heal quickly. For the sooner she looked like one of his staff and less like a prisoner, the better. Until her hair grew out and the bruises on her face and hands faded, she was in constant danger.

She emptied her bowl and then patted her mouth with her linen napkin. He noted a marked improvement in the healthy pink color of her lips. So full of promise . . .

"I'm finished, Herr Kommandant."

A note of pride touched her voice. Aric let his report slide to the table. She sat perfectly straight in the chair with her hands in her lap, looking secretly pleased with herself.

Her fear of him had disappeared . . . or at least abated. A promising start. "Soon you'll grow so fat you'll be wearing my clothes," he teased.

Roses bloomed in her cheeks, and her mouth curved upward. "I would need a lot more oatmeal, Herr Kommandant."

Stunned by her first shy smile, he quickly recovered. "Then I'll have a convoy of trucks deliver the paste each week, and two cows and a beehive for the backyard!"

Her smile blossomed at his words. So lovely . . . even with red hair. He rose from his chair. "Come, time to rest." He held his hand toward her. She hesitated, but then took it.

Despite her frailness, she looked smart and sleek in the houndstooth. She would be lovelier still, given time.

Aric repressed the hope as swiftly as it began. Time was no longer a luxury he could afford. Nor was sentiment; it meant having to be human, to *feel*. He was a soldier, a machine, lacking the substance to change what he'd become, or the will to change what he must do.

Stella would get her wish; the phone call with Eichmann had ensured it. Yes, his stray dove *must* heal swiftly, for in a matter of weeks he would become the monster of her dreams.

Before that happened, he would set her free.

5

And Mordecai walked every day before the court . . .
to know how Esther did. . . .

Esther 2:11

TUESDAY, FEBRUARY 15, 1944

Needle-sharp barbs cut into Morty's flesh as he grasped the *Pflanzengarten* fence. He immediately let go and cursed his impulsiveness. Sparing a glance at his fingers, he was relieved to see no blood leaking from the wounds. God knew there wasn't enough of the red stuff greasing his frozen limbs to squander in the snow.

The vegetable garden took up an acre of land just outside Theresienstadt and was surrounded by perimeter fencing and a dozen searchlights. Only the lucky residents of the ghetto—those who tilled the soil and collected food for the Nazis' plates—were allowed a glimpse of the world outside the fortressed walls.

Nothing grew now. Instead, only cold white drifts stretched across the earth that once gave birth to squash, carrots, and those precious red-tipped heads of lettuce. Nothing flourished except the hope that a few potatoes had escaped earlier notice and still lay hidden within their frozen womb.

The biting wind made Morty's eyes water as he stared back

at the Mercedes pumping dirty white smoke into a leaden afternoon sky.

The new commandant closed the latticed gate and strode toward the waiting car. Where was she? Morty squinted, as if his gaze might penetrate the ochre and chalk walls of the brick house. He'd heard it from Saul Goldmeier, who'd heard it from little Joseph Witte by way of a secret message that there was a new guest in the house.

Saul was so eager to impart his gossip that the stingy sculptor had willingly shared leftovers from the commandant's table, his coveted reward for gathering kindling in the wooded lot behind the property. According to Joseph's note, the commandant had returned the previous night accompanied by a beautiful young woman—at least by the boy's standards—with eyes the color of a Judean sky and hair so light it shone gold. *Like Hadassah's* . . .

"Psst!" a voice whispered behind him. "Get over here and help us dig before the *Hauptsturmführer* sees you!"

Morty glanced at his friends. Yaakov Kadlec and Leo Molski each held a pick and bent to the task of penetrating a mound of snow. Leo, a lanky middle-aged Pole, wheezed from the effort, while Yaakov bore the ruddy-cheeked, barrel-chested sturdiness of his Czech ancestors and emptied his lungs with even breaths. Steamy tufts curled beneath the brim of his felt cap as he ground the pick's head into the snowbank and wiggled it.

"You're thinking about her again, aren't you?" Yaakov said, pausing in his labors. "I know you well, Mordecai Benjamin. Don't try to deny it." He shot a sidelong glance at Leo. "He's convinced Herr Kommandant's woman is his *maideleh*."

Leo's rheumy eyes focused on Morty. "Is it possible?" he said through clotted breaths. His skinny arms raised the pick only to drop it with an ineffectual blow. "This woman . . . could she be your little girl?"

"Ech!" Yaakov snorted. "If you believe that, Leo, I'll convince you this is freedom."

With a furtive sweep he indicated the barbed-wire fence. "We've been here years now, and this *yukel*"—he shot an impatient look at Morty—"still thinks she'll come. He watches the gate every time a trainload of women arrives in the ghetto. Black hair, brown hair, green eyes, gray, it makes no matter—each of them is his precious niece. I doubt he can even remember what she looks like."

Morty turned back to the fence.

"Ja, you don't like what I have to say, Morty. But I tell you, you're turning some kind of *meshugeh* over this nonsense."

"I'm not crazy," Morty called over his shoulder. "She'll come."

Yaakov muttered something under his breath to Leo, but Morty ignored them both. How could they understand? God sent *him* the vision.

The commandant climbed inside the back of the Mercedes. Why didn't the woman leave with him? Perhaps she sat warm and cozy before the fire inside his house. Morty smiled at the possibility. If Joseph was right, if she was beautiful, she could be Herr Kommandant's wife—or his mistress. Either way, she was lucky to have landed on the safe side of the fence.

And who knew this Nazi, anyway? He seemed unlike the other SS policing the ghetto. Since his arrival weeks before, he'd already exercised a measure of decency in the most obscure of instances: the collection of firewood.

Morty still wasn't certain if the commandant's offer of table scraps was a genuine act of kindness toward Jews collecting wood for his hearth or a sadistic brand of cruelty. Didn't he know that the hungry masses inside the ghetto assaulted those Jews returning with food?

Nein, not just food; food was watery broth with a few potato peels thrown in. The commandant's table hosted cuisine: *Linzertortes* and buttered noodles, apricot dumplings, all rich and decadent. Even the soldiers didn't eat so well.

The Jews drew lots so that each Tuesday and Friday five prisoners got to leave the fortress and collect kindling. Once selections were made, Morty always wondered which of them would stuff his or her face before returning at the end of the day.

Some, like Saul, avoided molestation by pretending to have eaten it all, packing his cheeks full and licking his fingers as he walked through the main gate. Only Morty knew that the rest of his meal was stuffed down the front of his pants or lined the inside of his felt cap . . .

"Morty, quick! The Hauptsturmführer's coming!"

Morty whipped around to see the familiar officer in black moving in their direction. His aching muscles stiffened. "Hermann," he growled under his breath.

"You! Why aren't you working?" the captain shouted from a distance.

Morty stood silent, his back to the fence. He snatched off his cap and dropped his gaze.

"You're supposed to be here on kitchen detail, Jew. Digging in the dirt for your food." The captain shoved Yaakov and Leo aside to plow past them through the heavy snow. He came to a halt in front of Morty. "What are you doing this close to the fence?"

Before Morty could form an answer, the roar of the departing Mercedes rent the air.

"Spying on Herr Kommandant, eh, Jew?"

Morty took a fisted clout to the head, making him stagger.

"Do you know what we do to spies, you filth?" Hermann's fist came down again, knocking Morty to his knees. "Shall we visit the *Kleine Festung* and find out?"

The Little Fortress. Morty's battered senses rang with the threat. The small garrison outside Theresienstadt was rumored to be a place where the SS practiced various means of torture.

"Answer me!"

Morty ground his teeth as he felt his right arm twisted in its socket. He dared not meet Hermann's gaze—his own anger was too great. "Herr Captain, I saw something . . . near the fence."

He opened his other hand to reveal a sharp-edged metal object that gleamed in the dull sun's rays.

"A Grand Cross?" Hermann released his arm and snatched up the shiny piece. "Who did you steal this from, Jew?"

"I found it."

"Liar!"

Another blow knocked Morty backward. Dazed, he struggled to his knees. "Here, in the snow," he said, masking his pain and fury. "Is it valuable, Herr Captain?" He swallowed bile. Of course he already knew the answer.

"This Grand Cross is from the First War." The captain turned the medal in his gloved hand. "Less than twenty of these were ever awarded." He looked at Morty derisively. "You soldiered in that war, didn't you? You know that to earn such a decoration, a man must demonstrate remarkable courage in battle."

Hermann's taunt failed to hide his grudging admiration. "Too bad that man will never see this again." He closed his fist around the Cross. "It will look splendid framed on the wall of my office. Below my picture of der Führer, eh?"

Morty schooled his expression despite Hermann's malicious grin. Inside, he fought cold-blooded rage, letting it wash over him, beyond him, taking with it this latest assault on his pride.

"Now, get back to digging. All of you, or I'll begin to think you don't appreciate my generosity." Hermann's look promised retribution before he turned and tramped back to the one-man guardhouse at the entrance of the Pflanzengarten.

"How could you give the Hauptsturmführer your Grand Cross?" Yaakov hissed as soon as the captain was out of earshot. "You're a fool, Morty."

Morty glared at him. "I'm a fool who will live another day! You both heard what he said. I had to think of something—or face the inside of the Little Fortress." He shivered against more than the bitter cold. "No one leaves there in one piece."

He struggled to his feet, dusting the cold white powder from his clothes. "Besides," he said, trying to muster conviction, "what do I need with that medal now, anyway?"

"But you went to such lengths to keep them from taking it. When you told me where you hid it during the initial strip search . . ." Yaakov's shoulders bunched. "It still makes me flinch."

"This time my hide was at stake. And I believe God would agree it the more worthy cause."

Leo leaned against his pick, wheezing. "But it seems such a . . . crime to just hand it over to them now, Morty. Especially to that . . . pig Hermann, of all people."

"What has that medal ever done for me?" Morty demanded. "Bought me freedom, or at least given me my own bed to sleep in? Does it clothe me in something warmer than this summer jacket while I root around in the snow like an animal—for worms, rotten potatoes, anything I can shove down my throat to ease the craving in my belly?"

"What about your pride, Jew?" Yaakov waved a callused fist in the air. "What about your dignity as a soldier?"

Morty let out a rusty bark of laughter. "Jewish pride is a luxury we can no longer afford, my friends. As for a soldier's dignity," he went on, his voice turning bitter, "that no longer exists. These soldiers do not fight for Germany. They fight for Hitler, who fights for a place that doesn't include us filthy Jews."

Yaakov relaxed his stance. "Ja," he admitted. "Hitler has taken my own Czechoslovakia and turned it into a war zone. Even our beloved city of Terezin."

He stared at the fortress behind them, then spit at the frozen ground. "The Nazis have shamed her, turning her into a holding pen for Auschwitz." He jabbed the head of his pick against the snow. "Resort, my foot."

"Paradise . . ." Leo echoed in wheezing disgust.

"I'll take over for a while, Leo. You rest." Morty grabbed the other man's pick by its handle. Teeth clenched, he drew on all his strength to raise the axe over his head and let it fall again, chipping away a large chunk of unforgiving earth.

He understood their resentment; the Nazis had also deceived Morty into believing he was bound for a spa resort, a *Paradies-ghetto*, in Czechoslovakia. "Hitler's Gift"—a reward for affluent Jews the Reich considered prominent figures in Europe: an eclectic assortment of artists, musicians, writers, and like himself, a few highly decorated heroes from Germany's first big war.

Any expectations had vanished once he arrived. Behind Theresienstadt's stone walls lay squalid living conditions, disease, and death—like a festering boil the most expensive cosmetics could not hide. And food . . .

Morty actually feared thinking about it. That he never had enough to eat filled him with such despair, his tenuous hold on sanity often stretched to the point of pain.

Yet at night, in his dreams, he recounted in intimate detail his favorite dishes. *Wiener Schnitzel*, the lightly breaded veal cooked extra tender and served with red sauerkraut, onion *Kuchen*, palffy dumplings, glazed fruit bread, and of course plum-filled *Zwetschken Strudel* for dessert.

Food had been such an integral part of family life. It brought loved ones together in communion with God's gifts, shared laughter mingled with the exchanges of news, while problems were unburdened onto the shoulders of those who, above all, understood.

Each morning as he awakened from the dreams, Morty felt a sense of comfort, of being *normal*. It sustained him with enough rational thought to face another day in the place Jews called "Hell's Gate."

He glanced back to where the commandant's Mercedes had been. All that remained was a depression of tire tracks in the snow, like the heaviness that pressed against his heart as he thought of the woman inside that house. She with the blond hair and blue eyes of his beautiful niece . . .

"You keep standing there holding that pick like a golf club, and the captain will surely be back," Yaakov warned. "Then we'll all end up in the Little Fortress and Mrs. Brenner won't have anything for the pot."

Morty raised the pick for another blow.

"Here, give me that." Yaakov snatched the pick from his hands. "Already you've mangled two potatoes, see? You'll need to dig out the rest by hand."

Morty arched a brow. "You know I have bad knees," Yaakov grumbled. "Leo's too weak to dig. You must do it."

Morty crouched beside the furrowed hole. "I miss her, Yaakov. The young woman Joseph wrote to us about this morning? She sounds so much like Hadassah."

"But you'll get . . . your chance to see her, won't you?" Leo spoke up. "Yaakov said because you are Elder of the *Judenrat*, you are invited to a welcoming party for the new commandant at the end of the month, ja?"

"*Invited*, Yaakov?" Morty shot a withered look at his stocky friend. "As Elder, my only obligation is to organize the musicians for the party. A guard will escort them to the house. I doubt I'll even be allowed outside the ghetto walls."

"Too bad. Joseph could smuggle you some of that delicious food they'll be serving." The Czech looked wistful. "He is a clever one, that boy. Sometimes too clever—like that dangerous game he plays with you sending secret messages back and forth."

Morty's cheeks flushed. Even though Joseph had devised the plan, Morty found himself too starved for news from the outside to object. As for danger, well . . .

One risked death by simply existing in this place.

"Ech! What's the use of talking to you?" Yaakov said in exasperation. "Stop thinking so much." He smiled then, displaying a row of widely spaced teeth. "I'm sure your maideleh is safe. Probably tucked away in some warm, safe place with a full belly and a happier disposition than the three of us."

Like the woman in the brick house? Morty forced a smile. "You're probably right."

He breathed the chill air, feeling it sear his lungs as he bent to dig out potatoes. His thoughts returned to Mannheim. The Nazis had appeared without warning. They herded his people into a part of town that formed a *shtetl*, a ghetto separating Jews from the rest of the Gentile community. Hadassah had gone to work in Heidelberg that morning. He hadn't seen her again. How long had it been? Weeks? Months? Years? He struggled to remember.

"Hand me those potatoes, Morty. I'll . . . carry them," Leo called out.

Morty stared at the ground. He'd unearthed ten of the little jewels. His numbed fingers managed to grasp them and toss them one by one into Leo's aproned shirt. The rankness of the wrinkled, wet skins filled his nostrils, but he didn't care. Any addition to their daily ration of watery gruel would be an improvement.

Food had been scarce in the shtetl as well, and housing cramped—as many as fifteen people stuffed into a single room.

A luxury compared to what he had now.

He scrambled to his feet. "Let's get these to Mrs. Brenner." Snagging Leo's pick, Morty led the way past the guardhouse toward the main gate of the fortress . . . and back into their world of hopeless existence. He turned and cast a last glance at the brick house. A heavy sigh rose in him. *I do not doubt your message, God. But I do wonder when . . .*

He told himself to be patient. Many events in the vision had already taken place. Yaakov was right. Hadassah was alive. With her false identification papers, she must have escaped.

A sudden calm settled over him. The prophecy would be fulfilled.

She would be their salvation.

6

*Then on the thirteenth day of the first month the
royal secretaries were summoned.*

Esther 3:12

Monday, February 21, 1944

Death lists.

A chill swept through Stella as she scanned the papers
in her hand. She'd been impatient after her week of mandated
bed rest and arrived at the library that morning sharply at eight
for her first day of work. Nervously anticipating her employer's
summons, she'd removed the gray cloth cover from the typewriter, then sorted through a mound of folders on top of the
green filing cabinet beside her desk.

Stella spied one folder marked FINAL SOLUTION, along with a
terse note to re-file it. Peering inside, she found scores of pages
with names, presumably those of prisoners inside Theresienstadt. Typed headers ran the length of each sheet:

Name   Prisoner Identification   Arrival   Departure

Arrival dates varied for each name, but the same departure
dates continued for several pages. The second of November was
the last recorded, almost four months ago.

A chill ran along her spine at the word *Auschwitz* scrawled in pencil across the top of each sheet. Rumors had spread as far away as Dachau of a place where Jews were sent and never returned. Where Krematorium fires burned day and night . . .

"Fräulein Muller!"

Stella jerked at the sound of the colonel's voice. She quickly shoved the lists back into the folder. Grabbing up her steno pad and pen, she rushed from her desk into his office.

After a week's absence, the colonel still looked formidable. Seated behind his large mahogany desk, elbows against its top, he gestured her toward a chair across from him.

She edged onto the leather seat and waited. He said nothing as he studied her a long moment. She wondered when he'd left the note to re-file the Auschwitz deportation lists.

"Anxious to get this over with?" He nodded at her death grip on the steno pad and pen.

Stella's cheeks warmed as she eased back into the chair. "I'm merely eager to get started, Herr Kommandant."

He exposed her lie with a sardonic smile. She raised her chin, refusing to back down.

"I'm glad to see the shadows gone beneath your eyes. You're sufficiently rested, then?"

She'd slept almost nonstop for days. "Yes, Herr Kommandant."

"And your cheeks are starting to fill out." He scrutinized her as though she were a ripe tomato at market. "Helen's food must agree with you."

The brusque woman brought increasingly larger meals to her room each day, and she seemed to enjoy Stella's discomfort at having to force down every bite. "As you see," she said curtly, then thought to add, "Thank you."

"You're welcome."

His gentle tone affected her like an unwanted caress. Traitorous heat rose in her face. She felt as if she'd lost some unspoken battle between them.

"Nightmares?"

She shook her head and flipped open the steno pad on her lap, unwilling to continue this one-sided laundering of vulnerabilities. "Shall I take dictation now?"

"Ah, yes, to work." His sigh could have been amusement or exasperation. "To SS-Obersturmbannführer Adolf Eichmann, SS Headquarters in Berlin. Heil Hitler . . ."

When he'd finished dictating his letter, Stella read her notes:

. . . after our meeting in Prague, I received new information that the International Red Cross plans a "surprise" inspection of Theresienstadt as early as March. In light of this important event for the Führer and Herr Reichsführer Himmler, you will agree we must postpone the final matter we discussed.

What final matter? She glanced up to find the colonel had left his chair to stand in front of the barred window of his office. Watery light filtered through narrow panes of glass, casting him in ethereal shadows.

He seemed pensive. She wondered which of the letter's contents he found more disturbing, the Red Cross visit or the postponement of some unnamed "matter" with Lieutenant-Colonel Eichmann.

The colonel moved slightly, and Stella glimpsed his face in the light.

His abject misery shocked her.

She envisioned him as a young man leaving his father's house; perhaps he'd vowed for some painful reason never to return. Not until the older man's death forced him back.

Sudden empathy seized her. She rose from her chair to reach out to him, to . . . to . . .

The deportation lists flashed in her mind. "Will that be all, Herr Kommandant?" She gripped the back of the chair, shaken by what she'd nearly done.

"Yes." He turned to her, his breath coming fast, uneven. "We are finished."

Ten minutes later, Stella sat at her desk typing, unable to shake the colonel's last remark. Did his words hold some double meaning? Why did his mood bother her so much?

Each day that she grew stronger fueled her determination to leave—with or without his permission. If she chose the latter, she would need time to work out the details of her escape: what supplies to take, where to go once she managed it, and how to survive the coldest part of winter.

The folder on the green cabinet caught her eye. She dared wonder about her uncle: Could he be here, at Theresienstadt? Was Morty's name on those lists?

Stella had made discreet inquiries after him in Mannheim before her ill-fated abduction. Her efforts had never borne fruit. Maybe he lay dead in some other camp . . .

But what if he *was* here? She glanced at the finished letter in the typewriter, torn between risking the colonel's wrath by delay and her desire to search the file for her uncle's name. Anxious thoughts plagued her. Was Morty sick? Did he have warm clothes . . . and what about shoes?

A bittersweet ache pierced her. Mannheim's cobbler, Herr Schiffel, had made a special pair every year for her uncle, who happened to own the largest pair of feet on the Roonstrasse. The neighbors always gave Morty a ribbing on that day— "Flatboats," "Toe skis," "Yaks"—but he endured their jibes with good humor.

His last pair of shoes must be in tatters by now. The Nazis wouldn't bother to have others made for him. What if he was barefoot in this weather?

Her cheeks felt hot as she wiggled her bare toes under the desk, having freed them from the too-tight shoes. Morty wasn't the only one risking death in this cold.

Joseph told her about the clothes. "SS surplus," he'd explained on her second morning when she discovered the various sizes in her armoire had been replaced with clothing that fit her perfectly. Stella browsed through the expensive garments, noting the occasional outline of a star over the left breast on several sweaters and jackets.

Her clothes had been stolen from Jews.

She didn't want to imagine the woman who had owned such beautiful clothes. Likely she now wore a thin cotton dress much like the one Stella had arrived in.

Even her shoes were stolen goods. Stella ignored their discomfort as she slipped them on and rose from the desk. Their previous owner likely now wore chafing clogs—if she still lived.

Gripping the colonel's letter hard enough to crease it, Stella marched into his office. She envisioned those suffering behind Theresienstadt's walls, people huddled together like shivering sticks in the cold while her employer indulged in the luxury of his own melancholy.

He hadn't moved from the window. "Your letter, Herr Kommandant," she said, banking her hostility.

He turned to her, his stony features back in place. "Wait while I proofread it."

Stella barely breathed as he took the letter and returned to his desk. He fished his glasses from his pocket and perused the document for several minutes.

Then he reached for his pen and scrawled his signature in flawless, bold script. The air eased from her lungs.

"Impressive." He handed the letter back to her. "Have Sergeant Grossman post it immediately."

Pride and relief flowed through her.

"I think your job is safe enough for the moment." He made an effort to smile, but she could tell it cost him; her wisp of satisfaction surrendered to another unwanted pang of compassion. Or was it more than that?

Days without his company hadn't dampened her awareness

of him; his rough, uneven features were pleasing to the eye, and though he had the strength to crush her, he'd shown her only gentleness and consideration . . .

He walked around the desk to her, his troubled eyes searching her face. "Stella . . ."

He placed a hand lightly against her shoulder, and heat emanated from his touch. She pursed her lips as a pang of unwanted tenderness threatened to overpower her better judgment.

His hand fell back to his side. "That will be all for now."

Stella felt a ridiculous urge to cry. Heat suffused her face as she spun away from him, desperate to leave his presence before he witnessed her condition.

Back at her desk, she took deep breaths until the ache in her throat subsided. She couldn't rid herself of his haunted look—a desolation that threatened to penetrate her caution, breaking down every survival instinct she possessed.

She would be a good secretary. She owed him that much. Anything beyond that . . .

Through the shadow of her memories rose a face with long dark lashes and golden brown eyes. Then the loud shot of a pistol, a child falling to the frozen earth . . .

Stella's eyes burned. *It should have been me.*

Angrily she glanced toward the colonel's open door. No, *he* was the enemy. Aric von Schmidt may not have pulled the trigger, but his brethren had.

Leave him to his own torment.

7

*Then Esther summoned Hathach, one of the king's
eunuchs assigned to attend her. . . .*

Esther 4:5

TUESDAY, FEBRUARY 22, 1944

Stella glanced out at the predawn sky. The violet-gray light
pulled into focus the ghetto's towering stone bastions. The
immutable island she'd once imagined now looked like the prow
of an advancing ship, a ship full of Jews.

Where was their final destination?

She'd finished sorting through the deportation lists, relieved
that Morty's name was not among those sent to Auschwitz. Sleep
had evaded her, however. Stella felt a pressing need to winnow
truth from rumor about the horrible place, and to know how
much of a monster her employer really was.

Freshly showered and dressed, she sat on the edge of the bed
and reached toward the nightstand for the wristwatch Joseph
had given her.

The Bible lay beside it. Stella felt a prickle at her nape. The
book hadn't been there when she'd awoken this morning. She
hadn't seen it since she'd put it away in the drawer last week.

Had someone been in her room?

Joseph. Likely he'd removed it from the drawer while she was in the shower. He'd asked her to pray for his parents, and since she denied being Jewish, he must have assumed she was a Christian. Did he intend to give her a little inspiration?

Faintly amused, Stella picked up the book. Marta might call its mysterious appearance "Getting the Holy Nudge." Her best friend had had lots of sayings: "The road to heaven is paved with potholes," and "When you fall from grace it's a hard landing."

Stella felt a wave of homesickness. How she missed Marta! They had grown up together on the Roonstrasse, inseparable despite their different beliefs. In their teens, Marta confided to a motherless Stella the facts of life. Years later, Stella helped Marta find an apartment in Heidelberg when they started working together at Schnellpressen AG. Through the years they shouldered one another through boyfriends, bat mitzvahs, and overbearing bosses. And when the Nazis invaded Mannheim, Marta risked everything to keep her friend safe.

She must have been frantic when Stella didn't return that night—a lifetime ago. Where was Marta now? What was she doing?

No doubt praying for me, Stella thought as she stared at the Bible in her hands. Not that it was doing any good . . .

A soft rap sounded at the door. "Come in."

"You're already up!" Joseph stated the obvious as he gaped at Stella's fully clothed form.

The boy's reaction confused her. If he hadn't been in her room this morning, then who had? The colonel? Helen?

She patted the place beside her on the bed. "Joseph, I'd like to speak with you for a few minutes." Stella couldn't count on prayers, Marta's or anyone else's. She could only rely on herself. Right now she intended to find out from Joseph more about the deportation lists—without making him any the wiser. Then if the colonel did question him later, he would seem innocent enough.

Joseph sat down and eyed the Bible in her lap. "What do you want to talk about?"

What ruse could she try? Coercing the colonel rested so much easier on her conscience. "As you know, yesterday was my first day working for Herr Kommandant," she began.

"Did you have to work hard?"

She smiled at his obvious concern. "Not too hard."

Joseph had been her dutiful champion during the colonel's absence. He stood sentinel at her door while she slept, and when she longed for company, the boy happily chatted with her about mundane household matters. Only when she broached the subject of life inside the fortressed walls of Theresienstadt did he become quiet.

"I found papers in a file that mention a place called Auschwitz. I wish to know where it is," she said, hoping to sound only mildly curious.

His body went still beside her. "Why don't you ask Herr Kommandant?" he whispered.

Slipping an arm around his shoulders, she pulled him close, ignoring a stab of guilt. "You know how busy he is. I can't waste his valuable time with such questions."

She met with success when he relaxed against her and said, "It's a bad place where people die. In the east, I think. The Judenrat picks who must go there on the train."

"Judenrat?"

"The Council of Elders. Jews that run the ghetto."

She was surprised. "Jews actually get to control what happens behind those walls?"

"Only when the Nazis say so," the boy clarified. "Mostly the Elders just break up fights, divide up the food, and call prisoners for *Appell*. Work that Herr Captain and his men don't feel like doing."

"Like making deportation lists?" She couldn't imagine any Jew willing to send his own people to a place like Auschwitz.

"Ja," he said, staring down at his palms. "Herr Captain makes them choose."

Stella roughly fanned the pages of the Bible she still held. No doubt Hermann enjoyed forcing her people to turn against one another like cornered rats. "Joseph, you say 'they' and 'them' when you speak of this council. How many Elders are there?"

"Only one right now. The others got too sick."

Anger flared inside her. One Jew must carry the weight of so many upon his shoulders? "Is he a friend of yours?"

Joseph nodded. "I haven't seen him for a while, not since Herr Kommandant came here and gave me a place to stay in his house."

"You said Herr Kommandant has only been here a short time?"

He counted on his fingers. "Five weeks," he said. "Kommandant Rahm left a long time ago. Then Captain Hermann lived here in the house. He ran the camp until Herr Kommandant came to take his place."

Tension eased from her limbs. She had her answer; the last deportation occurred well before the colonel arrived at Theresienstadt. He hadn't sent those people to Auschwitz.

He was far from exonerated, however. "Tell me how you came to be in this house, Joseph," she said.

The boy flexed the worn leather tips of his boots as if to study them. "It was God's doing," he said, then nodded with the certainty of innocence. "Herr Kommandant came to the ghetto that first day with Captain Hermann and some other SS. I stole two potatoes the day before, from the barracks kitchen, and Lieutenant Brucker did this." He angled his head to show the scab where his ear had been. "Mrs. Brindel works in the ghetto infirmary. She wrapped my head in an ugly pink towel." His hands fisted in his lap. "I looked silly."

"I'm sure you didn't," Stella said soothingly while her heart filled with hatred for Lieutenant Brucker.

"Herr Kommandant thought I looked silly, too." Joseph lifted his face to hers. "Do you know why?"

Stella shook her head.

"'Cause he stared at me and said, 'What's wrong with that boy?' Captain Hermann told him how I got punished. Herr Kommandant said, 'What was his crime?' Then the captain told him I took the potatoes. Herr Kommandant's face turned so red he looked sunburned. I thought he was going to tell the captain to kill me."

When he paused, Stella absently clutched at the Bible and whispered, "What did he do to you?"

"Nothing." Joseph lifted his skinny shoulders. "All he said to Captain Hermann was, 'I need a houseboy. Delouse that one and send him to me.' I came here after that." A smile kicked up one side of his mouth. "Helen gave me a clean bandage. Herr Kommandant told her to burn the pink towel in the fireplace."

Unsettling warmth spread through Stella. It seemed her employer's compassion extended beyond rescuing half-starved secretaries. She planted a kiss on top of Joseph's tousled crown. "Well, I'm certainly glad you're here. You happen to be my only friend in this place."

Joseph gave her an earnest look. "You will always be mine."

He surprised her by grabbing her around the waist and burying his face against her. She hugged him hard, her maternal instincts savoring the pressure of his small body against hers.

"You smell nice," he said against her shoulder. "Like the spices Mama and Papa used after Shabbat."

Stella started to agree before she bit her tongue in silence. She must keep her secret, for his sake if nothing else.

The mention of his dead parents triggered another worry in her. "Do you have any other family?"

He shook his head and squeezed her harder. All at once her dreams of escape withered against a new, more powerful emotion. She couldn't leave him behind. "When the war is over, you'll come home with me," she said with a smile.

He leaned back and eyed her in disbelief. "You mean, live with you . . . as long as I want?"

"Absolutely." A wistful ache pierced Stella's heart. She'd offered the same to Anna.

"Where will we live? Do you have a house?"

Her smile faltered. During *Kristallnacht* the Nazis had shattered the storefront window of her uncle's smithy. Then they used Morty's forging tools to destroy Herr Kinzer's Furrier next door, stealing mink coats, sable wraps, and a jeweled muff from his broken glass display. The destruction hadn't ended there. All along the Roonstrasse the monsters ransacked apartments above her neighbors' shops, tossing out everything from women's lacy undergarments to fine Dresden china plates, family photographs, and furniture—even a baby's crib. Below in the street, their comrades laughed as frantic Jews tried to reclaim their possessions. *They divide my garments among them and cast lots for my clothing. . . ."*

Psalm twenty-two again. Stella felt the weight of the Bible heavy against her lap. "We'll find someplace," she said reassuringly. "How about a castle? I know of a palace with ceilings of gold and velvet draperies and so many mirrors you can look into any of them to see all the way through to the rest of the rooms."

"There's a real place like that?"

She nodded. "And great golden lions spout water into a blue pool beside a beautiful garden. There's even a grotto built inside a cave. We'll sail our own little boat while actors perform onstage across the water."

"Golden lions?" Joseph breathed. "Our own little boat?"

"I promise." Stella would make it a point to take him to Bavaria's famed Linderhof Castle. "You will also go to school."

Faint color stained his cheeks. "Papa showed me a little how to read and write and add numbers. I've never been in a real school."

Of course not—he'd been held captive like an animal instead. She kissed his brow. "Once I was a teacher at Dachau," she said gently. "Our International Committee—a lot like your Judenrat, I think—decided the children in the camp needed an education. They chose me because I was teaching Anna her numbers."

"Who's Anna?"

Stella gazed at him, then said, "My very special little girl."

"Where is she?" He seemed to tense. "Did you have to leave her at Dachau?"

"No, she died when . . ." Stella cleared her throat. "Anna died trying to save me."

"Then she's in heaven." Again he spoke with the conviction of an innocent heart. "Mama told me going to heaven would be wonderful. She said she would never need a coat, 'cause it's always summertime and there's lots of Strudel so you never go hungry. They would never have to dig holes or shovel dirt, and they could sing and dance all day 'cause the angels would play music on accordions and trumpets." He gave her a shy look. "I think Anna is with them now. Since God brought you to me."

Stella said nothing as she brushed back a curly lock of his hair. She didn't know what she believed anymore, only that when Joseph was with her, the ache of losing Anna didn't hurt as much. Somehow she and this child had been brought together and they needed each other.

They would be a family—her and Joseph. And Morty . . .

The last required faith, didn't it? A belief that God still listened.

She reached around the boy and placed the Bible inside the nightstand drawer.

"You and me," she said, giving him another hug. "Just you and me."

8

*And the king gave a great banquet . . . for all his
nobles and officials.*

Esther 2:18

SUNDAY, FEBRUARY 27, 1944

She felt like a harlot.

Pausing at the top of the stairs, Stella adjusted the red
wig, then fidgeted with the daring neckline of her aqua chiffon
dress. She felt conspicuous and vulnerable.

In two weeks' time her bruised hands had healed. They swept
nervously across the gauzy skirt, while her toes curled inside a
new pair of soft kid pumps that fit well and matched her dress
perfectly. A double rope of creamy pearls hugged the column
of her throat. Stella imagined them choking her.

This wasn't the dress of a secretary. Her employer had purchased the blue confection during his week in Prague. When he'd
presented it to her just that morning, he informed her they were
giving a supper party tonight. She would need clothes suitable
to her position.

It was at this mental juncture that Stella paused. What exactly
did he expect from her?

The distinct hum of voices rose from downstairs. Apprehension clawed Stella's insides as she fought an urge to return to the sanctuary of her room. Taking a deep breath, she resumed her descent. An unexpected wave of nostalgia rose in her as she heard lively strains from Verdi's "Triumphal March" coming from the living room. It had been so long since she'd heard music, and the melody made her miss her uncle even more. In Mannheim, she and Morty shared such an appreciation for the classics.

Reaching the bottom step, her gaze flew to the familiar castle painting. The misty wooded setting offered an inexplicable comfort that worked like the music to soothe her frayed nerves.

Such a tranquil place. Why had the colonel never returned? Stella hadn't forgotten the morning at breakfast when she glimpsed a boy's bitter yearning—

"So, what do you think, Captain? Lovely, isn't she?"

Stella spun around to find the colonel eyeing her with appreciation. He held two glasses of pale wine. "*Pouilly-Fuisse. My personal favorite, Fräulein.*" His deep voice swept over her like Verdi's dulcet notes as he offered her a glass.

"Danke, Herr Kommandant." Stella accepted the wine with cursory politeness, ignoring the traitorous flutter of her pulse. Despite his black SS uniform, he seemed hardly threatening as he stood before her, tall and distinguished, his smile softening the hard angles of his face.

She'd already completed her first week of work and so far had managed to keep their relationship on a strictly professional plane. The colonel, however, seemed to have other plans, laying siege to her emotional armor with battlefield vengeance.

A day didn't go by that he failed to compliment her, and his apparent fondness for Joseph had her wondering by the hour if he wasn't more human than monster after all. And when the warm humor in his eyes darkened to unspeakable despair, she felt an overwhelming urge to reach out to him, to offer comfort as though he was a friend and not her vilest enemy.

It took all of her discipline to maintain the wall that must remain between them if she was to survive. But the colonel was gaining ground.

"Fräulein Muller, you remember Captain Hermann?"

Stella tensed as she turned to meet the captain's hazel-eyed stare. Joseph had told her of his brutal treatment toward the prisoners. Hermann's hatred of Jews seemed only surpassed by his desire to inflict pain. "Herr Captain."

"Fräulein." Bowing curtly, he swept off his peaked cap to reveal a mowed thatch of white-blond hair. "We finally meet again. I was beginning to think you were a phantom."

Stella *had* managed to avoid him after that first night. Each afternoon as he arrived to give his daily report to the colonel, she fled for safety—any room in the house far enough away from his presence.

Like a mouse scurried the instant the cat was near, she thought in agitation. Now the "cat" was joining them for supper, and she had nowhere to hide. "As you can see, I'm no ghost."

"Hardly that," he agreed. Stella felt rather than saw his prurient interest as he stared at her. Or perhaps crudeness had become permanently etched into his glacial features.

Either way, she clenched the stem of her wineglass while heat from indignation and fear rose above her choker of pearls.

"See how beautifully she blushes, Captain? I believe even the Führer would envy my good fortune at having such a secretary." The colonel winked. "Especially when he has so many letters of complaint to deal with."

Oblivious to the veiled blasphemy, Hermann continued to stare at Stella. "I agree Fräulein is beautiful." He finally glanced toward the colonel. "But I am certain our beloved Führer envies no one. Shall we join the others, Herr Kommandant?"

"You go ahead, Captain. We'll be along."

With another curt bow, the captain departed. Stella breathed a sigh of relief. Even in company, he made her skin crawl.

"Shall we make a toast before dinner?"

The colonel drew her attention with his raised glass. "To beauty?"

His teasing smile was like balm after Hermann's icy appraisal, and she tried to smother the growing intimacy she felt for him. She didn't want to trust this man; he was as much the enemy as the captain. Yet unlike Hermann, she felt safe with him—at least for the present—and he knew it. Even now he sensed her weakening resolve and tried to exploit it.

The thought roused her dislike of him long enough to raise her glass. "To ability," she countered, "which far outlasts beauty."

Ignoring his startled look, she sipped her wine, savoring the fruity Chardonnay. Like the music, it had been too long since she'd indulged in such pleasure.

"Ability." His smile bore the hint of approval.

A myriad of delicious smells drifted in from the kitchen. Stella's stomach growled.

"And to appetite." He eyed her above the rim of his glass. "No sweeter sound."

Stella blushed.

"Shall we join the others?"

He took her hand and led the way. Near the dining room, the din of voices grew louder, echoed by the *clink* of glass and silverware. The music in the living room had shifted into energetic measures of Schubert's *Unfinished Symphony* while the tantalizing aroma of rosemary potatoes, sauerkraut, and fried onions assailed Stella's senses.

Even the colonel inhaled deeply and said, "The Führer may lack nothing—nothing except the finest cook in the land. Wouldn't you agree?" He appraised Stella with a look far less predatory than the captain's. "In the two weeks you've been here, I believe Helen has performed a miracle."

"I like a meatier dish." The pearls at her throat seemed to tighten as she recalled the words he'd spoken two weeks ago in

the car. She shot back without thinking, "A miracle for whom, Herr Kommandant?"

He jerked her to a halt. "You are still ungrateful for the food?"

"Nein." Regretting her rashness, Stella looked down at their still-joined hands, vaguely aware of the contrast of skin—hers pale against his darker tones—before his fingers squeezed hers in a painful grip.

"Gut. Then I expect you to eat and not embarrass me in front of my guests."

Her heart sank. They must be having pork again. It shouldn't matter any longer, yet she still found it difficult to break faith with a divine heritage that had been hers from conception. And though she tried to avoid eating what her people considered *traif*, pork was a favorite meat of the colonel's, and despite the difficulty in obtaining it, they ate it often.

She consoled herself with having finally realized his criticism stemmed more from an aversion to wasting food than it did over what she was reluctant to eat. Her secret was still safe.

In the dining room, Captain Hermann, along with five others—three men and two women—already sat at the table. Each man wore a black tunic sporting the silver *Tresse* and collar patches of an SS officer. They rose in unison when she and the colonel joined them.

"Our man of the hour has arrived!" the tallest proclaimed, raising his wineglass in salute.

"*Prosit!*" echoed the others, raising their glasses.

The women remained seated at the table: a wispy blonde in a white satin V-neck dress, and a brunette with hair piled into a French roll and revealing her generous bosom beneath a strapless red taffeta gown. Stella's skin felt hot as both turned their painted faces toward her, then glanced back at each other, giggling.

"Danke, my friends." The colonel led Stella to a place near the head of the table. She was dismayed to find Hermann seated directly opposite her on the colonel's left. He flashed her a cold, catlike smile.

"It's not every day we get a war hero in our midst. Or one so young," the tallest officer continued. He winked at the blonde beside him. "At only thirty, you make the rest of us look like doddering old reservists, Herr Colonel."

"I doubt that, Major." The colonel smiled, pushing in Stella's chair. "Herr Reichsführer informed me that you run a tight camp at Litomerice."

The major flushed, clearly pleased. "I imagine that after Kommandant Rahm took ill and departed, the captain here appreciated your timely arrival. Running a camp is no easy task."

Every head turned to Captain Hermann. Stella wondered if anyone else noticed the muscle in his jaw flinch at the major's remark.

"Yes, well, I am equally grateful, Major, to have such a capable officer. The captain has made my transition quite comfortable."

The colonel straightened to stand beside Stella. "I appreciate everyone braving this weather to come and officially welcome me to Theresienstadt." His hand settled against her shoulder. "I'd also like to introduce the newest member of my household—"

"Comfortable transition indeed, Herr Colonel!" the major boomed, tipping his glass in Stella's direction. The other men chuckled.

". . . my secretary, Fräulein Muller."

The colonel's tone held an edge as speculation lit the four pairs of male eyes focused on her. A titter of female laughter erupted from across the table, fading with the final strains of Schubert. Only the gurgle of running water and clatter of metal pots from the kitchen remained.

Stella met their looks with forced calm while anger seethed in her like an acid tide. Darting a glance at her neckline, she felt her skin burn beneath the lavish pearls at her throat.

How convenient she'd dressed the part of the "Kommandant's

mistress," since it seemed everyone assumed as much. And the colonel only encouraged the assumption, showing her off like a conquering king's spoils.

Though she lacked the courage to glare at the men, Stella glowered at the heavily made-up faces across from her. She knew what these women were. Many times she'd taken the train home from work and seen the scantily dressed *zoinehs* loitering along Heidelberg's bar district.

She was no prostitute!

The colonel pressed his fingers gently against her shoulder. Stella tensed. Did he offer an unspoken apology for their blatant insult, or was he showing possession over his goods?

"This is Dita," he said, gesturing to the smirking blonde in white, "and Marenka. They're here with Major Lindberg and Lieutenant Neubach." He indicated the tall major, then a stocky middle-aged officer standing beside the voluptuous zoineh in red.

"Captain Hoth is Berlin's attaché to the Prague office."

"A pleasure, Fräulein." The soft-spoken captain with sable hair and blue eyes seated beside her looked much younger than the other two.

Stella acknowledged each of them with a single nod. To her relief, Helen chose that moment to arrive from the kitchen, and all eyes turned to food. She bore to the table an appetizing platter of *Sauerbraten*, the marinated roast beef smothered in tangy brown gravy, along with carrots and potatoes. Her second trip yielded silver serving dishes filled with relishes, golden fried Käsespätzle, and freshly baked rolls, followed by dried fruit and a board of cheese.

Within minutes the feast was laid before them. Burgundy wine glistened in heavy goblets of Austrian crystal, and not an ounce of pork was in sight.

"You've been here mere weeks, Herr Colonel. How is it you've already become the center of our Führer's attention?" The major stabbed at several slices of roast beef and piled them onto his plate. "I hear he's chosen Theresienstadt as his showcase for an upcoming International Red Cross inspection?"

"Correct, Major. Never let it be said our Führer ignores the rules of Geneva." The colonel failed to hide his sarcasm. "Berlin informs me the Swiss should arrive in less than two weeks."

He spooned a small portion of Käsespätzle, followed by carrots, onto Stella's plate. She flushed at the snickers from the zoinehs across the table as they selected their own food.

"Will you be ready by then?" the major asked.

The colonel reached for a slice of the Sauerbraten and cut it in half on his plate. He glanced at Captain Hermann. "How is construction coming on the children's schoolroom?"

"So far we're on schedule, Herr Kommandant. Rebar for the new floor in the barracks has been laid and the concrete poured. But with this weather, it will take more time to cure."

"Is our labor holding up?" The colonel placed half of his roast beef portion onto Stella's plate, and she was relieved to note that he'd only served her as much as she could manage to eat.

Gratitude battled with her mounting resentment.

"A dozen have refused to work." Hermann turned his cold, covetous gaze back on Stella. "They have been taken to the Kleine Festung."

Her hand shook in reaching for her fork. Joseph hadn't told her about any "Little Fortress," but the captain's tone implied that it must be a terrible place.

"I could loan you some Jews, Captain," the major offered. "They're healthy enough, and you can keep them as long as you like."

"That won't be necessary, Herr Major." Hermann finally turned his focus from Stella. "We received a fresh shipment from Dachau a few weeks ago. All renovations will be finished by the second week in March."

"Not good enough, Captain," the colonel interjected. "We only anticipate a surprise inspection by then. All must be ready ahead of schedule."

Hermann's brittle features reddened. "All will be ready, I assure you, Herr Kommandant."

"We will accept your offer of Jews, Major." The colonel held Hermann's gaze. "I cannot afford to take the chance, Captain. The Swiss are not stupid, nor is this a routine visit."

He glanced at the other men around the table. "Denmark put them up to this. They're upset that Herr Reichsführer moved hundreds of Danish Jews here last fall."

"Because it spoiled their plan to steal them out from beneath our noses!" Hermann growled. "Now our Führer must tolerate the Red Cross interfering in our affairs—"

"To see how the prisoners fare, Captain," the colonel explained. "A reasonable enough request. Nevertheless, I'll inspect the ghetto myself. Tomorrow." He glanced at Stella. "You will accompany me, Fräulein Muller, and take note of any last-minute details needing attention."

She drew a startled breath. "Jawohl, Herr Kommandant." Though it sickened her to hear them speak of Jews like farmers discussing workhorses, she burned with curiosity to see for herself what lay beyond those walls—without the peril of being a prisoner.

There were still risks, of course. Jews from Mannheim might live there. Someone could recognize her . . .

"I welcome your inspection, Herr Kommandant, but you'll find everything in good order," Hermann said in clipped tones. "That is why our Führer entrusted this important task to the SS alone."

"Did he? I was told a *Wehrmacht* general, *Oberstgruppenführer* Feldman, has been assigned as the Führer's attaché for this inspection."

Irritation creased Hermann's frozen expression. "No doubt,

Herr Kommandant, our Führer wishes to enlighten the Wehrmacht on true SS efficiency."

"So you believe the German Army needs instruction from the SS, Captain?" The colonel reached for a helping of potatoes.

"Come now, Herr Colonel, quit baiting your poor captain." The major grinned. "Your years of service do you much credit, but even in your brief time with us, you must see how greatly the SS differs from Germany's other plebeian forces?"

"I see certain differences, Major," the colonel conceded, cutting a wedge of cheese and offering it to Stella. "A Wehrmacht soldier, for example, fights where he is called, whether knee-deep in snow on the Russian Steppes, or in sand, marching across a North African desert. He fights other armed soldiers."

He flashed each man at the table a challenging smile. "Forgive my frankness, but from what I've observed so far, the SS draws its battle lines inside the concentration camps, fighting unarmed Jews, Catholic priests, and a handful of dethroned politicians."

The dining room's warm, festive atmosphere turned chill with tension. Stella fell back against her seat, stunned. The colonel's ridicule of the SS was only eclipsed by the startling realization he'd been a Wehrmacht soldier, just like her uncle. Did he embrace Morty's same principles of honor, or was he like the other Nazis at the table?

"I served in the Waffen-SS two years, Herr Colonel." Stocky Lieutenant Neubach leaned back, arms crossed against his chest. "I fought armed men."

"I was at Babi Yar, Lieutenant. I saw Heydrich's *Einsatzgruppen* in action." The colonel's tone turned to ice. "We both know what kind of men your Waffen-SS gunned down."

"We were once the elite guard of der Führer!" Hermann's voice rose as he pressed his hands flat against the table. "Handpicked, highly trained Aryans of the purest race." He glanced to the others. "That was before Herr Reichsführer's office started recruiting anyone who could carry a gun. Italians, Czechs—"

"Wehrmacht castoffs, Captain?"

Hermann's hands slid from the table. "Herr Kommandant, I meant no insult . . ."

"Of course not." The colonel smiled, and Stella shivered at its lack of warmth. "Besides, it doesn't change what we've become"—he met each man's gaze—"chatelaines for the dregs of war, gentlemen. Dregs the SS created with their first camp at Dachau ten years ago."

"If I were to put a smell to that statement, Herr Colonel, I'd say it stank of sedition." The major tossed his linen napkin onto his empty plate.

"Treason, Major?" The colonel cocked an amused brow. "I sacrificed my body for Germany and have the bullet holes to prove it. The Fatherland has my allegiance."

He tossed down his napkin, as well. "Mine are only the sentiments of a world-weary soldier. Each of you mourns the day the SS enlarged its ranks to include mongrel curs in what was once the Führer's prized litter. I mourn the day I got out of bed and decided it wasn't enough being the son of a gentleman farmer." His acerbic humor vanished. "I believe on this point we can all agree that more is not necessarily better.

"This war holds us all in its grip, one way or another. We can only hope for a quick end." He lifted his glass of wine. "I myself long only for the blissful silence of peace."

"To peace." Dita raised her glass, followed by a smiling Marenka. Soon everyone at the table held up their goblets, restoring a measure of warmth to the party.

Except for Stella. She stared at her plate of half-eaten food while coldness permeated her. "*O Lord, how long will the wicked be jubilant? They pour out arrogant words; all the evildoers are full of boasting. . . .*"

The colonel wanted peace? How utopian, how simple, how . . . arrogant! Peace and quiet—like a nap in the afternoon, or curling up in a chair with a good book. And why shouldn't he? He had lost nothing in the war except a desire to return to his home.

At least he had one.

"Stella? Will you not drink?"

She glanced up at his frown, then lifted her glass with reluctance. The suffering wouldn't end with the war. Even if the Allies won, Jews would have nothing to go back to. Death would continue to stalk them, hunger and disease decimating their numbers. And if Hitler won . . .

She closed her eyes and sipped the Burgundy. If that monster won, he would make certain not a single Jew breathed air in all of Europe.

"Now, we have at Theresienstadt the world's finest musicians," the colonel announced as he rose from his seat. "Since the ladies have finished"—he gave Stella's plate a censured glance—"I'm certain they would rather enjoy dancing than listening to tedious politics."

"Ja, we want to dance!" chorused the two zoinehs across the table. Each vaulted from her seat to grab the hand of her date and pull him laughingly toward the lively music in the other room. Hermann and Captain Hoth followed. When the colonel reached for Stella, she hesitated.

"What's wrong?"

"Nothing, Herr Kommandant," she said, trying to bury her anger.

He read her too easily. "I think my wounded dove has turned into a fierce hawk," he said, smiling. "You look as if you would claw out my eyes."

She turned away, but he gently forced her chin back. "I told you from the beginning, Stella. There must be honesty between us."

What could she say? That she felt incensed by his arrogance and indifference toward the suffering of her people? That what he considered merely a disruption to his peace of mind had devastated the lives of thousands of Jews?

Stella pursed her lips. She must remain silent unless she chose to barter away what freedom she had left.

"You will tell me later." He spoke with confidence. "Now dance with me."

She was too stunned by his command to object and allowed him to usher her toward the living room. Captain Hoth halted them both. "Herr Colonel, may I speak with you privately? I have information from Herr Obersturmbannführer Eichmann. He asked that I relay to you the newest details for your upcoming project."

Stella felt the colonel's grip on her hand tighten. "Of course. In my office." He indicated to the captain the set of double doors off the living room.

"I'm afraid we must postpone our dance." He gently rubbed the back of Stella's hand with his thumb, and her pulse took an unexpected leap. "Go and enjoy the music. Helen is setting out brandy and glasses. I won't be long."

The idea of mingling with the butchers in the next room *and* suffering the captain's lurid gaze made Stella's insides clench. Still, she nodded and then quickly sought sanctuary in one of a pair of new leather chairs arranged alongside the hearth.

The chandelier overhead blazed with light. At the far end of the room a dozen men played a range of instruments: violins, cello, flutes, and accordions, while a thin woman in black provided accompaniment on a piano.

Stella absorbed the warmth from the fire as she listened to the music. Blocking out the other guests and their laughter, she soon lost herself in the sprightly notes of the "Berlin Dance." Her eyes drifted closed as she imagined herself and Morty back in Mannheim attending the local concert hall, hearing the lovely strains of Schubert, Mozart, and the daring Wagner.

She began tapping her foot to the music—when someone grabbed both of her wrists.

"Care to dance, Fräulein?"

Her eyes flew open, and she gasped into the frightening, cold face that had plagued her all through dinner. Captain Hermann didn't wait for her answer. Hauling her from the chair into his arms, he jogged her from side to side across the carpeted floor.

Stella's body stiffened against his embrace, her panicked senses reviled by the stench of his onion breath mingled with the odor of unwashed wool and woodsmoke. Far from the clean pine scent of the colonel . . .

"Tell me about yourself." He swung her back and forth like a rag doll to the lively polka. "Do you have family back in Germany?"

Trapped in his arms, she arched her spine to keep distance between them. She loathed him with every fiber of her being as he gazed at her chest with candid interest. She forced words from her throat. "M-my family is dead, Herr Captain."

He didn't bother with condolences. "Were you at Dachau?"

Paralyzed by his question, her mind scrambled for the right response. Thinking of the colonel's far-flung explanation to the Gestapo, she whispered, "A m-mistake, Herr Captain. I was secretary to Herr Kommandant's brother in . . . in Linz."

Abruptly he halted their dance to stare at her. "Herr Kommandant has no brother."

The room spun as Stella fought for air.

"When you arrived with your shorn head and bare feet, I had my suspicions." He leaned close, his grip becoming painful. "But I know better than to argue with Herr Reichsführer Himmler's shining star. Now, tell me the truth, Fräulein." His hazel eyes seemed to cut through her. "Tell me you are Jew."

9

*Just as the king returned . . . Haman was falling on
the couch where Esther was reclining. The king ex-
claimed, "Will he even molest the queen while she
is with me in the house?"*

Esther 7:8

Morty turned his attention from the kitchen doorway to
glance at the three zoinehs dancing with SS officers. Disgust at their display dampened his pleasure at being warm and
dry for the first time in months. He felt disappointment too as he
realized the woman he'd been so eager to see was not Hadassah.
Even from his position at the back row of musicians, he could
tell the blonde dancing with the tall major had brown eyes, not
the Judean blue Joseph spoke of in his note. Perhaps she'd left
the house . . .

A loud, discordant note rent the air. Morty hastily withdrew the
bow he'd let slide along the strings of his borrowed Stradivarius.
Asa Lokeran, a tall, wiry Belgian who once held first chair in the
Orchestre National de Belgique of Brussels turned to glare at him.

Morty ignored the look as he uttered a silent prayer and
scanned the room for Sergeant Koch. When he noted their escort's temporary absence, he breathed a sigh of relief and focused again on the kitchen doorway.

He'd been foolish to let Yaakov talk him into this crazy plan. Yet the lure of food was impossible to resist, and Leo's poor state had finally convinced him. The man was in desperate need of more than the potato peels and watery broth they'd been fed all winter. His cough had worsened; it wouldn't be long before he was sent to the infirmary. Then Auschwitz . . .

Morty clutched the neck of Leo's prized violin and pretended to slide the bow back and forth across the strings. If he'd listened to his mother and learned to play an instrument, perhaps he wouldn't feel so conspicuous among his fellow musicians. He was a danger to them all!

Yet while Morty had loved classical music from his youth, his creative passion had taken a more tactile approach, using metal instead of abstract notes. As a farrier, he produced more than tack and shoes for horses; in Mannheim his popular ironworks decorated many verandas of the upper apartments near the *Parade-Platz*. Even the *Bürgermeister* owned one of his ornamental creations: a pair of swan gates enclosing the entrance to the mayor's country home.

He crouched behind Asa Lokeran as Captain Hermann sailed by with his dancing partner. The red-haired zoineh looked terrified, her slim back ramrod straight while the captain jogged her across the floor.

Pity mingled with Morty's contempt. Even prostitutes didn't deserve such company.

A sudden movement flashed at the kitchen doorway. Morty straightened as Joseph smiled at him from the threshold. The boy held up Leo's violin case, now filled with the night's feast.

Morty's mouth watered in anticipation. All night he'd had to swallow away the delicious smells filling his nose and tempting his belly. He nodded at Joseph, who hefted the case and began to cross the room in their direction.

Pride strengthened Morty's aging bones. He'd laid out his plan in a secret message to Joseph the week before. The boy possessed more courage than the best man in camp—certainly more than the likes of that coward Hermann.

The polka was nearly over. Morty glanced back at the dancers and spied the commandant enter the living room. That alone wasn't remarkable, nor was the direct path he took toward Hermann and the redhead.

No, it was the rage contorting his aristocratic face that held Morty's complete attention.

The commandant looked ready to do battle. The woman appeared to sag with relief. Morty grinned in spite of caution, then turned back to check the boy's progress—

Sergeant Koch held the back of Joseph's collar. As he jerked the child off his feet, the violin case stuffed with food crashed to the floor.

Panic flooded Stella's senses even as she fought an urge to wrestle free and run upstairs to her room. Had Hermann discovered her secret? This monster sent Jews to Auschwitz. If he knew the truth, he would send her there, too.

"Tell me, Fräulein," Hermann hissed against her ear.

Stella glanced wildly around the room, hoping for rescue.

The colonel was closing the distance between them. Filled with new strength, she pulled back to stare at Hermann. "I'm no Jew, Captain."

"I don't believe you. Convince me."

He hauled her back into his arms. Stella understood his meaning. Memories of Dachau were still painfully fresh; her anger overrode fear as she opened her mouth to retort—

"Where are you going with that case?" a male voice boomed behind her.

Stella whipped around. Dita and the major, dancing beside them, also paused to stare.

"Herr Captain, I think our potato thief needs another lesson."

Gold flashed from Sergeant Koch's grin as he held Joseph in the air. "Answer me, Jew!" He shook the boy. "Or do we need to cut off the other ear?"

A violin case rested on the floor. Stella thought she glimpsed slices of Sauerbraten and Käsespätzle noodles protruding from its jarred opening.

She next glanced at the musicians; comically tragic gazes locked on the evidence while their fingers launched by rote into vigorous measures of Tchaikovsky's "Russian Dance."

Time froze, like a breath waiting to be released. With a flash of insight, Stella realized only she, Joseph, and the musicians had noticed the contents of the case.

The colonel was nearly upon them.

"Would a Jew do this?" She grabbed Hermann by the collar points and brought his mouth to hers for a kiss. He jerked in surprise at first, then crushed her against him, trying to deepen the contact. Stella gagged as she locked her lips against his further advances.

"CAPTAIN!"

The colonel's roar seemed to bounce off every wall in the house. Stella jumped as Hermann released her with a shove, his expression a mix of alarm, confusion, and desire.

The music stopped. The colonel's outburst held everyone's attention. Sergeant Grossman charged in from the kitchen, his pistol poised. Lieutenant Neubach and the buxom Marenka stood next to the sideboard of brandy, clinging together, their mouths agape at the scene playing out before them.

Even Sergeant Koch had dropped his small charge to stare openmouthed at his captain and the commandant.

Every eye in the room was focused on them—and no longer on Joseph, who clambered on hands and knees to retrieve the case. Stella caught a movement at the back of the orchestra. A thin man wearing a camel jacket crawled out to switch cases with the boy and then retreated from sight. A man with unusually large feet . . .

"What in blazes are you doing, Captain?" A broad hand seized Hermann's shoulder and spun him around. "Explain yourself!"

The colonel looked thunderous as he loomed over the captain. Hermann backed up a step, hands raised in supplication. "Herr Kommandant, I was only dancing with Fräulein—"

"That kind of dancing is better left for the bedroom, Captain, and not with my secretary."

Nervous guffaws erupted near the sideboard of brandy.

Hermann flashed Stella a seething look. "I did not realize Fräulein was spoken for."

Stella flushed. "I am not—"

"Silence!" The colonel turned his fury on her. "While you work for me, I expect you to comport yourself with more decency than some streetwalker."

Stella drew back as if struck. How dare he dress her up and parade her in front of these Nazi pigs like some prize of war, and then humiliate her for it!

His green gaze never left hers as he said, "In future, Captain, you will refrain from fraternizing with my household staff. Verstehen?"

"But I did nothing—"

"Do you understand?" The colonel turned to him.

Hermann straightened. Resentment creased his icy expression. "Jawohl, Herr Kommandant!"

"Go have a drink."

Hermann stalked away. The colonel growled at her, "I'll deal with you later."

His murderous expression made her look away—and she observed Joseph once more in the soldier's grasp.

The colonel also noticed. "Sergeant, why are you molesting my houseboy?"

The sergeant released the child. He then lifted the case Stella knew had been switched. "I caught him with this. I thought he meant to steal it, Herr Kommandant."

"Why would you think that, Sergeant?"

A heartbeat of hesitation. "Because he is a Jude," the sergeant said, blinking. "They are all clever liars and thieves."

As he spoke, the case fell open. It was empty. Amused chortles rippled around the room. Sergeant Koch flushed pink against the faint light from the kitchen.

"So you think a clever Jew would risk losing his warm bed, hot food, and a daily bath to steal an empty case?"

The colonel's remark produced more laughter. Sergeant Koch shifted. "Nein, Herr Kommandant."

"You will leave the boy alone, Sergeant."

The sergeant clicked his jackboots together. "Jawohl, Herr Kommandant."

The colonel turned his attention to the musicians. "Play!"

Yet the first notes were barely struck when the major approached them. "Herr Colonel, while I thank you for a most entertaining evening"—he flashed Stella a look of amused sympathy—"my driver tells me that new weather is moving in. We must leave for Litomerice."

Lieutenant Neubach and the two women followed in his wake. Captain Hoth added, "I should also return, Herr Colonel, if I'm to reach Prague before the snow starts."

Within minutes, Stella offered her perfunctory farewell to the bundled-up officers and women departing the house. The colonel then ordered a chastened Sergeant Koch to return the musicians to the ghetto.

Afterward he disappeared into his library, leaving Stella torn between a desire to escape to her room and the fear of angering him more by doing so. In the end she stayed and reclaimed her chair near the hearth. She lamented over the evening's events. She'd behaved like a brazen hussy—worse than the two women she'd branded as zoinehs. Revulsion tore at her, and she buried her face in her hands. Even the memory of Captain Hermann's touch made her ill. She could still smell his odor of onions.

He'd flashed her a killing look before leaving the house with the rest of the guests. She had humiliated him; it wasn't something he would forget.

And how would the colonel punish her for tonight's performance? Would he send her back to Dachau, or would he have his captain deport her to Auschwitz?

She raised her head to stare blindly at the flames in the hearth. There had been no other choice. If they caught Joseph stealing food again, he would lose more than the other ear.

The echo of dissonant notes drew her attention to the foyer. None of the musicians packing away their instruments wore enough clothing to fend off the freezing temperature outside. Their summer coats were thin and worn. The pianist's knitted black shawl barely covered her shoulders. Occasionally they stole glances at her. What did they see?

She scanned the room—from the chandelier with its crystals glittering like diamonds in the firelight to the lush Aubusson carpet at her feet. On the walls hung expensive oil paintings, their gilt frames gleaming like golden hues of the sun. Even the linen tablecloth in the colonel's dining room, now cleared of the night's repast, shone like first snow beneath a pair of tapered candles glowing from its surface.

Did they think her as frivolous and callous as the zoinehs who had just left?

The fire's heat branded her in guilt, and the words of the prophet Amos rose unbidden in her mind: *"Hear this word, you cows of Bashan on Mount Samaria, you women who oppress the poor and crush the needy and say to your husbands, 'Bring us some drinks!'"*

They had begun queuing up at the door. Stella flinched, reminded of her own hours spent in line, awaiting roll call at Dachau with the other prisoners. Like lambs for the slaughter . . .

How could they know that she was one of them, merely trapped in gilded surroundings?

Stella eyed her lovely blue gown. She, the best dressed of the flock.

Asa Lokeran bent to the task of returning his precious Amati to its case—the same empty case used to humiliate Sergeant Koch. Morty clutched the other, now filled with precious food. Behind them, safe from view, Mrs. Brenner wrapped Leo's Stradivarius in the folds of her shawl.

Morty savored the room's warmth and cast a wistful glance at the crackling fire in the hearth. He noted the redhead still seated in one of the commandant's fine leather chairs. Why hadn't she left with the others? She looked so sad with her head bowed and hands folded in her lap. Somehow defeated, not like the other boisterous women. He hadn't gotten a good look at her face, but he doubted she wore the same heavy paint; there was also a grace of movement about her, far from suggestive. A beauty oddly familiar . . .

"Line up!" Sergeant Koch ordered.

Morty started to turn away when the commandant reentered the living room. The tall man strode toward the redhead, yet she didn't look up. He'd been furious when she kissed that coward Hermann. Morty hadn't clearly heard their exchange, what with his crawling on all fours like a donkey to save their necks.

He felt a moment's pity for her and sighed. It seemed even a zoineh could be fickle. He'd been so certain the captain repulsed her as they danced, yet in the next breath she'd thrown herself at him, creating an uproar. In fact, the timing couldn't have been more perfect.

"Move out!" barked the sergeant.

The door opened, and Morty shot a last look over his shoulder at the woman before bracing himself against the frigid outdoors. Yaakov had always accused him of thinking too much. Maybe his friend was right. Wasn't it enough that God oversaw the night's efforts? Leo would finally have decent food to eat.

He trudged with the others out into the snow-filled night, unable to forget the miraculous sequence of events that had rescued them that evening—or the red-haired zoineh who, unconsciously or not, set them into motion.

Stella sensed the colonel's approach, and a shiver of the old fear raced along her spine. She flinched when the front door slammed behind Sergeant Koch as he herded the musicians outside. The slow tick of the foyer clock mingled with the crackle of logs in the hearth, the only remaining sounds to disturb the tense silence.

"Stand up."

He sounded calm. Perhaps his anger had abated? Stella's relief wavered as she rose from her chair.

"So you prize brains over beauty, do you?" His gaze traveled her length with insulting deliberateness. "A comfortable assertion for an attractive woman, isn't it? I assumed that when we toasted your ability earlier, we spoke in professional terms." His smile lacked warmth. "Apparently I had the wrong profession in mind, which leaves me to wonder what you were trying to prove here tonight."

"I . . . nothing, Herr Kommandant." Stella's voice vibrated with the erratic beat of her heart.

"Then you feel genuine attraction for the captain?" He advanced on her, his voice dangerously soft.

"He disgusts me!" Stella retreated from him until the backs of her knees brushed the chair. "I didn't want to kiss him."

"He forced you?"

The clock on the wall magnified the seconds. More lies, this time for Joseph. "Yes."

"I don't believe you."

His hand shot out to grasp her chin. Pulling her to him, he said angrily, "Tell me, Fräulein, if you give your kisses so freely to a captain, what will you offer a colonel? A Kommandant?"

Like a blow, his words roused such pain in Stella that she forgot her fear. "Is this what you want?" She grabbed at the buttoned front of her dress and ripped away the delicate cloth. Blue beads popped and flew in every direction. "The same thing the Gestapo pig tried to take before he shipped me out on a cattle car, or at Dachau when they beat me, then gave orders to have me shot because I refused to surrender to the Block leader's depravity?"

The front of her dress gaped open, exposing the white lace camisole beneath and the agitated rise and fall of her breathing. "Go on, take it, Herr Kommandant." Bitterness choked her. "Because I've learned it's much *safer* to submit than to fight back."

He stared at her, his taut features easing into an expression she couldn't identify. "I had wondered why you were taken to the shooting pit."

And you saved me from that death. She averted her eyes from his, wanting to nurse her resentment. Then she felt his touch, and a thrill coursed through her before being trampled beneath devastation. He was no better than the others.

She looked up at him, stunned, when he merely drew the rent cloth of her gown together. "Perhaps," he said, "your spirit isn't so wounded after all."

She felt wounded enough. "The scars have only made my spirit more resilient, Herr Kommandant."

Stella realized she'd been baited when he flashed her a dazzling smile. "You're a part of my staff now, Stella, and under my protection. You will *submit*"—he discharged the word with distaste—"to no one. Verstehen?"

Amazed and relieved, she nodded.

"Are you certain you grasp my meaning?" His voice took on a slight edge. "If Hermann touches you again, I will kill him."

Stella's reassurances faltered. What if he questioned the captain and learned the truth, that she had initiated the kiss? It would be her word against Hermann's. Who would the colonel believe?

Drawing a steady breath, she nodded. Her path had been chosen, for the boy's sake. There was no turning back.

The clock chimed to strike the hour. Ten o'clock. "It's late. We have a long day planned for tomorrow," he said.

"Of course, Herr Kommandant."

Stella started to move away, eager for the sanctuary of her room. He stayed her with a hand on her shoulder. "I've discovered one truth about you in our time together, Fräulein."

She held her breath.

"You've got quite a temper."

Her cheeks warmed.

"You also have passion. Probably more than you should." As he leaned closer, his spicy breath grazed her cheek. "Remember, there's a fine line between passion and foolishness. Be careful you do not cross it."

A warning? She should have been alarmed by his words, angry at the very least. But his nearness overwhelmed her, the heat of his hand on her shoulder, the smell of his skin. He turned his face into hers, so close that their lips almost touched. She studied the features she once thought so hard and unyielding, now generous, encouraging . . .

He'd promised her protection. *And who will save me from you, Colonel, or from myself?* She felt her resolve weakening against him, her savior, her champion . . . her jailer.

She dropped her gaze to the front of his tunic. The Knight's Cross and his broad array of medals blazed in the firelight. Glittering prizes for murder.

"No." She pushed at him, mortified that she'd nearly participated in her own seduction. How could she forget who he was and what he represented? "Please, I can't!" she whispered.

"Stella, I only want—" He stopped himself and released her. "Be downstairs for breakfast at seven," he said, his hard mask back in place. "We leave for the ghetto at eight."

He spun on his heel toward the dining room. Stella stood unmoving. When he glanced back, she saw fury etched into every hard-edged plane of his face. "For pity's sake, go to bed!"

Then he disappeared from view.

Stella slowly made her way up the stairs. She should feel relieved; the colonel had kept his word. He hadn't forced her. Yet any consolation she might harbor felt dampened by an inane sense of loss.

Back in her room, she saw the Bible had again materialized atop the nightstand. She sat on the edge of the bed and held the book in her lap, letting it fall open to a random page: Solomon's Song of Songs. *"Let him kiss me with the kisses of his mouth—for your love is more delightful than wine."*

Stella quickly closed the book and tucked it back inside the drawer. With a furtive movement, she pressed a finger to her lips and tried to imagine how his kiss might have felt, allowing herself a candid glimpse into her own traitorous feelings.

10

Now the king was attracted to Esther more than to
any of the other women. . . .

Esther 2:17

He'd nearly kissed her.

Aric extracted the cork from the chilled bottle of Pouilly-Fuisse and brooded over his recklessness. After pouring himself a glass of pale wine, he returned to the living room and sank into the chair Stella had vacated. Stretching out his legs in front of the hearth, he massaged each thigh with his free hand, working to relieve the agonizing cramps in his muscles.

He'd nearly kissed her—and murdered his captain in front of witnesses. The lingering rage he felt both disturbed and gratified him. Aric toyed with the idea of going out to the barracks to jerk Hermann from a sound sleep and put a bullet through his head; not unlike the urge he fought little more than an hour ago, but then only Stella's lack of resistance had saved the man's useless life. The devastating possibility that she'd wanted Hermann's attentions . . .

You're such a fool, Schmidt, believing your actions had to do with good deeds.

Again he recalled his first sight of her standing before her executioners. Tall and reed thin, her delicate features drawn while bruised lips pursed over her chattering teeth. Yet it wasn't her raw-boned features that had compelled him as much as her eyes. Dove's eyes, large and slightly tilted, filled her entire face. Cerulean pools drenched his memory with images of boyhood summers in Austria. Startlingly clear, like the stream rushing along the backside of his father's estate.

Those eyes . . . Aric released a self-deprecating laugh as he tipped his glass to swirl its golden contents. He should have realized his folly then, that he'd intended more than to simply feed her, dress her in new clothes, and send her on her way. Erasing one or two black marks from his soul—that is, if he still had one.

He downed the last of the wine, hoping to dull the incessant pain in his legs and the tightness in his gut for the task that lay before him.

Eichmann issued the command. During the first of the year, the Red Army had gained force while Germany lost substantial ground. In the event the enemy managed to break through Wehrmacht lines, the Reich had decided to minimize any visible wrongdoing.

Aric was ordered to get rid of the evidence.

So far, he'd been able to stall—until tonight when Captain Hoth informed him the aggressive Allied bombing in the East had prompted the SS-Obersturmbannführer to move up the date for the "cleanup" process.

In approximately two weeks—once the Red Cross departed—Aric must act. Even now he wasn't sure he had the stomach for it. And Stella, being raised by Jews . . .

He stared into the fire. She'd refused him tonight, mocking the attraction he'd seen in her brightened eyes and flushed cheeks. Still, he hadn't pressed her; he'd given his word to protect her, noble idiot that he was.

But he couldn't shield her from his duty. Once he executed

his orders, she would loathe the very sight of him. How could she not, when he would despise himself?

He remembered his foolish vow to set her free. Either way, he would lose her.

Desperation hit him with brutal force. Aric leaned forward and bowed his head in an action he hadn't performed since boyhood, at his mother's bedside.

Prayer hadn't worked for him then, either. Still . . .

11

Mordecai had a cousin named Hadassah, whom he had brought up because she had neither father nor mother.

Esther 2:7

Monday, February 28, 1944

"Walk faster!"

Morty felt a hard shove at his back and he staggered, losing his grip on the bundle of wood. Without thinking, he turned to glare at the perpetrator—and received a blow to the head that drove him to his knees.

"Your days grow short, Elder." Hatred infused Captain Hermann's tone. "Soon you'll grovel for me. I'll make you eat that Jew pride."

Morty didn't dare speak as he gathered up the fallen kindling and struggled to rise. He plodded through the snow, sensing Hermann close on his heels. His big feet cramped inside a tight pair of shoes while the bitter cold morning stiffened his joints. And if that wasn't bad enough, now his head ached where the coward had struck him.

A black Mercedes drove into the ghetto. Morty forgot his discomfort and watched the car halt in front of the old barracks.

The commandant exited first, his imposing height a full head taller than the two SS guards piling out from opposite doors. Emerging next was a slender woman in black wool; her familiar red hair drew a splash of color against the dismal black-and-white scene.

What was the zoineh doing here? Morty had lain awake the night before mulling over the evening's events. Each time he came to the same conclusion—that she'd purposely created their much-needed diversion.

The zoineh and her group of SS walked to the front entrance of the barracks. Morty decided to follow, increasing his pace toward a door at the back.

SS-*Untersturmführer* Brucker blocked his passage. Nearly as tall as the commandant, the lanky second lieutenant's inky black hair stuck out from the edges of his cap. "What do you want, Jude?"

As if it wasn't obvious! Morty hid his disgust. "I must replenish the fires inside."

"Let him pass, Lieutenant."

"Herr Captain." Brucker acknowledged Hermann over Morty's head and opened the door.

Inside, the blast of heat nearly buckled Morty's numbed joints. Barrel fires rigged on wooden planks above the floor quickened the drying of the concrete below.

He spotted the redhead at the front door of the building. A quick glance behind him confirmed that Hermann was still speaking with his lieutenant. Morty hugged his bundle of wood and shuffled across the planks in her direction.

She gripped the commandant's sleeve while she picked her way through the debris. She also clutched a notepad and pen. A secretary? Morty eyed her more closely, working to reform his first impression. In daylight she seemed more frail than slender.

When she glanced up, he noted her face, stark and bloodless beneath that blaze of red hair.

His heart lurched in his chest as he scrutinized her blue eyes . . . the high cheekbones . . . the way she pursed that expressive mouth . . .

His beloved maideleh!

Bracing his feet against the plank, Morty tried to steady himself. He'd almost given up hope of finding her, yet it *was* Hadassah—he felt it in every nerve and fiber of his being.

His euphoria died as he took stock of her wan complexion, and the fragility that seemed to shroud any youth or exuberance. *What have they done to you, daughter?*

His throat worked as he realized why she might need to wear what was now obviously a wig. He imagined her beautiful blond head shorn beneath the red strands. A thousand questions rose in his heart. Where had she been before this? How long since she'd left Heidelberg? And why was she with the commandant? Was she his secretary . . . or his mistress?

Morty ground his teeth. Must she sell her body to a Nazi in order to stay alive?

The commandant and his party mounted the planks, making their way to the east side of the building where Morty stood. His pulse pounded as he lumbered forward to close the distance as much as he dared.

The commandant leaned close to speak with Hadassah, and Morty tensed—until he noted the SS officer's gentleness with her. Apparently the man had rid himself of last night's rage.

His maideleh seemed unafraid of the colonel, as well. Her head dipped in concentration as she scribbled away on her pad of paper.

Feeling marginal relief, Morty continued to drink in the sight of his beloved niece, quenching his parched heart. It had been so long. Would she be able to recognize him—

Pain exploded in his skull from the unexpected blow.

"Jude *Schwein*!" Hermann snarled. "You dare to stare at that woman?"

Morty groaned and dropped to his knees, still clutching the kindling. His punishment would be worse if the wood fell into the wet concrete.

"Insolent filth!" Hermann raised his fist for another blow.

"No!" Stella shouted. She remembered all too well similar beatings when she'd been the victim. She turned to the colonel. "Please, make him stop!"

He stared at her, his eyes clouded with anger. "Captain," he finally called out, "if you knock the Jew into the wet concrete, it will require more time to cure. Time we do not have."

She drew back at his callousness. He winked at her. "You've also upset my secretary. Now I must repeat my dictation."

Hermann left the fallen old man and came forward. "Herr Kommandant, I apologize for the disruption." He flashed a derisive glance at Stella. "But it is necessary to keep discipline among the prisoners."

"What wrong did that man do to deserve your 'discipline,' Herr Captain?" Stella challenged him directly. She knew she played a dangerous game, but in the face of such cruelty she refused to back down.

Hermann's eyes narrowed. "He looked at you, Fräulein."

"That's a crime?"

"No prisoner is allowed to look upon an *Aryan* woman."

His emphasis on the word made her edge closer to the colonel. She hadn't forgotten Hermann's inquisition of the previous night. "I see no harm—"

"Enough!" The colonel shoved her behind him and advanced on Hermann. "You're bordering on surly, Captain. Dismiss the Jew so we can concentrate on more important matters. Major Lindberg promised laborers from Litomerice, but Berlin will also supply a shipment of fresh Jews for our Red Cross visit. That train arrives Friday—leaving only four days to make preparations.

"General Feldman of the Wehrmacht will be here a week from today to inspect our readiness. I rely on you, Captain, to impress him with this efficiency you boast about. See that he leaves here with a satisfactory report."

"Jawohl, Herr Kommandant."

Peering around the colonel's shoulder, Stella had a moment's unobstructed view of the prisoner before Hermann barked his dismissal. Struggling to his feet, the old man stole another glance at her.

Then he smiled.

Awareness electrified her; she swayed, grabbing for the colonel's sleeve. Her eyes darted to the prisoner's shoes. Huge . . .

"Fräulein?"

Stella all but ignored the colonel, for she couldn't stop staring at her uncle. Morty's honey-brown eyes were shadowed in hollow sockets, and his aquiline nose perched like a beak between sunken cheeks. Only his smile remained the same, and his enormously large feet!

"Stella, what's wrong?"

As the colonel gripped her shoulders, Stella forced her attention back to him, scouring her mind for a plausible excuse. The truth would be fatal.

Fumes billowed from the fire pits, coloring the air in white haze. "It's the smoke."

"Let's go outside."

He led her back toward the door, but not before she shot a final look at Morty, wanting assurance that he escaped before Hermann cornered him again.

Her uncle ambled to the rear door of the building, his shoulders straight, his gait marked with a perceptible bounce. Love welled inside her. He'd recognized her, too.

The cold, clean air outside offered little relief to Stella's real distress. Morty looked starved and beaten; no doubt Hermann took his fists to her uncle regularly. She fought back her frustration as the colonel supported her shoulders, leading her to the car. "Breathe deeply, Stella," he said. "You'll feel better in a moment."

She jerked away from him. "You're always telling me that, Herr Kommandant."

"If you showed more sense than a turkey, I wouldn't have to, would I?" he snapped. "For example, provoking my captain—especially after what happened last night."

He opened the car door and retrieved her coat. "You surprised me in there, braving his wrath to champion an old Jew." His harsh tone lessened as he helped her shrug into the heavy black wool. "But then you're partial to them, aren't you? You said that you were raised by Jews."

Before she could form a response, he turned her around and buttoned the top edges of her coat. "In future, you must tread carefully with Captain Hermann. The man's an arrogant cur. You saw his rage when he looked at you."

Afterward he grabbed his brass-topped cane from the back seat of the car and slammed the door. Stella longed to defend her earlier actions but knew she didn't dare. "I'll be more careful," she said.

"I won't always be there to keep him on a leash. I promised you last night, if he touches you again, in any way, I *will* kill him." He grasped her chin. "Remember that when you next decide to bait the bear."

Despite his censure, he leaned in close. Stella felt his warm breath against her cheek, smelled the faint Kaffee lingering from his breakfast and the woodsmoke from the fires that permeated his coat. Afraid to encourage him, to trust her own reaction in return, she held perfectly still.

"I won't *take* anything, Stella. That's my promise to protect you," he whispered. "But I want everything you're willing to give."

She heard the longing in those words and felt blood pounding in her ears. He wanted her kiss, and this time she was in danger of giving it to him. *You're a traitor, Hadassah.*

She quickly pulled away. "We . . . we can go back inside now. I'm feeling much better." Her voice shook, and she wondered if he noticed.

His rueful smile failed to mask his regret. "I think we've seen enough of the barracks. Are you warm enough?"

She nodded as she fished in the pockets of her coat for gloves.

"I'll get the captain so we can continue our inspection." He brushed her chin with his thumb before leaving.

Stella watched him go, her despair at Morty's situation warring with her growing attraction toward the man responsible. Had God planned this new anguish to replace the physical torment she'd suffered at Dachau? And how could she possibly help her uncle?

Stella thought of her promise to Joseph. How naïve to think she could leave this place.

She jammed her hands into the gloves, then surveyed the ghetto. Like a picture postcard, the city rose among cobbled streets swept clean of snow. Storefronts freshly painted and draped beckoned imaginary shoppers to their doors. Park benches and wrought-iron tables and chairs framed the town's Colonial-style square, while streetlamps blazed cheerily in the morning's gray light.

A handful of prisoners had ventured out into the cold dawn. They wore dirty, threadbare clothes, and flocked and disbanded in the square like fractious birds. A few were content to perch on the shiny new benches; others hovered at the fringes, beneath the freshly mended doorways of shops and *Gasthäuser*. A dozen ragged children played under a slush-lined stairway. A pair of women pulled a handcart filled with cans of paint, roofing materials, and lumber.

She quietly ached for them. How absurd they all looked,

like mourners at a wedding. Their somber presence cast a pall over the bright new city. But it wasn't so bright and new, was it?

Joseph had told her the truth, that beneath Theresienstadt's façade—quaint prosperity—lay dirty, straw-filled stalls crammed with too many Jews. Dysentery preyed on the elderly and weak, while hunger preyed on everyone else. This city that held her uncle and thousands more behind its bastioned walls merely wore a disguise, the sound of a hammer's distant pounding proof the masquerade was being set into place.

The creak of wheels grew loud as the handcart lumbered past her. Both women kept their eyes downcast. It took only a moment to understand their reaction before Stella tore the runic armband of the Hakenkreuz from her sleeve and stuffed it into her pocket. She didn't care that the colonel ordered her to wear it; she wasn't about to look any more despicable than she felt.

When the colonel returned with the captain, Stella avoided Hermann's gaze as she followed the pair deeper into the ghetto. The faint hammering she'd heard revealed three prisoners mounting a new sign over an old storefront. Beyond the large window glass, two women in kerchiefs dusted shelves and cleaned the floor.

"Foodstuffs and supplies for the stores and Gasthäuser will be stocked just before the Red Cross arrives, Herr Kommandant. We'll also issue new clothing that day. The children have been warned to stay clean—we don't want them soiled before the Swiss get here." The captain waved a hand toward the prisoners. "As you can see, every shop and room is being cleaned and painted, depending on the need for visibility."

Painfully thin men struggled on ladders to raise the heavy sign above the door and nail it into place. The air reeked of fresh paint, unwashed bodies, and the tang of cut timber. Shame pricked at Stella, observing their frayed cotton clothes while she remained snug and warm beneath layers of wool. How she wished she could help them!

The dilemma continued to plague her long after they'd left the scene, and the hammering faded against the crunch of boots in new snow. They walked some distance before the faint sounds of music drifted toward them. Stella paused to listen.

"The Jews are preparing a program for the Red Cross," the colonel explained. "I understand Obersturmbannführer Eichmann and his aides visited here last year and were given a full-length performance of Verdi's *Requiem*." He inclined his ear, then turned to her. "It sounds like they're rehearsing *The Bartered Bride*. Would you like to go and hear them practice?"

"Very much, Herr Kommandant." Thrilled at the possibility of again seeing her uncle, she started to walk toward the music.

"Fräulein, where is your armband?"

Stella paused, blinking at the force of Hermann's sharpness. She looked askance at the colonel, but he too seemed to await her answer. "It became loose. I have it here." She dug into her pocket and withdrew the offensive piece of cloth.

Hermann stepped forward. "I'll help you."

"Allow me." The colonel cut in front of him and refastened the band to her sleeve. "Captain, don't you have a certain matter to attend to?"

Stella could feel Hermann's rancor as he watched them. "Jawohl, Herr Kommandant."

Swiftly he departed, leaving her and the colonel to continue on until they reached a large Gasthaus with a painted window sign that read TEREZIN CAFÉ.

Stella peered beyond the entrance. High-arched ceilings hosted dimly lit chandeliers. Bistro tables and chairs, newly painted and gleaming, sat in rows on either side of the cavernous room. A lighted stage held a quartet of seated musicians with instruments—horn, drums, cello, and violin—playing lively music from one of the scenes of the opera.

She felt a sentimental rush; it was so much like Struber's—a cozy nightclub at the north end of Heidelberg, where she and

Marta often stopped after work for hot, sweetened Kaffee and to listen to local bands play. Stella had developed a crush on a particular saxophone player, a young man named Kurt, whose soulful music made her spirits soar and her heart sing.

It seemed so long ago now, back when the world still held hope.

She entered the café, the colonel right behind her. The music halted. A hushed silence fell over the room, followed by an explosion of scuffling chairs as both musicians and patrons rose to their feet. They stood at attention, arms woodenly at their sides, their shocked expressions fastened on walls, floors, tables—anywhere but Stella and her escort.

She blushed as she scanned the sea of pale faces. Like the musicians last night and the women in the square, these people thought she was the enemy. They seemed as afraid of her as they were of the colonel.

"Continue," he ordered the musicians. Then he turned to her. "I believe you owe me a dance, Fräulein."

She had no time to object as he hooked his cane onto the back of a chair and dragged her through the swiftly parting throng toward the front of the stage. Humiliated at his display in front of her people, she stared straight ahead; their unspoken condemnation pierced her with a surgeon's precision while her mind screamed denial at the wordless charges.

"Play the 'Blue Danube Waltz,'" the colonel instructed, before taking her into his arms.

The musicians didn't move. As the colonel narrowed his eyes on the four, Stella grew afraid for them. "Please," she called out. "We wish to hear the waltz now."

Possibly they detected her urgency, or perhaps they were roused from their stupor by the chafing look from their commandant. Either way, the dulcet strains of the waltz began, sluggish at first until fear finally succumbed to their love for music. The notes echoed strong and radiant throughout the whitewashed grotto, drenching the air with vibrant melody.

The colonel sailed with Stella across the floor, and her pleasure in their shared love of the waltz dampened her fervent wish to end the ordeal. Forcing herself to relax, she followed the colonel's lead, noting his slight limp as their steps eddied back and forth together.

"I apologize for my awkwardness," he said, reading her thoughts, "but I promise your toes are quite safe."

"You dance well," she admitted, drawn by his quiet dignity.

"Considering that a year ago I couldn't walk, I'll agree with you, Fräulein."

Stella hid her shock. "What happened to you?"

"The war," he said dismissively. "But I'm content to be here now, dancing with you in my arms. And I prefer this kind of exercise to the daily dose of pain from my sergeant."

"Sergeant Grossman causes you pain?"

"In a manner of speaking. Since Sevastopal, he's been the relentless advocate for my strengthening exercises." A smile touched his lips. "Certainly the inspiration for my success . . ." He glanced over her shoulder. "Ah, the captain is coming this way, and seems very determined."

Stella turned to see Hermann stalking toward them, his gaze leveled on her.

"Perhaps he wants to cut in?"

"Nein!" Stella cringed, watching his approach.

"Kiss me."

The colonel's words brought her head around. "What?"

He leaned in. "Please, Stella. It's the only way I can protect you."

She drew back. "What are you talking about?"

"If you kiss me, then he'll know you're off-limits. He'll never bother you again."

She gaped at him. The previous evening's nightmare seemed about to replay itself, only this time she was in the colonel's arms while the captain stormed toward them.

"Hurry," he whispered, a mere breath from her lips. "Or would you prefer that I kill him?"

His recent threat rang in her ears, and Stella thought of how the monster Hermann had beaten her uncle. Then there were the lists of countless Jews he'd sent to Auschwitz. *Yes, I could watch him die.*

But what of the colonel? Was she prepared to risk his death if Hermann won?

Taking no time to further consider her actions, Stella pressed a kiss to his lips. The colonel's response was immediate; his mouth captured hers, lightly at first, then more deeply as he drew her into the circle of his arms.

Stunned, Stella felt herself swept away by his kiss. Any fear she'd harbored was banished by his gentleness, and she relaxed against him, reassured by his tender embrace and the pleasing scent of pine and snow and spice that was so unlike the captain's onion stench of the night before. In fact, so unlike the captain . . .

He seemed reluctant to end the kiss, finally raising his head slowly. Dazed, Stella opened her eyes and saw him staring over her head at the captain.

His look made her shiver.

"Herr Kommandant." Thinly veiled fury threatened to crack Hermann's icy façade. He withdrew a packet of papers from inside his tunic and thrust them at the colonel. "The latest stores update—delivered into your hands, as requested. Do you wish to continue inspecting the ghetto?"

The waltz had ended. Stella tried to move away, shaken by what she'd done. The colonel maintained his iron grip on her. "Nein, I've seen enough. In fact, I believe everything is now as it should be."

His implied meaning was not lost on Hermann, who clenched his jaw in response. Stella seesawed between humiliation and anger. The captain hadn't intended to cut in at all; the colonel tricked her into that kiss. Well, she wasn't a meaty bone to be fought over by two hungry dogs!

"Carry on with your other duties, Captain. Fräulein and I will return to the car shortly."

"Very well, Herr Kommandant." Flashing Stella his contempt, Hermann clicked his bootheels and spun away to leave the café.

"Shall we sit?"

More command than request, the colonel placed his hand at the small of her back and urged her into the empty bistro chair where he'd left his cane. He sat down beside her.

The Jews continued to stand. Stella's resentment lessened as he motioned her people to resume their seats.

"What would you like to hear, Stella?"

He acted as though the kiss never happened, which only made her angrier at being the pawn in his game with the captain. Defiance overrode her fear. "'*Friling*,'" she blurted out.

A hushed intake of breath rippled over the sea of downcast faces. The Polish ghetto song, a man's lament to his beloved wife killed by Nazis, had traveled as far as Dachau, where Stella first heard it.

"I'm not familiar with that music. What's it about?"

Feeling the crowd's tension, Stella's sanity returned. Had foolishness goaded her to speak, or was it the need to gauge his reaction? Could she afford to exercise a bit of courage? "It's a Yiddish song of springtime, Herr Kommandant," she said at last. "And of love."

She held her breath, expecting his refusal. He surprised her when he said, "Love is a noble ideal, regardless of origin." He waved toward the musicians. "Play this song."

Sweet, melancholy strains floated across the vast ceiling to penetrate every corner of the room. Anxiety seemed to fade in the people around Stella as each man and woman drifted on the tide of wistful music, bodies swaying slightly with each measure.

Stella closed her eyes, and for a little while she forgot the harsh realities of the ghetto. At that moment she understood how these people, stripped of everything, could sit in a make-believe bistro and free their minds, if not their bodies, to the soft, lilting notes.

The music finally ended. Stella opened her eyes.

"Happy now?" the colonel asked.

She gazed out at their somber audience and it occurred to her to tell him she was miserable wearing the Jew Killer's badge in front of her people, and that the sight of these hollowed, gray faces filled her with despair. That they stood in the midst of war, and when it was over there would be nothing left for her or any of them.

But when she turned, she caught his eager look. Stella found she couldn't say the words, though they would hardly prove fatal. She thought instead of his kiss—manipulative, arrogant, gentle. Her anger ebbed, and she managed a smile. "Thank you, Herr Kommandant."

"Aric," he insisted. "I want you to say my name."

She leaned back against her chair, unwilling to breach another barrier with him.

"Just once." He reached across the table to cover her hand with his. "It would make *me* happy."

His face again wore that rare, unguarded look of expectancy. It seemed niggardly to refuse him. "All right . . . Aric."

His smile took her breath away. Dazzling against his bronzed features, it struck at the heart of her weakened state. Had she kissed him strictly for her own protection against Hermann, or was she putting herself more at risk than her keeping secrets?

"Let's return to the house." He rose, helping her to her feet. Everyone else stood, as well. Several cast furtive glances in Stella's direction.

She'd hoped for another chance to see her uncle. It dawned on her then that he'd been at the house last night, helping Joseph with the case of food. He'd also witnessed her disgrace with the captain, who had been furious; and at the barracks, the colonel had salvaged Hermann's pride only to shatter it here in this room.

Was Morty safe from the monster's wrath? "Shouldn't we visit the rest of the ghetto?" she asked, overcome with a need to resolve her fear.

He shook his head. "I'm certain Captain Hermann's pride in the SS will allow for nothing less than perfection when General Feldman arrives on Monday." A sardonic smile touched his lips. "Why? Was there something else you wished to see?"

Outside the café, Stella burrowed deeper into her coat and tried to conjure reasons to keep them in the ghetto without making him suspicious. But only angry frustration crowded her thoughts. "There is nothing else," she told him.

Back at the car, she observed Hermann directing soldiers to haul wooden crates into a garrison building across from the old barracks. Her uncle was nowhere to be seen. Still, her relief seemed elusive as she willed rather than believed him safe.

"We still have weeks before your 'Friling,' Stella. Let's get out of the cold."

The colonel stood at the open car door. His words brought Stella up short. He'd indulged her—indulged them all—with the Yiddish song. Had he also understand the lyrics?

She let him assist her into the back seat, and when he climbed in after her, he flashed a smile. Stella observed the generous lines of his mouth, then quickly looked away.

Danger took its many forms; her own seemed as decidedly grave as her uncle's. She must find a way to save them both before it was too late.

12

She begged him to put an end to the evil plan . . .
against the Jews.

Esther 8:3

TUESDAY, FEBRUARY 29, 1944

We are honored by your desire to visit Theresienstadt."
Aric adjusted his desk pad while he dictated his upcoming speech for the Red Cross. "We invite you to see for yourself that the prisoners interned here are well cared for. They receive plenty of food, clothing, and shelter, and we offer them intellectual and cultural activities. This facility is representative of all our other camps . . ."

He paused when Stella stopped writing. "Is there a problem?"

Her blue eyes blazed with condemnation. Was she still angry with him?

Yesterday he'd bullied her into a kiss. The opportunity to set Hermann in his place had been too good to resist. Yet Aric couldn't forget how wonderful Stella had felt in his arms, or the way she'd responded to him. Even later, when her face burned with resentment, she'd been unable to hide her yearning. He'd been consumed by his own.

The Jew song "Friling" with its haunting melody of love still lingered in his mind. She must have sung it as a child when she was raised by them.

She will come to hate you, Schmidt. A shadow of regret pierced him. He'd crossed the line, allowing himself to get too close before his better judgment kicked in.

He wouldn't make the same mistake twice. Nor did he enjoy her eyeing him like a stain she'd discovered on her sleeve. "Speak freely, Stella," he said, irritated at having to offer the liberty before she would tell him her thoughts.

She flushed a rosy pink. "Are you certain you want to say these things to the Red Cross?"

He noted her trembling hands. "Why not?"

"Because . . ." She hesitated. "Every word is a lie."

Leaning back in his chair, Aric covered his surprise at her blatant insult. Admiration doused the hottest sparks of his ire before he said, "You've certainly become the paradox. You sit and quail like a frightened rabbit, yet you condemn my actions with all the inflated conceit of the Gestapo. At this rate, you'll soon be running my camp, yes?"

Her color faded. "You misunderstand me, Herr Kommandant! We both witnessed Captain Hermann's cruelty yesterday, how he abused that old man. If you hadn't interceded, the prisoner might be dead now. Those people in the ghetto wear rags for clothes. Many looked as though they haven't eaten a decent meal in a long time."

"And you think you could do a better job?"

"I believe you are a man with compassion." She wore a look of earnestness. "Since you have not been with the SS very long, you must not be aware—"

"Compassion?" Her naïveté struck him like a fist. It was an aching reminder of his duty . . . and the fact he could have no future with her. "I have none, I assure you," he said, shoveling dirt onto the grave of his hopes. "Do you think me so duped by

my own officers that I believe we run a regular Gasthaus here?"
A second shovelful.

Her face crumpled. "But I thought—"

"Do you see an award for compassion among these?" He jabbed
at the decorations pinned to his breast pocket. "They represent
kills. Blood sacrifices to the Reich." Glaring at her, he tossed the
last shovelful. "Make no mistake, Fräulein. I understand far more
than you about what's happening in this war."

Through a haze of anger, Aric saw her fear and hated himself
in that moment. He'd admitted the truth about what he really
was—and he despised her reaction to it.

Desperate for even the illusion of escape, he rose from his desk
and strode to the barred window of his office. Against a backdrop
of searchlights and barbed wire surrounding the Pflanzengarten,
snow fell in heavy flakes, landing evenly against the white ground.

As a child, he'd marveled at nature's exactness. Aric tried to relive
the excitement of a first snow: as a boy, tossing snowballs with his
father, riding his pony through the heavy drifts blanketing the hills
behind their home, making snow angels. But those days were like a
sleeper's dream, indistinct yet inherently memorable, pleasurable.

He glanced back at Stella. Seated on the edge of her chair, she
looked poised for flight. Once more he'd dabbled in foolishness,
courting her at every step and yesterday nearly succeeding—when
he could never be fit company for her.

*Dear God, how can I survive this sordid trap of my own
making?*

But no answer came to him; it seemed his conversations with
God had gone the way of his childhood dreams.

Aric clenched his fists.

And he'd been awake far too long.

———

Stella glimpsed the anguish that wrestled for control in the
colonel's stony expression and thought of a wounded lion—
vulnerable and dangerous yet fiercely proud.

She understood pride. Pride held real fear at bay, the kind of terror that penetrated the mind, stripping away all reasoning. At Dachau the Nazis had tried to destroy hers.

"I believe you are capable of goodness," she told him quietly. "You saved me from death."

She saw him flinch. "My initial reason for saving your life wasn't so honorable," he said. "You were a mistake in paper work, a flaw in my otherwise impeccable, albeit brief, career as Kommandant of this camp. I wasn't about to let those guards kill you. I wanted no corpse on my manifest. That you had clerical skills or might be related to an old family friend was merely an afterthought. You were to be sent on the train with the others.

"Until you looked at me." He turned to her. "You were wearing that ragged shirt, and your hand still gripped the child's. I couldn't just leave you."

Stella's breath caught painfully.

"I had expected aversion from you, or at least fear," he said. "But your eyes burned with a determination I've rarely seen, an unwillingness to concede . . . even when everything seemed lost." A sad smile replaced his anguish. "It had been so long since I had that kind of faith in anything, you see. So I decided to kidnap you from my own train and smuggle you across the border."

His eyes shone like emerald glass, revealing a soul scarred by defeat. Stella understood that, too. Perhaps that was why she didn't tell him that she couldn't remember their first meeting, or that the faith he thought he saw in her was a mistake. "What do you really want from me?"

"The impossible," he said hoarsely.

Their gazes held a long moment before being broken by heavy footfalls outside in the library.

"That would be Captain Hermann." His tone lacked enthusiasm as he returned to the desk. "We'll finish the speech

126

tomorrow, Stella. Take the rest of the day for yourself—the captain and I have much to discuss."

Noting his haggard expression, Stella rose from her chair. He seemed as lost in his own tempest of emotions as she was, as if his silent anguish touched hers.

She fled from his office, and it occurred to her that perhaps Aric von Schmidt suffered even more than she did.

At least Stella *knew* the name of her demons.

Joseph stood at her bedroom door and listened for any stirring within. He glanced back toward the stairs, then down at the folded note in his hand. The torn half of an envelope, yellowed with age, felt damp from being wedged inside a piece of wet kindling that Yaakov Kadlec had collected that afternoon.

He fidgeted back and forth on his feet. She'd lied to him about being Jewish—he knew because he'd read the note. Joseph swallowed his hurt. Maybe she hadn't told the truth about other things, like caring about what happened to him, or taking him to live with her when the war was over. Maybe she would leave him one day and never return.

He rubbed at the unexpected sting in his eyes with his sleeve and put his ear back to the door. Should he knock or just sneak in? She wasn't going to keep any more secrets from him. He grabbed the doorknob and turned it.

She slept sprawled across her bed. Beside her was a pretty blue dress, the same one she'd worn *that* night, along with a needle and thread.

Joseph checked the bathroom for intruders before returning to her side.

"*Shalom*," he whispered, and felt a mean spurt of satisfaction when her eyes flew open and she bolted upright in bed.

"Joseph!" she gasped. "You nearly scared me to death."

He shrugged, though his conscience made him blush as he

handed her the wadded note. "Why didn't you tell me you were Jewish?" he burst out, hating that he sounded like a sulky girl, as if she had broken his heart.

She didn't say anything at first, her pretty face as white as snow. Air felt trapped in his lungs.

"I did it to protect you."

His breath came out in a *whoosh*. "Protect me?" He got angry all over again. "I'm not a baby. I can take care of myself." He sounded whiny, but he didn't care.

A smile traced her lips. "Of course you can, little man."

He straightened. He'd never tell her how much he liked it when she called him that. "So why did you lie?"

"I didn't know you, and I was afraid. Aren't you ever afraid, Joseph?"

He shook his head, dodging her gaze. He didn't want anyone to know how scared he got when he was in the same room with Captain Hermann.

"When you asked me about Morty, you could have said something then." He tried to hold on to his anger. "He's your papa."

She smiled at him. "He is like a father to me, but Morty's my uncle." The smile turned into a frown. "But I don't recall asking you about him before."

"When we talked about Auschwitz," he reminded her. "I told you the Elders of the Judenrat—"

"The man who makes up the lists for Auschwitz is . . . is Morty?"

Her sudden grayish color worried him. "Are you going to get sick?"

"No," she said, after taking a deep breath. "I just can't believe such cruelty."

"Morty?"

"The Nazis! They make my uncle choose from among his own people who will go to that horrible place."

He'd never seen her so upset. Then her shoulders sagged and

she looked tired. "I saw him yesterday morning. He was also at Herr Kommandant's party."

A black cloud descended over Joseph as he glanced at the mended blue dress on the bed. He didn't want to talk about the party—or the fact she'd kissed the captain, even though the note said she'd done it so they wouldn't get caught stealing food. "I know you saw Morty in the ghetto." He indicated the letter he'd given her. "He says so in there."

"This is from my uncle?"

She began to open the note when Joseph stopped her. "Nein! You must wait until I leave and then lock yourself in there." He pointed to the bathroom. "That way you won't get caught."

Her fingers stilled. "How did you get this?"

Joseph chewed at his lower lip. He had to be sure. "Did you mean what you said . . . Are you going to take me with you?"

She grabbed both of his hands. "I meant every word. You'll come and live with me, like we planned."

A thread of hesitation held him back. He wanted to believe her, but he felt . . . not scared, just uncomfortable—like he was still wearing the pink towel on his head. He didn't like the feeling. "Maybe you lied about those other things just so I would answer your questions. How do I know I can trust you?"

"Because, Joseph, I've given you my life."

He swallowed, his attention riveted on her.

"It's in your hands," she said softly. "It has been from the moment you learned Morty was my uncle. I am Mischling, half Jewish, and he's the only family I have left. It's a miracle I found him here, of all places." She seemed to hesitate, then added, "I carry false papers. And like you, I live on borrowed time.

"Now, you can keep these secrets safe in your heart . . . or you can use them as a weapon to hurt me." She searched his face. "Will you trust me?"

Joseph hesitated, then blurted, "But why did you have to kiss *him*?"

She seemed confused for a moment, before her expression cleared. "You mean Captain Hermann? I think you already know the answer to that. You needed the distraction." She made a face. "Believe me, it was awful. I only did it to help you, *kaddishel*."

Baby son. Only his mama had ever called him that.

The black cloud vanished, and he launched himself at her. She held him close, whispering soft words against his cheek the way his mama used to.

She had saved him the night of the party. "I'll never tell your secret," he promised. His voice shook, but he didn't care.

When she finally released him, he sat on the bed beside her and began his own confession. "On Tuesdays and Fridays, Herr Kommandant lets five Jews collect firewood for his hearth from the woods behind the house. They leave it at the kitchen door. If there's a message for me, it's always stuffed into one end of a piece of wood."

"Clever . . . and dangerous," she said.

He saw her worry and scoffed. "Not too dangerous, since I'm in charge of the wood." He didn't add that Morty helped him with that part of the plan.

"Can you send messages back?"

He nodded. "Herr Kommandant gives the leftovers from his table to the Jews who collect wood. Helen always gives them a loaf of fresh bread, too." He grinned. "She bakes my messages inside the dough."

"Helen? She's involved in this?"

He nodded again, enjoying her astonished look. Then his conscience made him add, "She doesn't know about the notes that come to the house, just the ones that go out. I told her I need to send messages to my sick grandma in the ghetto so she knows I'm all right. Helen helps me."

"What grandmother, Joseph? You lied, didn't you?"

Her voice cut into him like Herr Kommandant's razor. He

nodded a third time, his skin feeling hot and prickly beneath her stare. He was relieved when she asked, "Is Helen Jewish?"

"All I know about her is that she came here with Herr Kommandant." Joseph tried to think of something to add, then brightened. "And sometimes she gives me extra dessert to take to my room."

"I'll remember that." He saw her smile before she chewed on her lip. Then she asked, "How soon before you need my message for Morty?"

"Thursday night. That way Helen has time to bake the bread."

"Will she know it's my letter?"

Again he saw her worry. "She'll think it's for my grandma. She won't read it."

"I'll have my letter ready by tonight."

"Give it to me when I come and get you for supper at seven." Joseph heard a faint clanging downstairs and glanced toward the door. "I have to go. Helen's watching at the kitchen window for Herr Kommandant. He left with Captain Hermann an hour ago. She thinks I'm playing upstairs."

Again his face felt hot as he stood and fished a handful of colored marbles from his pants pocket. "I told her to bang on her kitchen pots when he returns."

"Be careful, little man."

He liked it when she worried about him. "You and me'll look out for each other," he said.

"That's a promise."

She caught him and gave him a quick hug before he headed toward the door. As he turned the handle, he remembered to call back, "Don't forget to flush the note."

Once he'd left, Stella rushed into the bathroom with the scrap of paper. Locking the door, she removed her clothes and stepped into the shower, turning on the water and aiming the spigot against the wall. Her fingers shook as she unfolded the note penciled in Morty's familiar scrawl.

Daughter,

God has surely answered my prayers, for He has brought you back to me. Please know I am well and have been here since I was first taken from Mannheim. I'm overjoyed you are safe. The new commandant must treat you kindly—I could tell by the way he championed your cause against Hermann, that horse's behind, whose treatment of us is abominable. And I know it was you, my sweet maideleh, who kissed that evil snake to save us all from disaster on the night of Herr Kommandant's party.

I will write again soon. I do not understand fully how you serve the commandant, but don't be discouraged by your circumstances. Earthly hearts cannot always fathom divine reasoning. Remember we live not in our time, but in God's.

Keep your faith, Hadassah. You will be our salvation.

M.

Scanning the cramped lines, Stella felt a mix of joy and anguish. Last night she'd wondered if the old man in the ghetto was her uncle and not just a vision conjured from her longing. Now, seeing his words, hearing his voice on paper, she knew he was alive.

She left the shower, toweled dry, and slipped back into her clothes. Holding the note over the toilet, she intended to heed Joseph's warning, but then hesitated. The handwriting on the back of a torn envelope was the only tangible link to family she had left. Would she see him again? Or would Hermann beat him to death at the next opportunity?

Taking a deep breath, Stella tried to calm her runaway fear. Perhaps her uncle would live, if for no other reason than to choose the next trainload of Jews bound for Auschwitz. How he must suffer! She couldn't imagine that kind of burden. Yet his belief in God remained strong. *Keep your faith, Hadassah. You will be our salvation.*

Morty had explained to her early on the precepts of faith and salvation. After she'd lost both parents in an automobile accident, her uncle had taken on the responsibility of her spiritual needs as well as her material ones. He taught that God offered deliverance to those with true faith, the same faith that made Jews indomitable, like the boy David conquering Goliath with a sling and a well-placed stone.

Stella held that belief once—they all had, at one time or another. But days of terror turned into weeks, and then months, until salvation took the guise of tired arguments from old rabbis looking as gaunt and lice-ridden as the rest of them in the concentration camp.

Doubt drove a wedge into her convictions like a needle pricks the skin, before anger festered in its place, each day their captors were allowed to rise out of bed to torment them. Each hour hunger and typhus swept through their numbers like a brush fire. When a child was torn from its mother's arms, and a little girl murdered in front of a bloodstained wall during the coldest part of winter . . .

Was that when she'd given up? Stella thought of the watercolor in her room and another little girl, lying amidst colorful flowers in a floppy-brimmed hat. Her eyes burned. What kind of salvation let monsters destroy children? What horrible sin had an eight-year-old girl committed to warrant such an end?

She reread the note. *You will be our salvation.* Morty believed the words. He wouldn't have risked them in a letter otherwise.

Her uncle was right about one thing. The colonel *had* championed her. And because she'd worn some obstinate look she couldn't recall, he'd brought her here to this house. She was very much alive, eating good food, wearing warm clothes . . . and struggling with emotions beyond simple gratitude.

Was God leading her in this, or was she merely a Maus awaiting the cat's final pounce? Aric von Schmidt was a Nazi, she was a Jew, and their kiss had been . . . ?

Stella touched her lips, reliving the memory. No monster's kiss, just a man's, who in brief moments revealed his compassion and his sorrow. A soldier burdened by his past—and it seemed, his future. Could he change? Would she be the one to change him?

Stella shredded the note and flushed it down the toilet.

~ 13 ~

And Mordecai came into the presence of the king. . . .

Esther 8:1

WEDNESDAY, MARCH 1, 1944

"You could get shot for speaking such nonsense!" Yaakov Kadlec whispered.

"It's true, I tell you." Morty shifted his rusted milk pail from one hand to the other. He glanced back at the hungry faces behind them as he and Yaakov stood in line for their turn at the day's ration of soup. "You just refuse to believe. My maideleh will save us."

"Pah! She'd save us, all right, *if* she were your niece and *if* she wasn't consorting with Nazis." They shuffled forward a few steps. "Your foolishness will get that boy Joseph into real trouble. They'll probably shoot him before the day is out, once he gives your note to her!"

"She saved our necks at the party. Why would she do that, I ask you? Joseph could have died because of your half-baked plan to steal food from beneath the Kommandant's nose."

"*Our* plan," Yaakov snapped. "Yours and mine, remember?"

Morty ignored him. "I tell you, it *is* her." He hugged the pail to his bony chest, conjuring the precious memory that had warmed him the past two days: Hadassah's clear blue eyes gazing

135

at him from across the barracks. He glanced at his friend. "I stake my life on it."

"And ours, as well!" Yaakov pinched the bridge of his bulbous nose. "*Oi*, I think we'll all be shot before this day is over!"

"Lower your voice! Do you want Brucker to hear?" Morty nodded toward the lanky SS officer strolling past the line of Jews outside the ghetto's kitchen. The lieutenant's baleful gaze speared them from beneath his black cap as he supervised their feeding.

"Even if such a coincidence is possible and this woman *is* your niece," Yaakov said more softly, "how can she help us . . . or poor Leo? I'm sure the commandant keeps her dancing attendance on him both day *and* night."

"She's his secretary, nothing more!" Morty cried, forgetting Brucker's presence. It was bad enough she was with the Nazi; he couldn't bear the thought she might have to barter more than her professional skills in order to stay alive.

Yaakov laid a hand on his shoulder. "Ja, Morty. His secretary."

"She survives, Yaakov. Like we all do." Morty felt beaten. Yaakov's words only served to underscore his own fears, and his doubt. Leo Molski still languished in the infirmary, too weak to leave his bed. The food from Herr Kommandant's banquet hadn't helped their friend's condition. All that risk for nothing! How could one young girl manage to save them?

He bowed his head, drawing a deep breath. *Give me strength, Lord.*

"Anyway, I doubt the Kommandant will grant her any special favors. He's a Nazi, after all," Yaakov insisted as they edged forward.

Morty glanced up. "But he *has* developed a fondness for her. I've seen it with my own eyes." He hated the words, but they needed to be spoken.

Yaakov shot him a dubious look. "So?"

"At least she's in a position far better than our own." *And a precarious one,* Morty thought. He tried to cast off his anxiety, knowing he was in no position to help her. "God will reveal His truth in good time. You'll see. She will be our salvation."

The line shifted again and they reached the kitchen and their turn at the soup pot. Warmth from the cooking fires thawed Morty's frozen limbs. Yaakov thrust out his bowl, an old tin-rations can. "When next you speak to God, Morty, will you ask Him to fill my bowl with hot beef stew instead of the usual spoonful of potato broth?"

While he spoke, Mrs. Brenner, the ghetto's assigned cook, ladled a pitiful dollop of grayish liquid from an enormous cast-iron pot into Yaakov's can.

He stared into the murky contents. "No potato skins, Mrs. Brenner? Surely you can give me at least one, since I braved the cold to dig them up."

The thin, hawk-nosed woman snorted. "I cook the soup, Yaakov Kadlec. I ladle it. Who does or doesn't get potato skins I leave to God. Besides," she added with a sneer, "I heard you ask Him for beef stew."

"Curb your tongue, woman," Yaakov retorted. "I want—"

"*Achtung!*"

The three turned in unison at the command. Sergeant Grossman flashed his silver hook as he cleared the way, allowing the commandant to enter.

All heads swiveled to gape at the unexpected guest in their kitchen.

"Herr Kommandant, you honor us. Heil Hitler!" A surprised Lieutenant Brucker offered a stiff salute from a few feet inside the doorway.

"Heil Hitler, Lieutenant . . . Brucker, isn't it?" The commandant dismissed him, then turned his attention to the line of people waiting to eat. As if one body, they dropped their gazes to the ground. Everyone except Morty—he continued to eye the tall man in the greatcoat, this Nazi who held the fate of his niece.

"What is that stench?" The commandant turned to Brucker and wrinkled his aquiline nose. "Rotten potatoes?"

"Jew food, Herr Kommandant."

"Show me this . . . food." The commandant strolled to the front of the line while Brucker hastened ahead, shoving at the throng to clear a path. Grossman stayed close.

Yaakov clutched his soup can, staring into it reverently. Mrs. Brenner stood beside the large cauldron, her ladle held loosely as she too dropped her gaze at the commandant's approach.

Morty refused to miss any of it, even at the risk of punishment. He watched the commandant lean slightly to take a whiff of the soup. His lips curled back in obvious disgust. "You, what's your name?" he asked the cook.

"Erna Brenner, Herr Kommandant, 145892," she whispered, head still bent.

"Yes, well, Erna Brenner, give me that spoon."

Mrs. Brenner obeyed and nearly thrust it at him. He dipped the ladle, stirring the contents of the pot. A hush fell over the kitchen while he examined the soup and the doubtless gray globs resembling potato skins that floated on top.

Morty hardly dared to breathe.

"Lieutenant, come here."

The commandant's terse order broke the stillness. Brucker rushed to his side. The commandant ladled a spoonful of broth and held it under the lieutenant's nose. "Taste this."

Brucker's eyebrows raised in alarm. "But, Herr Kommandant—"

"Taste it!"

White-lipped above his flaccid jaw, Brucker took the ladle and sipped at the concoction.

"All of it, Lieutenant," the commandant barked.

Brucker downed the entire spoonful. Then he gagged, doubled over, and threw up on the floor. Gasping, he straightened and wiped a sleeve across his mouth. His gray eyes shot pure hatred at the commandant.

The man in the greatcoat seemed unaffected. "I have a Red Cross delegation arriving in a week, Lieutenant Brucker. Your responsibility is to keep the prisoners looking fit and well cared for—at least until our guests depart. Make certain these people have ample, decent food, even if it comes from our own stores. If I find a repeat of the Jews eating this pig slop on my next inspection, the entire SS enlistment will eat it with them. Have I made myself clear?"

"Jawohl, Herr Kommandant."

"You smell, Lieutenant. Go clean yourself."

Brucker's fury suffused his pale features. Clicking the heels of his vomit-stained boots, he stormed from the kitchen.

The commandant also turned to leave when his attention shifted to Morty. A ghost of a smile touched his lips. "You again. I might have known."

Morty thought him a handsome man, one with impeccable authority. Did he also have a conscience? Gratitude warred with his outrage at the possibility his niece was being used unfairly.

Yet as he glanced at his people, their hungry faces drawn, eyes shadowed in despair, he wondered if Hadassah was so much worse off. He turned back to the man in the greatcoat and said boldly, "Thank you, Herr Kommandant."

Beneath the brim of his peaked cap, the commandant raised a brow. Morty detected in his eyes a glimmer of . . . could it be warmth? "Thank my secretary, old man," he said, then abruptly departed the kitchen with Grossman.

A slow smile spread across Morty's face as he heard Yaakov mutter to Mrs. Brenner, "She will be our salvation!"

"Good afternoon, Fräulein."

Hermann strolled out of the colonel's office toward Stella's desk. Her fingers froze on her typewriter keys. She'd left the room for only a minute. How had he managed to slip by her? "Do you need something, Herr Captain?"

He flashed his teeth at her. "What are you offering?"

Stella ignored his innuendo. "Typing . . . ?"

"As a matter of fact . . ." He hefted a burlap sack onto her desk. "I need these cards typed into numbered lists. Two copies each, one for me and the other for Herr Kommandant's file."

Stella opened the sack and withdrew a bundle of white index cards. She glanced at the top card; dread filled her at the sight of Morty's familiar scrawl.

"Herr Kommandant agreed to this?" she asked, trying not to panic. "With the snowstorm last night and still no telephones, he has given me many letters to type—"

"Of course he agreed!" Hermann snapped. "You possess the only working typewriter in this camp—my sergeant has informed me ours is suddenly useless. You'd think Berlin could provide us with a machine produced in this century! I would have made him telephone to find a spare, but as you say, Fräulein, the phone lines are down." He jerked his head at the sack. "These lists must be ready by morning. To try and send him to Prague and back in this snow would take too long."

Stella stared at the stack of cards, each marked with a single name and prisoner identification number. Her panic blossomed in earnest. She couldn't do this. "What are the lists for, Herr Captain?" she whispered, already knowing the answer.

"Friday's train."

"Train?" She held her breath, still not wanting to believe the ugly truth.

"Auschwitz, Fräulein."

His horrible statement sounded like a roar in her ears. Stella found herself back at Dachau, breathing in the pungent stench raining down from the Krematorium, her eyes and throat burning as the ash settled heavy in the air. "You want me to . . . to type deportation lists?"

He leaned over her desk. "I did not think you so squeamish, Fräulein."

She drew back from his searching gaze before he straightened and said, "For what it's worth, most of these Jews are too sick and lame to care where they are going. We must make room for the new ones arriving on Friday."

Stella felt sickened. "What time in the morning do you need these lists completed?"

"Eight o'clock." He smirked. "That gives you plenty to do this evening, Stella. See that you don't let Herr Kommandant keep you too . . . preoccupied."

As he left the room, she watched him go, loathing the sight of him. The colonel had said Hermann was an arrogant cur. Stella thought *pig* suited him better.

Countless names, all in Morty's familiar scribble, spilled onto the desk as she upended the sack. There were eight stacks of cards, each tied off with string. Counting out the first stack, 250, she glanced at the other identical bundles.

Two thousand Jews would go to Auschwitz. And she must type their death sentence.

A wild urge seized her; she would rush into the colonel's office, confront him with Hermann's cruel edict. Surely he wouldn't allow it. But then she recalled his remarks inside the ghetto: a trainload of Jews would arrive on Friday. He must have approved the captain's order.

Despair squeezed her chest with each breath. She imagined her uncle as she'd seen him in the barracks—his thin, stooped frame, the gauntness in his face. He'd shouldered this horrible burden of selection for years.

Stella retrieved a ream of paper and carbon sheets from her desk. Inserting them into the typewriter, she stared blindly at the keys.

Mrs. Bernstein once instructed her on a machine like this during summer's last days, after Rosh Hashanah. Stella had been seventeen, and the mornings unseasonably warm in Mannheim as she sat at Mrs. Bernstein's kitchen table while the retired school-teacher guided her fingers onto the keys for the very first time.

Stella could still picture the older woman. Her thin henna-dyed hair shone myriad shades of copper and brown, while a tortoiseshell monocle bounced from a silver chain against her white-laced bosom. Together they had typed the words *Hadassah Benjamin* in strokes so bold that the pudding flesh beneath Mrs. Bernstein's exposed arms jiggled with the motion, drenching Stella's senses with the heady fragrance of lilac water.

Their lessons had finished by Hanukkah. Mrs. Bernstein predicted that one day Hadassah would become secretary to a man of very important business, learning all sorts of marvelous things.

Stella punched the *1* key, and bile rose in her throat. Mrs. Bernstein could not have imagined such business as this.

Mina Keleman. The name glared at her from the top of the first stack. Stella's agonized fingers hovered above the keys. Did Mina have light hair or dark? Were her eyes brown or as blue as Stella's? Was she a teacher like Mrs. Bernstein or a secretary? Hermann said most of the people were ill. Did Mina suffer? Was she being cared for?

She would end up dead at Auschwitz.

Stella glanced back and forth from the blank page in her typewriter to Mina's name. Her heart began to beat faster. Mistakes happened, didn't they? An oversight in the list?

She thought of the birthday quilt she'd made to surprise her uncle. Stella had seen each and every flaw she'd made in sewing the squares together, yet when she'd shown the finished gift to Marta, her best friend had declared it perfect.

Could dropping a person's name from the list be as easy as hiding a bad stitch? What about several people? If she dropped, say, eight numbers from each page of 1 through 100? That would remove 160 names out of 2,000—less than two hundred Jews. She didn't dare risk more.

As it was, her plan would only work if the lists weren't carefully scrutinized. She fervently hoped the guards in charge of loading the train were as illiterate as those at Dachau. Appell often took hours simply because a guard couldn't count beyond twenty-five or read the prisoners' names from the ledger. The weather might even work in her favor. Any man standing out in the cold while the train was being loaded would want to rush through the process.

Stella refused to think of the Consequence as she poised her fingers over the keys. How could she have thought herself courageous in the ghetto just days before, boldly proclaiming a Yiddish song to the colonel? It seemed so insignificant now, compared with this.

Mina Keleman's card still lay on top. Stella bit her lip. The first card of each stack might hold some significance. While she couldn't be sure, it was more of a gamble than she could afford to take. Captain Hermann—or anyone else with half a mind—might notice its removal.

Forgive me. She typed Mina's name, each touch of the key like a knife in the other woman's back. Marta might liken this to the story of Jesus, how He'd given up His life to save the whole world.

Did that justify Stella's actions now? Was it right Mina should die so that others might live?

Stella continued to type, occasionally skipping a number until she'd deleted eight people from the first sheet. She began the second, then a third, each page offering hope to a few more lives. She felt a strange sense of empowerment as she neared the end of her task, a glimmer of the hope she thought she'd lost.

She *could* make a difference, even a small one.

At five o'clock, with her task complete, Stella retied the stacks as they'd been given to her, minus the 160 cards she'd eliminated from the lists. Those she would toss into the fireplace.

"Fräulein!"

She paused in restuffing the burlap bag to answer the colonel's summons. Inside his office, he sat behind his massive desk, his pen poised over a stack of letters Stella had typed earlier. "These must be posted tonight. Have Grossman see to it."

He handed her the correspondence. Most were requisitions for food—no doubt he wished to wine and dine the Red Cross while he made fools of them.

"Certainly, Herr Kommandant." Then, "I've just finished typing the lists for Auschwitz." Somehow she hoped he would deny any part in the obscene assignment.

Instead he removed his glasses and leaned back in his chair. "And?"

Devastation threatened to crush her. Still, she plodded forward. "I wanted to make sure you'd given Captain Hermann your approval for this task."

"And I suppose you have an opinion on that, as well?"

She met his challenging look. "Would my opinion change yours?"

His mouth flattened. "I can see that it bothers you. I only perform my duty. Disobedience is a luxury none of us can afford."

"But you are Kommandant. Surely you make the orders, and your officers must carry them out?"

"True, until one of them decides those orders are detrimental to the Reich. Then I'm conveniently labeled a traitor and any one of them, even the lowliest *Soldat*, would be justified in putting a bullet in my head. I've learned to trust no one in this war. Not you. Not even myself."

She wasn't moved by his embittered tone. "You won't save them, will you?"

"How can I?" He rose from the chair and tunneled his hands through his hair. "Shall I order Captain Hermann to send an empty train to Auschwitz? And afterward when I lie facedown in a pool of my own blood and Jews are still being loaded into trains, will you stop him?"

Frustration lodged like a knot in Stella's throat. The situation seemed futile. "I'll send these letters out right away," she whispered, clutching the papers.

He read her mood. Heaving a sigh, he came around the desk to meet her halfway. She tried to ignore him—and the battle of emotions warring within her.

"I feel no hatred toward your Jews, Stella. In fact, I feel nothing at all since they have little value to me. If it were my choice, I'd let them go free. They're nothing but a nuisance with which our Führer has hobbled the war effort. Good fighting men and countless resources are wasted dealing with the entire Jew issue. And it would be reasonable to say I treat them better than most in my position.

"But you must understand something else." He flashed a look meant to frighten her. "I am a soldier no longer fit for soldiering. Relegated to a pathetic flock of prisoners with what amounts to street thugs for guards. Until this war is over, I must perform my duty despite the lack of means at my disposal . . . or how distasteful it might seem. It's that or risk my own death."

Stella pretended to smooth a wrinkle from her skirt so he wouldn't see her anger. Beyond her impression that there was more at stake than he'd told her, she thought him callous, egotistical, and brutally frank.

He certainly didn't lie about his feelings. The man had so far spoken only truth to her, unlike the others of his kind that she'd encountered over the past few months. Unlike her own lies.

"Please understand, Stella." He reached to grip her arms, his voice slightly hoarse.

"I'll try." She wasn't sure whether she spoke the truth or simply yearned to unravel his shroud of misery. At least she finally understood that same sense of melancholy. *Only two hundred Jews saved . . .*

Whatever reasons had brought him to be in this place, in this time, he had no more choice in the matter of conscience than she did. And, it seemed, less hope of any deliverance.

14

During the time Mordecai was sitting at the king's gate, Bigthana and Teresh, two of the king's officers . . . became angry and conspired to assassinate King Xerxes.

Esther 2:21

THURSDAY, MARCH 2, 1944

"Permission to speak freely, Herr Captain."

"Granted." Captain Hermann stood at the open window of his second-story office. He stared down into the alley, watching snowflakes drift onto the half meter that already covered the frozen bank of earth.

"I'm going to kill that Jew-loving piece of *Kitch*."

"Trash, Lieutenant Brucker?" Hermann asked without turning.

"Er . . . pardon, Herr Captain, I meant no disrespect."

"What Jew lover has you so heated up, Frederick?"

"Our Kommandant, Herr Captain."

"He has become a problem, hasn't he?" Hermann took a drag on his cigarette, inhaling the fragrant smoke into his lungs. Exhaling, his mouth formed hazy smoke rings that floated out into the cold to collide with the falling white flakes.

"The task would be easy enough, Herr Captain."

146

Hermann closed the window and turned to eye Sergeant Koch. He and Brucker sat along opposite ends of his desk, a deck of playing cards between them.

"You should have seen him, Herr Captain." Brucker's normally flaccid jaw clenched. "He humiliated me, forcing me to eat that Jew slop."

His fist slammed against the desk, scattering the cards. "He comes limping into Theresienstadt waving that cane around like some high and mighty Wehrmacht hero, telling us how to run this camp as if we were idiots!"

"You *are* idiots." Hermann dropped his cigarette onto the scarred wood floor, then made a careless attempt to grind it out with the toe of his boot. He thought of the rich Aubusson rugs in the brick house and how lush they had once felt beneath his own bare feet.

"We could take care of his pet, the Jewess, at the same time."

Hermann glanced at Koch. "What makes you think the woman's a Jew?" He refused to admit that he'd held the same belief—until the night she'd grabbed his lapels and pressed a warm kiss to his lips. *Would a Jew do such a thing?*

Koch's eyes narrowed. "You and I both saw her that first night, Herr Captain. Without the wig, she looks Jew. And the night of the Kommandant's party she played the tease—"

"If she looks Jew, then so do you," Hermann growled, the undeniable pleasure of her kiss still warring with his subsequent humiliation. "She's got your blond hair and blue eyes, Sergeant." He smiled coldly. "Maybe she's your long-lost sister, eh?"

Koch launched at him, fists swinging. Hermann, taller and broader than his young sergeant, delivered a blow that sent him sprawling. "Stand down! And cease this foolish talk, both of you. Otherwise you'll end up dead with the Kommandant's bullet in your head. That, or face a court-martial." He turned to Brucker. "Don't let his injuries fool you. The man's a decorated soldier. He didn't receive the Knight's Cross for being stupid *or* cowardly."

"I've thought of this," Brucker said as Koch struggled to his feet. "My plan will still work. Are you in?"

Hermann hesitated. He'd lost so much: his command of the camp, the luxurious brick house, and now a woman with fiery blue eyes and sensuous lips. "I dislike the Wehrmacht as much as you," he said finally, "but I can't afford to risk my rank." He shot a pointed look at each of them. "After all, who would take over running this camp if something *was* to happen to the Kommandant?"

He fished another cigarette from his breast pocket and then grabbed a handful of papers from the desk. "I must see to the manifest for tomorrow's train."

Near the door he called over his shoulder, "I wish you good hunting."

Morty huddled at the far end of the room behind a stack of food crates earmarked for the arrival of the Red Cross. Pockets crammed with rations, he clutched a can of sardines in one hand while his other fisted the black metal object he'd forged only that morning.

He stole another glance at the wall behind Hermann's desk. Relief mingled with his indignation at the sight of his Grand Cross, now framed in glass below the Madman himself.

His legs began to cramp, yet he dared not move as Koch resumed the conversation.

"All right, Lieutenant, Herr Captain has more or less given us his blessing. What did you have in mind?"

"Tomorrow night you and I will replace the two perimeter guards at the Kommandant's house," Brucker said tersely. "When we're certain he sleeps, we'll make our move."

"Replace the guards? How do you propose we do that? Martin will do it for a few *Reichsmarks*, but Grossman is the Kommandant's man. He'll never leave his post."

Morty peered over the crate in time to see Brucker's malicious grin. "Did I say we were going to ask him?" The lieutenant plucked a card off the scattered pile on the desk and seemed to study it. "I'll make arrangements with Martin—"

"Leave Grossman to me."

Brucker eyed Koch as he tossed down the card. "Make certain he keeps silent on the matter . . . permanently."

Koch nodded. "And the Jewess?"

"She and the Kommandant will have a terrible lovers' quarrel." Brucker chuckled. "We'll make it look like she stabbed him with a kitchen knife. Later, we can report that we heard his cry and entered the house to find her standing over him with the bloodied blade in her hands. When she tried to turn on us"—he threw up his hands in mock fear—"what else could we do but open fire?"

"Like Romeo and Juliet," Koch said with a snort. "It will work. When do you want to meet at the house?"

Brucker rose from the desk. Morty ducked his head. "As soon as you take care of Grossman, come and find me at the barracks. We'll go over together."

Chills raced along Morty's spine as he heard the two soldiers leave the room. He tried to stand, but he'd been crouched behind the crates for the past twenty minutes and could barely move his legs. Hurriedly he rubbed enough circulation back into them to struggle to his feet. He had to warn Hadassah!

Hobbling across the room, he snatched the box frame from the wall behind the desk and removed his Grand Cross. After inserting the mock cross he'd crafted, he replaced the frame beneath the picture of Hitler.

Tucking his prized medal down the front of his pants, he slipped out the same exit as Koch and Brucker. Earlier, he'd snuck upstairs during the afternoon meal when the place was deserted; now the soldiers would be back at their posts.

Hugging the wall, he made his way toward the landing. He peered around the next corner—and spied a pair of Soldats at the foot of the steps.

Morty breathed a curse. How could he get a message to

Hadassah before Brucker and Koch followed through with their scheme? Though God *had* blessed him with the lucky draw to collect wood tomorrow, she might not get his message in time.

He retreated from the soldiers and moved back to the captain's office. Staring out the closed window to the alley below, Morty noted a lone sentry pacing back and forth.

Cold greeted him as he quietly opened the window. The distance to the ground seemed endless. He estimated how many of his bones would break in the fall. Even so, it was better odds than facing the guards downstairs.

A movement behind the sentry caught his attention. Joseph, his slight form darting in and out among the snowflakes, hid in a narrow space between buildings until the sentry turned away. Then he sprinted into the next pocket of darkness. His destination seemed to be Morty's quarters.

Perhaps he carried a message from Hadassah?

Morty stifled an urge to call out. How could he signal to Joseph without alerting the sentry? He turned to scan the room and noticed a wisp of smoke rising from the floor.

The captain's cigarette! He nearly shouted as he picked up the smoldering butt and blew on the ember until it glowed. His eyes darted to the desk and the papers that lay scattered along its top.

Kindling. He lit the papers. The thin trail of smoke quickly ignited into a stream of fire that rippled across the desktop. He fanned the blaze; a minute later, the dry wood surface of the desk began to burn.

Morty reached for the floor-length drapes at the window and touched them to the fire. Bright orange flames shot up the lace like vicious fingers clawing for the ceiling. A loud *whoosh* sounded as black smoke barreled outside into the frigid air.

He stood just beyond the range of burning drapes and billowing haze. *"Feuer! Feuer!"* he yelled, and risked a closer look when he heard an answering shout. The sentry abandoned his post and ran toward the front of the building.

Wasting no time, Morty climbed out onto the window's ledge. Hot cinders of burning fabric singed his hands and face.

He stared at the ground, hesitating. It was a long way down.

Frenzied shouts accompanied the thunder of boots on the stairs behind him. Morty glanced across the alley and said a quick prayer that Joseph still hid among the shadows.

He pushed himself from the ledge. As the ground rushed to meet him, he closed his eyes and curled into a tight ball, hoping to lessen the impact of his fall. Panic rose in his throat. Surely God wouldn't let him die . . .

The snowdrift saved him. Every joint in his body ached as he fell into a graceless heap against the soft stuff, but he was alive. *God be praised!*

"Morty . . . ?"

He raised himself on all fours, shaking his head to clear it. When he finally looked up, Joseph crouched over him, eyes huge. "What happened?"

"Help me up. Quickly!"

Joseph assisted him to his feet, and Morty groaned as he offered another silent prayer of thanks that his limbs were still in one piece. He pulled the boy across the street, and together they crept along the wall of the old barracks building until they reached a space that hid them from the ensuing chaos.

"Why are you here?" Morty asked when they were able to stop and rest. "Have you word from her?"

Joseph answered by shoving a note at him. "I must go," he said, then turned to leave.

Morty stayed him with a hand. "Answer me, boy. Why aren't you at Herr Kommandant's house?"

Joseph averted his gaze as he fidgeted with the brim of his bargeman's cap. "All children must help clean up for the Red Cross visit. We're taking . . . boxes down to the river."

"From the Krematorium," Morty finished grimly. Though Theresienstadt wasn't a death camp, it housed four large ovens that disposed of the hundreds of bodies dead from hunger and disease in the ghetto each day.

Such a task to be laid upon a child! Yet no worse than his own. As sole Elder in the Judenrat, he'd been charged with the deportation in preparation for the Red Cross.

He shoved it from his mind. "I started a letter today. I must finish it now and get it to her. Can you return later?"

Joseph shook his head. "Sergeant Grossman drove me here. He's waiting in the car at the main gate. Right now he thinks I'm still down at the river. Herr Kommandant told him to bring me back to the house as soon as all the boxes are gone."

"You must find a way to come back, boy." Morty paused, looked him in the eye. "Her life depends on it." Then he quickly sketched the details of the soldiers' plot. "You are the only one who can help them."

Brow furrowed, Joseph chewed at the edge of his lower lip for a long moment. Finally he said, "Bring your letter to the Krematorium and put it inside one of the cardboard boxes. Then wait for me and tap the box with your fingers when I return so I'll know which one. Before I sink the box into the river, I'll take out your message."

Morty nodded. "Do you know where to hide it—in case you get searched before you're taken back to the house?"

Joseph shrugged. "Grossman likes me. He won't search."

"Then take this to her, as well." Morty withdrew the Grand Cross from the waistband of his pants. "Have her keep it safe."

A distant cry caught their attention. More soldiers were running inside the burning building across the street. Black smoke continued to billow from the open window upstairs. "You'd better go," Morty hissed.

As the boy darted off in one direction, Morty hurried away in another, until the shouting and commotion across the street had faded into silence.

∼ 15 ∼

When he saw Queen Esther . . . he was pleased with
her. . . .

Esther 5:2

FRIDAY, MARCH 3, 1944

Dingy morning light penetrated Stella's eyelids, waking
her to a grayish dawn that filtered through the gossamer
lace at her window.

"You're even more beautiful when you sleep."

She yawned and stretched her limbs, only half aware of the
familiar voice that roused such comfort in her.

Awareness jarred her upright in bed. She glanced at the colonel with a sleepy, sullen look. He leaned against the doorjamb
and raised a brow. "Good morning to you, too."

His softened expression, paired with the amused glint in his
eyes, proved to be an irresistible force against her indignation.
She rubbed at her face, wondering why he was there.

"Have I overslept?" Her head shot up, and she swung her
legs onto the floor—before noticing that the colonel was out
of uniform. A chestnut crewneck sweater emphasized his broad
shoulders, while brown slacks replaced the usual black trousers,
though he still wore jackboots.

"What day is it?" she asked stupidly, bemused over his civilian dress.

"Friday. And no, you haven't overslept." He approached the bed, grabbed up her satin robe and tossed it to her. "I want you to see something."

He crossed to the window. She looked at the clock on the nightstand. Six a.m. She still had time to get dressed before breakfast. "Where's Joseph?"

"Still sleeping. Now, come."

Joseph was still in bed? She hadn't seen him since breakfast the day before. Disturbed by the colonel's answer, and her half-dressed state, Stella warily slid out of bed. When he didn't turn around, she hastily donned the robe and tied the belt snugly at her waist. "Is he sick?" she asked, struggling to hide her worry.

"No, just tired. Joseph's . . . task took longer than expected." He glanced at her and his expression eased. "Schnell, my dove, the day is wasting away."

Puzzled by his mood and his presence in her room, Stella shoved her bare feet into a pair of yellow satin slippers and walked to the window.

Snow fell from the tumid sky in crisp, tiny flakes, like iced petals blanketing the Ceaseless White as far as the eye could see.

"I thought we might play today, Stella."

She turned to him, dumbstruck. In his strange new clothes, he could have been any ordinary man. Even his rugged features held a boyish expectancy. "Play?"

He laughed, a genuine rumble that rose from deep in his chest and lightened Stella's heart. "You don't believe me?"

She could only shake her head.

"I'm tired of work." His gaze returned to the window. "Last night I spent hours in my office writing requisition reports. Captain Hermann's office caught fire yesterday afternoon, destroying crates of supplies set aside for the Red Cross inspection. The paper work had to be hand-dispatched to Prague early this morning since the telephone lines beyond Teplice are still under repair."

Stella wanted to crow over Hermann's loss. "Why didn't you wake me?" she asked instead. "I could have typed the reports for you."

"You needed your rest."

Stella felt both hot and cold as he reached to graze her cheek with the back of his hand. "Anyway, I've decided we're taking the day off." A mischievous smile touched his lips. "How long has it been since you played in new snow, Stella?"

"I . . . can't remember." His carefree mood stymied her. Only days before, they stood in his office sparring over whether or not to send her people to Auschwitz.

"Get dressed and meet me downstairs for breakfast. I've asked Helen to make your favorite, oatmeal. It will keep you warm while we're outside."

After he'd gone, she was still somewhat dazed. Stella retrieved a powder-blue angora sweater and gray ski pants from the armoire, then went to shower and dress. Afterward she stood at the mirror and noted the blond growth at her scalp just beginning to curl. Given a few more weeks, her hair might even look presentable; hopefully she could then rid herself of the red mop that lately itched whenever she wore it.

Back in her room, she searched out her shoes. Neither pair was practical for tromping outside, but she'd have to make the best of it. The idea of leaving a perfectly warm house to stand in the snow was beyond dismal. Hadn't she spent enough time outside at Dachau?

Crouching to retrieve the pair she'd tucked beneath her bed, she noticed the Bible again on her nightstand, an inexplicable occurrence that no longer surprised her.

She perched on the edge of her bed and stared at the book. Weary exasperation replaced her irritation. Though she was tired of being coerced by the colonel—or was it Helen?—Stella still felt wistful pangs of happier times spent with Marta, now long gone.

Nostalgia won out, again, as she reached for the tome. She held the Bible against her lap and let it fall open to a random page, just as she'd come to do so many times since her arrival. Stella wasn't certain why she bothered with the ritual; perhaps Morty's words on earthly hearts and divine reasoning had affected her, after all.

"Speak to me," she breathed . . . and froze when the open page revealed a passage in the Gospel of Matthew.

The New Testament? These pages were unchartered waters for Stella; her only prior experience with the Christian section of the Bible had been explained through Marta.

Stella shifted uncomfortably. Her uncle would likely disown her if he saw her now.

"*Love your enemies,*" the words of Jesus jumped out at her, "*and pray for those who persecute you . . .*"

Stella snapped the book closed. The beating she'd endured at Dachau before they dragged her off to the shooting pit had nearly killed her. Was she supposed to simply forget that? Or what they had done to her people? Should she pray for them while they continued to send death trains to Auschwitz like so much stock being shipped to the slaughterhouse? And what about the colonel? Should she pray for him, as well?

But her anger died abruptly, seized by a hailstorm of emotions she wasn't ready to face. He was unlike anyone she'd ever known: his warm sense of humor, the way he smiled at her. His kiss . . .

Stella banished the thought and returned the Bible to the nightstand drawer. Then she slipped her feet into the shoes and rose to cross the room. They were still tight on her feet, but the black pumps would hide water stains better than the blue ones—

How petty she had become! Stella scolded herself. What about the two women she'd seen earlier that week pulling a cart inside the ghetto? Each had worn threadbare clothes, without the luxury of decent shoes. She hugged the soft rabbit hair sweater against her skin in silent gratitude. Morty was right. The colonel did treat her kindly. *But should I pray for him?*

No. Not while her people rode the death trains to Auschwitz, or while her uncle suffered beyond those fortressed walls. It dawned on her then that Hermann must be furious over the fire. Had he taken to beating Morty again?

Stella forced away the tormenting thought as she descended the stairs to the dining room. Right now she could do nothing for her uncle except keep her wits. She was no longer a helpless prisoner at Dachau, but a woman living freely within this house, enjoying the amenities of her current position. But did she have the colonel's ear?

"Have faith, Hadassah," Morty's words echoed in her mind. If only she could.

The colonel rose from the table when he saw her. "You look stunning."

Stella blushed as she took the chair he held beside his own. "Thank you, Herr Kommandant."

"Aric," he gently corrected her. He returned to his own seat. "That sweater matches your eyes. Blue . . . like Austria." He continued his scrutiny. "And you look as though you'll be warm enough."

Nodding, Stella felt new tendrils of heat curl along her neck at his attention. She looked down at her breakfast while her mind raced. Could she really influence him? Two days ago, she'd asked him to stop sending Jews to Auschwitz. He'd refused. What if she requested something less . . . extreme? Taking a few bites of oatmeal, she mustered up her courage.

"Aric—" Her confidence rose when he smiled at her use of his name. "I'm grateful for the lovely clothes. I wish . . . the old man we saw in the barracks . . . well, that he and the rest . . . could also benefit from such generosity."

His smiled faded. "Are we back to that? I told you I have little choice in the matter."

"But couldn't you order your men to give them warm clothes? What about surplus or the new clothing to be issued for the Red Cross visit?" Her voice dropped when she thought of her uncle. "That poor old man had nothing but thin rags—"

"I'm tired of hearing about that old man!" He slammed a fist against the table.

Stella jumped.

"You seem obsessed with that Jew—for what reason, I cannot fathom," he growled. "But you'll be pleased to know I've had him transferred to a different project, one that keeps him out of Captain Hermann's way." He shot her a hard look. "I can do nothing else."

Relief washed over her. "Thank you."

"Stella, I don't wish to fight with you," he said in a tired voice. "Finish eating, and just for a little while we'll have no more talk about Jews or Nazis or wars. All right?"

His appealing look melted her obstinacy. She'd pushed him far enough . . . for now. "A truce then," she agreed grudgingly.

"Ah, like a queen granting her poor minion a boon."

Laughter returned to his voice, and Stella's pulse gave a light-hearted kick. In that moment—wearing beautiful clothes and feasting on her favorite, hot oatmeal—she felt like a queen.

"And now, Your Highness," he said, rising from the table, "I have a surprise for you."

He disappeared into the living room and returned with two packages wrapped in brown paper and string. Placing them on the table, he eased her chair back and offered her the larger of the two. "Open this first."

Too surprised to speak, she carefully untied the string. Brown paper crackled as she pulled away the wrapping.

Her breath caught in amazement.

The houndstooth coat was beautiful. Shiny black buttons

paraded down the black-and-white, full-length wool. As she lifted the coat from its wrapping, a pair of black kid gloves fell into her lap. "I . . . don't know what to say."

She fought to school her emotions before glancing at him. The boyish eagerness in his expression was nearly her undoing. "Open this one." He handed her the smaller parcel.

Tearing away the paper, she gasped at the expensive pair of calf-high black leather boots fringed in fox fur. "Herr Kommandant . . . I," she whispered.

"Aric." He reached to lightly cup her cheek. "And you're welcome."

His gaze held hers, and for a moment she leaned into the gentle pressure of his hand, irresistibly drawn. Searching his face, she saw his tender smile give way to the longing she'd seen before. Her pulse pounded in her throat as he bent his head to hers, and she half hoped . . . and feared that he might kiss her again.

"Shall we go and have our first snowball fight?" he whispered.

Stella blinked in surprise while relief and disappointment simultaneously swept through her. But then he grinned, and she found a sudden hilarity in the moment. Seized by an overpoweringly selfish urge to forget her present circumstances and simply feel normal again, if only for a little while, she smiled impishly. "I'll win."

He chuckled. "Is that so?"

"I have a pretty good arm."

"Let me see."

She held out her right arm, bent at the elbow. He tested the slight swell of her biceps, his brow furrowed in mock consternation. "I see now that I might have formidable competition."

"You've been warned."

She grabbed up her new boots, but before she could slip them on, Aric crouched in front of her. Removing her shoes, he slipped the boots onto her feet, and Stella's mind flashed with the memory of the day she'd passed through the checkpoint into Czechoslovakia and stood freezing in front of Pig-nose. Afterward the colonel—Aric—had warmed her numbed feet with his scarf.

He always seemed to be taking care of her. The new awareness made her cheeks warm, and as if on cue he raised his head and smiled knowingly. "I'm pleased to see your color back, Fräulein."

As he rose from the floor, he winced slightly. Again she wondered at the true extent of his injuries—both physical and emotional.

He helped her into her new coat, then brushed her hands away when she fumbled with the new buttons. "Let me," he said and deftly finished the task. Again she noticed his hands, strong and capable, the skin bronzed and the backs lightly dusted with russet.

"Come." He pressed the black kid gloves at her before leading her out through the kitchen. At the back door, Aric grabbed his greatcoat from a row of pegs against the wall. Then he snatched up a gray wool scarf and knit cap. "Helen won't mind if you borrow these." He winked at the housekeeper, who had glanced up from washing dishes to beam at him.

After fitting the scarf snugly around Stella's neck, he plucked away the red wig and tugged the knit cap firmly over her ears. "Now you won't have to worry about losing your head."

Stella smiled before the blast of cold air outside hit her cheeks. Aric took a moment on the landing to instruct Grossman and then pulled her along through the calf-deep snow toward a rise of bare-limbed poplars surrounding the deeper woods.

At the tree line, snow fell softly, surrounding them in a deafening hush. Against the Ceaseless White, tufts of steam billowed into the air from their labored breathing, mingling with the crystalline flakes that swirled around their shoulders.

Time slept, like the flowers drowsing beneath the ice, and the wild creatures dreaming peacefully inside their caves. It was a leap year, the second month of *Adar*—early March—yet spring still lay hidden. How could it be that in a matter of weeks, seeds would sprout, rivers would thaw, and forests fill with the urgent chatter of squirrels and the crows' menacing caws?

Aric lifted his face to the falling snow. "This country reminds me much of Austria. Don't you agree?"

Pulled from her reverie, Stella grimaced. She hated lying to him, especially in such a pristine setting. "It does seem like home"—she spoke the truth, as it did remind her of Mannheim—"but I spent much time in the city."

Deliberating whether to broach the subject of his past, she finally asked, "What was it like, living in the country?"

He glanced off toward the trees. "Thaur is the most beautiful place on earth." He spoke in a reverent tone that surprised her. "I was the son of a baron, who was also a gentleman farmer." He shot her a wry look. "Which is a pursuit of the titled wealthy when there is no wealth. Anyway, it suited my father. He loved commingling with the earth, feeling the dark soil between his fingers."

She saw the sorrow he tried to hide behind a smile.

"I had no such love of dirt," he continued. "When I was a boy about Joseph's age, I preferred to ride into the forest each day on the back of an old nag my father kept for heavy work. He even made me a small bow and a set of arrows, hoping to encourage me to hunt. I preferred playing games."

He grinned, and his sudden faint color surprised her.

"I pretended to be the son of a rich king, fearing no one as I went off in search of the fabled Magical River."

"Magical River?"

"You don't know the story?" When she shook her head, he explained, "A fairy tale by the Brothers Grimm. My mother often told it to me before bedtime. A king's fearless son goes in search of an apple from the tree of life and a golden ring with unimaginable power. He finds both and also recruits a faithful lion as his companion. The prince has promised the apple to a giant, but when the giant also demands the golden ring, the prince, with unbelievable strength, fights and defeats his enemy. He himself is wounded in the battle, and the lion takes him to the Magical River to be healed.

"Afterward, the prince comes upon a haunted castle with a maiden imprisoned behind its walls. He must spend three nights in the place and show no fear, uttering no sound, despite the horrors, in order to break the enchantment and save her."

He paused. "Well?" Stella demanded, eager to hear the rest of the tale. "Did he do it? Did the king's son save her?"

"He did. And each of the three mornings, after the devils that ruled the place tried to terrify him and beat him to death, the maiden came and washed his wounds with water from the Magical River."

His expression took on a faraway look. "I never told my father, but for a long time while my mother lay sick, I'd go out on that old nag in search of the Magical River, hoping to bring her back the healing waters."

Stella couldn't help but ache for his loss. "I was just a child when I lost both of my parents," she said. "It's a terrible feeling to know you can't help them, that you can't change things back to the way they once were."

He met her gaze. "I'm glad you understand," he whispered.

"What happened . . . afterward?"

"My mother died and I was forced to grow up." He brushed at the white flakes gathering on top of Stella's cap. "I went to the local school and worked the farm with my father until I had an opportunity to attend preparatory classes in Bonn. He took it hard when I left—he wanted me to remain in Austria. But already I had dreams of grandeur.

"In Bonn, I got caught up in the frenzy of Hitler Jugend, the new Resistance to create a perfect state. Everyone was promised prosperity. I thought to change my poor but noble father's situation and soften his attitude toward me." Bitterness edged his voice as he added, "After graduation, I enlisted in the Wehrmacht. I decided the infantry was where I should be."

Stella observed the shadows beneath his eyes, the sorrow etched into the corners of his mouth. In the fairy tale, the prince had only to endure the demons inside the castle for three days.

Aric seemed to live with them constantly.

Had the world been a different place, they might be on a first date, taking a stroll in the winter woods. Aric would have freed her from an enchanted castle, and in return she would have healed him with magical waters. Prodded by some unknown force, they huddled closer together, oblivious to the gentle falling of snow and the tangible stillness around them. The sun, hidden behind sullen clouds, made the air appear silvery gray.

"I have a present for you." He withdrew a cloth-wrapped bundle from his coat pocket and held it out to her. "I was going to surprise you with it later, but . . ." His lopsided grin struck her heart like a well-aimed snowball.

"Another gift?" She pulled away the cloth to reveal a jewelry case of shiny white porcelain, trimmed in gold and inlaid with pink and blue roses. When she opened the lid, the lilting notes of the "Blue Danube Waltz" broke the silence around them. "It's lovely," she breathed.

"It was my mother's. The music is my favorite. Maybe it will become yours, too."

Overwhelmed by the intimately personal gift, she reached to touch his cheek. It went against her conscience, defied even her bloodlines—yet she felt something for this man. He'd broken through her resistance, made her feel decent and human again, all the way down to her bones. It had been such a long time . . .

"Kiss me," he whispered. "This time no tricks, I promise."

Luminous flakes fell from a ragged sky, their only audience as he drew her close, the music box pressed between them. Stella ignored her numbing cheeks and nose as she leaned into him, knowing she shouldn't want to kiss him as badly as she did. Her own people would damn her; she would be a traitor to every Jew crushed beneath the Nazis' boot. Yet any objection she might have offered escaped her as Aric tipped her chin to search her face. With his mouth descending toward hers, she closed her eyes, anticipating his kiss . . .

The scream of a train's whistle tore through the air, jerking them apart. Stella turned to stare from the top of the rise at the train station of Bohusovice, where insidious cattle cars rolled to a stop behind an engine billowing steam. A bedraggled horde of Jews disembarked, trudging the miserable distance to the fortress gate amidst shouts from the guards.

Standing to the left of the train were exactly 1,840 souls ready to take their place. *Good-bye, Mina.*

———

Aric's pulse raced like a bullet. He watched Stella, waiting for her reaction. When it finally came, he wasn't surprised. The dove's eyes turned to him filled with accusation. She tipped her chin, just as she always did when she was furious. Her lower lip trembled.

"I appreciate the gift, Herr Kommandant, but I cannot accept such an extravagance. It wouldn't be right."

She shoved the music box back at him. It felt dull and lifeless in his hands.

"I'm cold. I want to go inside now," she said, then quickly turned to stumble back down the hill toward the house.

Aric didn't try to stop her. He'd seen the inevitability of his folly reflected in her eyes, a look of despair so hideously different from the blazing resolve she once offered him.

Frustration seized him, and he roared with it, but his rain of curses fell heavy and still against a quiet, snow-packed earth.

The spell had been broken.

"What have you found, Sonntag?" Captain Hermann trekked through the snow toward his young corporal.

Sonntag crouched beside the white drift beneath the window of Hermann's burnt-out office. "I discovered this, Herr Captain." He handed Hermann a rations tin. "Only a thin layer of powder fell last night, so we can make out at least one set of prints. Extremely large ones. They lead across the street and down along the far end of the building." The corporal pointed toward the old barracks.

"Unfortunately they disappear into an area where heavy foot traffic turned the snow into slush." He glanced up at his captain. "There are more prints here, much smaller and indistinct, which run in the same direction. And these boot prints"—he pointed to another set—"could easily belong to the sentry who stood watch along this alley."

Hermann grunted, glaring at the conspicuous sets of tracks. He pocketed the rations tin and then fished a cigarette from inside his black leather coat. An aide hurried forward with a match and lit it for him.

He drew smoke into his lungs and looked up into a swollen gray sky. The calm he sought began easing over him; he took another long puff before ridding himself of an overpowering urge to hit someone.

Arson, without question. Hermann easily recognized the larger set of footprints—just as it had taken little time in scouring his gutted office this morning to discover the phony cross in its charred frame. Formality made him question Koch and Brucker, yet there were few men at Theresienstadt who had the audacity to pull off such a stunt. It took the kind of courage his own men lacked, a certain amount of grit that earned a soldier such a prize as the Grand Cross.

Elimination of the problem was out of the question, at least for the moment. He couldn't afford to jeopardize his position with the commandant or Berlin by killing the only remaining

Elder in the Judenrat—not with the Red Cross inspection coming up. Besides, death would only martyr that Schwein.

Hermann took another drag off his cigarette. The Jew had been trouble from his first day at Theresienstadt, refusing to show proper respect. Even regular beatings had failed to cure that Semitic pride. His conceit was reminiscent of the Jew filth living in Hermann's hometown of Leipzig, lording their wealth and status over them all like a sour teat to suckling brats—

"Herr Captain?"

Hermann turned to face his all-but-forgotten corporal. "Sonntag, find the Jew, Mordecai Benjamin. Bring him to me for questioning."

Sonntag offered a hasty salute, then dashed off toward the prisoners' barracks.

Hermann crushed the cigarette in his fist and tossed it into the drift. His interrogation would require more than the usual degree of technique. Not only was the crime serious—the destruction of German property—but the criminal wasn't easily broken.

Hermann almost smiled as he slogged through the snow toward his temporary office in the garrison. *Well, pig, let's see how loud you squeal.*

$$\sim 16 \sim$$

*Mordecai found out about the plot and told Queen
Esther, who in turn reported it to the king. . . .*

Esther 2:22

She was desperate for a bath, a shower, anything to wash away the shame.

Brushing past Grossman at the back porch, Stella burst into the kitchen, slamming the door behind her. She wrenched off her new coat and gloves, followed by the borrowed knitted cap and shawl, shoving them onto pegs alongside her red wig.

She hadn't saved them. Anna was gone, now Mina . . .

Heat from the oven wrapped the house in a cocoon of fragrant smells, baked apples and spice, and the sounds of liquid boiling on the stove kept cadence with the *tick tick tick* of a hand-wound timer. Stella hardly noticed as she stormed from the kitchen toward the sanctuary of her room, and a bath.

She met the housekeeper on the landing, blocking her path. It seemed appropriate that above a pretty lemon-colored neckerchief, Helen wore her usual sour look.

Stella leaned against the banister. "What do you want?" she demanded, then felt foolish for expecting Helen to answer. "Sorry, I . . . I'm upset. I didn't mean to take it out on you. Please let me pass."

Helen refused to yield.

Stella met the formidable housekeeper's scowl—a woman not so heartless as to let a child's wound go untended or his belly go without food. So why did Helen despise her? Stella had committed no offense, at least that she knew of. And her friendly overtures had all been rejected. Did the woman believe her a threat to the colonel, or did she imagine Stella was his mistress? That notion made her angrier. The last thing she needed was Helen's misguided judgment of her. "Please," she said impatiently. "Get out of my way—"

Helen cut her off, thrusting a small package at her.

Stella took it. "Where did you get this?"

Helen's frown turned fierce.

Stella held on to her temper. "Just indicate yes or no. Did you get this from Joseph?"

Nothing.

It dawned on Stella that the day's firewood had not yet been collected. How had she received a message already? "He was inside the ghetto yesterday, wasn't he?" she asked uneasily.

For an instant, Helen's stony expression faltered. Apprehension swept through Stella. "Is he all right?"

Helen hesitated, then nodded.

"Did he return last night?"

This time Helen shook her head, jabbing an index finger toward the floor.

"This morning?" No wonder Joseph was exhausted! "Take me to him, please."

It was a moment before Helen's tight-lipped scowl relaxed. She motioned Stella toward another door off the kitchen that led to the back of the house.

Joseph's room was cast in shadow. A white sheet had been tacked over the only window inside the compact space. Helen stood at the door while Stella entered. Her eyes soon adjusted enough to detect the undersized lump buried beneath blankets on a bed against the far wall. Quietly she eased onto the edge of his mattress. A milk crate disguised as a nightstand rested beside the bed. Joseph's colored marbles lay scattered across its top.

Stella worked her hands over the boy's limbs, gently so as not to awaken him. She was relieved to find him still whole and un-broken. "I'm so happy you're back, little man," she murmured.

He didn't hear her, nor did his sleeping presence give her any real comfort. She knew that death awaited the Jews at the station outside the ghetto. Would Joseph one day be forced to board that train?

Stella reached to brush back his silken curls. Restless, he turned his head, revealing the angry scar where his ear had been. *Brutality is the Nazis' wheel, crushing everything in its path.* Was that what Aric tried to explain to her? Had the monsters become victims to their own destruction—killing with such ease and abandon that now, like cannibals, they preyed on each other? That meant no one was safe. Not even Aric.

Stella kissed the top of Joseph's head, vowing again to protect him. "Sleep well, kaddishel," she whispered, rising from the bed.

Helen stood at the door, a suspicious gleam in her sherry-colored eyes. The brusque housekeeper had never shown a softer side, except for the smiles she gave Joseph and the colonel. "Have you already opened this?" Stella held up the parcel.

Helen shook her head.

"Will you inform Herr Kommandant?" Stella eyed the other woman steadily, recalling the colonel's threat about deceit of any kind. He would send her to the ghetto in chains—or worse—if he learned of her deception.

Again Helen shook her head. Pointing toward the boy's sleep-ing form, she placed a fist over her heart.

For the boy, then, she would keep Stella's secret.

They formed a silent truce in that moment; each understood her precarious situation, as well as a responsibility to protect the child with her life. Stella resisted an impulse to embrace her new co-conspirator, unwilling to disrupt their fragile new balance. "I'll be in my room. Please let Joseph know I want to see him when he awakens."

Upstairs, she locked herself in the bathroom and turned on the shower. Leaning against the sink, Stella untied the package. Her uncle's Grand Cross slipped from the damp paper. Stella clutched the medal like a talisman as she read his familiar scrawl on the wrapping.

Stunned, she read, and then reread, Morty's adamant praises of the colonel. Laughter rose in her throat at his colorful tale involving Aric's visit to the ghetto kitchen. She sensed the relish in her uncle's words as he crowed over Brucker's humiliation. Her breath caught in the next instant as she read the words, *You can thank my secretary.*

An image of Aric standing alone on the hill pierced Stella with unwanted regret. He'd professed no compassion, yet with a simple edict like that of a grand king he'd eased the plight of thousands.

Murder. The word jumped out at her as she read about the intended plot Morty overheard. *Tonight, stay close to the commandant,* he wrote, *as you are both in grave danger. My dearest daughter, they suspect you are Jew.*

Stella's hands shook as she folded the paper into a thumb-sized square. Her dazed senses tried to digest the planned details of her own murder as she moved from the sink to dispose of the letter. Like the first, this missive was just as dangerous to keep.

Still, she hesitated. What if the worst happened, and she and Aric were found dead the next morning? Morty's message could be useful in implicating Hermann and the others—if a Jew's word could be believed.

The idea consoled her. Whether retribution for the sake of Joseph or her uncle or both, she needed to feel that some justice in this godless war would be served. Clutching the wad of paper, along with Morty's Grand Cross, Stella turned off the shower and returned to her room.

The Bible lay on the nightstand beside her bed. Someone had been inside her room again.

A knock at the door made her jump. She quickly hid the Cross and letter beneath her mattress. "Come in."

She expelled a relieved breath. "Joseph."

"Morty said you were in danger." He rushed to her, his features pale. She caught him in her arms and held him tight. "What can we do?"

"*We* can do nothing, little man. But I must somehow convince Herr Kommandant of this treachery . . . without revealing my source." She leaned back to examine him. "Why were you in the ghetto?"

"Herr Kommandant made all the children move boxes . . . to the river. Before the Red Cross arrives."

"Boxes?"

"Ashes."

A chill as brittle as the winter wind swept through her. She could never forget the tiny charred flakes soaring from Dachau's Krematorium. Souls of Jews . . .

"I gave Morty your last letter," he said.

Stella was relieved to change the subject. "That's how you found out about this . . . this plot?"

Joseph nodded. "Morty jumped from a second-story window!" His eyes grew round. "And he set fire to Herr Captain's office . . ."

But Stella barely heard the boy's rendition of her uncle's dangerous escapade. Arson! What if Hermann found out it was her uncle? Morty would be a dead man. "Why was he there in the first place?"

Joseph scrunched his shoulders. "I don't know. When will you tell Herr Kommandant?"

Heavy boot steps echoed up the stairs. "I suppose right now." She released him. "Go now, before he starts asking you questions."

He hesitated at the door, anxiety creasing his young features.

"All will be well, kaddishel." She forced a smile. "I'll convince him."

Joseph opened the door and nearly collided with the colonel. Aric stood on the threshold, still wearing his sweater and slacks. A lock of hair fell against his forehead, softening the hard-edged angles of his face. His eyes fixed on her as he said, "I see you're out of bed already, Joseph. Hungry?"

"Ja, Herr Kommandant."

He glanced down at the boy. "I've asked Helen to prepare *Kaiserschmarren*—it was my favorite when I was your age. You like powdered sugar and stewed fruit, yes?"

Clearly astonished, the boy nodded.

Aric smiled at him. "Go and eat. I need to speak with Fräulein."

"Danke, Herr Kommandant." Joseph wasted no time squeezing past him.

"May I come in?"

Again she felt the full impact of his gaze. "Of course, Herr Kommandant."

"I liked 'Aric' much better." He entered the room. In one hand he carried the music box she'd rejected. The other supported his weight with the cane. Climbing hills in deep snow must have left him exhausted and in pain.

He kicked the door shut behind him. Stella's heart raced with the same conflicting emotions she felt each time he was with her.

"Why did you leave me outside?"

"You need to ask?" she questioned.

"I need to know why you're so angry. The train?"

She gave a nod. "I typed the deportation lists for Auschwitz. Those people will likely die, and I did nothing to help them." Her throat worked with frustration. "You say you cannot help them, either."

"But you don't believe me." He made a grim face. "You think I've been courting you with excuses so that . . . what"—he advanced toward her—"I can seduce you into my bed?"

"Of course not! I just meant——"

"Or maybe I should martyr myself for your Jews. Would that be enough truth?" He came to a halt in front of her. "It won't change facts, Stella. Long after my carcass lies in the ground, your Jews will still board those trains. They will still die."

He reached around her to place the music box on the nightstand. He noticed the Bible. "Do you pray often?" he asked, retrieving it.

Jarred by the shift in conversation, she blinked. "Not anymore. Do you?"

He shook his head as he studied the book in his hand. "Once my mother died, it seemed pointless. The miracle I'd asked for didn't happen."

"The magical waters?"

He smiled at her. "Something like that."

Stella thought it ironic that she and Aric stood on opposite sides of the war, yet God chose to ignore them both. At least He didn't take sides. "I used to pray," she offered, "for an end to the war, and all its suffering and degradation . . ." Her gaze locked with his. "But God lets it continue while good people suffer and die."

"They do," he agreed. "Would you have me die, as well?"

"Nein!" Then, surprised at her vehemence, she added, "I don't want anyone to die."

"But as you said, the war *does* go on. You can't have it both ways, my dove. Man or martyr, which will I be? You must choose."

Her whole being ached as though bruised from the inside out. She searched his face. "You would abide by my decision? Die for this cause?"

"Would you?"

She flinched. How much courage had it really taken to distract Hermann at the party? Request a Yiddish song in the ghetto? Remove a few names from a deportation list? Every day she lived a lie to save her own skin. Still, honesty compelled her to answer, "If I thought it would make a difference, then yes."

"Like Jesus." He weighed the book in his hand. "According to the Bible, His death saved the world." He glanced at her. "Do you think mine will make a difference?"

Stella hesitated, then shook her head. Recalling how he had improved the food in the ghetto, she offered him a hopeful smile. "But I believe your living just might."

"Your continued belief in my 'goodness' has cast its spell." He returned the Bible to the nightstand and then propped his cane beside the bed. "It would explain my latest act of madness. Who knows? You may yet witness martyrdom in the making. I've no doubt incited murder in a few of my men."

Foreboding pierced her as she asked what she already knew. "What madness?"

He must have seen her worry; he placed his hands on her shoulders, and the warmth in his touch soothed her. "A small incident."

He said no more about what he'd accomplished for the Jews in the ghetto. "However, I imagine Sergeant Brucker will have dreams about me at night." He flashed a humorless smile. "Bad ones."

"Speaking of dreams . . ." Inspiration struck her. "I've had more nightmares."

His brow creased. "When did they return?"

"Three or four nights ago," she lied. "It's the same dream, but different from those I had before. Men are breaking into this house." She searched his face. "Men who try to kill you."

"Who are these men?"

"One is Sergeant Koch."

"And the others?"

"Only one other, but I've never seen him before."

"Do your dreams tell you why these men want to kill me?"

She could tell by his indulgent smile that he didn't take her seriously. "Because . . . you keep me here, with you," she whispered. "In the dream, I'm also in danger."

174

"What danger?"

His gentle touch had turned painful. Stella tensed. "These men, they think I'm Jew."

"Are you?"

His eyes narrowed, all tenderness gone. Stella raised a quivering chin at him. "If you believed that," she said with as much truth as she dared, "you would have let them shoot me at Dachau, regardless of your manifest."

"Enough nonsense, Stella." He gave her shoulders a light squeeze before releasing her. "Nothing will happen to either of us."

Stella hoped that he was right, yet her mind flashed with images of him lying in a pool of his own blood, and the devastation she felt made her angry. She must be insane. Aric von Schmidt was a hard-bitten man with an unpredictable nature. While he ordered children to bury the dead and hide the Nazis' hideous secrets, he was also defending the Jews' right to decent food in the ghetto—and endangering his own life.

He'd refused to stop sending trainloads to die in Auschwitz, and yet weeks ago he'd rescued her, a total stranger, from a firing squad at Dachau. Was she being fair? Was Aric such a contradiction, or just a man who'd seen too much of the world and understood its hard realities?

And why was she so desperate to believe the latter?

"Humor me, Aric," she said, placing a hand against his cheek. "Be on your guard. I have a strong feeling something will happen . . . tonight."

His hand reached to cover hers. "I'm pleased to know you care whether I live or die."

She pulled her hand away. "I . . . I've gotten used to you. It would be difficult working for someone else."

"Ah, Süsse, I think I mean more to you than that."

She felt her cheeks warm. "I'm your secretary, nothing more."

"And what if I said I don't believe you?"

"I . . . I don't know what you mean."

He laughed. "Would you like to find out?" He pulled her into his arms. "Give me your kiss, Stella," he said softly.

She leaned against him, unable to resist his tender touch.

"Please," he whispered, and lowered his head to hers.

Stella's body seemed to move of its own volition; her eyelids drifted closed as she raised her lips for his kiss. Just as before, the warm contours of his mouth fit hers perfectly. He tasted faintly of Kaffee, reminding her of their first breakfast together when he'd worn his gold spectacles and sipped from his cup while perusing his morning papers. Just like any other man might do.

She next tasted his sorrow. The barrier shielding her heart cracked a little as she slid her arms around his neck, wanting to give him comfort. Then as he drew her closer to deepen the kiss, Stella sensed a longing that matched her own. Suddenly nothing else mattered except the two of them, in that moment. The world outside could remain cold and unforgiving while in the circle of his arms she felt warm, cherished, and safe.

When their kiss ended, she rested her cheek against his chest, too moved to speak. Through his sweater she felt his heart beating as rapidly as her own.

"I've wanted to do that for the longest time." He sounded out of breath as he held her in his arms.

"You kissed me before, in the ghetto."

"That was unfinished business," he said softly, all traces of humor gone. "Now say it, Stella-only-my-secretary. I want to hear the words."

His gentle voice invited her response. Leaning back in his arms, she considered her surrender. No other man had ever made her feel this way. To deny the truth now would only make her look foolish. And it had been a good fight, if not a fair one.

"You win," she whispered. "I care."

17

The girl pleased him and won his favor.

Esther 2:9

She tasted so sweet. And time was running out.

Aric kissed her again to banish the thought; he allowed himself a few more blissful moments to simply *feel*. The enchantment she cast over him would warm the cold, bleak days that marked his future.

How naïve to think he could set her free or remain unaffected by those soulful eyes and the delicate line of her jaw that so often revealed her emotions. He wanted her for his own, despite his self-seduction and blind intent.

How could he let her go—even when she grew to despise him?

Her rapid pulse kept pace with his, and it pleased him that she was equally affected by the kiss. Her nature always seemed illusory to him; like the snow-covered earth, she appeared cool and unchanged, while passion—desire, frustration, and oftentimes anger—burned at her core.

Desire had surfaced as she surrendered to his kiss. He'd also sensed her inexperience and felt a kind of wonder that she was still innocent, untouched. A pure light, illuminating his dark existence.

She'd also deceived him. "You lied to me," he whispered against her ear.

177

She went still in his arms.

"The girl at Dachau. You told me she was yours."

Stella drew back from him, her features still flushed. Her eyes flashed apprehension, before clouding with grief. He sorely regretted his game.

"She was like my own daughter. I taught school to the children at the camp. Anna was my brightest pupil, very quick. After her mother's death, we were . . . inseparable."

"Exactly why were you both taken to the shooting pit?"

She released a tremulous breath. Aric felt it like a knife.

"The guard, a woman in charge of our Block, wanted . . ." She hesitated. "She said obscene things . . ."

"And you refused her." Aric knew she would never submit to that kind of degradation.

She nodded. "I was stripped of my clothes and taken to the pit. On the way, Anna ran up and tried to hand me a shirt to wear. The *Blockführerin* became furious. She screamed at the guards to take . . . the little girl, as well."

Misery seemed to shroud her like an old, familiar robe. Aric understood—he'd worn the same garment for many years. "And then I found you," he said.

She searched his face. "How could those soldiers . . . do that to a child? Where was God when it happened?"

How could a father destroy a son? "You're asking the wrong person," he said flatly. "I don't know the answer. I only know my duty."

"Does your conscience end when duty begins?"

Her reproach brought back his memories of Stalingrad and the blood of thousands—including his own—spilled across a frozen, white wasteland. "It would depend . . . on the stakes."

"What prize is worth the taking of human life?"

His smile took effort. "You've just described war. And in war, no other considerations are made—or deemed necessary."

Yet Aric remembered when those disciplines began to lose

their reverence. He'd been promoted to the rank of Wehrmacht major and ordered to command a battalion of artillery soldiers under General Paulus. Their planned victory had ended in slaughter. The entire Sixth Army lay trapped and starved-out during the harshest winter he could remember, picked off by Russian snipers better at street fighting than their German counterparts.

Each time Paulus requested retreat, Hitler had refused, insisting the army stand and fight to the last man. Aric could still smell the blood, still see the soldiers under his command, boys mostly, falling alongside the million other bodies littering the snow. Some died from gunfire, but more perished from disease, frostbite, and starvation. He'd been lucky enough to get shot—and get out—only days before retreat became impossible.

After his father's betrayal, he thought nothing else could alter him so deeply. Yet in those long, agonizing days of winter, his very humanity began to cease. God no longer existed for him. Aric simply shut down . . . until that day at Dachau.

"I cannot heal the past for you, Stella, any more than I can bring back the dead. I can only offer you this." He brushed his mouth across hers in a light kiss.

"Should that make me feel better?"

"Yes," he said with a ferocity that surprised them both. "Because in a world suffocated by death, you and I share something very much alive."

He kissed her again, losing himself in her sweetness and the budding hope that began to unfurl in his chafing soul—a need greater than flesh, calling him back from the darkness.

The future was rapidly closing distance. Aric would cling to the present as long as possible and let her make him human again.

He was such a fool.

~ 18 ~

"For if you remain silent at this time . . . you and your father's family will perish."

Esther 4:14

She was such a fool.

The persistent thought roused Stella from the enticing depths of passion. They could never be together, not as long as he sent her people to die. And she . . .

Everything about Stella Muller was a lie. How could he know the woman when she didn't know herself? "Aric, I can't . . ."

She broke away first and buried her face against his chest.

"Hush." He increased his hold on her, rocking her back and forth. "Don't say it. Please."

Stella heard his anguished tone. Did he understand the chasm that separated them . . . or was it something else?

She did care for him, as improbable and dangerous as that might be. His intelligence and humor, the quiet strength surrounding him—all drew her. He wasn't a man to boast of his accomplishments, nor did he follow the typical mind-set of his Nazi brethren. Instead he struggled to combine duty with an inherent compassion he still refused to acknowledge.

She smiled faintly. She, Joseph, Helen, and Grossman—Aric had rescued each of them, all broken sparrows.

But who would save him?

She gazed up at him with new affection. She must try her best to protect him from Brucker and Koch; she told herself it was because Aric was her best and only refuge in this war, a safeguard to all who lived in the house—

"Herr Kommandant!" A shout from outside the door broke them apart. Joseph burst into the room. "Please, come quickly. Sergeant Grossman is hurt!"

Aric bolted toward the door, Stella on his heels. "What happened?"

"Outside, he . . . he got stabbed."

"Has his attacker been caught?"

Joseph looked pale as he nodded. "Sergeant Koch's holding him at the back door."

"Who is it?" Aric's tone held ice.

"A Jew." The boy shot a miserable glance at Stella. "Morty Benjamin."

19

"Have a gallows built, seventy-five feet high, and ask the king in the morning to have Mordecai hanged on it."

Esther 5:14

Terror ripped through Stella as she rushed to keep pace with Aric's flying descent of the stairs. "Where is Grossman?" he barked to the boy behind them.

"He opened the back door and then fell down. Helen's with him."

Once inside the kitchen, Stella looked on as Aric knelt beside his prostrate young sergeant. He held the bloodstained handle of a paring knife. "Joseph, go to the front of the house and fetch Corporal Martin. Schnell!"

As the boy scampered away, Helen knelt on Grossman's other side and spread out a thick blanket. She and Aric worked to roll Grossman's body over onto the makeshift gurney.

Joseph returned with Corporal Martin. "Help me lift him, Corporal. We'll take him to the boy's room," Aric instructed.

Stella rushed forward to lift a corner of the blanket, and the four of them carried Grossman to Joseph's room, placing him on the cot. Even in her dazed state, Stella registered the housekeeper's efficiency: bowls of hot water, bandages, a needle and thread had all been laid out on a table beside the bed. With deft movements, Helen peeled away Grossman's bloodstained tunic. When the sergeant emitted a groan, Aric's tense features relaxed. "Hang on, my friend," he whispered. "Helen will take care of you."

He shot a meaningful look at the housekeeper before leaving the room. Aric went straight to the library and picked up the telephone on Stella's desk. After a moment, he slammed the dead receiver back on its cradle. "When will they get these accursed lines fixed?" He turned to glare at his corporal. "Take my car and fetch the surgeon!"

The soldier saluted and flew from the room. Aric looked furious as he stormed back to the kitchen. Stella raced to keep up with him. "I want to see the man who did this," he growled.

As if on cue, the back door to the kitchen burst open. A gold-toothed Sergeant Koch entered holding Morty by the collar.

Stella bit back a cry of panic.

"Herr Kommandant, I caught this Jew trying to escape to the forest. He wears Sergeant Grossman's blood on his hands."

Morty stood with his shoulders slumped, his eyes and cheeks swollen from recent blows. He glanced at Stella long enough to convey his defeat—and to warn her to silence.

Scapegoat, her mind screamed as pieces fell into place. Morty was being blamed for this attempted murder. But why hadn't he been shot down? Why did Koch keep him alive? Surely he knew Morty would deny the accusation. But then who would believe a Jew?

Her heart raced. "W-what are you saying? It isn't true!"

Stella's outburst garnered different looks from each man. Koch stared at her with blatant hatred, while Morty shook his head, his honey-brown eyes wide with fear.

Aric's icy stare was worst by far. "Go to your room, Fräulein."

"But, Aric—"

"Go now!"

Stella cast another despairing look at her uncle before she fled up the stairs so fast her heart nearly burst as she entered her room. Collapsing on the bed, she lay against the coverlet, suffocating with the building pressure in her chest, unable to purge what she felt. How long had it been since she'd cried or even screamed at the top of her lungs?

But her tears wouldn't come. And right now, more than anything, she wanted to bellow her rage like an irate newborn forced to leave its mother's womb, loud and lusty enough to echo downstairs. Let them hear the sound of her heart breaking.

But all she heard was the roaring in her ears, the rasping of her own breath.

Morty would die. She knew this because Aric was a man with few choices when it came to Jews. And Jews would always be made to pay.

She finally dragged herself from the bed after what seemed like hours. In the bathroom she splashed cold water against her face, then studied her pale reflection in the mirror. The beggar's eyes stared back at her, decidedly pathetic. She turned from the dismal image.

Back in her room, the music box caught her attention, along with the Bible that still lay on her nightstand.

She picked up Aric's gift to hurl it against the floor. But then the cover fell open, releasing the lilting notes of the "Blue Danube Waltz." Stella held the music box close as the soft, sweet tune eased the vise of her emotions. Eventually she trailed a fingertip across the tiny pink and blue porcelain roses that adorned its top and brushed against the red velvet interior—

She heard the soft *snick* of a latch before a hidden bottom panel sprang open. An old, worn photograph lay within, of a young dark-haired woman in a sleeveless dress, seated on a bench beneath an oak tree. Her slender arms hugged a wiry boy on her lap as she appeared to read to him from a book he held open for her. The boy, five or six years of age and with the same dark hair, gazed up at her just as the picture was taken. Adoration filled his tender expression.

Stella hardened her heart to a rush of unwanted sentiment as she examined the secret compartment. Aric must certainly be unaware of it, otherwise he'd have held on to such a precious keepsake.

It was the perfect hiding place.

She removed the picture, then fished beneath the mattress for Morty's note and Grand Cross. Her chest ached as she turned the medal over in her hand. Would she ever see him alive again?

After tucking her uncle's note inside the compartment, she added the Cross—and then changed her mind. Stella went to the armoire and rummaged through clothing until she found a length of white ribbon from one of her slips. She made a necklace of the Cross and slipped it over her head. The comforting weight eased her, and she clutched the talisman with her fingertips, the metal cool and unyielding like the valor it stood for.

Stella replaced the music box on the nightstand, and the Bible caught her eye. She thought of the cross Marta had worn. *"According to the Bible, His death saved the world."*

Aric's words; did he believe them, as Marta did?

Stella didn't think so. Her best friend had claimed the cross gave her strength and the knowledge that God was always with her. Aric seemed lost . . .

She shoved away the unwanted sentimentality. God might be with Marta, perhaps even Aric, but He'd left Stella and Morty to the wolves. Now her uncle would likely die.

She hid his prized medal beneath her sweater, close to her heart. She would keep her own vigil. Despite Morty's unwavering faith, he also believed in his niece. Stella would be his strength.

The old photograph lay on the bed. She picked it up and studied the sweet-faced child, the man who would now determine her uncle's fate.

Aric had improved the ghetto food. He'd also relocated Morty to a safer place in order to avoid Hermann's brutality. Was it possible his compassion would overrule duty in this instance?

Stella tucked the picture inside her sweater, next to the cross. She would keep vigil for him, as well.

"Can I come in?"

Joseph peered around the door. Stella rushed to him and pulled him inside. "What will they do to him?"

"Herr Kommandant is very angry." Joseph's young face wore serious lines. "And Koch wants to take Morty to the Kleine Festung."

Stella bit back a cry. The boy had told her of the Little Fortress, where the SS tortured Jews through beatings, amputation, drowning, or simply left them in a room to starve. Few ever returned to tell about it. Morty would never survive such a hideous place.

"I must speak to Herr Kommandant." She ran her fingers through her short, blond curls.

"What will you tell him?"

What could she say? That she'd lied to him all this time? That she was Jewish and Morty was her uncle? Stella collapsed to sit on the bed. Joseph hovered close. "Is it certain my uncle will be taken there?"

He shrugged. "The doctor is here and wants to take Sergeant Grossman back to his clinic. Helen's going, too. Herr Kommandant is helping to put Grossman into the back of the lorry." He paused. "Koch is still waiting in the kitchen with Morty."

She grabbed his shoulders. "Please, kaddishel, you must find out what will happen to Morty. His chances could improve if Grossman lives. But if the sergeant dies . . ."

It didn't bode well that the surgeon thought it necessary to take Grossman to hospital. "Either way, Herr Kommandant and I are still in danger," she said. "I think Koch has put his plan into action."

It would be so much easier if Morty could tell Aric of the murder plot he'd overheard in Hermann's office. But then Stella and Joseph would be at risk, and Aric wouldn't take the word of a Jew over his own man, especially a Jew with blood on his hands.

It didn't seem to matter that Morty had been beaten before they tainted him with false evidence. No, Koch and Brucker must go through with their plan tonight; it was the only way to expose them and perhaps save her uncle.

"Joseph, I need a weapon." Seeing his surprised look, she added, "An effective one. If I have to use it, I want it to hurt."

"Tonight, after Herr Kommandant goes to his room, I'll bring you the poker from the hearth." He eyed her anxiously. "Will that work?"

"Perfectly," she lied. She would have preferred a pistol but wasn't willing to give the child such a dangerous assignment.

"May I stay with you?"

Stella shook her head. "Hide—in a closet, the cellar, any-where they won't find you." She shot him her most stern look. "Whatever happens tonight, you must be safe. Give me your word you'll stay hidden."

His mouth twisted in obvious reluctance. "I promise."

"I want to show you something." She reached for the music box and opened it. Melodious notes broke the silence as she pressed the release for the hidden compartment and revealed Morty's last note.

Joseph sucked in a quick breath. "You must get rid of it!"

"This message is proof of the murder plot. If something happens to Herr Kommandant or to me, you must take it and give it to a person you trust." She pressed the secret panel back into place. "Helen . . . or Sergeant Grossman, if he survives."

"Nothing will happen to you," Joseph said fiercely. "Not if you hide, too!"

She reached to brush back a lock of his hair. "They would

only tear this house apart until they found me . . . and you, as well. I can't let that happen. Now go and see if you can find out what they plan for my uncle."

Stella stared at the closed door long after he left. Her thoughts focused on Grossman. Morty's only hope was that he might live, and the fact she must save Aric and herself tonight.

There was nothing left to do. Time would decide all of their fates. Yet the Grand Cross beneath her sweater no longer felt so steadfast and indomitable as it had earlier. She didn't know if she had the strength necessary to face tonight.

Stella's gaze drifted toward the Bible still lying on top of the nightstand. Maybe time had nothing to do with it . . .

She picked up the book and held it to her chest. "Speak to me," she whispered into the empty room. Then she closed her eyes and did something she hadn't done for a long, long time.

She prayed.

20

That night the king could not sleep. . . .

Esther 6:1

It was the first time he'd actually thought about running.

Aric reached for his bottle of morphine tablets on the nightstand, then changed his mind. Instead he opened the drawer and retrieved his gold cigarette case. He'd tried to quit smoking after the loss of his lung, yet the need for calm, whenever it struck, always seemed to outweigh his discomfort. And as far as habits went—he eyed the brown glass bottle on the table—it seemed the lesser of two evils.

Swiping a match against the table, he glanced at the alarm clock wedged between the pill bottle and a leftover cup of Kaffee from breakfast.

Midnight. Aric lit the cigarette and lay back against his pillow. Taking a long drag, he fought an urge to cough before releasing the billow of smoke. Moonlight from the window captured the haze as it curled and snaked and finally dissipated.

Desertion. Even the word left him empty, defeated before the fight. Mocking everything he once believed in. *This is what your life has come to.*

He fixed his gaze on the glowing red tip of the cigarette. Without fully comprehending how it happened, he had reached a

189

crossroad. He could follow orders and allow the monster within to completely take him, or he could rebel for Stella's sake and martyr himself as some righteous fool.

Or he could simply turn tail and run.

"Coward," he breathed into the darkness. Aric tossed back the covers and swung his feet onto the floor. How often had he barked the insult at one recruit or another? Never had he considered applying it to himself, not Aric von Schmidt, whose bold stratagems and reckless penchant for success had raised him through the ranks of the Wehrmacht. He was a man who had taken part in enough horror and butchery to last lifetimes, and for the sake of his ideals, and his vengeance, had stood by and watched as they killed his own father for a "Greater Germany."

He took another long pull on the cigarette. Perhaps what frightened him most was becoming a man who wavered on the edge of his own regret. If he abandoned the Cause now, it would mean he'd spent years living a lie—an admission he wasn't certain he could face. What little remained of him would have nothing to cling to, not the tattered remains of his idealism, jaded as it was, and not the vindicating anger he fostered against his father's duplicity. He would have no country, no money, and no possessions. There would be no place to hide from the Allies or the Germans.

And still he would lose her.

Stella's anger over the fate of one old man still confounded him. Aric's mind flashed to the Jew—the same prisoner whom Stella championed their first day in the ghetto, the same one who witnessed Brucker's humiliation when Aric had inspected the ghetto food.

How different he'd looked this afternoon: resignation pooled among bruised features, his bloody hands clenched at his sides. Why would the only remaining Elder of the Judenrat risk all to murder a single German soldier? And how did he get a knife past the guards, if in fact he was searched before leaving the ghetto?

Stella believed him innocent, while Aric still had his doubts. Enough to have instructed Koch to safeguard the prisoner at the Little Fortress until further questioning. Hopefully when Grossman returned from the clinic, he'd be recovered enough to clear up the matter.

His friend *would* recover. Aric's relief at the surgeon's prognosis had cooled some of his rage. Young Rand Grossman's laughing blue eyes and breezy nature reminded him much of Georg Zimmer, once Aric's closest friend at Bonn. And like Georg, Rand had proven his loyalty.

The doctors had said Aric would never walk again. Then Rand, a young corporal at the time, arrived to share his room at the hospital after losing his left hand to a grenade. The two discovered they'd fought together at Kiev. Rand's indomitable faith and hero worship in his former commander helped to restore Aric's confidence. Soon he moved with the aid of a walker and, some days later, mastered the use of a cane.

By the time they discharged him from hospital, he walked out on his own two feet. *Wundermann*, the medical staff had called him. Miracle Man.

But miracles no longer existed for him. Like his virtue, they'd perished with the past, buried in the foxholes he left behind, lost in the vacant stares of countless boys he'd watched die—on both sides.

Plunging his cigarette into the cup on his nightstand, Aric rose and walked to the window. The snow had finally stopped. Clear black sky held the three-quarter moon like a beam in a tunnel. The orb had been just as bright the night he'd brought Stella home. He remembered carrying her in his arms, enjoying her undisguised pleasure over the simple brick structure as she looked at him with those breathtaking eyes. Aric's pulse quickened. She made him want to believe . . .

A sudden movement below caught his attention. A sentry stepped away from the house onto the shoveled walkway.

Corporal Martin. Aric started to turn from the window when the guard glanced upward. Moonlight caught the soldier's familiar features.

Lieutenant Brucker.

Where was Martin?

Aric's hackles rose as he grabbed his pants from the wooden valet and pulled them on. He retrieved his Browning 9mm pistol from its holster on the bedpost. Drawing back the slide, he resumed his surveillance at the window.

Brucker chose that moment to turn and aim a Mauser in his direction. Aric jerked back into the shadows. The lieutenant grinned and relaxed his stance, then returned the machine gun to his side. Marching back toward the house, he disappeared beneath the eave of the porch.

Aric went to his bedroom door and opened it. The stillness broke with faint sounds of a lock turning downstairs. Edging the door wider, he slipped behind it and observed the hall through the space between its hinges. What would Brucker do next?

He heard another noise, this time from the back door at the kitchen.

The lieutenant wasn't alone.

A minute later, the banister creaked. Intruders were mounting the stairs.

Stella slept unprotected in the bedroom closest to the landing. Aric clenched his teeth as he gripped the Browning and waited.

Two of them—shadowy faces first, then torsos and legs—ascended into view. No one else appeared on the landing. In the darkened hall, Aric couldn't make out the man with Brucker except that he was taller and bulkier than the lieutenant. He carried a butcher knife in his free hand.

Both men approached noiselessly. Pistols raised, they scanned all directions. When they paused at Stella's room, Aric bolted around the door to face them. "Halt!" He aimed his Browning at the taller intruder.

Light flashed into the hall as Stella's door flew open. Like an avenging angel in white, she wielded what appeared to be the fire poker from his downstairs hearth. Screaming a warning—Aric thought she called his name—she landed a blow across Brucker's midsection. The surprised lieutenant doubled over, dropping his pistol and knocking his accomplice against the banister.

Brucker caught his breath and let out a roar as he plowed toward Stella like a Panzer on maneuvers. The other man straightened and raised his pistol. He aimed for her head.

An earsplitting *crack* rent the air. Brucker froze as his companion dropped to his knees. Swaying once, twice, the other soldier finally tumbled sideways onto the floor. His pistol skittered across the carpet, the knife still clutched in his grasp. Vacant eyes stared upward while his slackened jaw exposed a gold tooth that glittered in the light from Stella's room.

Koch? Aric swore under his breath.

The gunshot made Stella freeze. For an instant she was back at Dachau. A terrified whimper caught in her throat as she stared down at her clenched fist.

The fireplace poker, not the limp hand of a child, lay in her grasp.

"Scratch an itch, Brucker, and you'll join your friend."

She dragged her gaze from the weapon to see Aric only a few feet away, his gun aimed at her assailant.

"Stella, get back inside and shut the door."

She turned to go. Brucker was faster. His arm snaked around her waist and pinned her to him like a human shield. Snow from his coat soaked through the back of her thin nightgown, and the acrid smell of his violence attacked her senses. He wrenched the poker from her and pressed the lethal tip to her throat. "All right, Jew lover, come and save her."

Aric fingered the trigger of his weapon as he saw Stella's fear, watched Brucker's hands defile her innocent flesh.

But he wouldn't let the monster loose. Not yet.

"I see you never learned to fight like a man, Brucker. Maybe you spent too much time beating up on children and weak old men. Even now you hide behind a woman."

"You think to teach me?" Brucker's grip jerked another gasp from Stella.

Aric shrugged while the creature inside howled to rip out Brucker's throat. "You won't learn it all in one night, but we have time for your first lesson."

"Why should I?"

Aric drew a bead with his pistol on Brucker's head. Silence filled the hall. "Come, Lieutenant, you know if you harm her, I'll give you a third eye." He smiled. "And all that pent-up anger dies with you."

"So does the woman."

Aric stepped forward. "I'm offering you a chance—your fists against mine." He cocked his head. "Or are you afraid I'll beat you?"

Brucker anted in. "I'll show you fear." He kept his eyes on Aric as he dragged Stella toward the banister. He kicked his own pistol along with his partner's over the side. "Your turn, Kommandant."

Aric dropped the Browning at his feet. "Let her go."

For a long moment Brucker didn't move. Then he shoved Stella away. She rushed toward Aric, hesitating when he kicked his own pistol over the ledge. His eyes remained fixed on Brucker. "Go into my room and lock the door," he told her.

She froze and he glanced at her. Clearly she understood what was about to happen. Then she nodded and brushed past him into his room.

Tossing the poker over the rail, Brucker shrugged out of his jacket and shirt. Aric assessed his opponent. The lieutenant was tall and lean and younger than Aric; still, he lacked skill in combat. It must be quick. Aric's legs wouldn't hold out for long.

Every nerve in his body pulsed with anticipation.

The lieutenant stood bare-chested, his fists thrust forward as he prepared for Aric's attack. "Very well, old man. Impress me."

Aric's fists shook as he held himself in check. He smiled. Brucker was impatient; it would ultimately be his downfall.

True to nature, Brucker let out a cry and barreled toward him. Aric stood unmoving until the last possible moment—then sidestepped the lumbering lieutenant.

Brucker hit the wall with a loud grunt. Aric saw an opportunity, and with a snarl he jerked Brucker around. Cold rage ruled him as he sank his fists into the lieutenant's soft belly once, twice, three times. He became deaf to the grunts and groans of his prey, ignoring the occasional fist that found its mark against his own flesh.

Brucker finally managed to free himself. Rolling sideways, he scrambled to his feet. He rammed his head into Aric's gut and stole his breath as he shoved him against the rail. Wood cracked and splintered at Aric's back; he twisted away as the banister collapsed. Sections of railing and debris pitched to the floor below.

Sweat trailed Aric's body, making it easy to slip from Brucker's grasp. He landed another fist to the lieutenant's face. Brucker toppled backward, falling over the dead body of Koch.

"No more," the younger man begged in a hoarse whisper. He'd curled into a fetal position. Aric staggered forward to stand over him.

"Get up."

Brucker made to rise . . . then surprised Aric with a knife. It was Koch's. *Schwein!* he screamed, lunging for Aric.

Aric kicked the knife from his hand. The blade catapulted toward the end of the hall. Clenching his bloodied fists, he glared at Brucker. "Now get up. We haven't finished our lesson."

Brucker struggled to his feet. His eyes, the right one nearly swollen shut from Aric's blow, looked toward the stairs.

"Think to run from me, coward?" Aric said, breathing hard. "Where will you go that I won't hunt you down?"

Brucker stumbled toward the open section of banister and spit a glob of blood over the side. "Curse you and your Jew harlot."

He hurled his body over the edge. Aric leaped after him, falling the several feet to land beside his prone, dazed lieutenant.

The discarded Browning lay between them. Both attempted to seize it, rolling across the carpeted floor as they grappled for possession.

A muffled shot rang out, followed by another. Aric froze beneath Brucker, every nerve attuned for the burn from the slugs he was sure had lodged in his gut.

The fire never came; only the butt of his pistol dug painfully into his flesh. He stared into Brucker's lifeless eyes and realized which direction the gun's muzzle pointed.

"Aric!"

Stella's voice. Aric looked up to see her kneeling at the edge of the open banister. Her white nightgown seemed to billow around her.

"Please, God . . . no!" she cried, her arms outstretched.

Something warm and fierce exploded inside of him. Aric shoved Brucker's corpse aside and rolled to his feet. His body ached. Grinding his teeth against the pain, he bounded up the stairs and grabbed Stella. He held her tightly, desperate for reassurance that she was safe and unharmed.

She was crying. "I thought you were dead."

"No, Süsse," he said, then kissed her, tasting the saltiness of her tears while her trembling limbs matched the shaking of his own. He tried to be gentle with her, yet he couldn't seem to curb his anger or the fear he'd felt when Brucker pressed the weapon to her throat. He'd nearly lost her.

Stella weathered his punishing kiss, her fingers brushing over his temples, his cheeks, the back of his neck as she worked to soothe the violence that gripped him. She sensed the moment when he finally calmed; the hard press of his mouth against hers eased into an onslaught of tiny kisses, each butterfly soft as if begging pardon for his roughness.

Afterward she slid her arms around his neck and simply held him. His breathing gradually eased, along with the tremor that shook his limbs. She knew he must be in terrible pain and pressed closer to him, as though her touch could take away his suffering.

She'd told herself she wanted to keep him alive so that Morty had a fair chance at release when the facts came to light. But then she'd seen Aric lying motionless beneath Brucker's hulking form, and a part of her had wanted to die.

When he rose from the tangled heap—a modern-day Lazarus, to Marta's way of thinking—Stella knew then that she felt more than simple affection. Crossing the boundaries of war and hatred, and the Jewish blood running in her veins . . . she'd fallen in love.

"You will be our salvation." As she held Aric close, Stella wondered how she would ever save her people.

She couldn't seem to save herself.

21

It was found . . . Bigthana and Teresh, two of the king's officers . . . had conspired to assassinate King Xerxes.

Esther 6:2

Activity filled the next hour. With the telephone lines down, Aric had sent Joseph into the ghetto to fetch Captain Hermann. The house now swarmed with SS in charge of hauling away the bodies. Several women prisoners had been dragged from their beds to clean the carnage out of the commandant's expensive carpets.

Joseph returned to find every light in the house on. He wriggled past the throng of soldiers on the stairs and reached the landing where Brucker's body lay sprawled. Seeing the corpse, Joseph rubbed a hand over the scar where his ear had been. Herr Kommandant had avenged him. Someone else thought his ear worth more than the price of two potatoes.

He dismissed the body and scrambled up the remaining steps. Fear for his pretty Fräulein gnawed at his belly. The sooner he found her and saw she was all right, the better he'd feel.

Reaching the top step, he turned at the sound of angry voices below. Two men stood nose to nose in the foyer; they reminded

Joseph of the rutting red stags his papa once took him to see at a *Naturpark* south of Hamburg.

Herr Kommandant loomed over Captain Hermann. Joseph could tell by the swift hand gestures and shouted words such as *discipline, chain of command*, and *loyalty*, that the commandant was very angry.

Joseph felt a rush of perverse pleasure. Maybe Hermann would feel as ashamed as the pretty Fräulein did when she had to kiss him at the party.

He continued padding down the hall toward her room. Alarm outweighed his triumph when he saw two women crouched on the floor at her open door, scrubbing at a bloodstain with stiff broom brushes. The room was empty.

"Where is she?" he demanded of the pair. He thought his heart might be choking him.

Their tired, leathery faces glanced up at him in unison. One woman jerked her head in the direction of Herr Kommandant's room.

Stella paused from pacing long enough to listen to the chaos belowstairs. Oddly the buzz of voices and activity from the soldiers gave her a measure of comfort. Their noise broke the silence of her memories, easing the fear that tore at her outward calm. It seemed like hours since Aric had left her here. He'd promised to return and give her news. And where was Joseph?

"Fräulein?"

A frightened face peered around the half-closed door. "Kaddishel, I was so worried!" Stella rushed to him and pulled him into her arms. His grip made her wince despite her relief.

"I hid in my room, under my cot. Was it bad?"

"Awful." She still shuddered with the memory of so much blood, the image of Aric lying motionless beneath Brucker's body. "If it weren't for Aric . . . Herr Kommandant . . . the killers would have succeeded." She pulled away to look at him. "Is Herr Kommandant downstairs?"

Joseph smirked. "He's yelling at the captain."

She didn't share the boy's obvious pleasure. "He should be more careful of that man."

"I pray Herr Kommandant will send him away so he can't ever touch you again."

Stella gave Joseph's shoulders a quick squeeze. "Hermann won't get near me." *Unless he learns that I warned Aric about tonight's events,* she didn't add. She reached to smooth back his silken locks. "I'm supposed to stay here for now. Would you mind going down and heating water for tea? I'll meet you in a little while."

He readily agreed and bolted for the door. Stella was pleased to steer him from the disturbing subject of Captain Hermann.

Joseph paused at the door. "I think Herr Kommandant likes you very much. Will you tell him the truth about the letters?"

She shook her head. "Too dangerous, kaddishel."

His hopeful look vanished. Then he was gone.

Stella sat on the edge of the bed and watched the door for several moments. She hadn't told Joseph the whole truth—that if she revealed the letters, he and Helen would be implicated in the conspiracy, as well. She couldn't let that happen, even if it meant Morty's life.

"What kind of circus are you operating in the ghetto, Captain?" Aric faced off with the man in the foyer. "It's a disgrace to our Führer when one of his officers cannot control his men." He raised a bruised fist. "If I hadn't been forewarned of this treason . . ."

He stopped himself, refusing to repeat Stella's ludicrous talk of dreams.

"You had . . . knowledge of this attack, Herr Kommandant?" Hermann's sullen mouth wilted in shock. "But who told you—?"

"Suffice it to say, Captain, it wasn't you." Aric forced an end to the topic. "General Feldman will be here on Monday. Herr Reichsführer and Obersturmbannführer Eichmann arrive three days after that. Hardly the time for your ranks to fall apart, wouldn't you agree?"

"Jawohl, Herr Kommandant!" Hermann's icy features radiated contempt.

Aric's jaw clenched while too many memories fueled his rage: the night of the party when Hermann dared to touch Stella with his filthy mouth; and tonight, when Brucker mauled her and threatened to kill her. He thought of Rand, lying on the kitchen floor in a pool of blood, stabbed by whom he now suspected was the late Sergeant Koch. His own men . . .

He fought an urge to plant his fist into Hermann's obnoxious sneer. "How do you plan to deal with this insurrection, Captain?"

For a moment, Hermann looked startled. "What more can I do? Both men are dead."

"Years ago in a more primitive world, criminals were executed and their bodies impaled on pikes in the town square," Aric said, ignoring Hermann's look of shock. "It served as an effective warning to others. And since I'd hardly classify our present situation as civilized, this weekend you will display Brucker and Koch in much the same manner. Hang their corpses from the old gallows next to the parade grounds inside the ghetto. See that your men march past them twice a day. At dusk on Sunday, you may get rid of the bodies. I don't want General Feldman reporting this embarrassment to Herr Reichsführer."

"Heil Hitler, Herr Kommandant!" Hermann flung an arm upward in salute, his murderous eyes fixed on a spot just beyond Aric's left shoulder.

Perhaps he might also relish a good brawl, Aric thought. "See to it, Captain," he said instead, and swung around to head for the stairs.

As he began the climb, his thoughts returned to Stella's dream . . . and how contrived it all now sounded. Had she lied to him?

Suspicion mounted with each step, and his gut churned at the possibility she knew more than she was telling him. Treacherous thoughts began to prey on him as he thought of his father, then Georg Zimmer, and the old humiliation, the paralyzing sense of madness . . .

The women had finished cleaning the second-story landing. The smell of carbolic stung in his nostrils, flooding his mind with more recent memories. *Stark white walls and bed sheets. Helen and the other nurses padding in and out on their rounds. The rise and fall of shadows, marking endless days of disillusionment, despair . . .*

He opened his bedroom door and found Stella perched on the edge of his bed, her slight figure cocooned in his heavy cotton robe. The loose sleeves all but hid her fingertips while she examined his brown bottle of pills.

She glanced up at him and fumbled with the bottle before setting it back on the table. A rose-colored flush stained her cheeks.

Guilt? Aric's chest felt tight. Even culpable, she was a beautiful woman.

She rose to meet him. "You've been gone a long time."

The mild accusation washed over him. "Did you miss me?"

She hesitated, then nodded.

Closing the door, he turned and opened his arms to her. She rushed to him, and he pulled her close. Aric heard the faint sounds of Hermann downstairs barking orders with his usual éclat of self-importance, and the shuffling of feet as the last of the soldiers and cleaning women filed out of his house. Proof the events of the past hour were real.

He tried to console himself in Stella's embrace and escape the burden of his own distrust. But sedition, like cancer, had infected his ranks; he didn't know how far it spread, only that it had come dangerously close to fruition.

The woman in his arms harbored secrets. "Tell me again how you knew those two men planned murder this night," he whispered against her ear.

She tried to draw away from him, but he held her in place. Aric didn't want to see her face. He couldn't bear to look upon the guilt he knew his words inflicted.

"I told you," she rushed to say. "From my dreams—"

"The truth this time." He increased his hold on her. "No more lies."

Stella went rigid with apprehension. The ruse she'd concocted now seemed foolish and dangerous. Aric was a logical man. How had she supposed he would believe a ridiculous story about dreams of murder?

Or had he discovered her uncle's note?

Cold fear coursed through her. "I . . . cannot prove any of it," she managed in a calm tone. "But what reason would I have to lie to you?"

He pulled back, searching her face. "I'm not certain. Perhaps you protect someone?"

Stella relaxed in his grip. Morty's letter was still safe. Still, she hated lying to Aric, now more than ever before. "I tried to protect *you*." She grasped at what truth she could. "I knew you wouldn't believe my dreams, so I armed myself with the fire poker from the hearth as a precaution. I thought I could save us."

Her cheeks flared with heat. Brucker had used her own weapon against her, and then she'd been the one needing rescue! "I didn't do a very good job, did I?"

"Yes, you did." He sighed, all traces of anger gone. "Thoughts of you kept me awake tonight—so much that I even got out of bed and went to the window. I realized something was wrong when I saw Brucker had taken Martin's place on watch."

He raised her chin with the crook of his finger. "Because of that, we're alive. If I'd gone to sleep, neither of us would be here, talking about it." He kissed her lightly. "I shouldn't have doubted you. Forgive me."

Could she possibly feel any more wretched? Stella leaned her head against his shoulder. Exhaustion fell upon her like a sodden blanket—from the night's ordeal and the knowledge her uncle still languished in the Little Fortress. From the lies she must continue to speak, each tasting more bitter and foul on her tongue. She longed for some truth between them, a heartfelt thought left whole and unguarded, never having to be sacrificed in weaker moments.

"I knew you would keep me safe," she said finally. She then lifted her face, again catching sight of the rust-red cut just above his brow, and realized the veracity of her own words.

Taking his hands in hers, she inspected the bruised knuckles and torn flesh much the way he'd once studied hers. She'd heard his fistfight with Brucker from behind the door; she could now easily imagine the violence, especially as she glimpsed the streaks of blood across his chest, half concealed beneath the hastily donned uniform jacket.

Was he hurt? Alarmed, she pushed the jacket off his shoulders—then relaxed when she realized the blood was not his own. Still, he bore all the other marks of a warrior: muscles like carved stone beneath his bronzed skin; a long scar that ran from his sternum to the right side of his back, while another cut diagonally from his lower left side across his stomach.

Flesh as bruised and battered as his spirit. Stella laid a palm over the area of his heart and felt his thundering pulse. To the left of her hand was an oval mark, almost hidden by the russet hair that covered his chest. She ran a fingertip along its roughened edge. A bullet hole . . .

Aric grasped her fingers, unable to catch his breath. Her touch felt as soft as meadow grass and just as sweet; her warmth was like the sun, penetrating the icy wall of his self-imposed isolation. She was his glimpse into heaven, a haven of light and love, purity and innocence. The joy of his youth, a place he could stay the rest of his life. *God, do not tempt me with such false hope.*

Stella gazed up at him, while concern—not ethereal light—clouded her features. "At the banquet you told the other officers you'd given your allegiance to Germany. You said you had the bullet holes to prove it. Are there more?"

Her anxiety washed over him like gentle rain. "A few stray shots. Nothing of import, except this one." He glanced down at the scar. "It punctured a lung and grazed my spine on the way out. Bought my passage out of Stalingrad."

"Is that why you couldn't walk . . . for a time?"

He nodded. When she freed her fingers from his and again gently probed the mark, Aric shuddered at the contact. She looked up at him. "Does it still bother you?"

"Only when you touch me," he whispered, straight-faced.

Her blue eyes widened in distress . . . before she flushed, smiling. He grinned back at her, pulling her hand to his lips as he kissed each fingertip.

She leaned to kiss his scar. Aric's humor fled as emotions more poignant than pleasurable engulfed him. The caress, light, almost reverent, gave silent tribute to the mark that had altered the course of his life, as though she understood his displacement in a world with little compensation for crippled war heroes. As though she accepted him, despite his failings . . .

An ache began where her lips touched him, racing upward to constrict his throat. He blinked as he tried to assuage the unfamiliar burn in his eyes. Then he cupped her face and she lifted her gaze to his. "Thank you." His words sounded strangled and so he kissed her again, this time slowly, tenderly . . .

"Herr Kommandant?" A knock sounded as a voice hailed him from outside the door.

"In a minute, Captain," Aric called out, annoyed at the disruption.

The moment between them was lost. He gave Stella a last quick kiss and then donned his jacket. "I must see what he wants, Süsse. Why don't you stay here tonight and get some sleep?"

She shook her head, lips still rosy from his kiss. "I'd prefer tea, in my own room, after the captain leaves the hall."

He smiled. "Maybe you aren't as innocent as I thought."

"There's a difference between innocence and naïveté," she retorted with a blush. Her expression sobered as she wrapped his robe more tightly around herself. "Aric, who was the other soldier?"

"Sergeant Koch." Her earlier brush with death renewed his anger. "Like your dream."

"Do you think he had something to do with Grossman's injury?"

She looked so soft and appealing. Warmth flooded Aric's heart, dispelling his irritation. "It's possible. I'll speak with Rand when he returns." He realized the direction of her questions, and his joy dimmed. "We're back to that old man again, aren't we?" Her face flushed and he had his answer. "If I determine the Jew is innocent, he'll be sent back to the ghetto."

She raised her chin. "And if it can't be determined?"

Aric gave her a hard stare. "Then he'll be punished."

She turned away, and Aric sensed her sudden distance. It was their same argument, the breach that remained forever between them. He sighed. "Remember what I told you, Stella. You can't have it both ways. Not in war. The risks are too high."

When she said nothing, he left the room, the warmth of his pleasure lost beneath a frozen blanket of despair.

He couldn't have it both ways, either.

22

*And when the report was investigated and found to
be true, the two officials were hanged on a gallows.*

Esther 2:23

Saturday, March 4, 1944

Bright light stabbed Morty's eyes as he stumbled outside
the Kleine Festung.

His bruised cheeks and forehead itched in the bitter cold
while his battered feet ached inside his too-tight shoes. Still, he
lifted his face to the gray afternoon sky and praised God for
his freedom from that horrible place—alive and in one piece.

A pair of SS guards held him up on either side as they dragged
him back the kilometer's distance to the ghetto. The one on his
right cuffed him each time he tripped over a stone or a tree root
impeding the path.

Morty ground his teeth with each painful step—a reminder of
the thrashing to his insteps with a cane three centimeters thick.
The commandant's order to safeguard him had been ignored.
Was it any surprise? It seemed his fate was sealed the moment
Grossman's body landed on the floor of the commandant's
kitchen. Even before that . . .

They had been collecting firewood at the edge of the forest behind the house when Morty spied the glint off Koch's knife. The sergeant stole up behind Grossman from the cover of trees. Morty broke from the rest of the group and rushed to tackle Koch . . . but then Grossman turned and Koch plunged his blade into the man's chest.

Koch noticed Morty then; he'd swung his machine gun off his shoulder and took aim at Morty's head. Just about the moment he intended to pull the trigger, Corporal Sonntag bounded up the hill and called to Koch to halt.

Blackness had fallen over Morty, no doubt from the butt of Koch's gun. When he awoke, the bloodied knife lay in his grasp, with more of the red stuff smeared on his clothing.

Koch had stood over him, shouting that Grossman was murdered.

So why hadn't they killed him? And why was he being released? The commandant hadn't asked for his side of the story. In any case, Morty planned to hold his tongue. A Jew didn't go around accusing Nazis and live to tell about it.

And what about Hadassah . . . was she safe? Morty groaned and received another cuff to the side of his head. Shaking his dazed senses, he realized he could do nothing for his maideleh, at least not at the moment. He must cling to his vision. God would provide.

They arrived at the ghetto entrance. Morty's upper lip beaded with sweat as he squinted up at the arched gate, reading the black wrought-iron letters welded in place: *Arbeit Macht Frei.*

Work Makes You Free. Pah! Work only made a man hungry. And if he was lucky and got a morsel of food for his trouble, he might have enough strength to keep on working. Besides, no amount of work would change the fact they were all prisoners digging their own graves.

He and the others had toiled for weeks putting a good face on the town so the Red Cross could come and go with a clear conscience and the Nazi agenda could proceed unchecked. But when it was over, thousands of Jews would continue being transported east.

Inside the gate, the two guards released him. Morty promptly collapsed to the ground. One soldier gave him a parting cuff before they turned and retreated from the ghetto.

Like a chubby baby learning his first steps, Morty used his hands as leverage to rise up onto his feet. Air whistled through his teeth as his traumatized soles took the full weight of his body. Nausea roiled in him as he took one teetering step after another in the direction of the ghetto kitchen. Several notorious gossips were likely crowded around the trestle table even now; they would know any details from last night—and whether or not Hadassah was safe.

Fire shot up his legs with each step, and though he prayed to block the pain, Morty was eventually forced to stop and rest.

He spied a flock of black uniforms marching near the old parade grounds at the far end of the ghetto.

A procession? It looked as though Theresienstadt's entire company of SS were goose-stepping back and forth in tight formation, their steel helmets shining dully in the gray light. Crimson flags with the black-and-white Hakenkreuz writhed like fire-breathing serpents against the frigid gusts continually sweeping through the compound.

Morty's pulse raced. Never before had they amassed in such a manner. As if they paid homage to some great man. The commandant . . . ?

Grunting with pain, he hobbled in their direction.

The broken remains of an ancient pillory stood near the Appellplatz close to where the soldiers marched. Next to the pillory was a gallows. Morty froze at the sight of two dark shapes swinging from the main truss. Like twin pendulums of a clock, they moved in counterpoint to each other, back and forth, back and forth . . .

Hadassah? Morty choked on a cry and stumbled onto the parade grounds. Dear God, let neither of them be his niece!

Dodging half a dozen soldiers, he finally got close enough to get a good look. The corpses were bound in black cloth, much like a burial shroud—except for their hands and faces.

Another gust rose up, and the bodies swayed slightly. Ropes creaked. The stench of blood and excrement touched his nostrils. Morty craned his neck to stare into the faces, doughy and bloated by exposure. Two pairs of vacant eyes bulged back at him. Koch and Brucker . . .

Relief drove him to his knees. He offered up a prayer to God for His miracle of justice. Then Morty rose and shot a glance at the marching soldiers.

Their backs were to him. He turned to hurl a glob of spit at Koch's swaying body. "For your disgrace upon Germany," he muttered. "And for my feet."

It was then dawning struck. Had the commandant been victorious? Did that mean Hadassah was safe?

"Get away from there, Jude."

A sharp object dug into his back.

"Turn around," the voice said.

Morty obeyed. A young Soldat stood with his pistol leveled on him, an old Mauser C96 "broom handle" from the Great War.

"What were you doing there, just now?" The SS man waved his weapon toward the hanging bodies.

"Nothing." Morty tried to ignore the alarm prickling along the back of his neck.

"Ja, for you, *Juden*, it's always nothing," the soldier sneered. "Now move. Herr Captain wants to see you."

Prodded at gunpoint, Morty led the way to the building that housed Hermann's office. He stared up at the charred remains of his handiwork before they passed inside the set of double doors. Instead of going up the stairs to the captain's old office, however, Morty was directed down a narrow hall to the back of the building. At the last doorway on the right, the soldier shoved him inside.

"Leave us, Corporal."

Hermann spoke from behind a rustic pine desk. Morty heard the soldier close the door behind him, then cast a covert glance about the room. Hardly bigger than Morty's coffin-sized office above the old bank, the chamber was just as sparse. A gray filing cabinet hugged the wall, while the room's only window sat adjacent to the captain's desk.

Behind Hermann, just as in the old office, the face of the Madman with his toothbrush mustache glared from the charred frame. Morty noted the absence of a Grand Cross, phony or otherwise. Satisfaction flowed through his aching body like balm.

"You look somewhat worse for wear. The Kleine Festung doesn't agree with you?"

Morty pulled his attention back to Hermann. His legs shook as his feet throbbed.

"Come closer."

Morty shuffled forward, biting the inside of his cheek.

"Herr Kommandant thought to pamper you, but I can see my men made good work." Leaning back in his chair, Hermann retrieved the brass-handled letter opener from his desktop. It had the novel shape of a miniature Spanish sword.

"I would have preferred you dead," he said, toying with the dagger-like blade. "I should kill you myself after the stunt you pulled. Not only did you steal *my* Cross"—he paused as if daring Morty to object—"but you burned up my office in the process.

"I also suspect you know things. Information that, depending on your answer, could either grant you safe return to your friends in the ghetto . . . or land you back in the Little Fortress."

Steel flashed as Hermann thrust the blade into the desk's smooth surface. "Tell me who helped you. Who spoke to Herr Kommandant about . . . certain issues?"

Morty's heartbeat drummed so loud in his ears he feared the

captain might hear it. Still, he would die before betraying Joseph or Hadassah. "Herr Captain, I know nothing."

"Of course you don't. My men said as much after they questioned you about the fire." Hermann's gaze lit with mocking humor. "Believe it or not, Jew, I find your courage admirable, but I know you were in my office the afternoon of the fire. We found your footprints below the window." He stared over the desk at Morty's swollen feet. "Big as U-boats. And you dropped this." He produced from the desk a rations tin that Morty clearly recognized.

"Did you enjoy your punishment at the Little Fortress?" Hermann sneered. "I thought it appropriate, since those oversized hooves got you into trouble in the first place. That, and the Cross.

"Now. Give me a name." His humor evaporated. "Tell me, who else in this world is willing to aid an old Jew"—he arched a brow—"besides Herr Kommandant's woman?"

A guttural sound rose in Morty's throat.

"Ah, you care something for the pretty Fräulein?" Hermann looked eager as he rose from the chair. "Because she saved you that day in the old barracks?"

Lightning fast, Hermann's fist shot out to connect with Morty's jaw. Morty crumpled to the floor. "You're vermin," Hermann snarled down at him. "Unfit for the likes of her. Now give me a name!"

God save me. Blinding pain seized Morty as he struggled to his feet. Whether he answered or not, he was already a dead man. "I do not know—"

"What I'm talking about, yes, yes," Hermann said impatiently. "Well, your accomplice will reveal himself soon enough." He jerked the letter opener free. Morty stared at the gaping wound in the wood. "For now, I find it convenient to keep you alive. Later on . . ."

He held the blade's razor tip to his finger, pricking the skin. "Now get out. Your animal stink fouls my office."

Morty was astonished at the reprieve. He limped toward the door while pain from his jaw battled the trauma in his feet. Even so, his spirits rose, for he'd held death at bay, at least for the moment. So long as Joseph's identity remained his secret. And Hadassah's . . .

Despite his renewed determination to get news from the kitchen, Morty was forced to stop and rest after taking only a few steps. He leaned against the wall outside Hermann's office and wiped his face with the back of his sleeve. As he drew away blood, he glanced back inside at the Nazi standing at the window. *Who is the animal, I wonder, Captain?*

Mrs. Brenner greeted Morty at the kitchen door with a bowl of thick vegetable stew, two biscuits, and a loud kiss on the cheek. "God be praised, Morty Benjamin, you were right!"

Morty glanced toward the kitchen table, where several others sat, including his friend Yaakov Kadlec. Each clutched a small cup of diluted ersatz, which passed for ghetto Kaffee.

They nodded and smiled in agreement. Morty shifted uncertainly. "I was . . . right?"

"Come, sit down, you poor man. Eat, eat," Mrs. Brenner said, herding him into a chair. She placed the steaming bowl and biscuits in front of him. "What's the matter with your legs, Morty?" she asked. "And your face!" Before he could answer, she added, "We heard about the Kleine Festung. You're lucky to be alive." She leaned to inspect his swollen jaw, clucking her tongue in concern.

"Ja," Morty murmured, his attention completely absorbed by the smells of beef lard and spices rising from the bowl. He ripped off a chunk of biscuit and stuffed it into his mouth. "They beat the soles of my feet," he managed between painful chews.

"That commandant is a devil!"

Morty shook his head. "I heard him order Sergeant Koch to

keep me intact for questioning—no abuse. But Koch chose to disobey those orders."

"Ja, and just see where that got him," Mrs. Brenner huffed in a righteous tone.

The bread turned to a dry lump in Morty's throat. "I saw what remains of him, in the yard with Brucker. Is my girl . . . is she all right?" he asked.

"Not only all right," Mrs. Brenner said in a conspiratorial whisper as she glanced at the other faces around the table, "she's our salvation!"

Morty's head jerked up. Mrs. Brenner stood beside him, smiling, her straight white teeth a startling contrast to the rest of her neglected features.

He looked around the table. Everyone grinned.

"I'm sorry I ever doubted you, my friend," Yaakov spoke up. "I should have believed your vision from God, especially after our food improved. But then she saved them—one hundred and sixty of them—including Mrs. Brenner's daughter, Clara." He nodded toward the beaming aproned woman.

Morty gaped at them, confused. "My . . . maideleh . . . saved . . . ?"

"The lists, Morty!" Mrs. Brenner's excited tone filled his ears. "Ask Lenny, he'll tell you!"

"Lenny . . . ?" Helplessly, Morty turned to the lanky twenty-five-year-old seated at the table. Lenny Buszak had been an engineer's apprentice with the railroad in Krakow. Tall and sallow-faced, the young Pole's oversized Adam's apple made him look skinnier than he actually was.

"Ja, what she says is true, Elder," Lenny said, doffing his cap in respect. "I was cleaning the toilet down the hall from Captain Hermann's office on the day his sergeant's typewriter broke. Herr Captain was very upset—I think it was the same day the phone lines fell down."

Lenny swallowed, and his Adam's apple slid along the column

of his throat like a bobber tugged beneath the water. "I heard the captain say he would take the cards to Herr Kommandant's secretary to be typed."

"Don't you see?" Yaakov interjected. "One hundred sixty people who were originally notified to transport never got called to actually board the train!" He slammed his hand down against the table. "I don't know how she did it, my friend, but your girl even fooled that motherless whelp Hermann!"

Yaakov seemed to gurgle with pleasure. The spoonful of stew Morty had raised to his lips fell back into the bowl with a loud *plop*. "You think she . . . my niece . . . purposely shaved the lists?"

They nodded at him in unison.

"Oi!" Morty launched from his chair to gape at each of them. Fear squeezed his chest like a vise. "Dear God, what if she's caught? What if they deport her?" His memory flashed to the two men at the gallows. "Or worse!"

Narrowed glances rebounded at him from around the table. Mrs. Brenner snatched away his half-eaten bowl of stew. "Which is worse, Morty Benjamin, your maideleh or my Clara?" Her voice turned acrid. "It's no secret you're the one who makes up the lists. You get to decide who stays and who goes."

She tried grabbing the remaining biscuit. Morty was faster. He popped it whole into his mouth and glared at her.

Mrs. Brenner gave an indifferent shrug. "So if she wants to be brave and save you the trouble of a few more names on your conscience, who are you to stop her?"

Morty nearly choked on the biscuit. "You think I like the responsibility they have given me?" he questioned, spraying bits of dough across the table. "What would you have me do, give Hermann blank cards?" He slid back into his chair, feeling the old misery weigh like a stone against his heart. Selection was the most agonizing, offensive chore he'd ever performed. He culled first from those too ill to survive any length of time, then chose from the elderly—husbands and wives often wishing to accompany each other.

They were never enough to fill the train. So the rest of the names he pulled at random from the card file in his office, until the body count Captain Hermann demanded had been met.

Morty thought of the times afterward, when such impotent rage filled him that even the most ardent prayers failed to bring him peace; the days, oftentimes weeks, that would pass before he could look into the shard of glass above his cot and tell himself there was nothing he could do, that it was God's will. "At least I try to keep the healthy ones here," he said on a ragged breath. "At least I try to save the children."

Through a blur of unexpected tears, he saw the bowl of stew reappear in front of him. Mrs. Brenner pushed another biscuit in his direction. "We know, Morty." She let out a weary sigh. "But if your maideleh wishes to lighten your burden, if she desires to be our salvation, then we think . . ." She looked to the other faces, receiving their nodded agreement. "We think you should let her."

23

When Haman saw that Mordecai would not kneel down or pay him honor, he was enraged.

Esther 3:5

Captain Hermann stood at his office window, letter opener still in hand as he carefully traced a finger along its honed edge. It galled him to set the Jew free. Even now the old goat was likely laughing over Hermann's empty threat to send him back to the Little Fortress. But the commandant had ordered his release, stating that as sole Elder of the Judenrat, he must be kept alive to speak with the Red Cross delegation should they desire it.

Hermann left the window and returned to his desk—the size of a footlocker compared to the one burned to ashes. Tossing the blade aside, he pressed his palms against the wood and fought to curb his anger . . . and uncertainty.

Nothing had gone as planned. The commandant not only lived, but somehow he had foreknowledge of the attempt on his life.

Koch and Brucker dangled outside like *Rindfleisch* for the butcher.

Who had warned the commandant? Obviously the Jew was

217

involved; he must have been inside the room when Hermann and his men held their little conference. Hidden behind the food crates stacked along the wall? A daring feat, but not so dangerous to one who had earned a Grand Cross.

Hermann thought of his own encouragement in the murder scheme and flinched. Did the commandant know the truth and merely waited for the arrival of General Feldman? Or worse, Himmler and Eichmann? Charges made in front of such illustrious personages of the Reich would kill Hermann's hard-won career . . . perhaps even his life. "Sonntag!" he bellowed.

"Good news, Herr Captain!" The young corporal rushed into his office and offered a crisp salute. "The telephone lines are working." Sonntag hesitated, apparently realizing Hermann's black mood. He dropped his arm to his side. "I . . . I thought you would be pleased, Herr Captain."

"Pleased?" Hermann bared his teeth. "When I don't even have a phone available to me in this broom closet?" Grabbing up the letter opener, he pointed toward the window. "When I must stand here and watch my troops as they gawk all day on two of their comrades swinging by their necks and stinking up the place? You think that should please me, Corporal?" Furious, he hurled the miniature sword at the open doorway.

It caught a surprised Sonntag on the chin, nicking his flesh.

Hermann's face heated with rage and humiliation. How dare the commandant censure him like some green boy in short pants before the schoolmaster's whip!

A single crimson bead rose against Sonntag's milk-white flesh and dribbled along his jaw. Hermann took a deep breath and clutched the back of his chair, absorbing the cold steel against his palms. "Follow that Jew, Benjamin. Find out who he talks to—Jew and German alike. I want to know who he eats with and sleeps with. Report back to me every twelve hours."

Wide-eyed, Sonntag stood transfixed.

"Go!" Hermann roared.

Sonntag jerked from his stupor. He spun and fled the small office without a salute or backward glance.

Hermann eased into his chair. He now had a plan. He could only hope it proved successful. Torturing the Jew would have been preferable, but instinct told him the old man would die before giving up any secrets. There must be someone else—and once Hermann received Sonntag's report, he could eliminate the loose end before Himmler and Eichmann arrived. The commandant wouldn't dare accuse him without more reliable corroboration than the word of an old Jew.

Hermann planted a fist against the desk. Koch and Brucker had screwed things up, but what did he expect? He was amazed the pair actually went through with their plan. Crippled or not, Aric von Schmidt was a seasoned warrior. They were naïve to go up against him, believing they could win.

I would have succeeded. He reached for the leather pistol strap at his side. While he hadn't spouted off the way Neubach did at the commandant's banquet, Hermann soldiered fourteen months in the Waffen-SS; he'd ranked in the top twenty percent for marksmanship in the entire B Division. Fritz Beidermann, an old schoolmate, and Lagerführer at Mauthausen, had then offered him a promotion to second lieutenant. Hermann transferred into the political SS and further promotions came swiftly—a year at the concentration camp of Mauthausen, then on to Chelmno, where he rose to the rank of SS-Obersturmführer, first lieutenant.

Theresienstadt finally won him his captain's bars. Despite duty in a transit camp, he had no regrets. He'd surpassed the rank of his own drunkard of a father, a *Stabsgefreiter,* "career corporal" in the Great War. And he could still rid the world of Jews each time he loaded a train for Auschwitz.

I could have taken on Aric von Schmidt last night and won back what I lost—including the woman. Resentment failed to wipe away the memory of her softness against him as they danced, or the smell of her exotic perfume. And her kiss could warm more than a man's heart during a cold, dark night . . .

She was a veritable sorceress, able to bewitch a camp commandant into becoming a Jew sympathizer. Hermann planned to be on his guard when it was his turn. And he had no doubt that after his nemesis tired of her, Stella *would* come to him. Women were weak-minded creatures, mere vessels for a man's use. Even his own mother, after seven children, continued to breed one empty stomach after another into a house where hunger remained an unwanted guest.

Poverty was a concept the noble commandant had likely never experienced. Maybe Schmidt felt akin to the Jews, those mongering Christ-killers who bought up everything during the Great War, enjoying their rich tables while Hermann and his family starved.

He swiveled his chair around to the wall behind him and looked up at his picture of der Führer. His nostrils filled with the acrid traces of smoke still clinging to its charred frame.

His own father returned from the Front defeated. He'd chosen to face life through a haze of drink rather than work to support his family. Hermann's mother tried to make ends meet, laundering for a Gasthaus in Leipzig, but the grueling work—and bearing so many brats—finally killed her. He'd left home after that, and at fifteen he joined the Labor Service.

Hermann had no idea what became of his father or his siblings. He didn't care. Adolf Hitler was now his father, the men of the SS his brothers.

Had one of those brothers betrayed him?

He pushed himself up and returned to the window. Turbulent gray clouds scudded eastward, away from the camp. The only evidence of Tuesday's storm lie in the cold, white drifts blanketing the streets.

Hermann went completely still, his mind racing. The storm had knocked out the telephone lines. Whoever warned the commandant of Koch and Brucker's plan must have gone to the house to do so. Mentally he rifled through the list of his own men but couldn't believe any of them would be in league with the Jew.

Grossman, perhaps? The sergeant *had* been in the ghetto the day of the fire. He could have forewarned the commandant and told him everything, including the fact that Hermann allowed Koch and Brucker to talk of insurrection and had done nothing to stop it.

Sweat beaded along his forehead, beneath his cap. He cursed his overactive imagination. It couldn't be Grossman; otherwise Schmidt would have roasted Hermann on a spit *before* the attempted murder.

Impatience ate at him. Twelve hours . . . would that give the Jew enough time to hang himself? And who else would be named on Sonntag's report? The accomplice was definitely clever. Someone who had been in the ghetto during the time of the fire but who also had access to the commandant's house. The smaller set of prints could belong to a woman—

Shrieks of laughter from the alley below caught his attention. A cluster of ragged urchins chased each other, creating a quagmire of slush in the snow.

Dawning struck. Hermann smiled.

A woman . . . or a potato thief.

24

When Esther's maids and eunuchs came and told her
about Mordecai, she was in great distress.

Esther 4:4

MONDAY, MARCH 6, 1944

Anger and frustration churned in her. After an interminably
long weekend, Aric had returned from the hospital last
night with Grossman and still hadn't told her of his decision
regarding Morty.

Stella glanced at her watch. Time for breakfast. She'd confront him—

A knock sounded at her door. "Come," she said coolly.

Joseph entered, and a little of her resentment subsided.

"Are you ready to come downstairs?"

"Is there any word about Morty?"

"Not yet." The boy jammed his hands into his pockets, and
she could hear his marbles rattling in agitated synchronization.
Her own nerves felt stretched; the inability to do something,
anything, for her uncle made her want to shriek.

"What about Grossman? Do you know if he's spoken with
Herr Kommandant?"

Joseph chewed at his lower lip and shrugged. "Last night when the sergeant returned, he acted very sleepy. He's in my bed again. Helen sat with him through the night."

Stella crossed her arms and eyed him sharply. "Where did you sleep?"

"Herr Kommandant told me I should stay downstairs with Grossman." His face flushed, and he nodded toward the door. "But I slept outside your room."

Oh, how she loved this boy! "Come here, little man."

He rushed to her, and she hugged him, kissing the top of his head. "You didn't have to do that, kaddishel."

"I don't want anything to happen to you. Herr Kommandant didn't send the captain away. He could still hurt you."

"It's all right." Stella gave him a hard squeeze, refusing to admit her own alarm. What would Hermann try next? And what ridiculous excuse would she contrive this time in order to warn Aric?

Still, it was Morty's fate that preyed uppermost on her mind; he was in danger of being tortured, perhaps killed—while Grossman slept. "If only that man would wake up long enough to acquit my uncle," she muttered.

The boy looked up at her. "We must hurry. General Feldman arrived very early this morning. He's downstairs with Herr Kommandant. I was sent to get you."

"Herr General . . . but he wasn't supposed to be here until this afternoon." Stella hid her agitation. Now she must wait to confront Aric about Morty. The farce was about to begin. "Let's go meet him, then."

"I already have."

The slight tremor in his voice brought Stella's head up sharply. She glanced at his scar. "What happened? What did he do to you?"

"Nothing." The child stared at his feet. "Captain Hermann escorted the general to the house and then ordered me to bring his bags upstairs to the guest room." His soft brown eyes glanced up at her. "It was just . . . the way he looked at me."

"How did he look at you?"

"Like I was a cockroach."

Stella smiled and released a pent-up breath. "I think you're adorable."

His cheeks blossomed with color.

"Besides, he's a Nazi and probably hates all Jews. Why should he like you?"

The boy shrugged again. "I think Herr Kommandant likes me."

"Of course he does. That's different."

"Why?"

Why indeed? At a loss for a ready answer, Stella improvised. "Because he's taken the time to get acquainted with you, and now realizes what a fine young man you are."

Joseph beamed. Stella didn't share his pleasure, however, as they headed downstairs to the main floor. She wasn't looking forward to meeting the general. "What will you do today?"

"After I finish my housework, I have to go inside the ghetto. The captain needs help getting the children ready for Herr General's inspection."

Anxiety prickled along her spine. "What inspection? Does Herr Kommandant know about this?"

"Don't worry." He squeezed her hand with his smaller one. "Today the children get to dress up in the nice clothes they will wear for the Red Cross. Herr Kommandant called it a 'dress rehearsal.'" He turned to grin at her. "I get to wear a new suit."

Dress rehearsal—that sounded safe enough. "I'm certain you'll look splendid, Joseph."

At the dining room he disappeared into the kitchen, leaving Stella with Aric and a highly decorated officer in military gray uniform.

Aric was the first to rise, seated in the place normally occupied by Stella. The general had taken over Aric's chair at the head of the table. "Guten Morgen, Fräulein Muller. I'd like for you to meet Herr Oberstgruppenführer Feldman from the Reich Chancellery in Berlin."

Disquieted by Aric's sudden formality, Stella forced a smile and tipped her head in acknowledgment. "Herr General."

General Feldman rose to greet her. With a shock of white hair receding at his temples, he looked about fifty years of age. He stood centimeters shorter than Aric, but his girth was much wider; years of rich food had produced a paunch that strained at the gold buttons of his tunic. Colorful ribbons decorated his chest, along with several crosses and medallions that gave evidence to his high rank.

She heard the snap of jackboots beneath the table as he bowed to her. "A pleasure to make your acquaintance, Fräulein." To Aric he said, "Now I know why you spend so much time in your office, Colonel." He chuckled. "Your working conditions seem quite . . . satisfactory."

Heat crawled up Stella's throat.

Irritation flashed in Aric's features, though he smiled when he said, "As you say, Herr General. I cannot complain."

"Indeed." Another chortle escaped the rotund man. "You must join us, Fräulein Muller."

Aric motioned Stella into the chair beside his own. "I hope your room upstairs is satisfactory, Herr General?" he asked while seating her.

"You have fine quarters for a mere *Standartenführer*, Schmidt," the general retorted with another guffaw.

"Herr General will stay with us until Wednesday morning," Aric informed Stella. "Then he'll return to Prague and bring Herr Reichsführer Himmler, Obersturmbannführer Eichmann, and the Swiss back on Thursday."

He turned to the general. "Will there be photographers?"

"The Red Cross will bring their picture-takers." The general tucked a white cloth napkin into his collar. "Of course we have our media people, as well."

Aric resumed his seat beside Stella. "After breakfast I will take Herr General to the ghetto so he can begin his inspection."

"Perhaps your lovely secretary would care to join us?" The general was carefully arranging his knives and forks against the linen tablecloth.

"That won't be possible." He glanced at Stella. "I've left several drafts on your desk, Fräulein, which need immediate typing."

"Jawohl, Herr Kommandant," she answered crisply. She was still angry over his cavalier treatment of Morty's situation; now she wasn't even allowed to see the dress rehearsal? Joseph would look so handsome in his new clothes . . .

Stella had no more time to brood. Helen appeared toting a silver tray laden with fried eggs; *Tiroler Gröstl*, a dish of meat and fried potatoes Stella knew to be Aric's favorite breakfast—pork links, freshly baked bread—and blessed oatmeal.

As the housekeeper rounded the side of the table, Stella flashed her an appreciative smile. Helen, looking spry in a blue-and-white-striped neck scarf, gave her a wink before gliding back out of the room.

"The yolks are broken on these eggs." The general frowned at the platter of food. "I gave your cook specific orders to prepare my eggs soft. These are unacceptable. Get rid of them and give me new ones."

"My apologies, Herr General. Helen!"

Helen rushed in from the kitchen.

"Please prepare new eggs for Herr General."

The housekeeper reddened and removed the platter, then bowed a silent apology to the general before retreating into the kitchen.

Stella felt outrage for the other woman. There was nothing wrong with the eggs, just a slight puncture in one of the yolks.

Now they would likely be thrown away because the general insisted on perfect ones.

"There is another matter I wish to discuss with you, Fräulein." Aric's sober tone drew her attention. "The package sent to the Fortress"—he shot her a meaningful glance—"has been returned."

Morty! Stella's hand flew to the Grand Cross hidden beneath her blouse. "Was the package . . . damaged?" she whispered.

Tight lines edged his mouth. "I'm afraid so. However, the contents are intact."

She clenched her fist against the table. "How could this happen?"

"I think we both know the answer to that."

Touché. "Could I inspect the damage?"

"Nein, I will see to it." His look suggested she not argue.

"Give me the names of these imbeciles who destroy German property and I will deal with them."

Stella and Aric both turned to the general. The Oberstgruppenführer held a pork link to his greasy lips.

"We cannot afford laxity on the part of these Czech locals," he said before stuffing the entire sausage into his mouth. Chewing noisily, he added, "Especially when the Swiss will arrive in four days."

"I assure you, Herr General, the matter has been taken care of." Aric shot Stella a look of warning. "We'll have no more trouble."

"Better be certain of that, Schmidt," the general said once he swallowed the meat. "Because this 'Embellishment' we are orchestrating is of paramount importance to the Führer. He will not tolerate any mistakes or excuses."

"You'll find everything in perfect order, Herr General."

The general grunted. Helen returned with new eggs, and he continued to fill his face until the meal was finished.

Stella remained at the table after Aric departed with Herr Sausage. She toyed with the spoon in her half-eaten bowl of oatmeal. Pleasure over Morty's release from the Little Fortress dimmed against her fury at his brutal treatment. How badly was he injured?

"Well?"

She turned to find Aric standing in the archway wearing his greatcoat, gloves, and peaked officer's cap. He resembled a modern-day Charlemagne, like the statue she'd once seen at the fountain in Aachen.

She rose from her chair. "Of course, Herr Kommandant. I'll start typing those letters."

Stella tried moving past him, but he stayed her by grasping her upper arms. "Herr Kommandant, is it? I thought you'd be happy at my news."

Ignoring the comfort his touch evoked, she clung to her precious anger. "Is he hurt badly?"

"He'll live."

"What does that mean?"

He released her and stepped back. "The soles of his feet were beaten. Koch was in charge of the arrest. He ignored my order to safeguard the prisoner."

Stella ground her teeth to keep from shouting at him. Why hadn't he believed her about Koch and Brucker? "Can he walk?" she finally managed after a moment.

"Yes. I believe he'll recover."

"Did he return to the ghetto this morning?"

"Saturday."

Two days ago? "But you left that morning," she said, confused. "You went to see Sergeant Grossman at hospital. How did you—?"

"I had him released beforehand."

Warmth filled her as she searched his face. "You . . . let him go? Because of me?"

"Partly," he admitted, removing his cap. "After Friday night's fiasco, it became obvious more was going on than a random attack by one of the prisoners. I believe Sergeant Koch intended to remove any obstacle in his path to get to me—to us. With Grossman gone, he and Brucker had easy access to the house." He paused. "I decided then the Jew should return to the ghetto."

The joy that eluded Stella for so long now flowed through her with heady sweetness. Like champagne, the feeling bubbled up into her nose and throat, threatening laughter and making speech impossible. She could only beam at him.

"I take it you're pleased."

His smile was filled with such tenderness that Stella's eyes burned. He'd saved the only family she had left . . .

"Love your enemies . . ." It hadn't been so difficult with this man after all, she realized. Despite his accurate logic, he could have left Morty to his tormentors in the Kleine Festung a few more days. No doubt untold others had died in that place without the commandant of the camp giving the slightest notice. Yet her uncle had been spared because Aric was a fair man, and though he denied it, a compassionate one, as well. And he *had* done it for her.

Did she truly have his ear? "I'm very pleased," she said, moving into the circle of his arms. He lowered his head and kissed her deeply, and once more Stella sensed the sadness and desperation beneath his passion. She slid her hands around his neck and kissed him back. She wanted him to understand how much he'd come to mean to her: dangerous, irrevocable feelings that touched her heart with the purity and wonder of a first snow.

Afterward she held him tightly, as though they could meld together as one. Her heart lay pressed over his old wound—that place most vulnerable in each of them. She imagined for a blissful moment their pulses beating as one.

Aric finally raised his head. "I believe you," he said with an expression of genuine wonder.

Stella wanted to laugh. It seemed her prayers had been answered. "Thank you."

"You're welcome." He kissed her again quickly, then set her away from him. "I'm certain the general grows tired of waiting in the car. I told him I had to get this . . ." He moved to grab the brass-topped cane from beside his place at the table. "I also wanted to warn you to keep your bedroom door locked while that pompous rooster stays upstairs." He grimaced. "The general seems to run a steady course toward overindulgence . . . in all areas."

He brushed a finger along her cheek. "You could always stay in my room."

"No, Aric, I won't be your mistress."

He flashed her a wounded look.

"I won't have the general thinking so, either," she added.

"Nor will I," he agreed in a chastened tone. "See you later."

"Wait." She wanted to ask about the dress rehearsal. "When you return, would you please tell me . . . ?" A prickle of caution made her pause.

"Tell you what?" He donned his cap.

Trust him, Hadassah. "Tell me . . . how nice Joseph looks in his new suit?"

Aric visibly tensed, and Stella longed to call back the words. Had she put her kaddishel in danger? *Trust him*, her inner voice insisted. "He told me about the inspection."

"Ah, yes. The inspection." He offered a tight smile. "Of course."

Hefting his cane, he turned and strode through the archway. Stella felt suddenly anxious. Why did he seem to dread this dress rehearsal?

A soft noise behind her made her spin around.

Helen leaned against the table, her normally hard expression yielding concern. How long had she been standing there? "What's wrong?" Stella asked, watching for a sign that would explain the woman's obvious distress.

The housekeeper worked her jaw as if in thought, then shoved away from the table and propelled herself toward Stella. Pointing a finger at the area over Stella's heart, she nodded toward the opening where Aric had departed.

"Yes," Stella breathed, stunned at the woman's silent question. "He matters to me."

Helen shook her head vehemently. She reached to press a fist against Stella's breast and then thrust her chin again toward the archway.

Stella felt unable to tear her gaze from the housekeeper's. She wasn't ready to confess aloud what her heart already knew, yet Helen understood. The woman's hard mouth softened, and she clasped both of Stella's hands, giving them a hearty squeeze.

Then, in what seemed Helen's natural motion, she wheeled around and left the room.

Stella headed toward the library and her office. She wondered at the relationship between Aric and the gruff-mannered housekeeper. Joseph had told her that Helen accompanied Aric to Theresienstadt. But how did they meet? And how did Sergeant Rand Grossman fit into the picture of their shared past?

Impulsively she veered off course and went to Joseph's room at the back of the house. As she stood on the threshold, Stella noted the sheet had been removed from the window, allowing dull, gray light to illuminate the tiny room.

Grossman's sizable lump lay buried beneath a heap of blankets. Beside his narrow cot, a mahogany end table abducted from the living room sat cluttered with pill bottles, one empty drinking glass, and an untouched slice of Helen's Apfelstrudel. On the floor next to where he slept lay a stack of books bound in ochre-red leather.

"Helen?"

The sergeant's voice rose groggily from somewhere beneath the blankets. A steel hook prowled from beneath the bedding to tap the side of the empty glass. "Thirsty."

Stella retrieved the glass and took it to the kitchen. Helen was up to raw elbows in soapy dishwater and hardly gave her a glance.

Stella poured water from the tap and then returned to find that the patient had shucked off his blankets. The pajama-clad Grossman was as solidly built as Aric, though not as tall, and closer to Stella in age. Without his *Stahlhelm*, he looked more like a man and less like an armed machine. He wore his sable hair shaved close at the neck and above the ears, while a sweep of dark locks hung limply against his forehead. Beard stubble shadowed his lean, flushed face.

She moved toward the cot, and his eyes opened. Glazed with fever and blue as ice, they watched her steady approach. "Not Helen . . ." he growled hoarsely.

Stella clutched the glass of water. She shouldn't have come—they had never been formally introduced. The only dealings she'd had with him since her arrival was to give him mail to post. They had never actually conversed.

His mouth widened in sudden recognition. "Fräulein, welcome. Wel . . . come," he sang.

"Your water."

She thrust the glass at him. Droplets splashed onto his beige flannel pajama top. He didn't seem to notice as he struggled to sit up. "My throat feels like I swallowed sand."

Stella glanced at the shiny prosthesis. "If you'd like help . . ."

"I'm no cripple." He snatched up the glass with his good hand and took several long gulps before placing it on the table. The exertion seemed to exhaust him. Wiping his mouth on his sleeve, he said, "Sit awhile, Fräulein. Keep me company."

"Just for a few minutes." She dragged over a ladder-backed chair from beside the door and sat down. "How do you feel today, Herr Sergeant?"

"Like the Fourth Panzer Army ran practice maneuvers across my chest."

Stella smiled. His stoic humor was much like Aric's. "Can I get you anything else?"

His steel hook tapped at the brown bottle of pills on the end table. "Would you mind . . . ?"

Stella picked up the nearly full bottle, identical to the one on Aric's nightstand. She unscrewed the cap and shook out a single morphine tablet and handed it to him.

"I am grateful to Herr Kommandant for these. That idiot surgeon gave me nothing." He popped the pill into his mouth and retrieved the half-empty glass to wash it down. Afterward he settled back against the pillows. "Do you play chess, Fräulein Muller?"

"I never learned." She looked down at the stack of books on the floor. "What are you reading?"

"See for yourself."

Stella reached for the top book and hid her surprise. *Poems of Alfred Lord Tennyson*. She hadn't imagined Grossman to have an appreciation for poetry . . . or a disregard for the law. The Third Reich forbade possession of such literature.

Flipping open to a ribbon-marked page, she couldn't contain her astonishment. "'Ulysses'?" she said, glancing up at him.

"I *can* read, Fräulein."

She blushed. "I didn't mean . . ."

"It is my favorite. Would you read a few lines aloud?"

Stella scanned down toward the middle of the poem and read:

"How dull it is to pause, to make an end,
To rust unburnish'd, not to shine in use!
As tho' to breathe were life! Life piled on life
Were all too little, and of one to me
Little remains. . . ."

"Ah, how that speaks to me, Fräulein. Danke," he said when she paused.

"It's a lovely piece, Herr Sergeant."

"Herr Kommandant has excellent taste in poetry."

Stella glanced up. The book belonged to Aric? "But I thought
. . . it's forbidden by the Nazis!"

"How do you think literature survives war, Fräulein?" He
grinned. "And call me Rand, if you like. Under the circumstances"—he glanced down at his bedclothes—"we don't need
to be so formal."

Stella allowed herself another smile. "Call me Stella."

Rand shook his head. "Herr Kommandant would not like it."

"Why should he care?"

Her cheeks ignited at his sudden burst of laughter—followed
by several moments of phlegmatic coughing. "Come now, Fräulein," he wheezed. "I am his man. He is quite taken with you."
His eyes took on a faraway look as he added, "And don't I know
he deserves happiness."

Her curiosity overrode embarrassment. "He's had a difficult
life, hasn't he?"

"More than you can imagine. We shared a hospital room at
Sevastopal, on the Crimean Peninsula. We played a lot of chess."
His fevered face softened. "He usually won."

"How long were you in hospital together?"

"I was released after four months. I was on patrol outside
Sevastopal last August when a few of us got showered with par-
tisan grenades." He raised the ominous hook for her inspection.
"When I was admitted to the hospital, Herr Kommandant—a
major at the time—had arrived a month earlier from the city of
Lemberg, in the Ukraine." He gave her a weighty stare. "He'd
been in hospital there since December of forty-two."

"When did he get out?"

"We took a train to Berlin together in January of this year."

Stella fell back against her seat. Aric had been hospitalized
for over a year? Her heart ached for him. "I imagine you became
good friends, at Sevastopal?"

Rand loosed another grin. The morphine made his eyelids heavy. "We fought together with Army Group South, under Field Marshall von Reichenau back in forty-one. At the Battle of Kiev."

"On the night of Herr Kommandant's party, he mentioned a place called Babi Yar. Is that where you met?"

He grimaced and shook his head. "Our division was already in Kiev two weeks." The drug's effects seemed to be loosening his inhibitions. "Terrible place, Babi Yar. 'Old Wives' Gully.'" He closed his eyes and jerked his head to one side as if avoiding a blow. "The baby . . . I'll never forget . . ."

Stillness rose between them like an impregnable wall. "Tell me about the baby," Stella said softly. "I want to understand."

Rand opened his eyes. Even dulled by morphine, they held anguish. "Can't possibly describe. Ravine was an open grave, miles of rotting flesh." He dropped his head. "Blood and excrement . . . so strong I got sick all over myself. And the baby . . ." His deep voice broke. "He jus' kept nursing while his mother lay dead in the ditch." With a groan, Rand rose up off his pillow and reached for Stella's hand on the book. "His tiny black head . . . soft hair, stuck out all over. Jus' like my sister's boy, like little Karl's hair." He fell back onto the pillows, clearly exhausted.

Dread clawed at Stella's heart, recalling Aric's conversation the night of the banquet. "Was Herr Kommandant a part of this?"

"Nein!" Rand sat up again, all visible signs of the morphine gone. "Our divisions went in first, killing Russian soldiers only. Then Heydrich's SS-*Sonderkommandos* followed. They killed women and babies and old men just hours after we had taken Kiev. They boasted of how they 'led the sheep to slaughter' with promises of relocation—"

"Stop!" Stella covered her ears. "No more, Rand. Please!"

"Forgive me." Haggard lines rimmed his features. "I should not have spoken of such things."

"Lie back before you damage your stitches." Her voice shook

as she nudged him against the pillows. "It was my fault. I shouldn't have pried."

Yet she felt driven to know the rest of the sordid story of Aric's past. "After what you saw . . . at Babi Yar . . . why did you and Herr Kommandant join with the SS?"

"By forty-three the Reds and the Americans had started to squeeze us in. The Wehrmacht wanted only able-fighting men." He frowned. "They had no use for invalids. We had nowhere else to go."

"You could have gone home," she accused.

"I have no home left, Fräulein, except with my widowed sister and her baby. In the city, work is scarce. Food is rationed. And this"—he raised his steel hook—"does not help my chances for employment. So I stay here and send her what money I can."

"And Herr Kommandant?"

"Worse for him, I think. I was only in service three years. He spent a decade in the German Army. He was a major when the fighting at Stalingrad almost killed him. It killed his career, anyway. Last December, when he began to walk again, Himmler sent his personal courier to Sevastopal. The SS-Reichsführer offered him the rank of colonel and commandant of this camp."

"And you came with him."

"He made a place for me. Promoted me to the rank of sergeant," Rand said proudly.

Frustration tore at Stella. While she understood Rand's limited options, she wondered why Aric had taken a position in the SS. Why hadn't he gone home to Thaur, anywhere beyond Hitler's reach? Or did he too feel he had nowhere else to go?

Her own entrapment seemed precarious at best. Did Aric simply try to survive, as she did? He'd spent a year of his life in hospital, unable to walk, at least until those last few weeks. Then he was abandoned by the Wehrmacht.

Stella tried to imagine his sense of loss. "You helped him," she said to Rand.

He shrugged. "Herr Kommandant is a great man. Have you noticed the Knight's Cross on his uniform? Few men receive such an honor, but I have seen his courage and strength. He actually led a band of soldiers to the west of Cherkassy, right beneath Ivan's nose. Took out their Thirty-eighth Rifle Army and freed up our Seventeenth, which had been holed up for days at Uman." Rand smiled. "The man is afraid of nothing. I just let him win a few games of chess."

Stella smiled back. She suspected Rand had done much more. "You're loyal to him, aren't you?"

"I would gladly give my life for him." His blue gaze met hers. "And you, Fräulein? Are you as faithful?"

Such a complex question. Stella considered her sham life and the 160 Jews who did not board yesterday's train. There was also the fact she knew Captain Hermann wanted Aric dead but said nothing. She nodded at Rand, and the answer rose from deep inside her. "I would die for him," she said.

He slid his good arm beneath his head and smiled a dreamy smile. "Please read to me some more, Fräulein."

She picked up the book and read from the last few lines of Tennyson's "Ulysses."

> "We are not now that strength which in old days
> Moved earth and heaven, that which we are, we are;
> One equal temper of heroic hearts,
> Made weak by time and fate, but strong in will
> To strive, to seek, to find, and not to yield."

Stella glanced up. Rand was asleep. She closed the book and ventured back upstairs before going to the library. Removing Morty's Grand Cross from around her neck, she stuffed it inside the hidden compartment of the music box. Her vigil was over. Morty was safe.

Taking the photograph from inside her shirt, Stella gazed

at the child with his mother. The tenderness he'd stirred in her earlier returned, filling her heart with hope . . . and uncertainty for the future.

She considered the lines from the poem she'd read to Grossman. The lamentations of an old warrior seemed appropriate for Aric's life. He'd sacrificed the best part for his country and now, far from the excitement of battle, he was sending innocent Jews to be slaughtered at Auschwitz—an untenable task for one whose nature inclined toward fairness and decency.

Would Aric uphold those same qualities when all secrets between them were revealed?

Stella glanced toward the nightstand. The Bible, as usual, had mysteriously reappeared. She retrieved it, feeling no animosity this time, only a jarring sense of wonder. Had God truly listened?

She sat on the edge of the bed and let the book fall open against her lap.

The book of First Kings, part of the *Nevi'im* in her own Jewish Tanakh. Her eyes went to chapter nineteen on the page, and she felt the first flutter of recognition. It was the story of the prophet Elijah, whom God told to wait in a cave at Mount Horeb for His passing. A great wind arose, and Elijah came out of his cave, but God was not in the wind. An earthquake followed that shook the ground, but God was not in the earthquake. A fire ensued, but God was not in the fire.

After the fire, a whisper. And God spoke to Elijah.

Stella gently closed the book. Why had she assumed God would speak to her in some great audible sign, like a thunderclap, lightning, or a burst of fire from the sky? Had anger and bitterness made her deaf to His whisper?

"Tell me, Lord," she pleaded softly. "I promise to listen."

~ 25 ~

In every province to which the edict and the order of the king came, there was great mourning among the Jews. . . .

Esther 4:3

Aric might have imagined the human display out of an American motion picture. Men and women dressed in their Hollywood best: expensive suits sporting tweed caps or crisp felt trilbys, and colorful jewel silk dresses trimmed in matching pillbox hats and wrist-length gloves.

He trudged through the snow beside Hermann and General Feldman as they approached the lineup at the center of the ghetto's *Marktplatz*. In addition to the borrowed surplus garments, each Jew had donned a frozen smile for the occasion. Only the infrequent darting glance or shifting of feet revealed their anxiety.

Most of the women wore cosmetics. Like circus clowns, they had charcoaled brows and heavily rouged cheeks, imbuing their gaunt flesh with a kind of grotesque hilarity. Aric felt acutely relieved at Stella's absence. He couldn't bear her look of condemnation for what he must do. And the boy . . .

His chest tightened as a frigid gust blew across his face, lifting the hem of his heavy greatcoat. The endless line of bodies huddled closer together, their lightweight garments barely protecting them against the cold.

"Captain, are there no coats in surplus?" he demanded. "I doubt we'll convince the Red Cross of the prisoners' comfort over their loud chattering of teeth."

"Excellent suggestion, Colonel." The general penned another notation into his diary.

Feldman had turned out to be the biggest surprise of all. Once they'd reached the ghetto, the general stepped from Aric's Mercedes, retrieved a small journal from his breast pocket, and began making copious notes. Obnoxious joviality had been replaced by hawk-eyed determination—a man ambitious to impress his Führer, Aric decided.

The transformed ghetto now looked more like a winter ski resort than a transit camp for Auschwitz. Feldman still managed to find flaws. "That sign above the bank needs to be straightened, Colonel," he said. "And I want a snowman built over there"—he whipped a leather crop from beneath his arm and pointed to the park beyond the square—"complete with eyes, nose, and stocking cap. We want to impress our visitors with the wholesome activities of the children."

"My captain will see to it, Herr General," Aric said.

Feldman scribbled another note and then glanced up, scrutinizing the perimeter of the square. "Where are the propaganda posters we sent from Berlin? Why are they not hanging in plain view?"

Aric turned to his captain. Hermann flushed. "I will take care of it immediately, Herr Kommandant."

"Have all remains been removed from the Krematorium?" the general demanded.

"Last Thursday, Herr General," Aric said. "The children worked late into the night dumping them into the lake."

"Herr Kommandant even sent his houseboy to participate in the removal," Captain Hermann spoke up.

"The little Jew from this morning, Captain?" The general nodded. "Hard work is good for him. He'll be out here today, yes?" He glanced at Aric.

Aric jerked his head in assent as he silently cursed Hermann for drawing Feldman's attention to the boy. He'd planned to keep Joseph out of view until the general departed. Did the captain now use the boy to get even with him? "You waste Herr General's time with tedious details, Captain," he bit out.

Hermann eyed him coldly. "Forgive me, Herr Kommandant. I merely wished to bring to attention your dedication and inconvenience. For the good of the Reich."

"Your captain does you credit, Colonel," the general interjected. He turned his attention to the line of prisoners. "Who was in charge of screening?"

Aric looked away from Hermann to answer, "Instructions came from Obersturmbannführer Eichmann, Herr General. We were ordered to present only the healthy ones to the Swiss during their visit."

"Hmmph. Let's see how healthy they are." Feldman replaced the diary in his pocket and gripped his leather crop as he strolled past the long line of well-dressed candidates. Aric walked beside him. Hermann and two SS guards followed at a respectable pace.

The general paused in front of a thin woman clad in a royal blue jacket, skirt, and matching pillbox hat. Black netting hid most of her face except the vermilion lips that smiled at him tremulously.

Placing his crop beneath her chin, the general smiled back. "What is your name, pretty Sarah?" he asked, using the Nazi slang for Jewess.

Her smile faltered. "Sophie . . . Sophie Lettenberg, Excellency," she said, revealing a mouthful of rotted teeth.

"Sophie. A lovely name. My cousin's name." The general slid his crop around her nape and gently prodded her out of line toward the two guards.

"No, please!" she cried. "I won't open my mouth, I swear it!"

But the general had already moved on to the next person.

Aric followed, fighting to breathe against an invisible noose. He eyed Feldman's gray Wehrmacht uniform and wondered when an honorable soldier's days had been reduced to eliminating Jews from a dress lineup much the way one discarded old clothes from a closet.

He tilted his head toward the gray wash of sky. Perhaps the same time his own had been debased to the point of eliminating an entire camp.

The general stopped in front of a short, gaunt man with ruddy complexion.

"Give me your handkerchief, Colonel," he said pleasantly. Aric complied, and the general took it and wiped at one of the man's hollowed cheeks.

He stared at the crimson stain left on the white cloth. "Do you enjoy using women's rouge?" he asked.

The Jew shifted, staring at the ground. "It is not rouge, Excellency. It is . . . my own blood."

"How resourceful." The general wrinkled his nose and tossed the stained handkerchief onto the snow. Then he pulled the Jew from the line. "You may show them that trick at Auschwitz."

Two hours passed in bitter cold while the general winnowed out those adults bound for the next train east. The rest would remain to take part in the Embellishment.

"Now, let me see the small ones."

At the general's order, hundreds of children were marched single file from the renovated "recreation center" to stand in front of the remaining Jews. Aric scanned the assembly and found Joseph, dressed in a brown wool suit and felt cap, standing toward the end of the line.

He shot another hostile glance at Hermann. The captain merely cocked a brow, his eyes gleaming. Aric ground his teeth and turned back to the general, who now examined the teeth, hair, and appendages of each boy and girl.

He finally reached Joseph. Aric held his breath. Perhaps Feldman had already forgotten what the boy looked like. *Leave your cap on, Joseph.*

"Smile for me, child."

The general spoke in a jovial voice. Joseph grinned up at him. "Ah, what nice teeth. You are the *Hausjunge?*"

Aric's hope evaporated. Joseph glanced over at him, then bobbed his head eagerly.

"Do you like working for Herr Kommandant?"

Another enthusiastic nod. "Ja, very much, Herr General."

"But he hasn't taught you manners?"

Joseph's expectant smile faded. He flashed an uncertain look at Aric and then back at the general. "Herr General?"

"Has he not taught you to remove your hat in the presence of an Oberstgruppenführer?"

Joseph snatched away the felt cap and bowed his head. "Please forgive my bad manners, Herr General," he whispered.

But the leather crop was already pressing his head to one side. "What is this?" the general asked. "Where is your ear?"

Aric's senses reeled. This wasn't happening . . .

"I . . . I lost it over a month ago, Herr General," the boy whimpered, keeping his eyes downcast.

"And no one has found it yet?" A loud guffaw shook the general's protruding belly. "Too bad, little Hausjunge." He nudged Joseph from the line toward the two guards.

Aric fisted the brass top of his cane. He wanted to hit something—Hermann, Feldman, both of them—even as the rational part of his brain warned caution. "Do you intend to take my houseboy away from me, Herr General?" he tried to cajole.

"Ja, and I commend you, Colonel. Your personal sacrifice in order to ensure the goals of the Reich will set a good example for soldiers and Jews alike."

"But, Herr General, surely you know how long it takes to train one of these Jews."

Feldman reached into the line and pulled out another boy, a shorter one with reddish-brown hair and gray eyes. "Teach this one. I am certain he'll be a quick learner." His challenging gaze seemed to bar any further argument. "Now, let me see the infirmary."

Leaning against his cane, Aric worked to draw breath. Feldman walked with Hermann toward the ghetto hospital, having dismissed the issue of Joseph's life like so much negligible paper work. He stared into the faces of those remaining Jews and saw relieved smiles pass between them. Relieved . . . and unaware.

Dread consumed him like a fever. Himmler had coined the "cleanup project" *Wolkenbrand*, or Firecloud, and Eichmann was going to ensure that Aric carried it out. At least those leaving for Auschwitz might have a chance at survival—

Liar. He glanced over at the Jews bound for Wednesday's train. Joseph stood among them. Aric's head began to pound as he spun away to follow the general. Eichmann would bury the evidence at Auschwitz, too. Just like Heydrich had done at Babi Yar . . .

His cane went flying through the air to land in a distant drift of snow.

26

*When this day is done, I will go to the king, even
though it is against the law.*

Esther 4:16

Stella finished typing her last letter as General Feldman
marched into the library. Aric followed. "There are still too
many unsuitable prisoners," the general growled. "I want them
all out of here on Wednesday's train."

"Of course, Herr General." Aric looked harassed and barely
tossed Stella a glance as the two men disappeared into his office.

Stella's insides twisted. Another train? Had something happened in the ghetto?

"Fräulein Muller!"

At the general's booming request, Stella grabbed her steno
pad and pencil and hurried into Aric's office. Herr Sausage sat
behind the massive mahogany desk. Aric stood at the barred
window. He didn't look at her. Stella's gnawing sense of alarm
increased. "Yes, Herr General?"

The general thrust a pocket-sized diary in her direction. "I
want you to type this list of entries, my dear. They must be sent
to our Führer in Berlin. Please sit and I will dictate a cover letter."

Stella took the chair in front of the desk. Before the general started, he called to Aric, "Where is your captain, Colonel? I want to speak to this man of the Judenrat now and rid myself of him before supper."

Morty was coming here? Again Stella looked toward Aric. What did they want with her uncle?

"Herr Kommandant, I have brought the Jew."

She twisted around to see Morty being dragged into the room by Hermann. His face still carried yellow bruises from Friday's beating, and his feet . . .

Stella bit the inside of her cheek to keep from crying out. His red, swollen ankles bulged from the tops of his shoes.

The general seemed equally distressed. "How do you expect the Red Cross to believe our ploy, Colonel von Schmidt? This one looks like he was hit by a train." He glared at Aric. "Did you suppose that a few cosmetics might make him look as convincing as the others?" He slapped his crop against the desk. "Bring me another!"

"Herr General, there is no one else." Aric moved toward the desk. "The other members of the Judenrat died in a recent outbreak of typhus. I haven't yet had time to interview replacements."

"You'd better find someone," the general ground out. "I want this . . . this mess"—he pointed at Morty—"on Wednesday's train."

No! Stella stifled a cry as her steno pad fell against her lap. She couldn't let her uncle go to Auschwitz! She edged forward in her seat. "Your pardon, Herr General, but I may be able to offer assistance—"

"That won't be necessary, Fräulein," Aric cut her off sharply.

"Let her speak, Colonel." The general eyed Stella with congenial amusement. "What do you propose, pretty one?"

"You spoke of cosmetics, Herr General. I . . . I am very good with them. I believe I can hide this man's bruises."

His gaze raked over her. "Yes, my dear, I imagine you are

good at many things." His expression then soured as he cast a negligent wave of his leather crop in Morty's direction. "But I doubt a little face powder and rouge will keep him on his feet."

"I believe, Herr General," Stella pleaded, "you have just given him the incentive to try his best."

A chortle escaped the portly man. "Perhaps the lovely Fräulein should pose as our Judenrat representative, eh, Colonel? She is clever as well as pretty." Then his eyes narrowed on her. "Why do you wish to go to all this trouble, Fräulein? It is after all just a Jew."

Aric drew up beside her. "I fear my secretary, like most women, suffers from a soft heart, Herr General."

"You are tenderhearted, then?" the general said with a grin. "You speak of incentives, Fräulein. What is mine? Giving in to this compassionate whim of yours?" His gloved finger trailed slowly back and forth along the leather crop.

"Why . . ." Stella braved her best smile. "You would have my utmost admiration, Herr General."

The general leaned forward and chuckled. "And who could resist such a prize?"

Stella could sense Aric's anger beside her, but she didn't care. Nothing mattered except saving her uncle.

"Very well." The general rose from his chair and turned to Morty, all joviality gone. "You had better be waltzing by Wednesday morning, Jude," he said, "or you will be on that train."

Aric barely tasted his food at supper. Occasionally he shot blistering glances at Stella, who knew she'd either upset him or realized her folly because she seemed to share his lack of appetite.

The general sat at the opposite end of the table, plowing industriously through a bowl of *Leberknödel* meatballs.

Licentious pig. Aric envisioned Stella screaming in the middle of the night because the general had broken into her room and tried to ravish her. Even now, the fat man's beady gaze bore into her. Aric stabbed at his fried potatoes with his fork. He wasn't going to let anyone—general, field marshal, even the Führer himself—lay so much as a hand on her.

There was the other issue to deal with, as well. Sooner or later, Stella would question him about the boy. Aric wished to avoid the conversation until tomorrow. By then he hoped to convince the general to change his mind. "Perhaps, Herr General, you would care to take a drive into town after supper?" he said.

The gluttonous man glanced up and mumbled through a mouthful of food, "The ghetto?"

Aric forced a smile and shook his head. "I'll take you to Litomerice. Major Lindberg runs the camp in that city and tells me they have a fine *Schenke* where we can have a drink." He winked at the general. "And perhaps a little entertainment."

The general paused, a meatball halfway to his lips. A slow smile transformed his features.

Take the bait, you degenerate. "After all you've accomplished today, Herr General, surely an evening off will not hurt?"

Setting down his fork, the general wiped his mouth with the napkin tucked in his collar. He cast an appraising look at Stella, who seemed to have enough sense to ignore him and keep her attention on her plate—before he shot a wink back at Aric. "I believe I'd enjoy a drink, Schmidt." Too eagerly the general vaulted from his chair, the buttons at his midriff catching a corner of the tablecloth and clanging the silver. "I'll be ready after I make a call to Berlin. Why don't you ask your captain to join us? He can drive."

"Of course, Herr General." Aric also rose. "I'll go and make the arrangements. Please use the telephone in my office."

When the general disappeared, Aric moved to stand beside Stella's chair. "Sweet little idiot, what were you thinking this afternoon? Do you realize the game you play with that lecherous ox?"

She looked up at him with frightened eyes. He had to struggle to hold on to his anger.

"I can distract him tonight, but that won't stop him from trying to get to you tomorrow—"

She stole the rest of his words with a finger to his lips. "I'm sorry. I only wanted to save the old man from the train."

He grasped her hand. "By saving that old Jew one more day, you made a deal with the devil." He leaned in so that his nose touched hers. "And the pound of flesh he has in mind will be very much alive and waiting for him in his bed." Satisfied to see her look of shock, he straightened. "Finally you understand."

"I . . . I realize what I did this afternoon was foolish—"

"And dangerous."

She nodded. "What can I do now?"

Hearing her anxiety, Aric squeezed her fingers. "He'll have to get past me. You might still consider sleeping in my room."

"And where will you sleep? I told you, I won't be your mistress."

He'd half expected her response. Still, her guarded look had the ability to sting. He smiled past his injured pride. "Marry me, then."

Stunned silence fell between them. Aric, shocked by his own words, saw the solution to his dilemma. He could get her safely out of Theresienstadt before Friday, and perhaps the boy, too.

"Be my wife," he urged, turning her chair so that she faced him.

Her face whitened. "M-marry you?"

"Yes." For an instant, he considered—and discarded—the notion of merely sending her away with the Red Cross. She would still be alone and unprotected. If they married, she could have a new life in Switzerland, with access to his money and under his legal protection. "It's the only way."

Before she might object, he pulled her out of the chair and kissed her with a desperate passion meant to overwhelm her. Time was short; he had to make certain she never found out about Wolkenbrand or his part in it. She began to relax in his arms, meeting his passion with her own. Aric nearly crowed in triumph.

"We can marry within two days, in Litomerice," he murmured between kisses. "Thursday I'll arrange for you to leave with the Red Cross. I have enough funds so that you can accompany them to Switzerland and wait for me. At least until this business is finished."

―――――

Stella's senses reeled as much from his marriage proposal as his intoxicating kiss. She struggled to marshal her thoughts— and her emotions. "I cannot marry you," she said finally.

"Yes, you can." He dipped his head to kiss her neck.

She closed her eyes and shivered at the contact. "We hardly know each other," she said weakly. "We need more time."

That gained his attention. He pierced her with a look. "We're at war, Süsse. Time is a consideration we do not have. As for our length of acquaintance . . ." His sober expression softened. "I know what I've wanted for a long time now."

Want. Not love. Stella knew it wasn't enough, and some deeper part of her grieved for him, grieved for them both. Yet when he kissed her again, she surrendered. For a wild moment she imagined being swept away from the war and its lingering ghosts of death and disease.

Yet Stella knew she couldn't abandon Morty and Joseph. And whether he knew it or not, Aric needed her, too. "What I want isn't the point." She drew back from him. "There are so many issues at stake."

"What issues?"

His sharp gaze made her falter. "I can't leave without Joseph—"

"Or the old man, or every other Jew in that ghetto!" He gripped her arms and held her. "Do you love them so much that you would turn down my offer?"

"Nein!" Alarmed at the turn of their conversation, Stella

tried a different tack. "I just imagined my wedding day would be a beautiful ceremony with flowers, a cake . . . a honeymoon. Not some hurried affair among strangers, within sight of a concentration camp, in the middle of a war."

"I do apologize for the lack of amenities." His regret seemed real enough as he relaxed his grip on her. "But you have until Wednesday to get used to the idea of being my wife. Then we'll go to Litomerice to be married. On Thursday you must leave with the Swiss."

Her panic rose. "Why can't I stay? I don't understand—"

"The war is winding down. I don't want you here when . . ." He paused, his features tense. "It won't be safe. This is the last opportunity I'll have to get you out."

She couldn't imagine leaving her uncle and the boy behind. "You could protect me," she persisted. "I trust you—"

"No!" His loud bark made her jump. Then more gently he said, "Please, my dove, do this for me. I won't rest until I know you're safe."

"What about Joseph?"

He hesitated, but before Stella could demand an answer, the creak of library doors signaled the general's return. "We'll talk later," Aric said. "I must fetch Captain Hermann. Remember to lock your door tonight." He kissed her once more and left.

Stella wandered into the living room to stand in front of the blazing hearth. But the flames did little to assuage the cold that permeated her.

Aric had given her no choice. He'd simply commanded that she wed him and leave Theresienstadt as if she were one of his soldiers. Never mind that the ceremony would be a farce. Stella Muller didn't exist, except on paper. And her uncle would never approve of a Jew marrying a Gentile. No, this couldn't possibly be God's plan to save them all. If she left with the Red Cross, her uncle would slip beyond her reach. And Joseph . . .

251

The house seemed quiet except for the crackle of flames. Too quiet. She left the hearth to seek out the boy, going first to his room at the back of the house.

Helen sat beside the softly snoring Rand, her fingers moving rapidly over a beaded rosary.

Stella felt the first stirrings of fear, seeing the housekeeper's normally stout features drawn with worry. "Joseph's not in the house, is he?" Before Helen could indicate her answer, Stella said, "Did he come back from the ghetto this afternoon?"

Helen shook her head, gripping the black beads tighter. Stella darted from the room toward the kitchen. Joseph was probably freezing!

Reaching for her coat on the peg, she hesitated. The idea of entering the ghetto on her own terrified her. What if they locked her inside with the others?

Perhaps the guard outside knew what had become of her boy. Stella shrugged into her coat, then snatched Helen's hat from the wall peg before opening the back door.

A blast of bitter cold stung her cheeks as she stepped onto the porch.

"Achtung!" shouted a voice from the darkness.

Stella startled. "Herr Corporal . . . Martin?"

The soldier's figure took shape in the inky haze. "Fräulein Muller?" He stepped onto the porch, his Mauser submachine gun poised to shoot. "Is something wrong?"

"Joseph's m-missing," she said through chattering teeth. "Do you know w-where he is?"

The soldier relaxed his grip on the gun. "The Hausjunge sleeps in the ghetto tonight, Fräulein."

"Why?" Stella imagined little Joseph, cold and frightened. "Is he all right?"

Martin gave a snort. "I doubt it. Not after Herr Captain finished with him."

"What are you saying?" she cried, as terrifying memories of

252

Anna engulfed her. She thought of Joseph's missing ear. "What has the captain done to him?"

"Enough to make him regret his mischief." Martin scrutinized her. "Why should you care, anyway? He's just a Jude."

Just a Jew. Stella's whole body began to shake, this time with fury—an all-encompassing rage that eclipsed her fear. Her little boy could be near death.

She advanced on Martin. "Take me to him."

Martin set his jaw. "You cannot enter the ghetto, Fräulein. Now go inside and wait for Herr Kommandant's return."

Stella was unfazed. "You *will* take me to him, now, Corporal. Or shall I tell Herr Kommandant that you were paid to shirk your post the night Koch and Brucker attempted his murder?"

Martin stepped back, his alarm visible even in the dim light from the kitchen. "How did you know?"

"Do we have an understanding?" Chin raised, she waited, her heart drumming so fast she could hardly breathe. He would either argue—or shoot her.

Martin did neither. "Follow me," he growled, and spun away into the darkness.

Stella closed the door and hurried after him, trekking the snowy half-kilometer distance to the ghetto. By the time they reached the main gate, her feet felt frozen. So did her courage.

She stood behind Martin as he addressed the guard, "Let us pass. We are here on Herr Kommandant's business."

A young pocked-faced sentry sat in the lighted booth. He eyed Stella while chewing on the inside of his lip. "Herr Kommandant sent her?" He glanced back at Martin.

"That's what I said. Now open the gate."

The barred doors swung wide to let them enter.

The night air was cold and crisp as they walked along the cobbled Marktplatz of the ghetto. Silence had descended along with dusk. No streetlights were lit. Only a three-quarter moon illuminated the make-believe village with its festive storefronts and painted park benches.

A music pavilion built of pine had been added to the town's square since her last visit, and inside the park a snowman in stocking cap and vest seemed to dance among the shadows of barren birch trees. Stella burrowed deeper into her coat. Where did her uncle sleep tonight? Was he warm enough? Were his feet healing?

"The boy will be in the children's quarters." Corporal Martin made a turn and halted at the arched entrance of a two-story brick building.

"Not the infirmary?"

Stella felt only mild relief when he shook his head. "In there." He pointed toward the murk of an unlit hallway. "I'll give you ten minutes."

"Twenty," she shot back.

"Ten. Then I'm leaving."

She glared at him before climbing the steps and walking through the open entrance. Groping her way through the blackness, Stella ran her palms along icy stone walls until she found an opening to her right. She stepped inside.

The sounds of soft breathing mingled with an occasional whimper and moan. Stella felt overpowered by smells of mildew and unwashed bodies, vomit, and the briny stench of urine. Moonlight flooded the cavernous chamber from a pair of windows across the room. A dozen rows of beds, each stacked four high, stood along either wall.

Small dark shapes were huddled two and three to a bed. Stella crept forward and whispered into the dark, "Joseph?"

"Mama?" A thin, fearful voice cried from the shadows.

"Joseph . . . is that you?"

One of the shapes in the bottom bunk nearest her shifted. Stella moved close and saw that a little girl with shiny dark hair had kicked her covers onto the floor. With eyes still heavy from sleep, she shivered violently against the thin mattress.

Stella knelt to retrieve the blanket.

"Mama!"

Tiny arms like bird's wings shot out to encircle her neck. Stella reached to embrace the little girl. Her skinny torso and limbs stank of lice powder and sour clothing.

"Mama, I had a bad dream," she whimpered. "Hold me."

Stella gently rocked her. "Shhhh, it's all right." The child felt so small and fragile against her. "Have you seen a boy . . . Joseph?" she asked.

But the child merely tightened her grip on Stella, silently shifting her nighttime monsters onto adult shoulders.

While Stella held her, she called out to the room, "Joseph, are you here?"

Only a few muffled sobs answered. Beds creaked with restless children, perhaps fighting the same nightmares. Stella wanted to protect them, but felt helpless to do so.

And she still had to find Joseph.

"You must go back to sleep now, maideleh," she whispered to the little girl in her arms.

"Mama, don't leave me!" the child cried anew.

"You must be a brave girl for Mama." Stella's voice trembled as she extricated the tiny arms from around her neck and put the child into bed. Then she covered her with the blanket and gently massaged her limbs until the child's tremors subsided. She'd done this so many times with Anna.

"I'll stay with you awhile," she said in a hushed voice. "Sleep now, and dream good dreams for me, all right?"

The child closed her eyes, and Stella tucked the blanket up beneath her chin.

"Unter . . . Yideles . . . vigele . . ."

She began to croon the lyrics of an old Yiddish lullaby.

"Shteyt . . . a klor-vays . . . tsigele . . ."

At last the whimpering ceased, the restless sounds growing still in the darkness. Stella sang on as she brushed back the matted dark locks from the child's temples.

"Dos vet sayn dayn . . . baruf Rozhinkes mit man-
dlen . . . shlof zhe, Yidele, shlof . . ."

Stella rose and moved away from the drowsing child. She continued to hum the sweet lullaby while she quietly searched each bunk for Joseph.

She didn't find him.

"Fräulein, we must leave!"

Martin's shout echoed from down the hall. Stella only hummed louder. She refused to give in to despair as she scanned the rows of huddled forms. Loath to abandon the children, she knew if she didn't, Martin would leave her behind.

She neared the door when the little girl sobbed, "Mama . . ."

"You must sleep now, *Liebling*," Stella whispered around the knot in her throat.

Shading her eyes against the beam of Martin's flashlight, she emerged from the arched opening.

"Are you satisfied now, Fräulein?"

Stella fought an urge to slap his face. She hated these Nazi monsters—for their cruelty, their self-proclaimed superiority, for treating little children worse than dogs. "Joseph wasn't inside," she bit out.

"What took you so long?"

"It was dark. I could have used that." She glared at his flashlight. So much precious time wasted in trying to make out each child's face. "We must try another place. Are you certain he's not in the infirmary?"

"He wasn't there earlier. Now, we need to get back—"

"I must see him!"

"Fräulein, it could take hours to find him." Martin sounded

exasperated. "And even you wouldn't dare to be caught inside the ghetto when Herr Kommandant returns."

He was right. Aric would be furious. Still . . . "I thought we had an agreement, Corporal?"

"I brought you here, as agreed," he shot back. Switching off the flashlight, he attached it to the strap at his shoulder. "If I hear any news about the Hausjunge, I'll let you know. It's the best I can do. Now come. Herr Kommandant and the others could return at any time."

Stella plodded after the corporal toward the main gate. She'd promised to protect Joseph, yet she'd left him behind. Left them all . . .

Her chest ached, remembering the little girl's thin blanket, the smell of her clothes. The lice that Stella couldn't see but knew infested her bed.

How could she save them? To speak out about the injustice she'd witnessed would only reveal her whereabouts tonight. Aric's anger would be nothing compared to losing the general's latest boon—her chance to save Morty.

Stella ground her teeth in frustration. She must keep silent . . . and suffer the shame of her own impotence.

But Joseph was another matter, she decided fiercely. Aric wanted her safely tucked away in Switzerland? Well, she wanted the boy. And despite God's plan or her uncle's approval, she would agree to anything so long as the child was returned to her.

Even marriage.

27

Having learned who Mordecai's people were . . .
Haman looked for a way to destroy . . . the Jews. . . .

Esther 3:6

TUESDAY, MARCH 7, 1944

"Are you ready to give me a name?"

Dawn had not yet shown itself as Morty stood in Hermann's office. The pain in his ankles had wiped away the last dregs of sleep. "Herr Captain, I have no name to give you—"

"What a relief it must have been yesterday when Herr Kommandant's woman once again came to your rescue." Hermann paused. "Provided, of course, you can still walk." He rose from his chair and picked up the thick wooden dowel lying across his desk. He moved closer to Morty. "I could arrange for another treatment."

Morty lowered his head and stood perfectly still. The hatred oozing from Hermann burned his nostrils. He tried to control his fear with quick, shallow breaths, making himself dizzy while he waited for the blow.

The beating didn't come. Hermann instead surprised him by saying, "I've decided against it. A man of your courage would no doubt walk on bloody stumps if necessary." He paused.

Morty could feel his stare. "I just gave you a compliment, Jew. Have you nothing to say?"

Morty swallowed. "Yes, of course. Thank you, Herr Captain."

"I've also found an inducement to make you much more responsive to my questions." He went to the door and snapped his fingers. "Sonntag, bring me the boy!"

Queasiness settled in Morty's gut. *Nein* . . .

A shuffling of feet sounded behind him. "Leave him, Corporal." When the door closed, Hermann said, "Look at him, Jew."

Morty swung around—and choked back a cry. Bruised welts ravaged Joseph's face; he eyed Morty through two swollen slits along either side of his nose. A cut on his lower lip wept, trailing blood into the cleft of his small chin.

"As much as I discourage this type of violence, I can see it's proving effective." Hermann grabbed a fistful of Joseph's jacket and hauled him forward. "Now, you will tell me what I want to know. It would be a shame to see this boy die before Wednesday's train."

Morty's jaw clenched to the point of pain. He ached to knock Hermann's teeth to the back of his throat. Instead he caught and held the boy's gaze. A confession might spare Joseph only as far as Auschwitz. Still, he had to try. "You know I set fire to your office, Herr Captain. I also took back my . . . your Cross." He nearly spat the words.

"Where is that Cross, by the way?" The captain sounded bored as he held the child.

"Lost," Morty lied. "It must have dropped in the snow . . . when I escaped." He shifted to ease the ache in his feet. "I've gone back to search for it several times, but cannot find it."

"And our potato thief?" Hermann lifted the scrawny boy off his feet. "He warned Herr Kommandant of the attack?"

Morty went still. Even faced with death, he would never implicate the boy or Hadassah. "I don't know what you mean, Herr Captain—"

"I grow tired of this, Jew. You and this one were hiding in my office when Koch and Brucker had their little discussion."

Morty dared to raise his head and look the captain in the eye. "I was in your office. The boy wasn't involved."

Hermann seemed to consider his words. "Then you must have told him what you overheard. And he warned Herr Kommandant."

Morty felt at a loss. If he tried to acquit Joseph, he would endanger Hadassah, and the boy would still be punished. His involvement as go-between would not be overlooked. He sank to his knees, ignoring the ache in his joints. "Please." He glanced at Joseph's limp form, then at Hermann. "I'll do anything—"

"The truth!" Hermann gave the boy a hard shake. "Swear to your God and tell me what I want to know!"

Pain stabbed at Morty with each breath, and he grabbed for the edge of the desk. There seemed no hope, after all. His vision, a foolish dream . . .

"It . . . it was me," Joseph said. His voice came out more croak than whisper.

"Go on."

"I told him," the boy added while Hermann dangled him like a puppet. "Herr Kommandant has been good . . . to me." He raised his bloodied chin. "I was glad Brucker died."

"Mmmm, yes, I imagine you were." Hermann eyed the boy's scar. "What exactly did you say to Herr Kommandant?"

Joseph turned swollen eyes to Morty. "I told him . . . when I was moving boxes from the Krematorium, that I overheard Brucker tell Sergeant Koch that he was angry about having to eat the Jew's food. That he was going to get even with Herr Kommandant." The boy ran his tongue across his bloody lip.

"Nothing else?" Hermann demanded.

Joseph shook his head. "I could not say more without . . . without Herr Kommandant wanting to know about the fire."

"I always suspected you were a clever Jew." Hermann grinned. "Sonntag!"

The corporal reappeared. Hermann handed off the child by his collar, like a rat caught eating stores. "Take him to the infirmary."

Morty rose and watched the boy being carried away by the soldier. Rage battled with his pride at Joseph's quickness of mind and his courage.

"I want cards for twenty-five hundred by noon today, Elder," Hermann said, returning to his desk. "Include yesterday's selections as well as those still in the infirmary. Everyone must go on tomorrow's train—no exceptions."

Twenty-five hundred souls. Morty swayed on his feet.

Hermann flashed him a sharp look. "We both know there was more to that little discussion in my office last Friday, don't we? Perhaps the boy knows, as well? But then, after tomorrow, he'll no longer be a problem." He leaned across the desk. "Which leaves only you."

He looked down at Morty's bludgeoned feet. "By the looks of it, we'll be adding your name to the list, too. I admit Herr Kommandant's woman has many fascinating *attributes*"—he eyed Morty with a smirk—"but she's no reincarnated messiah who can make you walk again."

Morty's eyes burned. *Dear God, give me strength . . .*

"Maybe I'll put you in with the boy. That way you can enjoy the stench of the same car. You can watch his face, knowing you take him—all of them—to meet their death. They'll probably kill you before you even get there." Hermann shrugged. "And if they don't, the gas will. I hear it's running all the time now."

~ 28 ~

Esther again pleaded with the king, falling at his feet and weeping.

Esther 8:3

A loud knock at her door brought Stella straight up out of another nightmare. This one had been about Joseph. She hadn't been able to save him.

Stella tried to catch her breath, blinking against the drab light of morning. She lay in bed, still in her clothes, the black wool suit she'd worn yesterday now rumpled beneath a blanket—one she didn't recognize.

Someone had been in her room. Aric?

She grabbed up the music box from her nightstand. Sweet notes of the "Blue Danube Waltz" filled the air as she stared inside at the pearl necklace nestled undisturbed.

Stella eased out a breath. Morty's Grand Cross, and his messages, were still safe.

Another rap on the door. "Fräulein?"

"Joseph!" Stella replaced the music box on the nightstand and bounded out of bed. "Come in!"

She flung the door wide with a burst of relieved laughter. "I was so worried . . ."

The red-haired boy was a stranger. His deep-set eyes stared at her, gray like the leaden sky outside. Not brown. Her pulse hammered too fast, making her dizzy. "Who are you?"

"Simon Kessel, Fräulein," he said, looking up at her nervously. "I was told to come wake you."

She barely heard him. Grabbing his arms, she tried not to shake him. "Where is Joseph?"

Simon shook his head, eyes wide with fear. Stella wanted to scream. Last night was real. She'd gone to the ghetto to find Joseph and failed. She'd tried to stay awake, to question Aric.

She let the boy go and searched out her shoes. Then, snatching her wig from its stand in the bathroom, Stella sailed out into the hall and downstairs. Simon ran to keep up with her.

On the main floor she passed the painting of Thaur as she did every morning. Today, however, the light was wrong. "What time is it?" She turned to Simon.

He shrugged. "Afternoon, Fräulein."

"Why was I not wakened earlier? Herr Kommandant will be furious—"

"But, Fräulein, he told me not to get you up until now!" Simon started backing away from her.

"Where is he?"

The boy jabbed a finger toward the library. Stella hurried in that direction.

Inside her office, she halted at the sight of the familiar burlap sack on her desk.

"Ah, Fräulein Muller, you're feeling better?"

Her head shot up. General Feldman came out of Aric's office. "Why . . . yes, Herr General." She smiled to hide her confusion. "Much better."

"Gut, gut. Perhaps a little too much excitement last night?"

Stella went still. Did he know about her trip to the ghetto?

"I understand congratulations are in order, eh?" His chuckle sounded strained.

"Congratulations . . ." She felt more dazed and vulnerable by the moment.

"Your upcoming marriage, Fräulein." His snow-white brows narrowed. "Is this not so?"

Angry at Aric's heavy-handedness—he'd even told the general!—she considered denying it. But as Herr Sausage approached her, he reminded Stella of an overfed bear licking its chops. She would go along with Aric's madness. "Of course, Herr General. Thank you."

He stood so close that she could make out each embossed line of the gold eagle decorating his peaked cap. "Too bad you chose to be the wife of a mere Standartenführer." His tone held mild irritation. "You should have held out for a general, like myself." His gold eagle took flight then as he doffed the hat and leaned into her. "My consolation shall be a kiss from the bride, eh?"

He even smelled of sausage. Disgusted, Stella held her breath to keep from gagging. As he dipped his head to kiss her, she was quick to give him her cheek. His tongue felt reptilian against her skin. "You are too kind, Herr General," she managed through clenched teeth.

He straightened, his dark eyes chilling. "And you are a tease, Fräulein," he said without humor. "Perhaps I should reconsider my generosity of yesterday."

"Please, don't take offense, Herr General." Stella panicked as she scrambled to think of an excuse to appease him. "It's just . . . I am about to be married to one man and do not think it proper to be kissing another."

"As it should be," interjected a masculine voice behind them. Aric leaned against the doorjamb. Stella wilted in relief.

The general turned slowly. Aric started toward him. "First you take away the help, and now I find you trying to steal my fiancée?" He flashed a smile that failed to reach his eyes. "If you're not careful, Herr General, I'm going to think you don't like me."

The general let out a bark of laughter. "Ah, Schmidt, can you blame me?" He sidled away from Stella a respectable distance before adding, "You have stolen the prized plum from the tree."

"Indeed."

Stella basked in the warmth of Aric's gaze as he came to stand beside her. Taking her hand, he squeezed her fingers tightly. "Are you feeling better, Süsse? You were quite ill after supper last night."

"Yes, much better," she answered, taking her cue. She was grateful now, for his concocted story had kept the philandering general from coming to her room last night. Aric had likely announced their engagement for the same reason—a union she hadn't yet agreed to.

"Good." He pressed her fingers a second time, more gently. "We're leaving for the ghetto. Captain Hermann has arranged a preview rehearsal of Verdi's *Requiem*."

"Would you care to join us?" the general inquired. "The Führer himself told me it is a favorite of Herr Reichsführer Himmler." He eyed her speculatively. "And perhaps tonight you will feel well enough to share a glass of *Bier* in Litomerice? We are in need of another pretty face at our table."

"Unfortunately, Herr General, I must burden my secretary with another task." Aric nodded toward the burlap bag on her desk. "I'm afraid she must work most of the night."

Stella pulled away to eye him accusingly. "Lists for Wednesday's train?"

His gaze clashed with hers. "Pardon, Herr General, but perhaps you would give me a moment with Fräulein?"

"A lovers' quarrel?" The general's tone was mocking. "I'll be in the car. Don't keep me waiting, Schmidt."

Aric rounded on her after the general had gone. "You will not take that tone with me, Stella. I need the list of names typed tonight—the train leaves early tomorrow."

"Why must I do it? Surely Herr Captain has requisitioned a new typewriter by now."

"You still question my orders?" His tone pierced her like shards of ice. "Not a good beginning for husband and wife, I think." Then he seemed to read her distress and said more gently, "Typing the lists was Sergeant Koch's duty. And it would take Corporal Sonntag days to accomplish what you can do in hours. I regret allowing you to sleep so late, but now you must stay and work until the task is finished."

"Aric, please don't—"

"Nein!" He propelled himself away from her. "The only thing I wish to hear from you is that you've come to terms with my proposal. In fact, I should think you might be grateful at being rescued from such a fate as that one." He jerked his head toward the double doors where the general had just departed.

Stella clamped her mouth shut.

"Not yet?" he said. "Then I suggest you get to work. I'll be back in a few hours."

He turned to leave. Stella's heart felt as if it might break. He seemed a stranger to her. "Where is Joseph?" she called out.

"In the ghetto," he said without looking back.

"Why?" Her anger resonated in the single word. "What have you done to him?"

He swung around. "I said you will not take that tone with me!" More quietly he added, "He's well enough, back with his own kind."

"I don't understand—"

"Enough, Stella." Aric held up a hand. "Please. I am weary of this battle with you. Joseph is no longer your concern."

Stella's insides felt frozen down to her bones. The world she lived in, such as it was, had fallen apart. "Aric, what's happening?" she whispered.

He hesitated, then said hoarsely, "The end, my dove."

Before she could question him further, he disappeared behind the library doors.

Joseph was never coming back.

Stella sat unmoving in her chair, deafened by the silence of the empty library. Aric, the man for whom she cared deeply—no, the man she loved—had simply let the child go.

She stared blindly across the room at the mahogany bookshelves. Titles such as Hitler's *Mein Kampf* and Streicher's *Protocols of Zion* stood neatly beside stacks of the propaganda newspaper *Das Schwarze Korps*. She thought of Aric's copy of Tennyson, a book outlawed by the Nazis, yet one he'd seen fit to make an exception.

Aric would risk breaking rules over a book. Why not a boy?

"A fool is the lamb who runs with wolves." Another of Marta's favorite sayings. Stella's eyes burned. What an idiot she'd been to believe Aric was any different from his brethren. Or perhaps she'd just been a coward.

She turned to look at the heap of brown burlap on her desk—a mountain for the sheer effort it took to reach and open the sack. Stella retrieved the first bundle of cards. Her hands shook as she fed fresh paper and carbon into the typewriter carriage.

She'd obviously read too much into Aric's tender smiles, his kisses. The affection he'd shown to Joseph and Helen, his friendship with Rand, were simply a ruse to confuse and ensnare her. How could she forget Nazis enjoyed playing such games?

Animosity hardened in her like icicles hanging from the eaves. She grabbed the top card from the stack, wishing now she'd firmly rejected Aric's proposal last night; it would have saved her the trouble of refusing him tomorrow.

"No . . ." Shock hit her like a fist as she reread the name on the card. "Noooo!" Stella doubled over in her chair as though cut in two. "Please, God," she groaned, her head shaking back and forth in denial, "not my kaddishel. Not my baby boy . . ."

She gasped for air, grieving noiselessly in the quiet room. Afternoon shadows had begun falling across the carpeted floor before she finally roused herself, exhausted and spent, to stagger from the library toward the kitchen.

Helen stood angled in front of the stove, her pink floral neckerchief lending color to the otherwise drab uniform. The rich scent of hot chocolate filled the room as she turned from the pot she was stirring to glance at Stella.

"They've taken him!" She held up the white card to prove her words.

The spoon clattered to the floor. Helen rushed to her, wiping reddened hands against her stained apron. She snatched the card from Stella. Her squared features turned ashen.

"Joseph leaves on the train for Auschwitz tomorrow. What can we do?"

Helen's eyes welled with tears. She withdrew from beneath her colorful scarf the black rosary beads Stella had spied the night before. She tried offering them to Stella.

"He needs more than that," she said bitterly. Why had she ever supposed God would speak to her? Even in a whisper? "Joseph needs Aric, but Aric refuses to help."

Helen's expression crumpled. Clutching the rosary to her breast, she walked past Stella to the living room and sank onto a leather chair beside the hearth. Stella followed, eyeing the beads gliding rapidly through her work-roughened hands. She watched the housekeeper's lips move in soundless prayer. "Do you really believe God will save him?"

Her near shout rose above the crackling of logs in the hearth and the clicking of black beads. "Will God rescue a single boy . . . when He saves no one else in that ghetto?"

The housekeeper paused in prayer, lifting her face to Stella.

Stella held up the white card. "This is all Joseph's life is worth: a scrap of paper with his name on it . . . and a number like this one." She jerked up a sleeve to expose her wrist.

Helen's eyes widened.

"I know you're loyal to Aric, but he has made his decision.

Now you must choose." Stella ripped up the card. "I will not let those monsters kill my boy."

Tossing the bits of paper into the flames, she watched them blacken and curl. When she glanced back at Helen, the housekeeper's eyes glistened in the light from the hearth. "I will save him," Stella said fiercely.

Helen rose from the chair. Before Stella knew what was happening, the older woman pulled her into an awkward embrace.

Stella felt strength in the arms that held her . . . and faith, even as she yearned for her own. "Thank you," she whispered.

"I was telling Colonel von Schmidt this afternoon that he is fortunate to have such a disciplined officer in the captain here," General Feldman said to the table at large. "We could use more like him at the Chancellery."

"Captain Hermann *has* been quite an asset to the Reich," Major Lindberg said with perfunctory obeisance. Seated to the left of the general, he gave the giggling Dita beside him a playful squeeze. Marenka, heavily rouged, clad in royal blue satin and minus one Lieutenant Neubach, nestled close to the general's right. "What say you, Colonel?"

For the second night in a row, Aric all but ignored their conversation. He turned from scanning the sea of couples inside The Raging Boar to smile benignly at the major.

Feldman raised his glass to Hermann. "As I see it, you have only one conspicuous flaw, Captain." He paused to chug down half his beer, then wiped his foamy lip with an edge of checkered tablecloth. "You still do not drink with us!"

His loud guffaw erupted into an even louder belch—producing more laughter as well as giggling from the women.

When Feldman finally recovered, he rubbed at his teary eyes and tried offering the captain the remains of his glass of beer.

Hermann put up a hand of refusal.

"What kind of German are you that you do not like Bier?" Feldman demanded.

"Herr General, as I explained last night, the roads are icy. Since I am driving, I feel obligated to stay sober."

The general loosed a snort, his glass wavering in the air. "You see, Colonel? A remarkable man!"

Aric gripped the handle of his mug and shot his captain a disparaging glance. Hermann had wormed his way into Feldman's overindulged senses, just as he'd made certain the boy would go on tomorrow's train.

His own efforts to convince the general otherwise had merely increased the friction between them—as evidenced in Feldman's current pursuit of his captain's favor. "I agree, Herr General. Captain Hermann is always full of surprises," he said dryly.

Feldman set down his glass with a heavy thud. "I believe all is in readiness for Thursday. Herr Reichsführer will be thrilled with the *Requiem* performance we saw this afternoon. And thanks to your captain's efficiency here, the discrepancies I noted have been taken care of to my satisfaction."

Leaning toward Major Lindberg, Feldman confided in a loud whisper, "With the war going so badly for us right now, success in creating the illusion of a Paradiesghetto at Theresienstadt is critical. If things were to go sour, well . . ."

"I'm certain all will go as planned, Herr General." The major offered up his glass for a toast. "To success."

The two women joined him. "Success!" they chorused.

The general raised his glass and beamed. "I believe our Führer will be pleased." Then he slapped the tabletop with his palm. "In fact, I will telephone my report to Berlin in the morning, before I leave for Prague." His eyes narrowed on Aric. "It will be a shame to miss your nuptials, Colonel. But I'll be back on Thursday . . . to witness the radiance in your beautiful bride, eh?"

Hearing the general's mocking tone, Aric smiled over the

rim of his glass. "Like a beacon on a mountain, Herr General," he said.

"You're getting married, Herr Colonel? Congratulations!" Lindberg said in pleased surprise. "Who is this lucky woman?"

"His lovely secretary," the general supplied coolly.

"Fräulein Muller?" The major turned to Dita and winked. "She has thrown our poor captain over for a colonel, then?"

"She has, Major," Aric responded through a burst of female laughter. He turned to Hermann. "I hope there are no hard feelings, Captain?"

"None, Herr Kommandant." Hermann still looked more surprised than angry. "Where will this event take place?"

"Here, in Litomerice, with a private ceremony at noon tomorrow."

"In a matter of hours, Schmidt will lay claim to the most beautiful woman in all of Europe." The general took another swallow of beer.

Aric caught Marenka's frown. Feldman had been much more attentive to the buxom, dark-haired beauty last night. "Surely you take exception to the lovely woman beside you, Herr General?" he asked.

Like a petulant child, the general slammed down his glass. "I don't care all that much for brunettes, Colonel." His bleary-eyed resentment bore into Aric. "I much prefer redheads."

Aric masked his irritation and shot a quick glance at his watch. "It's getting late. I suggest we adjourn for the evening. Herr General, if you are ready . . . ?"

Feldman seemed to collect himself and rose from his chair. They all followed suit. Aric felt relieved to end another evening with the group. "What time will you load the train tomorrow?" he asked Hermann.

"One o'clock, Herr Kommandant, but if that is inconvenient—"

"Nein, I should arrive back at the ghetto by then."

"See that all is ready, Colonel," the general said, his tone more sober than before. "I'll arrive with the delegation on Thursday morning, eight o'clock sharp. That way the Red Cross will see everything fresh." Surprisingly his mouth curved into a rueful grin. "I trust by then you and your bride will be in some condition to greet us, eh?" He held up his glass one more time. "To your future."

The others raised their glasses, echoing the sentiment. For the first time in a long while, Aric allowed himself to hope. Tomorrow he would marry Stella. By Thursday night she would be well on her way safely to Switzerland. His bride . . .

Tightness edged his throat as he too lifted his glass. "To the future."

29

She sent clothes for him to put on instead of his sackcloth. . . .

Esther 4:4

WEDNESDAY, MARCH 8, 1944

Watery morning light seeped in through the kitchen window's sparkling panes, illuminating the shriveled lump of a man who sat on the footstool and faced her.

He was like a stranger to Stella. Bruised shadows hung beneath his eyes, and his skin wore the sickly, yellow cast of jaundice. She mourned the sight of him, ravaged more by hunger and exposure than Captain Hermann's abuse. There was a time when his face had been ruddy, his eyes and mouth creased with laugh lines from smiling too often at her childhood antics.

"You may start anytime, Fräulein. No doubt you are eager to prepare for your own wedding."

The general's annoyed tone sounded from the kitchen doorway. Corporal Martin stood beside him. "I leave you to your efforts while I go and speak with your future husband."

Stella glimpsed her uncle's shocked expression. "I will do my very best, Herr General."

"Let's hope it is good enough." He departed on that subtle

warning, while the corporal moved to position himself behind Morty.

Stella continued to study her uncle . . . or what remained of him. Beside her on the tiled counter lay pressed powder, grease paint, brushes—a magician's bag of tricks that would hopefully transform him from the general's "train wreck" into a healthy, happy Jew suitable for parading in front of the Red Cross.

Reaching for the foundation paint, she noticed her hands shook. Why? Hadn't she become an expert at covering up the truth?

Yesterday she'd worked into the night typing deportation lists for her masters and sending "undesirable Jews" to their graves. Pretending to be something she wasn't so as to eat good food and sleep in a soft bed. Falling so far from grace as to love a man who would abandon Joseph to monsters . . .

"Did I hear Herr General say that you are to be married, Fräulein?"

Stella turned at her uncle's quietly spoken question.

"You will not speak, Jew!" Martin raised the butt of his pistol to strike him.

"Stop!" Stella threw up a hand. "Do you think to make my task even more difficult?"

She raised a brow at Morty. In an airy tone she said, "Let the Jew talk. It might be entertaining."

The corporal's only response was to scowl. Retreating to the stove, he stared out the window.

"Are you . . . to be married, then?" Her uncle's gravelly voice faltered.

"Hold still." Ignoring his question, she applied foundation beneath his bruised eyes. Her touch lingered against his skin, hoping to convey to him what she dared not speak.

At five years old, Stella had often played alone in the storeroom of her uncle's metalwork shop. One time in particular she managed to climb—then topple off—several stacked crates of tools and split her head open on a crowbar lying next to them.

Morty had scooped her up in his arms; through a haze of pain she'd seen his strong face, taut and pale as she bled profusely from the gash on her head. His deep voice had soothed her with soft words as he ran with her the entire four blocks to Dr. Kerr's office on the *Tattersallstrasse*.

Stella's throat worked, along with her fingers. Now her uncle needed the soft words; he needed her to make his world right again. But she could do nothing.

She concentrated on her task, too ashamed to look him in the eye. "Herr Kommandant wants me to marry him," she said at last. "But I'm not certain—"

"I would think a woman foolish to pass up such an opportunity."

Stella glanced at him. "So you agree . . . ?" She turned to Martin. "Fetch me another hand towel from the Schrank in the dining room."

"I cannot leave the prisoner alone with you."

"Yes, Corporal, you can." She eyed him steadily, knowing her threat over him would eventually lose its power. "The cabinet is in plain sight of the doorway." She nodded toward the opening. "Watch him from there, if you like."

Martin swore under his breath as he crossed the kitchen and went to the cabinet. When Stella heard him rummaging through drawers, she whispered to her uncle, "Herr Kommandant also wants to send me to Switzerland tomorrow night with the Red Cross."

"Go!" Morty's features hardened, and for a sweet moment Stella felt like that child of long ago, receiving one of his parental lectures. "You must stay safe"—his gaze bored into hers—"above all other considerations."

Martin returned with the towel. Stella wiped her hands, then began to apply powder to Morty's face. Her uncle closed his eyes, leaning slightly as if to fully absorb his contact with her.

She whispered, "It is difficult."

"You can do it." He opened his eyes, and his mouth curved upward. "Keep faith—"

"I can't keep what I don't have."

Stella ignored his stricken look. Grabbing the last of her magic tricks—a tin of rouge—she dusted pink powder onto his cheeks and face with a horsetail brush. Morty's pallid features had transformed into a guise of glowing good health. "There. We're finished."

She searched his face, scrutinizing each feature. The general had made it clear that he would order her uncle onto the train if she failed.

"Fräulein, would you mind refolding my handkerchief?" Morty reached for the wrinkled wad of cloth in his left breast pocket. "I fear I've made a mess of it."

Stella took the handkerchief—and felt the crisp note within. Glancing at Martin, she was relieved to see him inspecting the contents of the kitchen cupboards.

"This one is stained. You can have mine." Without missing a beat, she stuffed the handkerchief with his message into the pocket of her wool jacket and produced another lace-edged cloth from inside her right sleeve. She tucked it neatly into his breast pocket. "Now you look splendid," she said softly.

"Thank you." His aged, brown eyes glistened with emotion. "I wish you a happy marriage, Fräulein." He reached to touch her hand, but didn't. "My maideleh," he whispered.

Stella's eyes burned. *I love you too, tatteh.*

The heavy thud of jackboots approaching drew her attention. As Aric entered with the general, Stella bristled. They hadn't spoken since she'd learned of his intent to send Joseph to Auschwitz.

"So tell me, does he need his train ticket, after all?" the general asked.

Stella pursed her lips as he strode forward to stand over her uncle. His dark eyes narrowed in scrutiny. When he shook his head, scowling, she blurted, "Please, Herr General, I . . . I am not finished!"

She made a grab for the face powder on the counter; it clattered to the floor, along with the tin of rouge. Stella dropped to her knees, frantic to retrieve the only magic that could save her uncle.

"I compliment you, Fräulein," the general said at last, his grudging tone at odds with his smile as he extended a hand to assist her. "This Jew looks like he just returned from a week's holiday on *Bodensee*, eh?"

Stella rose and leaned against the counter for support. "Danke, Herr General."

"I trust you can repeat this process tomorrow morning before the Red Cross arrives?" When she nodded, he turned to Morty. "Fräulein has given you a second chance, Jew. One you don't deserve. Have you memorized what you are to say when the Swiss question you?"

Morty immediately rose from his stool. "Jawohl, Herr General."

"And the consequence if you don't?"

Morty hesitated, then nodded.

"Then I am off to Prague." The general turned to Aric. "You will see me out."

"Of course. Corporal, take this man back to the ghetto."

Martin shoved at Morty with the muzzle of his gun. "Move."

Stella and her uncle exchanged a last glance before he left the kitchen.

"Herr General wishes the letter you typed for him yesterday to be posted this morning. When the corporal returns, he can take it."

She turned to Aric and nodded stiffly. His mouth compressed into a thin line as he eyed her for a second longer. He then swung around to follow the general out.

Collapsing onto the stool, she felt the weight of Morty's words press on her. He wanted her to marry and flee to Switzerland. Abandon both him and Joseph, the children. Aric . . .

In her heart Stella still loved him, though now it felt more like an affliction, some rare disease without a cure. Aric would have let them send Joseph on the train if not for her intervention. She didn't think she could ever forgive him for that.

The kitchen was quiet. Empty. Stella double-checked the door before withdrawing Morty's note from her pocket.

"Fräulein?"

She almost fell off the stool in her haste to hide the message back in her jacket.

The red-haired boy, Simon, stood in the archway. She let out a shaky breath. "Yes?"

He walked to her, one small fist outstretched. "I found these in the back room. Can I keep them?" His hand opened to reveal a half-dozen colored glass beads. Marbles . . .

A lump rose in her throat as she crouched before the boy. Stella knew she shouldn't get close to him; he wouldn't last long in this place. "Where are your parents, Simon?"

He pointed a stubby finger toward the front door.

The ghetto. At least they were alive. "How old are you?"

"Six." He eyed her openly for the first time. "How old are you?"

You should never ask a lady that question. . . . Stella blinked hard. "Why don't you go play with those marbles upstairs?" she finally managed.

A smile erased his worried look, and he dashed from the kitchen. Stella rose and trudged in the direction of the library. Later, in the privacy of her own room, she would read Morty's message. For now, she had the general's letter to post, then an absurd wedding to consider, and tomorrow . . . ?

She couldn't imagine leaving behind those she loved, yet she would be safe in Switzerland with Aric's name, his money . . . and freedom.

The temptation seemed too tantalizing to resist.

⤳ 30 ⤳

Haman went out that day happy and in high spirits.
But when he saw Mordecai . . . and observed that
he neither rose nor showed fear in his presence, he
was filled with rage. . . .

Esther 5:9

Hermann locked his fingers behind his head, tipped back in his chair, and smiled. The general's praise of the previous two nights made him almost giddy; he imagined himself one day an SS-Sturmbannführer in the Berlin Chancellery.

The new transport lists he'd retrieved earlier that morning lay spread across his desk. He'd barely given them a glance. Nor did he pay attention to the icy wind howling through the cracks inside his poorly insulated office.

He chided himself over his hasty first impression of General Feldman. Yes, the fat man drank as much as his father ever did, but the general countered that weakness with an ambition that frankly impressed Hermann—and seemed to irritate the commandant.

He lowered his hands and chuckled. What a surprise the Wehrmacht general must have been to Schmidt, who normally dragged his feet when dealing with the Jews. The general held no such qualms. Hermann had also sensed there was more to the animosity between the two men last night. Like the stench of the Krematorium at the onset of a hot day, it grew steadily stronger, to the point of being openly offensive. They fought over the woman, the commandant's wife-to-be.

Rising from his chair, Hermann began to pace. The announcement still amazed him. A man of Schmidt's distinction planned to shackle himself to the cow giving him free milk?

And how ironic the commandant had bested him for Stella, only to have the general toss his rank into the fray. Hermann had seen the envy burning in the general's eyes and understood that kind of yearning, wanting something so badly when the prize was just out of reach.

Still, their hostile tug-of-war made little difference to his own situation; the general would soon depart from Theresienstadt forever, while Aric von Schmidt remained in the warm house, bedding his warm woman, and eating warm food.

Hermann would continue as he had his whole life—standing out in the cold.

The room's chill finally registered, and he rubbed his hands together, nursing his old outrage. Himmler had tossed him over for an icon. Hermann had more experience in the SS and with the running of a concentration camp. Yet he'd failed to measure up to Colonel Aric von Schmidt, war hero, blue blood. A perfect decoration to set atop the SS-Reichsführer's prized cake.

A single, sharp rap at the door brought him up short. Corporal Sonntag entered, still wearing his parade black from the general's earlier inspection. He looked very smart, except for the white bandage across his chin. Hermann felt a moment's remorse for his earlier rashness.

"The Jew, Benjamin, has returned, Herr Captain."

Sonntag stepped back to let the prisoner enter. Walking now with a steady gait, the old Jew wore the silk suit he'd been issued. He appeared healthy and unblemished, despite his sunken eyes. Hermann had to admit the woman had done an excellent job with him.

"Have you rehearsed your lines for the Red Cross? Will you tell them how much you Jews flourish in this creative Paradies-ghetto?" Hermann flung his arms wide.

The prisoner stared at the floor. "Jawohl, Herr Captain."

The Jew's unruffled response annoyed him. He returned to his desk and began arranging the scattered pages of the train's manifest. "Have all the transports been notified?"

"I've issued their numbered tags, Herr Captain. They make ready to leave for the platform at Bohusovice."

"And the potato thief? He is ready, as well?" Hermann waited for the moment the old goat's cool insolence crumbled. It didn't come; only contempt ignited the sunken eyes, a look that had taunted Hermann in childhood, reminding him that he was no more than the miserable offspring of a drunken Stabsgefreiter and his laundress.

He exploded from his chair, his fury like a blast of frigid wind outside. "You can still board that train!" he bellowed. Then he rammed a fist into the old man's face.

The sunken eyes rolled before his body crumpled to the floor.

Hermann leaned across the desk, chest heaving, unable to stall the old memories . . . the Gasthaus owned by the Christ-killers where his mother lived and died scrubbing other people's soiled sheets . . . he and his snot-nosed siblings begging barrel scraps in the alley just outside the kitchens . . . the soles of his shoes tied together with string because the Jew cobbler, Mehrstein, refused to give his father credit . . .

Always they had treated his poverty like a stain against his skin, dirt that would never wash off or let him rise up to become a star like Aric von Schmidt.

"Get up," he demanded.

The prisoner grunted and rose to his feet. Hermann felt a spasm of satisfaction, seeing his bloodied nose mar the carefully applied cosmetics. So much for Jew arrogance now. "I will not ask again."

The Jew's silk suit hung askew on his scrawny frame like a warped coat hanger. "The boy is . . . ready."

"I want them leaving to board at one o'clock. Now get out."

The Jew hobbled toward the door. "And work on that limp," Hermann called out.

He turned his attention back to the manifest, the lists that *she* had put together for him. He imagined he caught the faint scent of cloves as he sifted among the neatly typed pages.

How easy it must be for a woman, he thought. He'd worked hard to ensure his position in the brick house after Kommandant Rahm's departure. Who wouldn't prefer eating delicious food and sleeping in a soft bed to the cot and tin rations reserved for soldiers? Yet despite all of his efforts, he still wasn't good enough.

Stella had only to exercise her charms on the right man to have anything she desired. Except for the boy. A smile touched his lips as he scanned the typed sheets for the potato thief's name. Like the commandant, she'd grown especially fond of him. Using the general had been the perfect plan; even Schmidt would not dare to override his decision. As for her other cause—the old man—he would get a one-way trip back to the Kleine Festung.

The mistake jumped out at him on the third page.

Hermann straightened. Number twenty-eight had been skipped. He counted off down the list.

Seven more numbers were omitted on the same sheet. He felt a tingling of comprehension. Sabotage?

He flipped back to the first sheet, then the second. More missing numbers! Excitement warred with his rage as he found dozens of discrepancies throughout the twenty-five pages.

"Sonntag!"

With thoughts of the Berlin Chancellery foremost in his mind, Hermann leaped from his chair, impatient for his corporal. He grabbed the manifest and charged into Sonntag's tiny office across the hall. "Who oversaw the transport loading for Auschwitz last Friday?"

Sonntag launched from his seat and saluted. "Sergeant Koch, Herr Captain."

"I want that train manifest. Schnell!"

Sonntag opened a gray filing cabinet and shuffled through countless folders before he found the sheets. He stood at attention while Hermann took the corporal's seat behind the desk and surveyed the pages.

"Hah!" He waved the sheets in the air. "We have a traitor in the camp, Sonntag. Over one hundred fifty Jews have been omitted from this list—even more from this one." He snatched up the morning's manifest. "Prisoners hiding within the ghetto walls."

He turned to his awestruck corporal. "I want four men— you, Martin, Zeissen, and Burke—to ferret out these Jews who missed the last train."

"Jawohl!" Sonntag began hauling out stacks of old cards from the filing cabinet.

"Never mind those," Hermann said. "It will take too much time to figure out whose names are missing. Besides, I'm certain our traitor already thought of that and destroyed the evidence." He paused to rub his chin, then said, "Which makes your task more difficult, but not impossible."

"How will we discover them, Herr Captain?"

Hermann checked his watch. "They'll be lining up to feed right about now. Take your patrol and go to the ghetto kitchen. Put out the word that we have the names. Those who come forward voluntarily will not be punished. Tell them if we must search them out, it will mean a trip to the Kleine Festung. That should collect most of them."

"Herr Captain?"

Hermann saw his corporal's confusion. "Jews are like cattle, Sonntag," he explained. "Easily led when you're good with the prod. They'll have no idea we're bluffing and will be too afraid to risk punishment. Visit the infirmary first. I suspect you'll get several confessions."

He rose from the chair. "Speak nothing of this to anyone. For now, we shall call it a 'mistake'—at least until I get all the facts. We cannot afford a scandal the day before the Red Cross arrives." He eyed Sonntag sharply. "Verstehen?"

"Of course, Herr Captain." Sonntag flashed a salute. "Who do you suspect as the traitor?"

Hermann grinned. Perhaps the real traitor was Schmidt. He'd allowed passion to do his thinking while she wooed him and made a laughingstock of the Reich. What's more, Sergeant Koch had likely been right about her. A Jewess, through and through.

"Soon enough, Corporal," he replied. "You will know soon enough."

∽ 31 ∽

"For I and my people have been sold for destruction and slaughter."

Esther 7:4

Wolkenbrand.

Stella glimpsed the strange phrase once more before she folded the general's letter to the Chancellery and stuffed it inside the addressed envelope. What did it mean, this Firecloud? And why had the general written that it would occur on Friday? The day after the Red Cross inspection . . .

Uneasiness stirred in her like snow flurries announcing a storm. The letter's contents revealed nothing specific. Still, she couldn't help feeling a chill of impending doom.

After sealing the letter, Stella rose from the desk. Where was Martin? It seemed forever since he'd left for the ghetto with her uncle. She felt inside the pocket of her jacket, reassured that Morty's unread note still rested there. Once the corporal returned for the post, she could slip upstairs . . .

The distant screech of a train's whistle made her jump. Captain Hermann had already taken back the burlap sack of cards, along with her typed lists. Her people must be starting to board the train. Had her deception worked, or would Joseph still be among them?

In a nervous burst she dropped the general's letter and rushed back to the kitchen.

Rand Grossman stood in pajamas and robe, blocking her exit out the back door.

"Why aren't you in bed?" she demanded.

He merely stared at her in equal surprise.

"I . . . I need fresh air," she muttered. Then, without bothering to grab her coat, she ducked beneath his arm and went outside.

Stella heard him call after her as she slogged up the snowy hill. Reaching the top of the rise, she hugged herself as she tried to fend off the brutal wind.

Beyond the ghetto's bastioned walls stood the one-room station of Bohusovice. Beside it, a train thirty cars long sat on tracks. Dirty coils of smoke blew from its stack.

The train wasn't moving. From her viewpoint, Stella couldn't tell if the cattle cars were loaded. Anxiety—or was it the frigid air?—threatened to cut off her breath. How could she know if Joseph was safe?

"Fräulein!"

Rand struggled up the hill toward her. He wore a greatcoat over his pajamas and used his machine gun like a walking staff. Guilt pricked her and she made her way toward him. "You shouldn't be out here!" she shouted above the wind.

"I think you . . . try to . . . kill me, Fräulein," he wheezed when they caught up with each other. He leaned on his gun and tried to catch his breath. Stella hefted his free arm across her shoulders. The steel hook loomed in front of her face.

"Let's get you back to the house." She helped him down the hill and fell twice in the snow when he collapsed against her in half-conscious exhaustion.

Stella finally managed to get Rand into Joseph's room. She wrestled the dazed sergeant out of his boots, then straddled his knees, working to extract his feeble limbs from the sleeves of the dampened greatcoat.

"Care to explain yourself?"

Stella jerked around. Aric stood at the door, jackboots braced apart, arms folded against his chest. She froze—before indignation scalded her cheeks. "It's not what you think . . ."

"Oh? Suddenly you know what I'm thinking?" His green eyes glittered. "Tell me."

Carefully she eased off the bed to face him. "You assumed we were"—her gaze darted to the barely conscious pajama-clad soldier on the bed—"that I was . . ."

"Seducing my sergeant?" He raised a brow beneath his cap. She nodded.

"But I distinctly recall explaining to you the consequences of betrayal." His voice took on a dangerously calm tone. "Only a fool would dare test me. And there was a time when I thought you were hardly that."

Stella looked away. Snow had melted through her clothes, her silk stockings. Even the abominable red wig clung in wet strands to the sides of her face. She clenched her jaw to keep her teeth from chattering.

"Look at you," Aric said irritably. "Cold, wet, shivering. You're mad to be out in this weather without a coat."

"I . . . sorry, Herr Kommandant, tried to get to her sooner . . ." Rand's weak voice rose from the bed.

"Rest easy, my friend." Aric grabbed Stella by the arm and pulled her out into the hall. "As I was saying"—his finger jabbed back toward the room—"you nearly killed my man in there, making him chase you down in this weather. And what if *you* become sick and jeopardize my plan to get you out of here tomorrow? Wouldn't you call that foolish?"

Feeling the chill of her own clothes, Stella thought of the man lying wounded inside on the bed. "Very foolish, Herr Kommandant," she said, realizing she meant it.

"So it's back to 'Herr Kommandant'?" Yet his anger had eased somewhat. "Why were you outside . . . without proper clothes?"

She flashed him some of her own anger. "I heard the train. I wanted to see Joseph."

Aric's face hardened. "I told you the boy is a closed issue."

"You knew he was being sent to Auschwitz, didn't you?"

Stella braced herself for another blast; she was surprised when instead his granite features collapsed. "I tried to convince the general that it was a mistake. He wouldn't listen." He grasped her by the shoulders, his tone almost desperate. "Please, Stella, I told you I can't—"

"Save Joseph? Save any of them?" She pulled away from him. "Yet you'll rescue me from Herr General by marrying me today and showing him proof tomorrow. Then I'm to be sent off to Switzerland . . ."

Her voice faltered with a sudden, horrifying thought. Aric's outlandish plan to remove her from Theresienstadt had something to do with Wolkenbrand.

Vaguely she recalled a letter he'd written weeks before—to Eichmann, postponing some project until after the Red Cross inspection. And then words he'd spoken to her the other night flashed in her mind: *"By saving that old Jew one more day, you made a deal with the devil."*

"This has nothing to do with the general, does it?" she whispered. "You're making me leave because of what happens on Friday."

Aric's mouth tightened. So did Stella's insides.

"Tell me about Wolkenbrand," she said.

Their eyes locked for several seconds. "The war is going badly for us," he said at last. "The Red Army is gaining ground at an alarming rate. They've recaptured Odessa, and the city of Lemberg in the Ukraine. Rumor has it the Russians will soon take Hungary.

"It's only a matter of time before the battlefield reaches us. I want you far away when that happens. With the Swiss arriving here tomorrow, it will be my only opportunity to get you safely out of the country."

He'd told her nothing. "What is this . . . Firecloud, Aric?" she demanded.

He ignored her question. "We leave for Litomerice in an hour. Go upstairs and get into dry clothes." His voice softened as he added, "It would please me very much if you'd wear the blue dress and your pearls." He smiled wryly. "As my wife, you must shine like a 'beacon on a mountain.'"

She started to object when he reached for her again. Pulling her into his arms, he brushed away the wet strands and laid a cheek against hers. "Please don't argue, my dove," he whispered urgently. "I'll tell you this much. I do not marry you simply to save you from the general. I . . . the truth is . . . I am a starving man who desires you with a hunger that defies mortal appetite." He pulled away to search her face. "The general will never have you. You are mine."

"I'm not some country to be fought over." Yet she mocked her own objection by leaning into his embrace.

"But you are, Süsse. You are Austria, my home."

When she gazed up at him questioningly, he merely smiled and then lowered his head to kiss her deeply, passionately. Stella surrendered to his desire, unable to think or catch a breath. Even her guilt failed to dampen the longing in her heart or compose her trembling limbs. Only when the kiss ended did she remember her anger . . . far safer to her peace of mind.

"You make me forget myself." She hated the sudden emptiness she felt as she withdrew from his embrace. "And you haven't answered my question."

He hesitated, then said, "*Wolkenbrand* is a code word. It means to ready ourselves for possible confrontation with the enemy."

She felt his continued evasion, yet understood enough. The end was in sight, and with it more bloodshed. Only one side could win. Either way she lost, because impossibly, irrationally, she loved this man. "I want to stay, Aric."

"You're going with the Red Cross tomorrow evening."

His tone brooked no argument. "I don't want to leave you here," she said.

His features relaxed, though his eyes held their familiar sadness. "Believe me, Stella, I'll fare much better knowing you're safe." He took her hands in his and kissed her fingers. "Now, you should go upstairs and get ready to be my bride."

∽ 32 ∽

"Do not think that because you are in the king's house you alone of all the Jews will escape...."

Esther 4:13

Aric paced the library floor wearing his full military regalia: black tie and a fitted brown shirt, pressed and starched beneath his uniform jacket; creased black slacks and leather jackboots hand-rubbed to a polished sheen. Even the aluminum buckle on his belt and cross strap gleamed in the amber light from the task lamp positioned over Stella's neatly arranged desk.

She would be difficult, he knew. Yet as a seasoned soldier, and Stella his unwilling adversary, Aric made it a point to know her weaknesses. His pulse quickened at the thought of this evening, when she would become his wife in truth. He'd desired Stella for so long that he felt a moment's gratitude toward God ... and that gluttonous fool, Feldman, for setting the course of his future into motion.

His future. Aric paused in his pacing. The truth was that he *needed* to marry her, not because of all his logical reasons but because he couldn't bear the thought of losing her. She had captured his heart with her smile, her innate goodness and belief in others, even the way she stood up to his anger. And despite their differences, he knew that she cared about him—the man, not the soldier, the machine.

Marriage would keep them tangibly linked. And once this terrible mess was finished, he could begin his life again, this time with Stella. Perhaps tonight they would even make a child together, a little girl to make her forget about the dead one. To forget about Joseph . . .

"Herr Kommandant, I must speak with you."

Aric turned to find his captain at the library doors. Hermann held a sheaf of papers. "There is a problem."

Aric noted an excited gleam in his eyes. "Come inside," he said, leading the way into his office. He'd just closed the door when Hermann slapped the papers down against the desk. "Take a look."

"Are these a few last-minute corrections that Herr General deigned to leave to SS efficiency, Captain?" Aric asked, fishing for his glasses.

He immediately saw it was not. Hairs rose on the back of his neck as he recognized the top sheet of the train manifest Stella had typed the night before. "What seems to be amiss?"

"She's a traitor."

Aric's blood went cold. He leaned against the desk. "What are you talking about?"

Hermann jabbed a finger at the sheet. "*She* has altered the lists. Here, and here."

He indicated several missing numbers. Aric's muscles eased. "You show me a couple of mistakes, Captain?" It surprised him that for years he'd cleaved to exactitude, ingrained in him by his father, and then throughout his years of disciplined soldiering. Now he felt only mild irritation. "Easily corrected," he said dismissively.

"You'll find Fräulein Muller's action very premeditated, Herr Kommandant." Hermann picked up the rest of the papers from the desk and waved them at Aric. "Eight numbers omitted from each page, and not just today's train. I've dispatched a detail to locate the one hundred sixty Jews who escaped notice last Friday. On this manifest"—he pointed to the sheet in Aric's hand—"nearly two hundred are missing." He paused. "Clearly sabotage."

Aric stared at the sheaf of papers, tasting the first bitter traces of treachery. *Georg* . . . Memories seeped into his brain, stabbing his insides as he scanned the pages of meaningless names and numbers, wanting to shout a denial at Hermann's words.

Yet his hopes for the future had already begun to recede, like the fading images of a dream . . . even as he clung to them. "How can you be certain—?"

"Herr Kommandant, please! You let your feelings for the woman affect your thinking. Surely you can see now that she's one of them?"

"You're out of line, soldier!" Aric's rage surfaced, and he pressed his face nose to nose with Hermann's. "You dare speak to me in such a manner or question *my* judgment? I am Kommandant of this camp!"

"It doesn't change the fact that your intended bride has committed treason against the Reich, *Herr Kommandant*," Hermann ground out with equal venom. "Any obstruction you present in this matter will be taken as complicity."

The captain was correct: Aric would face a court-martial if he so much as tried to interfere. Stepping back against the desk, he struggled to leash the fury that overrode his stupefaction.

"Where is she?" Hermann demanded.

"Upstairs. I'll get her!" Aric snapped when the captain made to step toward the door. He snatched the sheaf of papers from Hermann, then pushed past him out of the office, nearly knocking the captain off his feet.

Outside the library, he bounded up the stairs two at a time, ignoring the pain in his legs. *They had both betrayed him.* Aching visions of the past swamped him—the days just prior to the first failed attempt of *Anschluss*, in '33. Aric had been a teenager then, coming home for a holiday from university. He and his best friend, Georg Zimmer, along with several other boys from Bonn's Hitler Jugend, had marched proudly through Innsbruck's city streets, spouting off Hitler's ideals to passersby. Aric had been naïve in the belief he could convince his Austrian countrymen to adopt Germany's vision for a new future.

The first blow had struck him hard from behind. Uniformed Austrian *Landswehr* soldiers had seized him and his friends, meting out with bludgeons their intent to keep Austria free of Nazis. That night, as Aric lay in an Innsbruck jail barely conscious, he'd wanted to die with shame at the treachery of his own fellow Austrians. But it was Georg who had lost his life.

Pain from the past collided with Aric's present rage and threatened to explode as he reached Stella's bedroom door. When his father had come to arrange for his release the following morning, Aric learned the truth that Johann von Schmidt, always vehemently opposed to Hitler's ideologies, had turned in his only son to the police.

Even now, the memory of his father's betrayal pierced his heart. And Stella—

Aric let out a tormented cry as he rammed a fist through the paneled wood door.

Hers would forever brand his soul.

33

*"For how can I bear to see disaster fall on my people?
How can I bear to see the destruction of my family?"*

Esther 8:6

Stop taking risks. Morty's writing was bold, emphatic. *There are 160 possibilities you will pay for your actions.*

Standing clothed and barefoot in the bathtub, Stella stood just outside the range of hot spray and scanned the smudged contents of her uncle's note. He'd written to her on the back of a mimeographed advertisement for *Requiem*, to be performed for the Red Cross.

So he knew of her handiwork regarding last Friday's train. He couldn't yet know of this morning's list and almost two hundred souls, Joseph among them, who wouldn't be boarding the train at Bohusovice's station.

. . . cannot get caught, daughter, her uncle continued. *You will be our salvation. . . .*

Stella had grown to hate the word *salvation*. Morty had written to her before knowing her current situation, that in little more than an hour she would be the bride of a man who wanted her but did not love her, a man determined to win her away from another man's desire.

And afterward, when she'd given him what he wanted most, when she'd splayed her heart open for the price of a single night of passion, he would send her away to a safe place, where words like *deprivation* and *death* no longer seemed real but were merely unpleasantries discoursed among strangers.

And Jews would still die. She'd be useless to those left behind.

Steam rose from the hot shower, swallowing her in a damp haze. Stella breathed deep to ease the tightness in her chest and throat. She thought of Helen's faith, and Morty, with his prophetic vision. Why was she the only one who saw the truth?

There were no miracles.

She'd almost begun to believe when Aric championed the Jews' right to decent food, or each time he tousled Joseph's hair and smiled at him, treating him not as a pariah but like any other child.

She thought God had listened when she'd prayed for Aric's safety, and when, despite her convictions and against all reasoning, she'd fallen in love with him.

But the cold reality was that their bond was built on deceit. She was Jewish, and Aric was a man who would always bow to duty first, even if it meant death to her people. She must keep pretending—to be someone she wasn't; to do the right thing by leaving tomorrow and never look back. To be loved . . .

"Why won't you speak to me?" she cried, fisting the note and plunging herself beneath the spray. Liquid heat drenched her white blouse and wool skirt, and she tore at her clothes while the water's pressure pushed away her wig. The wet strands pooled at her feet. Like red tentacles caught in an eddy, they swirled round and round, unable to stop. Trapped . . .

Loud gasps shook her shoulders. Finally her knees gave out and she sank into the standing water, wearing only her slip, uncaring that her clothes were ruined—

Strong hands grabbed her from behind. Stella screamed as she was jerked from the tub. The wet ball of paper—Morty's note—flew from her hand to roll across the tiled floor.

While her assailant hauled her into the bedroom, she was
seized with a vague sense of familiarity, one she'd memorized
in her heart.

He finally spun her around. "Liar!"

Aric's handsome features contorted with rage. Stella fought
down her panic. He shoved her backward until she fell hard
against the mattress. "Tell me why?" he demanded in a near
roar.

She couldn't find her tongue to speak.

"Sabotage!" He swept up a handful of papers off the bed and
threw them at her.

Transport lists. Fear stabbed at her like icicles.

"I trusted you. I even saved your life—and you betrayed me!"

He raised his fist as if to strike her. Stella flinched, waiting
for the blow. Then he turned instead and grabbed the music box
from the nightstand. "I even gave you this . . ."

Hurling the delicate box against the wall, it shattered into
pieces. Pearls scattered everywhere, along with Morty's note
and his Grand Cross.

Aric didn't seem to notice. "Did you have a good laugh at my
expense, Stella . . . or should I call you *Sarah*, like the others in
the ghetto? You're a Jew, aren't you?"

She gaped at him even as giddy relief shot through her numbed
state. He knew the truth.

"Herr Kommandant!"

Hermann burst into the room and stared at the bed. "I heard
you shouting, I thought . . ." He gazed at her openly. Stella tried
to hide beneath the papers.

"Get out, Captain," Aric said through clenched teeth. "I
haven't finished my interrogation of the prisoner."

Hermann stared at her another moment before his attention
turned to the destroyed music box and its contents lying on the
floor. He leaned to pick up Morty's Cross, and she groaned.
He then retrieved her uncle's note, the one that proved Koch's

and Brucker's failed attempt at murder. He stuffed them both inside his jacket pocket.

"Get out!" Aric looked ready to kill. Hermann shot her a last glance before he backed out of the room.

"What other lies have you told me? Do you have a husband? Is that why you don't want to marry me?" Aric glared at her.

"No, please, I . . . I told you the truth!"

Terror filled her as he leaned over her, pinning her wrists against the bed. "I doubt you're even a virgin." Stark fury etched his rock-hard features.

"Aric," she said hoarsely, "you don't understand—"

"Oh, but I do. You bargained for this all along, didn't you? Using your beauty, your charm, to get what you wanted from me. For those Jews."

His face moved so close that their lips nearly joined, but anger—not desire—burned in his eyes. "You were even willing to bed the general for one of them, weren't you?"

"Would that have been worse than your dying?" She searched his harsh features for some sign of the man she'd fallen in love with. "You told me you couldn't help the Jews, that your own soldiers would kill you if you tried."

He paused, his breathing labored, his eyes clouded with anguish. Stella desperately wanted to soothe his anger and the despair that must match her own. She lifted her head a fraction of an inch and pressed her mouth to his, eyes open, imploring. His body went completely still. He stared back at her, then gradually she noted the faint dilation of his pupils; she felt the moment his lips softened, molding to hers. Her eyelids drifted closed as she gave herself up completely to the kiss, telling him with every fiber of her being how much she loved him—

"No," he growled, dragging his mouth from hers. With a single, fluid movement he pushed himself off the bed and away from her. "No."

Aric's fury gave way to exhaustion; he felt as though someone had bludgeoned him. He stared at her—she who had been his hope, his future. "Get dressed, Sarah."

"Not Sarah." She rose off the bed, her large eyes blazing blue fire at him. "*Hadassah*. Is that Jewish enough for you?"

Admiration warred with his anger as he stared at her beautiful form. "How could you do this?" he whispered. "To us?"

"How could I not? If they were your people, you would do the same." She stood before him, shoulders straight with the same natural grace that had first mesmerized him at Dachau. "We breathe the same air. We eat, sleep, and have the same hopes and dreams. We love . . ." Her gaze faltered, then returned to sear him. "In the most important ways we are the same, Aric. We want to live, just like you."

"But I warned you!" he bellowed, more enraged over her senseless sacrifice. He grasped her shoulders. "Nothing can help them, don't you see? It's too big now; it's gone too far."

"I had to try."

She sounded so calm. "Curse your soft heart!" He shoved her away from him. "Because of what you've done, I must arrest you."

"I'm not afraid."

"You should be." He glowered at her, then saw she really was terrified—the way her mouth trembled beneath those enormous blue eyes. Wolkenbrand would commence against the Jews as soon as the Red Cross departed. She would be among them.

Something inside of him collapsed. Shut down. "You were right about me," he said in a voice he hardly recognized as his own. "I am a monster."

He reached to trace the delicate curve of her cheek. Touching her was painful, but he endured it. He'd already endured so much.

Duty had always come first; he'd been a soldier too many years, a front-line commander. He'd seen too many of his own die on the bloody battlefields of Russia; he'd spent too many months trudging through snow and mud, suffering lice and freezing temperatures. And he could do nothing else until the war was over. Not until Germany either won or surrendered. He was conditioned for nothing else, knew nothing else. He had nothing else.

Aric let his hand drop back to his side. "Dress warmly." The words felt numb against his tongue. "Captain Hermann will escort you to the ghetto."

She walked to the armoire, and after retrieving the same houndstooth jacket and skirt she'd worn that first morning, she slipped into the bathroom to change. When she reappeared, she seemed more achingly beautiful than he could ever remember. He walked to the door.

"You're not a monster, Aric." Her voice came to him soft and steady. "Or a martyr, either. You're just a man, nothing more."

He stood with his hand on the knob, refusing to look back at her. He couldn't. Giving a rough jerk, he tore open the door and stormed from the room.

Back into the world that had suddenly crashed in on him.

34

*Then Esther sent this reply . . . "And if I perish, I
perish."*

Esther 4:15–16

I find I'm always entertained by coincidence. What are the
odds, do you think, with thousands of Jews scattered across
Europe, that you'd end up in the same camp as your"—Hermann
scanned the letter—"father, is it?"

Hadassah stood before his desk as he held up one of her
uncle's letters from the ghetto. It was the note she'd dropped in
the bathroom. The page was still wrinkled and wet, the mimeographed advertisement on the back now a blue smear.

Unfortunately, Morty's penciled words on the other side were
clearly legible. She didn't doubt Hermann had already destroyed
the other note, the one incriminating him in Koch and Brucker's
murderous scheme.

"'Dearest daughter.'" Hermann's hazel eyes narrowed on her.
"Who is this man? The old Jew you keep trying to save?" He
reached for the burlap sack on his desk and withdrew a couple
of the white cards. "The writing looks to be the same." He held
up one card, then another beside the note. "Is Morty Benjamin
your father, Sarah?"

Hadassah answered honestly, "Nein, Herr Captain."

"We shall see." He leaned back in his chair, a sneer touching the edges of his mouth. "So, does Aric von Schmidt know he's been playing house with a Jew?"

Hadassah's hands fisted at her sides. She refused to acknowledge him, glaring instead at the picture of Hitler mounted on the wall above Hermann's head. She wore no coat, only her houndstooth suit and the fur-lined boots Aric had given her. A shiver coursed through her as the room's chill overrode the popping oil furnace in the corner.

How foolish to have kept Morty's notes! Now her sentimentality would get them both killed . . .

"Nothing to say?" Hermann rose from his chair and moved around the desk to face her. His gloved hand reached to stroke her cheek. "A quiet woman is the best kind."

Hadassah resisted an impulse to shrink from his touch.

"You should have chosen me the night of the Kommandant's party. I could have shown you what you were missing. Perhaps I may still."

He edged closer to prove his point. Stella stifled a scream.

"Life in the ghetto doesn't have to be bad for you, Sarah." His breath reeked of stale cigarettes. "I can even overlook the tattoo. I saw it, you know, earlier, while you were in your room. Come and be mine," he murmured against her cheek, "and I'll even give you extra rations."

Unable to endure another moment of his repugnant speech, she tilted her head to glower at him with such loathing it made her limbs shake. "I would rather breathe the gas at Auschwitz than wake up to your face each morning," she ground out.

"As you wish!" He drew back and belted her across the cheek. Hadassah's head snapped to the side. Blinking against the pain, she felt blood flooding the inside of her mouth.

"Sonntag!"

The young corporal quickly materialized. "Return to the

house and get Fräulein's typewriter. Take it up to the records office."

Once the soldier dashed off, Hermann told her, "You'll type a supplemental to the manifest. It will contain all of the names you neglected to list—including those from last Friday. The train will load and leave tonight."

Her shock mingled with a vague sense of dread. "The cards . . . I destroyed them, Herr Captain. I don't remember the names."

"Then you'd better hope they come forward on their own, or that your *father* remembers, because for each missing name, a new one—a child, I think—will be chosen to take its place."

"You can't!" Hadassah gasped, horrified. "Please, I'll . . . I'll do anything!"

She moistened her lips, ignoring her aching mouth and the nausea churning inside her. She touched his sleeve. "Anything . . ."

He shoved her so hard that she fell backward onto the floor. "And I've decided," he said through clenched teeth, "that when I wake up in the morning, I would rather stare into the face of a bleating *Schaf* than a filthy Jew."

From the doorway of the ghetto's kitchen, Morty stared down the cobbled street toward the building that housed Captain Hermann's office.

"Some salvation," Yaakov called out behind him. "After those gullible fools turned themselves in this morning, the guards punished them anyway."

Morty kept his back to the group seated at the kitchen table.

"They rounded them up in the Marktplatz and beat them with clubs—as a warning to others," Yaakov continued. "And still they must go on today's train."

"Did you see what they did to my daughter?" Mrs. Brenner's high-pitched voice quavered between rage and hysteria. "Did you see the marks on Clara's sweet face when they got through with her? Their dogs tore at the hem of her dress, then her coat sleeves until nothing but shredded cloth lay at her feet. Now she has nothing warm to wear when she goes . . ." Her voice caught and she cleared her throat before she whispered, "And just look at that poor boy."

Morty turned then. Joseph lay cocooned in blankets on a bench beside the brazier. Even in the kitchen's dim light, his sleeping face revealed a wealth of bruises.

"I heard one of the soldiers tell the deportees they must give their names to Morty's maideleh so she can type the new list." Yaakov glanced at Morty. "Is she still in there?"

Morty jerked a nod and then returned to his vigil. Dread gnawed at him. He imagined what Hermann was doing to her and fought the impulse to rush down the street, break in the door, and confront the devil. Of course, he would only get himself shot for the effort, and Hadassah would soon need his comfort, what little he could offer her.

His mind flashed back on the scene of her being led by soldiers from the elegant brick house. She'd worn no coat or hat. In the gray winter light her short blond curls had seemed almost white. Morty had no idea why she'd been brought to the ghetto, only that her misfortune was the result of some convoluted logic that defied all but a Nazi's mind.

"It seems your vision was no more than a dream, old friend," Yaakov muttered. "Everything has gotten worse—except the food."

Morty glanced around in time to see Yaakov shove a biscuit into his mouth. "She can't help us now," he said around his chewing. "In fact, I'll be surprised if they don't make her go to Auschwitz, too."

"She should go," Mrs. Brenner piped up bitterly. "If my Clara has to go, it's only right she go, too—"

"Silence!" Morty snapped, before he swung his attention back to the street. One of the guards, Corporal Martin, had emerged from the building with Hadassah and now led her toward the square. Morty left his position by the door and followed them. When they mounted the steps and passed beneath a mock sign that read BANK, he realized they were going up to his own office.

Morty shadowed them inside and up another flight of stairs. They entered the small room, which held a table that served as his desk, along with a straight-backed chair and a desk lamp that was missing its shade. A dented brown filing cabinet stood in one corner; it contained all the prisoner records and other paper work he was required to provide.

"Can I help you?" Though he maintained a polite tone with Corporal Martin, anger coursed through him. He'd noticed the angry swelling around Hadassah's right cheek.

Martin ignored him, looking just beyond his shoulder.

"Out of my way, Jude," barked a voice behind Morty. Corporal Sonntag pushed his way past with a typewriter. After dumping it unceremoniously onto the table, both soldiers departed, leaving Morty alone with his niece.

Hadassah flew into his arms. She squeezed him so hard that his ribs ached. "Ah, my baby girl, how wonderful it feels to hold you again." He didn't care that his voice shook. He embraced her a long moment before finally, reluctantly, setting her away from him.

"Now, let me have a good look at you without the worry of getting clouted in the head." He was relieved to note that except for being a little paler and thinner, and the welt at her cheek, she seemed healthy and whole.

"Joseph?"

"He's sleeping right now."

"Please, *tatteh*, bring him to me. I need to know he's all right."

Morty breathed a heavy sigh and nodded. "He's been roughed up"—he held up a hand when she made a distressed sound— "but his bruises will heal quickly. He's young."

He scowled at the angry mark on her cheek. "Hermann, that *chazzerei*, he did this to you, didn't he?"

"Perhaps," called a voice from the door. "And once I translate that Jew gibberish, I imagine you'll have one to match. So . . . father and daughter reunited at last."

Hermann entered the room. Morty shot a glance at Hadassah. "There wasn't time," she whispered. "They found the notes. And your Grand Cross." She turned to glare at the captain.

"I retrieved these from your files. A carbon copy of yesterday's manifest." Hermann held up a stack of papers. "Twenty-five hundred names, minus the two hundred you omitted."

Then he withdrew from his coat pocket a packet of cards. "Here are two hundred cards from the Judenrat's files—all children. As I said before, you will provide *all* the missing names or supply an equal number of these." He handed Hadassah the cards along with the sheets. "I'll be back this afternoon for the new list. Make certain the potato thief is on it. I will station one of my men outside the door to ensure you stay at your task.

"By the way, you're fortunate my men were able to round up most of the Jews who evaded last Friday's train—or I'd have to provide you with more cards. They should be arriving shortly to give you their information." He smirked. "I wanted you to have a good look at them."

Hermann turned an icy stare on Morty. "In case you think to interfere, Jew—don't. I've removed your files from this office, in case you're tempted to make substitutions for the cards I've already chosen. There is also your dear daughter's safety to think about." He flashed a malignant smile before departing from the tiny records office.

Morty uttered an oath. His niece was now more of a prisoner than he was.

Hadassah glimpsed her uncle's anger. "I'm so sorry, tatteh. I failed you . . ."

"Hush, child." He opened his arms, and she returned to his comforting embrace. "You didn't fail. We can only do God's will—"

"Then God failed!" She jerked away, fury exploding inside her. "Are you so blind? There is no salvation!" *Only this ache in my heart that won't go away . . .*

"God did not fail." Morty caught her up again and forced her to meet his gaze. "Man fails. He fails God. He fails his brother. Himself." A sad smile touched his mouth. "Perhaps I expected too much from Herr Kommandant."

Her pain intensified. "He's no god," she bit out. "He's mortal, like the rest of us."

"Then we must hope for another miracle."

She stared at him. "Your conviction never wavers, does it? Despite everything that's happened—the brutality, starvation, and death—you never question God."

"And you know this for a fact?" He raised a grizzled brow at her.

"I've listened to your teachings since I was a child. You've always had your faith."

"It is still *your* faith too, daughter," he reminded her. "But in truth, I struggle with mine each and every day. A strong belief in God is like forging steel; it must be repeatedly tested in fire, then cooled in the waters of His mercy before becoming resilient enough to withstand evil."

"Not all," Hadassah countered bitterly. "In these past months I've seen such 'evil' as to defy even the stoutest faith."

"Nor will it go away, Hadassah. God gave His people free will, and so Satan will always try and tempt us. Yet we can be redeemed through our own weakness if we but have 'eyes to see.' Look at King David. He fell into sin by coveting Bathsheba for his own, and then arranged the death of her husband, Uriah. When God punished his evil deed by taking their first child, David repented and became even closer to God."

"I don't see the Nazis being punished," she shot back. "Nor do they feel a need to repent. In fact, they seem to enjoy our destruction."

Morty sighed. "Our truest test, daughter, is to wait . . . and persevere. What did God tell Daniel? 'Many will be purified, made spotless and refined, but the wicked will continue to be wicked. None of the wicked will understand, but those who are wise . . .'"

"Does that make me one of the wicked or the wise?" she asked. "Is my soul being 'refined'—by typing lists that send innocent people to their death? Or am I damned for all eternity? And if I refuse . . ." She recalled Aric's words to her. "The monsters will simply shoot me and find another to take my place. Is that God's will?"

Morty flinched. Hadassah knew he wrestled with the same dilemma, saddled with the burden of choosing those who would go. She suddenly felt tired. She didn't want to talk about faith or redemption. What would it change? She must still go through with this hideous task. "Please, tatteh, let's not argue. You'll bring Joseph to me?"

His sorrowful gaze held hers a moment before he nodded. After he left, Hadassah wandered toward the makeshift desk. Her limbs felt brittle as matchsticks as she eased herself into the only chair.

The typewriter still wore its protective gray cloth cover. Sonntag had placed fresh paper and carbon alongside it, as if she were preparing mundane supply requisitions in triplicate instead of sending hundreds to die.

Despair settled over her. How could she remember the names of each person she'd tried to save? And for the ones she couldn't . . . to force a child to take their place? Where was God amidst so much evil? *"Many shall be refined, purified, tested . . ."*

Unexpectedly, Abraham's story came to mind. He'd been given the ultimate test by God. Had he felt this heartsick, taking his son Isaac to the top of Mount Moriah? Knowing all the while what he must do?

But God had spoken out to him, releasing him from the gruesome promise. Hadassah stared at the cards still in her hand. Like Isaac, these children were blissfully unaware of the danger. Would God stay her hand and save them, too?

No, she thought miserably, because she lacked Abraham's courage. His faith . . .

"Hadassah, I've brought a friend," Morty called from the doorway.

She glanced up to find a short, stocky man standing beside her uncle. The stranger carried a large blanket roll over one shoulder.

"Yaakov Kadlec, meet my niece."

Yaakov bobbed his head in greeting, then shifted the wrapped weight in his arms. A soft groan emitted from beneath the blanket.

"Joseph?" Hadassah left the chair and rushed to them. "Let me hold him!"

Yaakov transferred the child into her arms. "Who did this?" she cried, seeing Joseph's bruised face. Glaring at the two men, she clutched the boy, rocking him back and forth. "How could they hurt my beautiful boy?" she whispered brokenly.

"Hadassah, sweetheart—"

"Don't tell me to 'wait and persevere,' tatteh," she snapped at her uncle. "Not while they shoot and maim our children!"

Before he could respond, a shuffling sounded as people began crowding into the room. Others queued up beyond the door, their shabby clothes and meager faces forming a long island of misery. "I can't do this," Hadassah breathed. "I can't send them to die."

"You already know it will happen with or without you," Morty said harshly. "So try and remember the names, daughter. Try to save some of the little ones."

Her attention returned to those waiting to surrender their very lives. She took several quick breaths to ease her panic, then kissed the top of Joseph's head before handing him back to Yaakov.

At the desk, she removed the gray cloth from her typewriter—and spied the black Bible from her room hidden beneath. A sob of hysterical laughter rose in her throat. How was it possible? It had been tucked away, in her nightstand . . .

She shoved the book onto the table beside her and signaled to the first person in line. A dark-haired young woman approached, with soulful brown eyes and a face as battered as the fingers poking through her frayed gloves. Hadassah jammed paper and carbon into the typewriter. "Name?" she said.

"Clara Brenner," replied the soft voice in heavily accented Czech, "137538."

Hadassah couldn't seem to move her fingers against the keys. She looked up at Clara and saw Mina, the woman she'd never met yet condemned to Auschwitz.

Her vision blurred and she quickly looked away. How could she obey the monsters? But then she thought of the little girl in the ghetto, reeking of urine and unwashed hair. And the other children who slept in the same room, wrestling their nightmares. If she didn't, they would all die.

She felt cornered; self-loathing washed over her. Why hadn't she been shot that day in Dachau instead of Anna? Why did God spare her . . . only to make her an accomplice to murder?

Tell me, Lord. I promise to listen. Hadassah cast a desperate glance at the Bible on the table beside her. The book had fallen open to a page, marked by the photograph of Aric.

His image brought fresh pain. She'd tucked the snapshot inside the Bible after reading about Elijah. She reached for the book now and withdrew the photograph, staring at the boyish features of the man. Never again to see him smile, only recall the anger of his words.

She'd been so foolish to believe that once Aric discovered the truth about her, his feelings wouldn't change. She thought he might even champion her cause. But in the end, duty had outweighed all. He was lost to her, and with him any hope, however slim, of saving her people.

As for Hadassah, Hermann would likely have her shot after today's task was completed. Or worse, make her languish in this place, typing more lists, sending more innocent souls to die. Was that how she wanted to live out her final days?

"For God so loved the world that he gave his one and only Son . . ."

Her gaze drifted down to a passage in John's Gospel, of the New Testament. Hadassah shot a covert look toward her uncle before returning to the words. Why did they seem so familiar? Was it because of Marta?

No. It was Abraham's story, she realized. God had spared his son, Isaac, yet according to the Christians, He later sacrificed His own Son for the love of His people.

"That whoever believes in him shall not perish but have eternal life."

She glanced up from the book. Aric had spoken of Jesus and His death that day in her room. That He had willingly died so that others might live.

The room had gone deathly quiet, yet Hadassah heard a Whisper as she glanced over at the precious bundle asleep in Yaakov's arms. Then she looked at Clara, and behind her the sea of hopeless faces lined up at the door. Her people . . .

She began to type.

35

So the king took his signet ring . . . and gave it to Haman. . . .

Esther 3:10

Adrenaline pumped through Hermann's veins as he pounded on the door of the commandant's office. When he received no reply, he boldly entered.

The room was cast in shadow. His nemesis stood at the window facing the Fortress. "Herr Kommandant."

The tall man at the window didn't turn. "Captain."

Spying the holstered pistol at the commandant's side, Hermann resisted an urge to taunt him for making himself the fool over a Jewess. Perhaps he already knew.

Anyway, it didn't matter. Once Hermann executed his plan, it would become a foregone conclusion. His damp fingers clutched the handle of his briefcase, which contained the sabotaged manifest as well as the secret letter sent from inside the ghetto to the commandant's woman. Both would easily implicate Schmidt. Even Hermann's men would testify—they still carried a grudge at being forced to give up half their food to the Jews.

Hermann forced a calming breath. His promotion would soon be forthcoming. General Feldman had been pleased to receive his telephone call, especially when Hermann explained how he hadn't told anyone else. He'd contacted Herr General first, asking for guidance in the matter.

His mouth twitched. That fat one was easy to read. His ambition to take full credit for the arrest and parade it before der Führer had been predictable. Though Hermann expected a just reward, he no longer held grand illusions of the Chancellery; it was probably overrun with men like Schmidt—or worse, the general. Instead he surveyed the office that would very soon belong to him. No longer in the cold, he would again have hot food and a warm bed.

After glancing over his shoulder at the pair of guards he'd brought with him, he stepped forward. "Herr Kommandant, you are under arrest for treason against the Reich."

From his place by the window, Aric slowly turned to Hermann. "You are joking?"

"Nein, Herr Kommandant. I've got all the proof I need here."

Aric eyed the briefcase Hermann held up for his inspection. "What proof?" he asked, trying to rouse his anger. Defeat already weighed heavy upon him—his beautiful dove, his future, gone. Yet he wasn't going to let this cur deliver the final *coup de grâce*. "By whose authority do you dare arrest a superior officer, Captain?" he demanded.

"Herr General Feldman. Surely you know, Herr Kommandant, that during wartime, no rank of office is exempt from a charge of treason."

Aric moved toward the desk, then halted as Hermann jerked his Walther from its holster. Pulling back the slide, he raised the barrel. "My man will take your weapon. Martin!"

Corporal Martin hesitated in his approach. Aric raised his arms, allowing the guard to relieve him of his pistol.

"Search him," Hermann ordered. "You, Zeissen, search the desk."

Aric's eyes locked with Hermann's while Martin combed him for other contraband. Finally he took a hasty step back. "Nothing, Herr Captain."

Zeissen closed the last drawer. "Nothing here, either."

"You two will make certain he stays in this office while I am in Prague. Now wait outside until I am finished."

"What, no stockade for the prisoner, Captain?" Aric mocked once the soldiers left, his wrath finally awakened. "I would have thought you eager to see me caged and cuffed."

Hermann grinned. "Herr General's instructions were specific. A delicate matter, he called it—for Himmler's prized bull." He chuckled. "Putting you in stocks would draw unwanted attention, especially on the eve of the Red Cross visit. The fewer tongues wagging, the better.

"He was very interested to hear about your little deception. When I told him how you've been catering to the Jews, he wasn't surprised that you would sabotage the train manifests and obstruct the Reich's progress toward the Final Solution. In fact, he's quite eager to see the proof." Again Hermann held up the briefcase.

"We both know I had nothing to do with those lists, Captain."

"Do we? You're a clever man, Wehrmacht. More likely you've deceived us all. But too much bed sport has affected your brain if you think you could succeed, using that Jewess and her father . . ." He grinned at the shocked expression that appeared on the commandant's face. "Ah, you're surprised, then? About the Jew Elder?"

Aric reached for his chair and fell into it. He didn't know the old man was her father. "What have you done with her?"

"Nothing, yet. But I do plan to discover what you find so fascinating—"

"Schwein!" Aric launched at him over the desk, but the muzzle of Hermann's pistol stopped him.

"Careful," Hermann warned.

"I'm a colonel! Why jeopardize my rank, my life, to delay the deaths of a few hundred Jews?" The callous words tasted bitter, but Aric needed to convince him. Stella was in danger.

Hermann shrugged. "War makes people do desperate things."

"You're insane. When Herr Reichsführer arrives tomorrow morning—"

"It's already too late for that. I'm calling my men back in here."

"Wait." Aric had to find out how much Hermann knew about Stella. "You seem convinced she's Jewish, and that the old man is her father. How do you know this?"

Hermann eyed him a moment, then shrugged. Holding his pistol with one hand, he slid the briefcase onto the desk and opened it. "Have a look."

Aric donned his glasses before inspecting the water-stained note Stella had received from the ghetto. "Is this the only letter?" He glanced up at Hermann.

"It's enough."

"You plan to show this to Herr General?"

"Of course."

Aric breathed a curse and, despite the weapon trained on him, stalked back over to the window. He stood several moments, a plan forming. Finally he said, "Leave it with me."

Hermann snorted. "Do I look stupid?"

Aric turned to him. "Leave it . . . in exchange for my full written confession. I'll prepare it for you now."

Hermann eyed him suspiciously. "Why?"

"Captain." Aric ignored the ache in his gut as he strode back to the desk. Time was running out. He had to save her. "We both know this arrest is a farce. But you want something . . ." His eyes narrowed on Hermann. "My position as head of this camp?"

He knew he'd guessed right when the captain smiled.

"I too want something," Aric said.

"You're in no position—"

"Do you know anything about Wolkenbrand?"

Hermann stood in flushed silence.

"Eichmann has ordered that on Friday, after the Red Cross leaves, all evidence of Theresienstadt will be removed," Aric said. "I want Stella gone from this place before then. Otherwise she'll be treated like the rest. That cannot happen."

Surprised anger flashed across Hermann's face. "What do I gain by protecting a Jew?"

"Offer General Feldman my full confession." The ache in Aric's gut intensified. "And give him Stella. I promise he'll reward you greatly—"

"Until he sees the mark on her arm?" Hermann sneered. "Now who is insane?"

"Her new papers are in my desk, reissued last week from Berlin. There is also a letter regarding the error of her incarceration at Dachau, which explains the tattoo." He returned to his chair. "Think about it, Captain," Aric continued, forcing the words. "Make the general believe it and he'll give you whatever you desire. Surely you've noticed how enamored he is with her?"

Hermann's hazel eyes gleamed. "Clever Wehrmacht. So be it."

Something felt terribly wrong.

From the kitchen archway, Helen watched Captain Hermann leave through the front door without his two soldiers. She returned to the stove and stirred the *Rahmkalbsbeuschel*—veal lights in cream being another of the commandant's favorites—then removed the pot from the heat and set it against the sideboard.

Not that awful things hadn't already happened, she thought, wiping her hands on her apron. She hurried from the kitchen toward his office, her head still swimming with events from the past twenty-four hours. Poor little Joseph had been sent back to the ghetto and was now bound for Auschwitz—no doubt due to that foul-smelling general who laughed too much and ate enough for three people. Then there was Stella's arrest this morning . . .

Helen sucked in a breath as her sense of dread turned into a tangible pain; she instinctively reached for the lavender scarf tied at her throat. She'd had this kind of sense before—five long years ago. Yet time hadn't erased those memories. Every moment of every day that she opened her mouth and tried to speak prevented it . . .

She'd left the hospital that night after working second shift, willing herself invisible to the Soviet soldiers prowling the streets in packs as she darted in and out of the shadows toward home. Her city was again being torn apart. Centuries had witnessed Lvov tossed back and forth between Russia, Poland—even Austria held a two-hundred-year claim.

When her people recaptured their city for Poland in 1919, they had assumed an end to it. But twenty years later, as Helen walked the lamp-lit sidewalks, she sensed the danger of another coup. The Reds needed only to smell the first drop of blood before creating a frenzy that would make the city run red with it.

She had no idea the first drop would be her own.

A mob of soldiers, boisterous from a night of too much drink and womanizing, descended on her without warning. When she tried to run, a group of young Poles saw what was happening and gave chase. She suddenly found herself in the midst of battle as tensions broke loose between civilians and soldiers. They wielded rifles, clubs, knives . . . and the broken bottle that sliced her throat when she tried to flee the scuffle.

That night, the Reds won. And while she should feel grateful she was one of the survivors, Helen found that even with constant prayer it seemed impossible to forgive those who had consigned her to a life of silence.

She reached the library and recognized Corporal Martin standing with another soldier outside the colonel's office. She nodded to him as she approached the door.

"Nein, you must stay out!" Martin's uniformed sleeve shot out to halt her progress.

Helen gave him her best smile. He was young enough to be her son, if she'd mothered one. Young enough to have his backside paddled, too. She pointed toward the door, then opened her mouth and gestured with her fingers.

"Time to eat?" Martin sniffed the air. The aroma of her Rahmkalbsbeuschel wafted through the house. "Zeissen, you smell that? We have to eat canned rations while that Jew lover gets home-cooked meals." He glanced at Helen. "Get us some food."

She smiled again, waving at them to follow her.

"We can't leave our prisoner," the one called Zeissen said. "Bring the food in here."

The colonel was being held against his will? Helen hid her shock as she bobbed her head and left the library. Returning to the kitchen, she pulled the rosary beads from beneath her scarf and said a quick prayer for what she was about to do.

There were advantages to being mute, she decided after she'd finished her prayer and headed toward the back of the house. People usually told her everything; some even gave her their deepest secrets for safekeeping. Others had the foolish misconception she was stupid as well as dumb. They underestimated her.

Not the colonel. He'd always appreciated Helen's intelligence. He would never make the mistake of thinking *her* stupid, and she'd known him for over a year.

She had thought him dead at first, when they brought him into St. Nicholas's hospital in Lvov on a gurney that night. Gunshots had torn up his right lung and bruised his spine so badly he'd been paralyzed from the waist down. He declined over the next few months and refused to eat. Helen became so concerned that she cooked for him at home—Apfelstrudel, Leberknödel, and *Tafelspitz*. She learned and prepared many Austrian favorites and brought them in, hoping to entice him over the bland hospital fare.

It worked. Slowly he'd regained his color and weight. When he departed for Sevastopal, she accepted his offer to accompany him as his private nurse. Then, when he miraculously healed and began to walk again, he asked her to join him at Theresienstadt as his cook.

A soft smile touched her lips. She'd been eager to leave the past behind, and he'd always been willing to make a place for her. Aric von Schmidt never asked questions and always treated her with respect and kindness.

Rand slept soundly on the cot inside Joseph's room. Helen retrieved the bottle of morphine pills from the nightstand before she ran a quick hand across his brow. She considered waking him, but then decided against it. He needed his rest.

She all but skipped back to the kitchen. At almost fifty, she couldn't remember the last time she felt so good. She even tried without success to hum an old polka as she ground the entire contents of the bottle with mortar and pestle, then dumped the white powder into the Rahmkalbsbeuschel.

Why the colonel ever decided to cast his lot with the SS she would never understand. They were all ignorant brutes; cruel and hateful, much like the Reds.

The colonel was nothing like them.

Ladling the tainted veal lights into bowls, she set them on a wooden tray along with forks and napkins and made her way back to the library.

"Food!" Zeissen rushed forward as she placed the tray on Stella's desk. Helen beamed like a mother bird watching her two young chicks while the soldiers each ate an entire bowlful.

"Danke," they said in unison afterward, rubbing their full stomachs. Helen picked up the tray and returned to the kitchen to wait. Fifteen minutes passed before she grabbed a spool of clothesline from the laundry. She was about to start back to the library when a knock sounded at the kitchen's back door.

A gate guard escorted the old man, Morty Benjamin. The

soldier seemed nervous as he cleared his throat and demanded, "We must see Herr Kommandant at once. The Elder of the Judenrat is here on official business."

Helen considered Morty a moment before stepping back and allowing him to enter. When the young guard tried to follow, she blocked his path—and gave him her most searing look.

"But, Fräulein—"

Slamming the door in his face, she turned and led the way toward the library. She found Martin and Zeissen just as she'd expected: both slumped over in chairs, their chins drooping onto their chests.

"You've been busy," Morty said, taking in the scene. He raised a brow at her, clearly impressed.

She arched a brow back at him and then handed him the length of clothesline. He bound the soldiers' hands and feet to their chairs. Helen removed their pistols, stuffing them into her apron pocket.

Her anxiety finally gave way, however, when she stood before the colonel's door.

Aric sat in his darkened office, his mind numb and his limbs wooden, like the pull toys he'd played with as a child.

Was he ever really that young? It seemed eons had passed since the boy had charged happily through Austria's green hills on the back of his pony. Aric had been warmed by the loving embrace of his mother's arms; even his hard-nosed father had tousled his hair, giving silent approval on those rare occasions when his son had done something to please him. Before the war. Before Anschluss.

They were dead now, his parents. Soon he would join them. It was unlikely he would survive, having offered up a full written confession to toadies like Hermann and Feldman. Aric had been in the party long enough to know words like *sabotage* and *treason* kept firing squads engaged in the lively business of shooting first and asking questions later.

No doubt he would be formally incarcerated, perhaps in the Kleine Festung once the Swiss departed. Then shot. He'd be written off as a bad example of discipline, a lack of fervency to the Führer's cause.

But Aric had his own cause.

He looked down at the single pearl lying on his desk. He picked it up, rolling it back and forth between thumb and forefinger. He could still see her and imagine that beautiful column of throat, where strands of the precious beads had rested against her soft skin.

And by tomorrow night she would belong to the general. He felt an invisible vise squeeze his chest. The idea of that lecher Feldman touching her made him want to die.

Still, he'd made his pact. Aric let the pearl fall from his fingers into the wastebasket beside his desk. It sank beneath the charred ashes . . . all that remained of her private letter.

Now she could continue to pretend with someone else, but at least she would stay alive. The *Endoslung* at Theresienstadt would certainly still happen on Friday; the wheel would continue to turn, with or without him. At least the mass killing would not be at his hands, nor would he live long enough to be haunted by the faces of those Jews murdered behind the walls. Pathetic, hopeless . . . human faces. *"We want to live, the same as you . . ."*

Aric thought back to Dachau and how one woman had clutched the hand of a dead child as though willing her back to life. Stella had captivated him, drawn him in. She'd given him hope. He hadn't figured it out until now—that he'd been counting on her to hold him like that, to resurrect him the same way she tried to save that little girl.

But she'd used him instead, to save her precious Jews. *Her people*. She must hate him now.

The chronic ache in his legs had become unbearable. Aric

rummaged through the top drawer of his desk for extra mor-phine pills. The bottle was empty. Slumping back in his chair, he closed his eyes. He seemed doomed to the pain . . .

His fingers curled beneath the seat, searching out the pistol taped to its underside. He retrieved the gun and laid it on the desk, running a hand over its short barrel. The *Westentaschen-pistole* was small enough to fit inside a man's vest pocket, yet quite lethal.

He'd already considered shooting his way out, but where would he go? What good would it do? She would still be gone, and he would still be the fool who had soldiered in a war fought for all the wrong reasons, sacrificing everything for another man's distorted perception of glory. He was a man who loved a woman he could not have.

Aric raised the pistol and released the safety. Grazing the bar-rel along his right temple, he felt cold steel against his skin. An alternative he'd not contemplated before, it now held appeal. There was nothing left for him. There would be no more pain. *Dear God, save me from myself* . . .

"Herr Kommandant . . . ?"

A soft knock sounded. Aric checked the safety and dropped the gun into his lap. In the next instant, the door burst open to reveal not his guards but Helen—and the Jew, Morty Benjamin. "Where are Martin and Zeissen?" he asked dully.

"Sleeping in the library, Herr Kommandant." Morty Benja-min smiled. "Your housekeeper is a woman of many talents."

Helen blushed before ducking out of the office. Aric barely registered the pair of pistols stuffed inside her apron. He placed his own gun back on top of the desk. "What do you want, old man?" he asked wearily.

"I've brought you the final manifest for tonight's train, Herr Kommandant."

He slapped a sheaf of papers onto the desk. Aric ignored them. "She's your daughter, isn't she?"

The old Jew shifted. His gaze fell to the pistol. "She's my niece. My brother's daughter."

Dry humor broke through Aric's misery. "No wonder she went to such lengths to try and save you."

Morty Benjamin seemed to take his measure before he said, "As you know, the manifest is always approved by the Kommandant of the camp. Herr Captain Hermann usually handles the matter, but in his absence, I've come directly to you."

"What do I care about your lists?" Aric pushed the papers toward him. "Go to Hermann's office and wait for his return."

Gnarled fingers nudged the papers back at him with challenging vigor. "You'd better take a look at these."

Surprised at the old man's insolence—and his piercing look—Aric picked up the sheets and sifted them into order.

He rose and went to the window where gray light filtered through the barred panes. Fishing his glasses from his pocket, he put them on and stared at the first name on the page.

Fury blazed through his chest as he whipped around. "Is this some kind of sick joke?"

Morty eased out a breath. For a moment he'd been afraid the commandant was past convincing. Beyond comprehension of what was at stake. "I assure you, Herr Kommandant, deportation is not something we laugh about in the ghetto."

"I made a deal with that mangy cur!" The commandant launched a fist into the wall next to the jamb. Plaster crumbled to the carpeted floor. He shook the papers at Morty. "She cannot go to Auschwitz, do you understand?" He marched back across the room to halt in front of Morty. "This list is unsatisfactory." He thrust the papers at him. "Revise it."

Morty pursed his lips. He knew he played a dangerous game. "I can do nothing about the list, Herr Kommandant." Boldly, he met the gaze of the man his Hadassah still loved, on whom their deliverance now rested. "She won't change her mind, my maideleh. God knows, I tried to dissuade her," he lied.

"I forbid it."

Morty's heart took a small leap. "If she must die, Herr Kommandant, why not allow her the right to choose her own way?"

"No! This is suicide—"

"Not suicide," Morty interjected softly. "Not when the enemy holds a gun to your head."

The commandant stumbled backward. In a seeming daze he returned to his chair and tossed the papers and his glasses onto the desk.

He stared at the small pistol still lying there. Morty followed his gaze. "Survival is the key instinct in all of us," he said gently. "Yet it never comes without cost. Each must pay a price. With intellect or strength, for pleasure or pain. Some even barter their self-respect." Morty leaned over the desk and caught the other man's attention. "What price have you tendered, my son?"

"The highest of all, old man." The commandant spoke in anguished tones. "I've sold my own soul."

Morty straightened and smiled. "Then you must buy it back."

36

All the royal officials . . . paid honor to Haman. . . .

Esther 3:2

Heil Hitler!" Hermann saluted the two men standing near the terrace window. He'd been ushered into the elegant suite at Prague's Hotel Europa.

"Heil Hitler, Captain," General Feldman returned the address.

The other man eyed him from behind a pince-nez glass. "The general has informed me of the situation at Theresienstadt. I commend you for reporting this . . . difficulty."

The SS-Reichsführer looked anything but pleased. Heinrich Himmler's ferret-like features flushed against a thin-lipped smile. No doubt he wondered what der Führer's reaction would be to discover Himmler's "war hero" a traitor who had nearly sabotaged their Embellishment project with the Red Cross.

"Herr Reichsführer, I recommend the captain here to take over as Kommandant of Theresienstadt." Feldman moved to join Hermann. "He has been at the camp over a year and proved most efficient in preparing for our visit—and he has been discreet. Colonel Schmidt will remain under guard and confined to his quarters until the Red Cross delegation has left. Afterward we can deal with the prisoner and minimize any embarrassment to the Reich."

Silence ensued as the general's well-aimed barb at the SS-Reichsführer hit its mark. Hermann's heartbeat raced. His eyes darted to the general, and he saw the mouth that had consumed liters of beer the night before flattened with determination.

"Very well, General." The SS-Reichsführer's intensity shifted to Hermann. "You'll be given whatever you need. Our visit with the Swiss tomorrow must proceed without event. I need not elaborate on our Führer's expectations for this particular success."

Elation robbed Hermann of speech. He bowed smartly, tapping his bootheels together.

"You're dismissed, Kommandant." The general sounded smug. "Telephone me with any problems."

Hermann found his voice. "Jawohl, Herr General. I assure you that all will be in perfect order for tomorrow morning." Saluting, he wheeled sharply and strode from the foyer into the carpeted hall.

He descended the stairs, taking note of the hotel's grand opulence. Wide, arched openings and colorful murals were painted into each alcove, while brass sconces depicting cherubs hung above beautifully cut glass, guarding each portal in the lavish style of Art Nouveau.

The lobby downstairs wore rich walnut paneling with floral brocade divans stretched like languorous felines across tapestried rugs. Crystal chandeliers glittered high overhead, while higher still, frescoes of seraphim and the heavens caught the afternoon's rays through a series of skylights along the canted ceiling.

Hermann appreciated the beauty; he envisioned the rich Aubusson rugs and plush leather chairs back at the brick house in Theresienstadt. The warm fire blazing in the hearth, the mouthwatering smells of Sauerbraten, Apfelstrudel, and freshly baked bread emanating from the kitchen—all of it would be his now, permanently. All except for the woman . . .

He'd kept his end of the bargain, allowing Schmidt to burn

her Jew letter after writing out his full confession. And the general was quite thrilled at the prospect of finally getting his dream girl. Hermann laughed aloud over the deception. The only way the fat general would ever know he'd been played a fool is if Stella refused to play her part—and she wouldn't, not if she wanted to live.

He wondered at her progress with the revised manifest. Father and daughter both must be sweating blood to come up with the missing prisoners' names. The notion felt like balm to his wounded pride. She would suffer for rejecting him.

Outside the hotel, Wenceslas Square seemed deserted. A pair of enlisted men, one wearing a non-regulation red scarf and mittens, huddled next to a fire barrel. Snow fell lightly from a muted gray sky. Hermann strode toward his car, impervious to the cold.

Kommandant! His senses reeled with euphoria. The feeling stayed with him as he drove north along the narrow snow-dusted streets of the Vltava River's east bank. At the Charles Bridge, with its thirty statue saints, he gazed with mounting anticipation across the icy waters toward his destination—the *Mala Strana*, the Lesser Quarter. He was glad he'd come alone.

Prague's imperial castle of *Hradcany* and the twin spires of St. Vitus went unnoticed as Hermann drove on, his mind replaying the scene at the hotel. He was now in charge of Theresienstadt. He imagined Himmler and Eichmann's pleasure once the Swiss were satisfied with the exemplary ghetto and its model prisoners. It could mean his promotion to SS-Sturmbannführer.

Excitement coiled in him as he tracked deeper into the Lesser Quarter. Towering stone buildings rose along either side of the narrow streets, while gingerbread façades, darkened with age, housed many of the city's small taverns and shops.

Hermann grinned as he mentally ticked off the remaining items to be dealt with at the camp. Aric von Schmidt must be made to try and escape, which of course would necessitate killing him. Thereafter he would remain "ill and unavailable" until after the Red Cross had left.

Grossman posed no problem; the Wehrmacht's loyal man was still abed with his wounds. Only the old Jew and his daughter remained. After tomorrow, Morty Benjamin would end his life in the Little Fortress—or the Wolkenbrand Schmidt spoke of.

Stella would go to Feldman willingly once she knew it meant her freedom. Hermann had yet to tell her of her good fortune. He'd make her get on her knees and beg for the new identification papers, however—then again for her opportunity to leave the ghetto.

He gripped the steering wheel hard as he turned onto a familiar street of tightly fitted houses. Wheeling the car up to the curb alongside a four-story building of blue-gray stone, he jammed on the brake and sat, jaw clenched.

He still wanted her. His mind began conjuring memories—of her kiss, then of Stella lying on the bed that morning, trying to shield herself with the proof of her treachery. He envisioned them together, yet he wasn't certain what compelled him more: the need to conquer his fascination of her or the desire to show her what a real man—an SS man—was like.

Exiting the car, he jogged up a flight of stone steps to the front porch. He rang the bell. Moments later the door cracked a few inches. A voluptuous woman clad in a yellow silk wrap—and little else—stood in the shadowy opening. Beneath her mop of bleached blond curls, eyes heavily lined with kohl raked him up and down. "It's been too long, Liebling," she purred. Hermann said nothing but just pushed his way through the door.

Reasons didn't matter; he would have Stella before the general did.

37

Then the king extended the gold scepter to Esther and she arose and stood before him.

Esther 8:4

Dim lamplight cast her shadow against the wall inside the Judenrat's compact office. Hadassah slid into the chair she'd placed beside the cot, which her uncle had brought for the boy. The room, previously crowded with Jews, now sat empty except for her and the sleeping child.

Hadassah paid the price for giving false hope; she'd spent hours enduring the despair in each voice, witnessing the quiet misery etched into each hollowed face as one by one they came forward to surrender their lives to a single line on a sheet of paper.

After much agonizing, she'd managed to recall only about half the remaining names on the cards she'd destroyed, forcing her uncle to draw from Captain Hermann's stack.

Morty had departed with the revised manifest nearly two hours ago. She remembered his moment of recognition, when he'd seen her name at the top of the first page. Despite his pinched mouth and narrowed gaze, he'd said nothing. Yet when he tried to offer his own name, she objected. Hermann wouldn't allow him to go on the train, not until after the Red Cross visit. No, the monster would much prefer the children to go.

She was still haunted by the image of the fretful little girl inside the ghetto. In a few hours, innocent children—perhaps her as well?—would be wakened from their beds and bound for a place where real nightmares awaited them.

She clutched the Bible to her chest. Would God save them from her arrogance, the ridiculous notion that she alone could make a difference?

In a burst of raw nerves, Hadassah rose from her chair to pace the length of the room. Waiting stretched her sanity to the breaking point, sowing seeds of panic that grew with each passing hour as the Consequence of her rash act crystallized into hard reality.

She was going to Auschwitz.

Pausing in mid-stride, Hadassah opened the Bible to a random page—the book of Hebrews, chapter ten, verse thirty-nine. She read:

"But we do not belong to those who shrink back and are destroyed, but to those who have faith and are saved."

Gooseflesh rose along her arms. She had taken a leap of faith. Would it save her?

A murmur of voices outside the door brought her up short. Hadassah's pulse raced as the guard outside her door, Corporal Sonntag, opened it wide. Aric . . . ?

Yaakov. Her last breath of hope died. "I've brought blankets," the stocky man said, moving into the room. "And dinner." He held up a liter-sized pail. "It's cabbage soup. Not the kind of food you're used to, but it will have to do—"

"Where's Morty?" Hadassah asked anxiously.

Yaakov shrugged. "He stopped by our Block about an hour

ago." He looked down at the book in her hand. "Is that a Christian Bible you're reading?"

Hadassah flushed.

"Where did you get it?"

"I . . ." She had no logical explanation for why the book continually sought her out, only that it had become her lifeline. "I can't tell you. It just . . . calls to me." Seeing his scowl, she raised her chin, adding, "It contains many of the books from our own Tanakh."

"It's not suitable—"

"Does it matter now?" She clutched the book tighter to her chest. "It gives me strength."

Yaakov seemed unmoved by her defense. He kept his frown while he eyed her steadily. Finally he said, "They are angry, you know. You gave them hope, then took it away." He paused, let out a sigh. "But they do admire your courage. Though they may choose to forget that you once tried to save them, they cannot ignore the fact that you now join them willingly."

"That doesn't mean I am not afraid."

He surprised her by placing a hand on her shoulder. "That's because you haven't been in the ghetto very long. After a while, here in this place, everything becomes lost to you: privacy, hopes and dreams. Your dignity." His dark eyes flashed pain. "And when you think there is nothing left, even the fear goes away."

She hadn't forgotten her months at Dachau. "I know, Yaakov."

"Besides, I suspect we will all be shipped to the east before long." He glanced again at the Bible, and his scowl eased. "Glean what strength you can."

With that, the stocky Czech swung around and walked toward the door. Hadassah called to him, "Thank you . . . for taking care of Joseph. And for being Morty's friend."

He turned, and his ruddy features softened as he doffed his felt cap. "God go with you, Morty Benjamin's maideleh."

As soon as he'd left, Hadassah retrieved her bounty and

returned to Joseph's side. Setting the pail of soup on the floor, she covered the child with an extra blanket and laid the other across her lap. She took up the Bible again and smoothed trembling fingers over the cover.

She'd told Yaakov it gave her strength, and it was true. Hadassah opened the book and for the first time began carefully navigating through each section of the Old Testament: the five books of Moses; the book of Prophets—or the Nevi'im, as she knew them in Hebrew; the Ketuvim writings—Wisdom books, including Psalms and Proverbs; and the Qohelet, the book of Ecclesiastes. *Shabbat Chol Hamoed Sukkot . . .*

Seized by an unexpected wave of longing, Hadassah pressed her hand against the cool pages of the first chapter. Each year on the Sabbath during Sukkot, the Feast of Booths, Morty, his head adorned in a *yarmulke* and wearing his *tallit* shawl, would read to her from Ecclesiastes, hoping to glean from King Solomon's words the truest meaning of human existence.

Sukkot had been her favorite celebration as a child. Each year she was allowed to help her uncle and a few other men construct a *sukkah* in the courtyard behind their apartments. The open-sided tent made of limbed branches would be covered with willow sprigs, myrtle leaves, hanging citron, and real palm fronds that Herr Mahler across the street had shipped directly from Palestine for the occasion.

Fat orange pumpkins, dried cornstalks, summer fruit, and gourd squash added decoration to their booth. It was there the small Jewish community gathered during the prescribed eight days to celebrate their meals together. At night, she and the other children slept in the garland-rimmed booth, decidedly just as their ancestors who fled Egypt had done. Long after her friends fell asleep, Hadassah would lie awake listening to the soft rustle of palm fronds, the early autumn breeze lifting their edges. She remembered inhaling the tang of ripened apples piled in a bushel basket outside the tent opening. She had felt such peace . . .

Scanning down the page, she paused to read the first verses of chapter three.

> *There is a time for everything,*
> *and a season for every activity under heaven:*
> *a time to be born, and a time to die . . .*

She gazed at Joseph. He looked so frail, his eyes terribly swollen, his baby-soft skin marred with cruel bruises. The gentle rise and fall of his chest assured her that he was only sleeping.

> *a time to weep . . .*

She blinked hard to keep the words from blurring on the page,

> *a time to be silent and a time to speak . . .*

A sense of calm unfurled inside her, penetrating the fear. It dawned on her then that she no longer had to cower behind secrets; the truth had found her out, exposed her, and oddly gave her back a measure of control. She had made the decision to go on the train, and it would be her choice, not the Nazis', on how she would meet the future . . . even if there was none.

Morty's vision of salvation had been no more than a dream, but Hadassah knew she could make one difference: Anna had died alone. Her kaddishel would not suffer the same fate.

"Mama?"

A head of mussed brown hair emerged from the blankets as Joseph tried to sit up.

"I'm here, little man." She slid from the chair onto the edge of his bed and gathered him close. Already she'd taken a thorough inventory of his cuts and bruises, carefully inspecting his arms, chest, and legs for damage. What she'd found made her want to scream. The monsters had all but beaten him to death. "You must be thirsty, sweetheart. How about some soup?"

He ran his tongue across swollen, cracked lips, and nodded. Hadassah reached for the metal pail Yaakov had brought. "It might be a little cold," she cautioned.

She held the vessel to his bruised mouth, felt her heart constrict when his little Adam's apple bobbed up and down with each huge swallow. "I think most of the cabbage must have sunk to the bottom," she said when he stopped drinking.

"Where is . . . Morty?" His voice sounded wraith-like.

"He's gone to notify those who will take tonight's train." Guilt battled her despair as she set the pail on the floor. "He hasn't returned."

"Yaakov told me what you did. You took all those names off the train list. Even mine," he whispered.

She couldn't look at him. "I was a fool, Joseph, to think it would work."

"What you did was good."

She looked at him. "Yaakov didn't tell you, but I failed. I made things worse."

"Papa told me a boy only fails when he does not try." Joseph eyed her through puffy lids. "I think it must be the same for a girl."

Hadassah couldn't help smiling even as she said, "Sometimes the risks are too high, and then it's too late to make things right again."

"You can't give up. You have to save us."

Bitter laughter nearly choked her. "You sound like Morty."

"There must be lots of people in the ghetto who still believe in you." His bruised face showed his earnestness. "I do."

The evident hostility in those who had passed through the room earlier seemed a far cry from this boy's unswerving belief. Hadassah breathed deep to try and ease the ache in her heart. "I want to believe, too," she whispered. Then she lifted him onto her lap and rocked him until his head finally dropped against her shoulder in sleep.

Easing him back onto the bed, she tucked him in. Words couldn't express how much he'd come to mean to her; Hadassah wished they might live long enough for her to show him. "You would have loved the golden lions, kaddishel," she whispered, knowing the promises she'd made must now be broken. "You could have chosen any castle—"

"An enchanted castle, Hadassah?"

Her head swung around as Aric entered through the open doorway. His presence filled the room. In his greatcoat and peaked cap, he cast an indomitable shadow against the backdrop of light from the desktop lamp. Slung over one arm was the new coat he'd given her.

Rising from the edge of the cot, Hadassah backed away until her knees touched the edge of the chair. This couldn't be real; it had to be a dream.

Unable to look him in the face, she focused instead on the brass-topped cane clutched in the palm of his hand, then at his polished Hessians.

The boots halted beside Joseph's bed. Aric passed her the houndstooth coat and then removed his hat and gloves before lowering himself to kneel beside the boy. "How is he?"

He still hadn't looked at her. His white-knuckled grip on the cane told her his legs pained him more than usual. Caution overruled any compassionate urge, however. He had yet to state the purpose for his visit.

"Joseph is as well as can be expected, Herr Kommandant." Her voice held surprising steadiness. "As you can see, your captain used him for boxing practice."

His hand faltered as he reached to touch the boy's crown. Joseph's dark lashes drifted open. "Herr Kommandant." The swollen lips grimaced in a smile. "I knew you'd come."

Aric smiled back. The hand on his cane wavered slightly. "You must hurry and get strong, Joseph. There is much to do and I need your help."

His gentle voice tore at Hadassah's heart.

The boy nodded. "Gut," Aric said as he settled his tall frame on the edge of the bed. "I overheard Fräulein mention castles. Would you like to hear a story . . . about a magic castle?"

"Ja," Joseph said through a yawn, his puffy lids already blinking against sleep.

"Once upon a time there was a king's son who lived in an enchanted castle," Aric began. "By day, he went out in search of love—the only magic that would protect him from the demons that stalked the castle's dark halls at night. They waited to torture his dreams."

"But, Herr Kommandant . . ." Joseph came suddenly awake. "Why did he return to the castle at night? Why didn't he just stay away?"

"The prince couldn't stay away. He was tied to the enchantment like the castle itself. Only love's magic could set him free and save him from the nightmares that were killing him little by little each night. They made him lose all hope of ever healing, or feeling anything but pain."

Aric looked up at her then. Time stopped as she drank in the sight of him: his rugged face pale with exhaustion, the taut creases framing his mouth.

"Did the prince ever find his love?"

The child's drowsy voice punctured the silence. "He did," Aric said, his gaze never leaving Hadassah's. "But by then it was too late. The castle demons had twisted it into something despised and ugly so that the prince could no longer believe in it." His voice dropped to a whisper. "He could no longer believe in himself."

Joseph had already fallen asleep. Hadassah searched the face of the man before her, feeling joy, frustration, even laughter. Most of all, she ached for the comfort of his embrace.

Yet she resisted the impulse. "He should have trusted in his love. It was always true, even though circumstances didn't seem that way," she said.

Aric rose from the bed to stand beside her. "You're right." Anger flashed in his eyes as he raised a finger to gently trace her bruised cheek. "Perhaps then he wouldn't have let others destroy it."

Hadassah's heart raced. "Are you so certain it's gone?"

Her words seemed to have a profound effect on him. The grim mask disintegrated, revealing an expression of longing and uncertainty. He took back the houndstooth coat and wrapped it around her shoulders. When he drew her close, she breathed in the scent of his spiced cologne, felt the damp snow that clung to him. "Love's magic never dies," she whispered.

"Then make me believe again," he said, his face mere inches from hers. "Save me, Hadassah . . ."

His voice broke on a plea so softy spoken it seemed more breath than substance. The words penetrated to the core of her soul. She raised a tentative hand to his cheek, then brushed her lips across his—once, twice, before his mouth seized hers with a desperation so fierce it threatened to shatter them both. His hands cupped the back of her head as he deepened the kiss, telling her without words that he would never again let her go.

Hadassah wrapped her arms around his waist, comforted in the solid feel of him. She kissed him back with equal passion, telling him without words that lies would never again come between them.

He cradled her face with his hands even after he ended the kiss. When Hadassah finally opened her eyes, she saw in his expression a look she'd never seen before.

Hope.

"Always love me," he whispered. He kissed the tip of her nose, then her cheek and the edge of her brow.

"Which woman do you love, Aric?" she breathed.

His only answer was to smile and kiss her again. "We don't have much time."

"Time for what?"

"He's got a plan, child."

Hadassah's gaze flew to the doorway, where her uncle stood. "Tatteh?" She blushed at seeing his smug expression. How long had he been there? "What plan?" she asked.

Morty beamed. "Salvation, of course."

38

"Now write another decree in the king's name in behalf of the Jews. . . ."

Esther 8:8

Hadassah followed Aric as he carried Joseph toward the door, where her uncle waited.

Outside the room, she glanced around for the guard. "Corporal Sonntag has been detained," Aric said at her questioning look. "Come, we must hurry. Our favorite captain will return in a couple of hours and there's still much to do."

"Where is he now?" she asked.

"In Prague, arranging my court-martial."

Hadassah gasped. "Why . . . ?"

"I'll explain later." To Morty he said, "Is everyone in place?"

Her uncle nodded as he led the way downstairs. "I've spread the word. Everyone wishing to board tonight's train will meet us outside the infirmary. I've recruited volunteers to distract the guards away from that area." He flashed a crafty smile. "A little fire."

"And the railroad man?"

"Lenny Buczak will be waiting for us in the ghetto's kitchen, as you requested."

"Excellent." Aric gently shifted the sleeping bundle in his arms. Hadassah carried Aric's cane. She'd also brought along her Bible. Morty glanced at the book but didn't say a word.

"What are you planning to do?" she asked Aric.

"Steal a train."

Before she could reply, he cut her off. "No more questions, love. Come, you'll see."

Outside, the snow had stopped. Morning's dingy light had faded to the soft gray pallor of afternoon. They reached the street and made their way to the ghetto kitchen where a welcome fire in the brazier and the smell of cooked cabbage greeted them.

Hadassah had expected to see Yaakov and was surprised to find Helen there, as well. The housekeeper rushed forward to wrap her in a crushing embrace. Then she took the sleeping child from Aric and moved with him to a bench near the brazier.

Two others sat on the opposite side of the kitchen table: a slender young man and a middle-aged woman, neither of whom Hadassah recognized. The woman clasped and unclasped her red-knuckled hands against the table.

Aric glanced around the room. "Where's Rand?"

"Herr Kommandant." Sergeant Grossman moved out of the shadows. He offered Hadassah a curt nod before facing his commanding officer.

"How are you feeling, my friend?"

The tall soldier's movements were stiff. "Much better."

"Thank you for coming. And you too, Helen." He flashed an amused look at the housekeeper. "But remind me never to make you angry. You cook a very wicked Rahmkalbsbeuschel."

Confused by the conversation, Hadassah nonetheless felt warmed at the loyalty of these people. She wasn't fooled—whatever Aric and her uncle had planned was certainly dangerous.

Aric retrieved his glasses before pulling a folded piece of paper from his coat pocket. He smoothed what appeared to be a map out on the table while Morty lit a kerosene lamp.

Aric caught up her hand and pulled her close. Only after he gave her fingers a quick squeeze did Hadassah realize she was tense. She took a deep breath, forcing herself to relax.

"This is Lenny Buczak." Morty indicated the slender young man at the table. "And Mrs. Brenner."

The woman with reddened knuckles nodded in their direction. Lenny vaulted from his chair and whipped off his cap. He was painfully thin and nearly as tall as Aric.

"I understand you're from Poland, Herr Buczak. You once worked for the railroad?"

Lenny's large Adam's apple bobbed up and down. "Jawohl, Herr Kommandant."

Aric leaned over the map. "We are here." He pinned a spot with his finger. "And we need to get there." He drew an imaginary line east through Poland, to a point in the Ukraine. "The Red Army has retaken a few cities east of the Polish border like Vilna, Bialystock, Brest Litovsk"—his finger paused on a mark south of the Ukrainian city of Lutsk—"and Lemberg, which is where we want to go."

"Lemberg?" Lenny asked. "You mean Lvov?"

Aric nodded. "The Reich renamed it when it fell into German hands. I'm well-acquainted with that city." He shot a glance at Helen. "Your job, Herr Buczak, is to figure out how to get us there . . . without alerting Auschwitz."

Lenny stared at the map, frowning while his Adam's apple convulsed. He finally reached out with a long finger and ran an imaginary line from Theresienstadt to Prague, then beyond to a city marked as Prerov. "Here—there's a switchback just north of the city. You can avoid Auschwitz and go east along the rim of the *Nizke Tatry* and cross the Carpathians." He indicated a daunting east-west stretch of mountains south of Poland. "The train will come out here, at Krosno"—his finger jogged northeast—"and then to Przemysl. It's only a few kilometers from the Ukrainian border. Beyond that is Lvov." He glanced at Aric. "But since we don't know the train schedules, switching tracks will be dangerous."

"This entire scheme is riddled with danger, Herr Buczak. Least of which is whether or not we'll encounter an oncoming train." Aric eyed the tall young man. "The question is . . . are you up to the task?"

Lenny looked about to swallow a snowball whole before he straightened and said, "I am, Herr Kommandant."

Aric turned to Helen, still seated by the fire. "You're certain you want to do this?"

Her answer was a vehement nod as she rocked the sleeping Joseph in her arms.

"Very well," he said. Then to Grossman, "You and Helen will be our decoy. Escort her in my staff car to this point—Bratislava." His finger moved back to the Austrian-Czech border. "I'll prepare a set of orders and we'll establish the story that the *Gruppenführer* there demands I share my exemplary cook. I doubt any patrol who stops you will question the order." Aric's mouth curved upward. "Those soldiers out there are freezing their pants off. They won't wish to leave their warm stations to detain you any longer than necessary."

He turned to Lenny. "You'll have to hide in the trunk of the car. When Sergeant Grossman arrives at the target point near Prerov, you must switch the track to change our course of direction. We should be well on our way to you by then. I'll use green flares to signal our approach. You'll wait until our train has passed before you leave.

"Rand, I'll give you and Helen what funds I have at my disposal. From there, my friend, you must smuggle Herr Buczak into Switzerland."

"Herr Kommandant, I would much prefer to go home to Krakow."

"As you wish," Aric said to the young man. "But I warn you, Poland is still in German hands. You would fare better in neutral territory."

"Will they be taking the boy, too?" Mrs. Brenner nodded toward the sleeping child in Helen's arms.

Hadassah's jaw set. "Nein."

Aric gave her a tender look. "Joseph stays with us."

"This plan is crazy, Herr Kommandant," Grossman said angrily. "Our own soldiers will shoot you down before you reach the border. And if they don't get you, Ivan will finish you off the instant you step onto Russian soil."

"I take no more risk than those who ride the train," Aric said. "And the only alternative for them is death."

"And yours, Herr Kommandant?"

"The same." He shrugged. "But I'd rather risk my life and what's left of my soul with these people than do nothing and prolong a miserable existence."

Hadassah squeezed his hand, overjoyed by his change of heart. She was also frightened by the realization he would be more likely to die than those he tried to save.

She gripped the Bible she still held, hoping to gain strength. Hours ago she'd put herself into God's hands; she'd accepted the possibility of her own death at Auschwitz for her people—but not Aric's. *Please, Lord, don't let me lose him. Not now . . .*

"Let's get going. We've got a lot to do," Aric said.

"Like stealing a train?" Hadassah tried for a halfhearted attempt at humor. Despite her fragile renewal of faith, she couldn't help being afraid.

"Freiheit, my love," he said, reading her concern. "Freedom for you, for them." He indicated those leaving the kitchen. "Even for me." He smiled and nudged her toward the door. "Quickly. Our future waits."

Outside the infirmary, Hadassah stood beside Aric and burrowed deeper into her coat. She tried not to think of the peril
that the next few hours would bring, yet it was impossible to
ignore—especially when she heard the distant shouts and observed coils of black smoke rising up from the proximity of the
Terezin Café.

"I believe Yaakov is keeping the guards busy, Herr Kommandant." Morty stood beside Mrs. Brenner, wearing the benign
expression of a fox.

"You're not burning down the whole city?" Hadassah asked.

His thin features took on a fierce look. "Let the Red Cross
take a good look at our Paradiesghetto now."

"Instruct the others to line up here outside the infirmary,"
Aric said. "I'll go inside and talk with these people."

"I'll come with you," Hadassah said. "They might find what
you're going to tell them very hard to believe."

"It would seem this entire day has been filled with surprises."
He smiled at her, and Hadassah nodded as she took the hand
he offered her.

Inside the infirmary, the cloying stench of sickness pulled her
back into the harshness of reality. Wooden bunks like those she
remembered in the children's quarters stood three levels high
and were packed tightly into rows along either side of the dimly
lit room. Each bunk held two people—the sick, the dying, and
those too elderly or weak with hunger and exhaustion to care
for themselves.

Hadassah leaned against Aric and felt his body tense. She
glanced up at his tight-lipped expression and knew that he too
was affected by the sight.

———

Aric opened his mouth to speak, but the words he'd intended
failed. The silence unnerved him as he and Hadassah reached
the center of the room. He looked around at the hundreds of
pairs of eyes watching him—many of them rheumy, frightened,

or simply too weak to care—and wondered how he could have been so blinded by duty.

How could a man allow such atrocities to occur, even in war?

"They want to live, the same as you." Hadassah's words returned to him. Yet most of these people would die from disease and hunger. His own negligence had taken care of that.

He managed to clear his throat, but it was Hadassah who said, "Everyone, please listen. I am Morty Benjamin's niece." A murmur of voices rose at her announcement. She held up the manifest. "Your names have been included on these lists, to leave on the next train. But that train will not go to Auschwitz." She flashed Aric a tremulous smile and said, "Instead, we will seek freedom across the border of the Ukraine, into the safe hands of the Russians."

The stillness shattered as everyone began speaking at once. Someone called out, "You are the one we have heard about! You have come to save us!"

Confused by their declaration, Aric shot her a curious look.

"Later," she said, blushing.

He held up a hand for silence. "We must prepare quickly if our plan is to have any chance of success. Right now, Captain Hermann believes I am still under house arrest. He left hours ago for Prague to inform my superiors. He'll return soon in order to oversee the train's departure. We must be gone before he gets back."

"Will everyone be able to go?"

Aric scanned the sea of drawn, pallid faces for the person who spoke. A thin, knobby-jointed arm shot out from one of the bunks.

"I am Leo Molski, Herr Kommandant. Friend to Morty Benjamin . . . and his maideleh." Leo poked his gaunt face from the shadows and gave Hadassah a toothless smile. "Will all of us be able to leave Theresienstadt?"

"There isn't enough room on the train for everyone. Just those on the manifest." Aric's gaze darted to the others. "This journey will be dangerous. I can't guarantee you won't be captured and shot before we reach our destination. I can't even be certain the Russians will protect you. But you must try." He turned back to Leo Molski. "To stay here can only mean death for you."

The room went still for several moments. Then Leo called out, "I have become . . . feeble, Herr Kommandant. I doubt I could even make such a journey." He propped himself up on one thin elbow. "So I would give up my place on the train for another. Someone young and strong, who will live long enough . . . to enjoy freedom."

"My place, too," offered someone—a white-haired woman across the room whose shrunken face held dark eyes glittering with purpose. "Give mine to a child."

Others began to murmur their agreement. Aric felt a sudden constriction against his throat as one by one the courageous held out their hands, giving up their places on the train to someone younger, stronger. Someone who would tell their story to the Russians.

He glanced at Hadassah. Her eyes were bright with unshed tears. Clearing his throat, he said, "Tomorrow morning my superiors will arrive with the Red Cross. They expect to see a perfect city, filled with healthy prisoners of war. But even now, we're torching some of the new storefronts in the ghetto to keep my soldiers occupied while we escape."

He turned to Leo Molski. "My superiors will be gravely annoyed. Those of you who choose to stay will suffer the brunt of their disappointment."

Leo looked to the others in the room. Each nodded at him, as if by some tacit agreement. When his gaze returned to Aric, it was bright, burning. "Then we'll give them a disappointment they won't forget."

39

Many lay in sackcloth and ashes.

Esther 4:3

Once the children were included, a lottery was held for the remaining space on the train. Hundreds lined up, their steamy breath creating a fog against the frigid air. Light snow began to fall again, and with the billowing smoke rising above the streets of the Marktplatz the afternoon seemed more like dusk.

Hadassah was given a key to the Nazis' storehouse. With the soldiers diverted, she and several others took blankets, food, clothing, and first-aid supplies before collecting all available hospital stretchers from the infirmary. Aric and her uncle stole into the armory. They retrieved armloads of submachine guns, pistols, knives, and assorted ammunition, including a kind of rocket gun, a *Panzerfaust*, which Aric explained could be used to attack enemy tanks.

The thought of having to use such extreme force gave her pause. It also underscored the real threat to them all. She could only hope Aric's plan worked. How would they convince the guards that they were the sick bound for Auschwitz?

Her answer came when Mrs. Brenner returned from the Krematorium carrying a single box of ashes. "These must have been overlooked," the older woman said in a quiet voice.

"I don't think they would mind the sacrilege."

Hadassah took the box and held it reverently. Reaching inside, she withdrew some of the ash and wiped it over her face, neck, and any other exposed skin. She thought of those who died in this place, and the many who must now stay behind to await death so that the rest of them could live. Moving from person to person, she offered each a handful of the ash, watching as they covered themselves in the only disguise that would fool the guards at the station. The souls of Jews . . .

Yaakov returned, his sooty features needing no further enhancement. Aric handed him a submachine gun and clips of ammunition. "When you depart for the train, lie on a stretcher and hide these until we board and get moving."

He outfitted others in the same manner. As he approached Morty, her uncle said, "I should stay behind, Herr Kommandant. Give my space on the train to someone younger."

"No!" Hadassah rushed forward.

Aric stayed her with a hand. "I believe this is yours, old man." He withdrew from his pocket a shiny metal object—her uncle's Grand Cross.

"Where did you find it?" Hadassah asked.

"I remembered seeing the Cross in your room this morning." Again their eyes met as each recalled the painful moment. "I found it when I searched through the captain's desk for my pistol and the lists. I realized it must belong to your uncle."

He offered it to Morty. "Our plan will only succeed if we have the best fighters. I cannot think of anyone I would rather have at my side than the soldier who has earned such an honor."

Morty straightened and accepted his Cross. "As you wish."

Relieved, Hadassah listened as Aric instructed her uncle that he too would be carried on a litter the two kilometers' distance to the station, with the Panzerfaust hidden among his blankets.

Finally, all seemed ready. "I must see to the fire damage," Aric said with a grim smile at Yaakov. "And I'll make certain

Rand, Helen, and Herr Buczak are ready to leave. Soldiers will be sent to escort all of you to the station at Bohusovice. When it's time, I'll join you."

Morty stepped forward and turned to the crowd. "Once, long ago, we Jews fought for the right to live despite the wicked ploys of Haman. Now on this eve of *Purim* thousands of years later, we are again called, through this man and woman"—he gestured toward Aric and Hadassah—"to defend our claim. Let us take a moment to thank God for His generosity."

A hush fell over the multitude as each man, woman, and child bowed their heads in prayer. Hadassah had changed into men's clothing earlier and now hugged the Bible beneath her leather jacket. She gave thanks along with them, sending up a silent plea to God to deliver them all safely into the hands of the Russians.

Afterward, her uncle put a hand on Aric's shoulder. "Thank you, my son."

Aric threw an arm around Hadassah and pulled her close. "Thank my secretary."

Soft chuckles echoed around them, easing some of the tension. Then Aric once more grew serious. "I let myself be blinded by a fool and his vision of glory." He gazed down at Hadassah, then out at the crowd. "What I have allowed to happen . . . I can only ask your forgiveness . . ." He cleared his throat. "But I wish you to know that I am proud to be among you now, fighting for our chance at freedom."

A soft murmur of approval rippled among those present, and many nodded in quiet understanding. Hadassah's throat tightened as she squeezed his fingers. God had surely opened Aric's heart. It was only by His miracle that they had come this far.

"I must check on the fires," he said quietly.

She glanced up at him. "Shall I go with you?"

"Too many know of your arrest, my love. You must take Joseph and go to the station with the others."

The gravity of their situation, and what they were about to

embark upon, struck her anew. It must have shown, for Aric led her to the side of the building where they had some privacy.

"If we get separated, I'll find you," he said fiercely.

"But what if the train leaves without you?" She clutched at the lapels of his coat while terrifying possibilities took root in her mind. She imagined him being arrested—or shot down—before he even made it to the station. "What if Captain Hermann returns . . ."

"You asked me earlier which woman I love." His gentle voice cut through her fear. "I love *you*, Hadassah Benjamin." He smiled. "So how could I ever let you go?"

Her eyes grew misty. "And I love you."

Wrapping her arms around his neck, she kissed him with all the tenderness she possessed. He tightened his hold on her and deepened the kiss, and Hadassah drew comfort knowing his heart would always belong to her.

"I suppose this means we'll have to postpone our wedding," he said when the kiss ended. His smile was filled with regret.

"What wedding?" Hadassah dropped her hands to his chest.

He pulled back to look at her. "Ours. You and me. Have you forgotten?"

"We aren't getting married."

"Since when?"

Hadassah almost smiled at his thunderous expression. "Since you haven't asked me."

"I didn't—"

She pressed a finger to his lips. "You demanded. Now ask me."

He eyed her a long moment. Slowly he lowered himself onto one knee.

Hadassah tried to stop him. "Don't . . ." she said, realizing how painful it would be.

"I'm doing it right this time," he said sharply, discomfort evident in the taut lines of his face. "No mistakes." He reached to take her hand. "Hadassah . . ."

"Yes," she whispered, even as she tried to pull him up.

"I haven't asked you yet," he growled. Then he gave her fingers a quick squeeze.

Hadassah blushed furiously beneath her sooty makeup. They weren't alone; her uncle, Yaakov, Mrs. Brenner, and dozens of smiling onlookers had come to the side of the building to watch Aric's progress. "We have an audience," she whispered.

"They can wait." Shifting his position, he looked up at her. His expression held such love that Hadassah's breath caught in her throat. "I admit now that I was first attracted by your show of determination that day at Dachau, and to the promise of outward beauty. Yet it was your inner light that captured my heart—your strength and willingness to sacrifice all for those you love, your sense of fairness and your compassion for others. But most of all, you never doubted the goodness in me . . . so much so that I began to see it again in myself. My darling Hadassah, I *live* because of you. Your love and your constancy have made me a man reborn."

He bent his head and kissed her palm before he said, "I cannot tell you what our future holds, only that I want to share it with you. Please be my wife."

For several seconds, Hadassah was too overcome to speak. Finally she managed a soft "yes," after which the spectators began to cheer and applaud. Yaakov and Morty approached to help Aric to his feet, all the while pounding his back in congratulations.

Mrs. Brenner gave Hadassah a hug. "God bless you," she said, teary-eyed. "I wish you both a long and happy life."

Hadassah squeezed her back. "For us all," she said.

"All right, everyone," Morty said as he began herding the masses away from the couple. "We have much work to do and little time." When he looked to her, Hadassah swore she saw tears in her uncle's eyes. "Shalom," he called to them, before turning to leave with the crowd.

"I need to go, as well," Aric said, though he made no move to leave. Hadassah rushed into his arms and held him tight.

"Don't leave me," she whispered against his chest.

He gently pried her arms from around his waist. "You and Joseph board the first car. I'll join you there." He tipped her chin up so as to look her in the eyes. "I promise."

"Have you ever broken a promise?" She didn't care that she sounded desperate.

He only smiled and said, "Hold on to these." He withdrew four signal flares and a flare pistol from the pockets of his coat. "Once we arrive near Prerov, I'll need them to signal Herr Buczak to switch the track."

Hadassah nodded and took the flares. He gave her another quick kiss, one that left her afraid as he departed for the ghetto's square, now ablaze with fire.

There was so much danger ahead that could jeopardize their happiness.

Hadassah said a prayer for their future.

~ 40 ~

Then let the girl who pleases the king be queen. . . .

Esther 2:4

Sheathed in tumid clouds, the sun spread milky rays across miles of whiteness.

Aric stood at his bedroom window and watched the headlights of his Mercedes toss a faint beam against the snow. Rand was leaving for Prerov with Helen and Lenny Buczak. He'd given his friend official orders and explicit instructions. He could only hope that, for all their sakes, the party would make it to the rendezvous point.

As the car disappeared into the east, Aric turned to stare toward Prague. He'd have liked a meeting with Hermann before the train left, face-to-face on equal ground. Aric would enjoy making him suffer—not only for Joseph's battered face but for Hadassah's bruises, as well.

Yet as much as he ached for a chance to retaliate, there wasn't time. He must leave it to God to exact His own vengeance.

Aric walked to his armoire and opened a drawer that held the clips for his Browning. After retrieving the ammunition, he glanced at the extra bottle of morphine tablets. Then he slammed the drawer shut and left the room.

Downstairs, he stopped at Joseph's room to check that Martin and Zeissen, as well as young Corporal Sonntag, were still securely bound and gagged. After finding they were, he went to the living room to survey one last time the possessions he would never see again.

His eyes came to settle on the painting of his childhood home. The country castle looked peaceful and content against the backdrop of snowcapped Alps.

He could never return; he would soon be marked a deserter—if he managed to stay alive. Yet it was such a small price to pay for his transformation to become human again.

Aric had been at Theresienstadt only two months, yet he agonized over the part he'd taken in sending Hadassah's people to Auschwitz. Nothing in this world could ever erase his actions; he only hoped that, in time, God would offer him absolution for his soul.

He closed his eyes, and unexpected warmth, like the sun's rays, touched his face. He envisioned his boyhood summers, the melting Alpine snow washing crystal water down from the mountains like a ribbon across the green valley. He could even smell the sweet tang of meadow grass and feel its softness beneath his bare feet. He saw then the face of his beloved, how Austria shone clear and pure in her blue eyes. *Thank you, Lord . . .*

The Warmth seeped into his heart, filling the last breaches of pain.

~ 41 ~

But Haman rushed home, with his head covered in grief. . . .

Esther 6:12

The ghetto was on fire.

Cresting the last hill, Hermann spied the black smoke snaking upward like serpents into the approaching dusk. The blaze seemed to be spreading through the center of town.

"What . . . ?" He punched the accelerator; the car slipped sideways across an icy curve and narrowly missed a ditch. Easing back on the gas, he managed to straighten the vehicle . . . then noticed that the train, to his left, was loading prisoners.

His heart pounded as he again increased his speed, more evenly this time. Who had given the order? He'd left Sonntag explicit instructions to wait until his return . . .

Another possibility occurred to him: Had the prisoner escaped? The one held a few kilometers away in the two-story brick house? The notion wasn't hard to grasp. Schmidt had won both the Iron Cross First Class and the Knight's Cross with Oak Leaves and Swords, given only to those frontline commanders who displayed exceptional bravery and skill. He was also the same man who killed Koch and Brucker as easily as two grouse in a bush.

"Wehrmacht!" Hermann roared, racing the car toward the house. He arrived minutes later to find the commandant's Mercedes gone. Alarmed, he rushed inside and burst into the library. Empty. After conducting a methodic search of the house, he located three of his men bound and gagged in a room off the kitchen.

"The old Hausfrau poisoned us!" Zeissen bellowed once his gag was removed. "Herr Captain, there was nothing we could do—"

"Shut up!" Hermann finished removing Zeissen's bindings. "Help Martin," he ordered before he bent to loosen the knots at his corporal's wrists. "Where is the Kommandant?" he asked Sonntag. "Did he take the car?"

"I don't know, Herr Captain. He came to the Judenrat's office hours ago and attacked me. He hit me over the head with something." Freed at last, Sonntag rubbed the raised lump on his scalp. "I woke up in this room."

"Then he and his Jew mistress have escaped." Hermann ignored Sonntag's surprised look. "Zeissen, Martin, go to the ghetto and put out that fire. Sonntag, come with me. I need to find out who's loading that train. No one goes anywhere until I say so!"

"Move, you lazy Jude!"

Hadassah cried out as the butt of the rifle landed hard between her shoulder blades. She lurched forward with her precious bundle, knocking the people in front of her off-balance.

"Mama . . ." the child in her arms whimpered.

"Hush now, it's all right." Hadassah regained her footing and pressed on. Shifting the little girl in her arms, she worked to adjust the Bible, flares, and flare pistol hidden inside her bomber jacket so that they didn't poke her in the stomach.

Perhaps she shouldn't have gone back; she could have stayed

with Joseph in the first car. But Hadassah couldn't ignore the child's tearful cry any more than she could that night in the ghetto. The little girl must have lost her mother in the throng making its way onto the ramps.

"I said now!"

Again the Soldat shoved his rifle into her. Hadassah stumbled forward before she realized he was herding her up a ramp at the middle of the train. "Please, I must get to the first car!"

She made a desperate attempt to swerve away.

"Eager to get there?" the soldier barked.

Her mind exploded with pain as the butt of the rifle struck the back of her head. Dimly she heard a child scream before her legs collapsed beneath her, forcing her to the ground. Then a man growled, "First or last, you'll all get there at the same time," before darkness seized her.

Hadassah heard nothing else.

42

On the thirteenth day . . . the month of Adar, the
edict commanded by the king was to be carried out.

Esther 9:1

Have you boarded all the prisoners?" Aric demanded.
"We are almost finished, Herr Kommandant."
"Hurry, Private, I want this train moving in five minutes."
"Jawohl!"
He returned the soldier's salute, then watched the young
man break into a run along the tracks. All thirty cars were now
filled with people wearing numbered tags, crowded together like
matchsticks. He glanced at his watch. Where was Hadassah?

Alarm compounded the uneasiness he already felt; he had to
stifle yet another urge to go in search of her. He couldn't afford
to let his emotions jeopardize the plan—too much was at stake.
Hermann would return at any time.

Still, Aric edged closer to the first ramp and stared into the
shadowed confines of the car. When he didn't see her face among
the dozens huddled together near the open door, his agitation
increased. His breath rushed out in a puff of warm steam, and
not for the first time he wondered at the lunacy of his plan. These
people would freeze to death before they ever saw freedom.

A small face peered around the opening. Joseph shouldered

a heavy woolen blanket and flashed Aric his pitifully swollen smile before a hand dragged him back inside.

Aric breathed a sigh of relief. Hadassah had made it on board with the boy. He continued along the tracks past each car, a renewed sense of expectancy rising in him as he watched the remaining fifty or so board. When he retraced his steps, Yaakov and Morty were being hauled up on stretchers into the first car.

Yaakov groaned like a man breathing his last. Aric's mouth twitched at the performance, until one of the two men that carried Morty and the prized Panzerfaust lost his grip.

The stretcher—and Morty—dropped to the ground. Aric's pulse rocketed as he hurried toward the scene. A guard beat him to it.

"You clumsy oaf! PICK . . . HIM . . . UP!" the sentry screamed.

Morty's blankets had unraveled. Aric's mouth went dry as he spied the bulging outline of the tank gun against the canvas stretcher.

The guard had also noticed. "What is that?" He leaned closer. "What have you got there, Jude?"

"Achtung, Private!" Aric forced his way up the ramp and faced the guard, effectively blocking his view. "Why are you causing delays?"

The young Soldat jumped to attention. "The Jude hides something beneath his blankets, Herr Kommandant!"

"Does he? And what could that possibly be?"

The guard shifted. "I don't know, Herr Kommandant, I was about to investigate."

Aric turned to Morty. "Are you hiding something?"

He expected Hadassah's uncle to deny the charge, but when Morty reached beneath the blanket, Aric's breath froze. Had the old man gone mad?

"My violin, Herr Kommandant." Morty held up a Stradivarius for all to see.

Aric leaned against his cane to steady his legs. "You have

sharp eyes, Private," he told the guard. "I'll note that for your next rank evaluation. Now go and see to the other cars."

The guard raised a salute, then hesitated. "Shall I confiscate the instrument, Herr Kommandant?"

"Let him keep it. I believe the Kommandant at Auschwitz has a fondness for music."

The sentry rushed off to obey his commandant's orders. Aric and Morty exchanged a grim look. "Carry on," Aric said. Only after the two men on stretchers were safely loaded and the guards closed the doors was he able to calm his heart rate. He cast another glance at his watch and then started for the single-room train station, where one soldier manned a wireless radio.

A woman's shrill scream brought him up short. Aric spun around and saw a tall dark-haired woman struggling to move past his soldiers into a full car. The same guard gave her a hard shove backward, knocking her off the ramp and onto the ground below.

"Halt, Private!" Aric strode toward the pair. Minutes were slipping by. "What is the problem this time?"

"She has no assigned number, Herr Kommandant." Again the Soldat straightened to attention. "There is no more room."

It was true. The car was so full that those inside could hardly breathe. The other cars were in the same condition.

"Please, Herr Kommandant! I dropped my tag and someone must have taken it!"

Aric glanced at the woman. Young and slim, she had a pretty face beneath the bruises. His chest tightened as he thought of his beloved.

He rechecked the time on his watch. "I'm sorry, Fräulein. You must go back."

"Wait, please!" A woman pushed her way forward through the packed bodies inside the car. It was Mrs. Brenner. "I beg you, Herr Kommandant." Her voice held panic. "She's my daughter, Clara. She must come with me."

The older woman's dark eyes were brimming with tears. Aric's gut ached. "Are you certain all the cars are full?" he barked at the soldier. Having watched nearly three thousand people cram themselves inside the train, he already knew the answer.

"Jawohl, Herr Kommandant. We had difficulty closing the doors."

Aric fought another urge to look at his watch. "I can't help you," he said to Clara. He turned to Mrs. Brenner. "The train must leave now."

She met his gaze, and Aric expected to see hatred. But Mrs. Brenner merely offered him a sad smile, then removed the numbered tag from around her neck. "She will have my place."

Aric worked his jaw. "See to it, Private," he said.

Mrs. Brenner was swiftly extricated from the car and led down the ramp. Clara let out a cry as she and her mother embraced, clinging fiercely to each other. Then Mrs. Brenner pulled back and said, "God go with you, child," and slipped the tag over her daughter's head.

The older woman watched as her daughter made her way inside the car. The soldiers then closed the door and moved to the next ramp.

Aric turned to Mrs. Brenner. "I regret . . ." His voice trailed off. He knew no words to comfort her.

"Succeed, Herr Kommandant," she said fiercely. "For all of our sakes."

The nightmare began.

"Schnell!" Hermann slammed a fist against the dashboard. The train was gathering steam as black smoke billowed in bursts against a dusky sky.

Sonntag pressed down on the accelerator. The car lunged forward on the snow and zigzagged for several meters before sliding sideways to a stop.

Hermann kicked the door open and leaped from the car.

"Herr Captain!"

He ignored his corporal's cry and raced for the station. Less than ten meters away, he slipped on the ice and staggered backward, regaining his balance only after he'd pulled a muscle in his right leg.

Eight meters.

He continued his breakneck pace.

Five meters.

The shaft of the locomotive wheels began to turn.

Four meters.

A screaming whistle—the train lumbered forward.

Two meters.

He burst into the lighted train station office. The radio he'd intended to use lay in a mangled heap on the floor. Beside it rested another heap: his station man, half naked and unconscious. Hermann ripped off his hat and wiped at the sweat along his forehead. His pulse threatened to explode. He had to stop the train.

As he turned to dash back out, he spied the black uniform on the floor behind the door—an officer's tunic with the unmistakable Knight's Cross in a beribboned pile beside it. The gleam of brass from a dark wooden cane . . .

"Wehrmacht!" He bellowed his frustration as he barreled outside to the tracks.

The train was picking up speed. Fury and panic sent a flood of adrenaline surging through him. He saw the house, the warm fire, the good food—all disappear with each belch of black smoke.

Three soldiers stood off the boot and gaped at him in wonder. With a desperate burst of speed he sprinted after them, his lungs burning by the time he neared the rail of the caboose.

Several pairs of hands reached out to him. He leaped forward like a human javelin, gasping at the excruciating pain in his left shoulder as the soldiers dragged him inside.

Aric stood inside the cramped engine room of the locomotive. His eyes darted between the guard leaning against the opposite door and the two engineers who stoked the fire and set the boiler to increase the train's speed.

Finally the soldier—a lance corporal—withdrew a crumpled pack of cigarettes from his coat pocket. "Want one?" He held out the pack to Aric.

"Danke." Aric withdrew a cigarette and returned the pack. The lance corporal also took one, then drew out a tin of matches. He lit his cigarette, taking it deeply into his lungs. "I do this 'cleanup' run all the time, but I've never seen you before. Are you new?"

"New to this job," Aric responded.

The soldier handed over the lit cigarette. Aric kindled his and handed it back. "Enjoy it."

The soldier paused to stare at him. "Why?"

"It's your last one."

Before the lance corporal could blink, Aric had his Browning poised on him. "You're going to jump."

"You're crazy!"

"You have no idea." Aric flashed a humorless smile. He stepped forward and commanded, "Now jump or I'll kick your corpse over the side with my boot."

The engineers froze next to the firebox. The lance corporal grinned at Aric. "This is a joke, right?"

Aric flipped off the safety. "I'm not laughing."

Seconds stretched. The whine of the boiler and the roar of burning tender echoed in the small heated space. Sweat beaded along Aric's brow beneath his steel helmet. "One."

"Lunatic!" The soldier dropped his cigarette as he reached for the rifle strapped at his shoulder. Aric ripped off a shot. The bullet whizzed past the lance corporal's ear to shatter a thick pane of glass in the door behind him. "Two."

"All right, all right!" The soldier moved to slide the door

open. A rush of frigid air swept through the compartment. Aric followed him out onto the plate, Browning in hand.

The soldier stared at the blur of track rushing beneath the train. He turned to Aric. "Please . . ."

"Three."

Giving out a strained yelp, the soldier jumped over the edge. Aric watched him land just beyond the track, tumbling against the white ground like a snowball gaining speed. He closed the door and announced to the two engineers, "I'm in charge now."

They each whipped off their caps and nodded vigorously.

"We're not going to Auschwitz," he informed them. "We'll be switching near Prerov. Do you have a radio?"

Both men were extremely short. The taller of the two—who looked remarkably like the other except for his height—pointed to a wireless set at the back of the compartment. Aric swung around and grabbed up the radio.

The engineers watched while it flew off the train through the now-windowless door.

"Any weapons?" He aimed his Browning at the taller of the two.

They both paled and shook their heads.

"Do either of you speak German?"

The shorter man nodded, twisting his cap in his hands. "We are not allowed to have weapons, Herr Corporal."

Aric smirked as he glanced down at his uniform, the one he'd taken from the enlisted man at the station. He lowered his pistol. "We're going to Lemberg, in the Ukraine. Do you have enough fuel?"

"We had the tender filled before we left," the taller man responded.

"Then get this crate up to speed. And no heroics—or you'll leave the train just like your friend. I'll be back in a minute."

Aric slid open the opposite door of the compartment. Stepping outside, he made his way past the tender. Darkness had settled in, dropping the temperature even more.

Freezing wind pierced his face and hands like needles as he scaled to the roof of the first car. He lowered himself over one side using the ladder-style rungs adjacent to the door, until he reached the mechanism that held the door in place.

Gritting his teeth—more against the cold than his efforts—he drove back the iron bar from its seat. He kicked at the door several times with his boot before it opened. Several pairs of hands reached to pull him inside.

Air, hot and stifling, blasted him like a furnace. The car was so overcrowded he had to grip the door with one hand to keep from falling out of the train. He tore off his steel helmet and waited while Morty and Yaakov squeezed forward through the wall of bodies. Yaakov held a submachine gun. Morty, the Panzerfaust.

"Where is she?" Aric had to shout over the icy gusts at his back.

"I don't know." Morty seemed weaker than he had an hour before. His arms shook with the heavy weight of the tank gun. "With so many people pressed together, it's nearly impossible to move."

Aric tried shaking off his anxiety. "We'll find her," he said, more to convince himself than to reassure her uncle. He took the Panzerfaust from Morty and, with the old man's help, strapped it onto his own back. "Let's go. We'll climb to the roof, then cross the tender to the engine room. It's the only way."

He replaced his helmet before turning to face the cold air that pushed through the open door. Bracing himself, he reached out to the nearest rung and began his ascent. Yaakov and Morty followed. He cast them backward glances, surprised at how easily the two older men kept up.

They had barely gained footing on the roof when a burst of machine-gun fire sliced over their heads. "Get down!" Aric yelled, but his words were snatched up by the furious wind. He turned in time to see Yaakov hit the deck—and Morty topple over the side.

Aric raised his head and tried to locate the enemy. Three German soldiers moved forward in a half crouch from the rear of the train. He reached for his pistol as another spray of fire passed overhead. Slamming the side of his face against the roof, he heard a loud *clang* as a bullet hit the steel tender car behind them.

"Move!" he bellowed at Yaakov above the tempest.

They belly-crawled across the slatted roof of the train before diving into the tender. Between the front of the tender and the locomotive, a meter of space would shelter them from the hail of bullets. He and Yaakov slipped down into the tiny opening.

"Stay low and get inside the engine room," Aric instructed. "Two civilian engineers are inside now, firing up the box. Make sure this train keeps moving. And take this with you"—he removed the tank gun and handed it to the other man—"while I settle up with these fools."

Yaakov retreated, and Aric turned his attention back to the three soldiers now hidden from view fifty or sixty meters back. Somehow he'd been discovered, despite the fact he wore the uniform of an SS-Corporal, and they clearly meant to kill him.

Aric could feel the train gaining speed. As it began to round a bend in the track, he rose up from his crouched position. The convex position of the cars offered a clear glimpse of the soldiers creeping steadily in his direction. It would be several minutes before his range was accurate enough to fire at them. Steady against the piercing cold, Aric crawled to the side of the tender and faced the direction of the first car. His heart almost stopped at the sight of Morty, clinging to the lowest rung along the siding.

The old man's feet dangled just centimeters above the clacking fury of wheels. The door to the car still lay partially open. Apparently no one had noticed his distress. Aric stuffed his pistol inside his coat pocket and then edged along the tender car until he gripped a support at the rear.

He extended a hand and held his breath. Morty tried to bridge the distance. It was no good—they were still too far apart. Aric unbuttoned his coat and released the buckle on his gun belt. He jerked on the black leather until it came free of the holster still strapped to his thigh.

KATE BRESLIN

It took Aric three attempts at tossing the makeshift lifeline before Morty's outstretched fingers grabbed hold. Wrapping his hand several times in the leather, Aric yelled, "Let go!" over the noise. His arm burned with Morty's weight; the old man swung for a moment, then rammed up against him. They gripped each other for a moment, clinging to the tender's support.

Morty offered him a weak grin before fainting.

Aric hoisted the frail man over his shoulder. His chest burned as he worked his way back to the front of the tender. Setting Morty down in the small space, he began chafing his limbs.

Relief overrode his agitation when he glanced up to find Yaakov hovering. "I'll take him inside, Herr Kommandant." With a grunt, the Czech hefted Morty into his arms. Aric, fairly assured his beloved would not be grieving the loss of her uncle, returned to hunting down the three soldiers.

The clouds that hovered earlier had disappeared. Against a coal-black sky the full moon rode high, along with the first stars of night. Aric huddled behind the tender and caught his breath, despite the acrid smoke belching from the locomotive's stack. Concern for Hadassah preyed upon his mind. Was she all right? Why hadn't he seen her?

Even as he watched the slow approach of his enemy, Aric's thoughts continued to churn. God willing, she would become his wife. He imagined his bleak existence colored in the glorious shades of her laughter and love. Their children . . .

He wanted a future with her—more than anything he'd ever desired before. The notion that he might never see her again needled at his sanity. She believed in him, the best about him.

He had to find her, but first he had to get rid of the three obstacles nearly upon him. Raising his pistol, Aric fired a random shot. As if on cue, two of the three soldiers tried to roll out of the way—and inadvertently pitched themselves over the sides of the train.

367

"Idiots," he muttered before ducking down to miss the middle man opening fire. Aric heard the shots ricochet against the steel locomotive casing behind him. He raised his Browning and fired off three rounds.

The shooting stopped. Aric peered over the tender. The soldier lay in a lifeless heap on top of the train.

Moments later, Aric shoved what he hoped was their last impediment over the side.

"Thank God!" Yaakov greeted him as he made his way back inside.

"Amen to that." Aric took the leather belt from Yaakov and re-threaded his holster.

Morty sat slouched in a corner of the engine room, lips blue with cold. His dark eyes gleamed in the dismal light of the car. "Thank you, my son," he managed in a whisper. "Did you solve the problem outside?"

Aric nodded as he cinched his belt and returned the Browning to his side. "They tried to copy your performance but forgot to hang on." He shook his head in wonder. "You're lucky I didn't drop you—that, or follow you under the wheels."

Morty offered a faint smile. "I had faith in you."

Aric's mouth kicked up. "A family trait, then?" He removed the steel helmet and combed a hand through his hair. Thoughts of his beloved and her whereabouts made his smile fade.

The train slowed. Aric's heart rate accelerated as he glanced out the engine room window. They were entering the city limits of Prague. "I take it you had no trouble with these two?" he asked Yaakov, looking at the two engineers.

Yaakov grinned. "Herr Kommandant, meet Karel Pavlik"—he turned to the taller one—"and his brother, Miko. They are my own countrymen!" He slapped Karel squarely on the back, and both brothers beamed at Aric. "They will take us anywhere we wish to go."

The brothers nodded enthusiastically. Aric eyed them with suspicion. "Why?"

"Yaakov told us you plan to free the prisoners who were at Terezin," offered Miko, the shorter of the two brothers. "Many of those prisoners are fellow Czechs."

"We hate the Nazis," Karel cut in, giving Aric's SS uniform an overall hard stare. "First they steal our country, then our jobs. Finally they take our men, women, and children. Those of us who are not Jewish are forced to do their dirty work." His tone held disgust. "We wear the stain of their sin on our hands."

"I'm a Nazi." Aric eyed the brothers. "How do you know I won't turn against you?"

"Karel and I saw the way you forced that soldier over the side with your pistol." Miko smiled shyly. "Either you didn't like the cigarette or you share our dislike for your countrymen."

"You also seem like a smart man." Karel spoke this time. "Tell me, Herr Kommandant—do you know the workings of a steam locomotive?"

Aric shook his head. Karel grinned. "See? You need us. And Yaakov says you're a good man, even for a Nazi." His long features sobered. "Czechs do not lie, you know."

"Of course not," Aric said dryly, recalling Yaakov's earlier performance on the stretcher.

"So we will help you," Miko stated solemnly. "We will help you . . . help them."

"Gut. I'm taking one of your pickaxes," Aric said.

Yaakov and the Pavliks gaped at him. Even Morty eyed him questioningly. "I need to go and find Hadassah," he explained, retrieving the tool mounted against the engine room wall. He withdrew his map and handed it to Yaakov. "Tell them everything."

A moment later, Aric was gone.

≈ 43 ≈

"Since Mordecai, before whom your downfall has started, is of Jewish origin, you cannot stand against him. . . ."

Esther 6:13

Prague's city lights loomed into view as the train slowed. Hermann sat against a leather seat in the boot car, ignoring the sharp pain in his left shoulder.

He glanced at his watch. Another minute stretched with still no word from his men. He swore under his breath, again regretting his lengthy dalliance in Prague. Things had soured for him after that, most bitterly when his efforts to stop the train had dislocated his shoulder.

One of the guards who had hauled him inside had realigned bone with socket, then fashioned a sling from an old blanket. The incessant throbbing angered him, underscoring his lack of control in a situation already grossly out of hand. He breathed deeply to offset the pain that pricked him like needles. It wouldn't be long before they stopped. Surely his men would bring him Aric von Schmidt, and then he could re-route the train to Theresienstadt.

Had Martin and Zeissen gained control of the fire? Thinking

370

of the black smoke he'd seen rising from the ghetto gave his gut a hard twist. Was the damage insubstantial . . . or more critical to tomorrow's success with the Red Cross? He ground his teeth. If Schmidt was involved, it promised to be much, much worse.

Why was the Wehrmacht on this train? The question had plagued Hermann from the moment he became certain he *was* on board—the gunfire overhead minutes ago proved it.

This train was bound for Auschwitz. Death would meet the Jews riding it. Did the Wehrmacht wish to die with them? If so, why had he taken the corporal's uniform at the train station? What was his plan?

Abruptly the train picked up speed. As he watched the yellow lights of Prague grow distant, Hermann's insides turned cold—like the freezing boy who long ago stood outside Tiern's Gasthaus in winter, begging food his mother couldn't afford to purchase; or the poorly heated stone barracks and tinned rations he'd endured each day back at the camp.

Like the expression on General Feldman's face when he discovered his newly appointed Kommandant had failed with the Embellishment.

With a grunt, Hermann vaulted from his chair. Why couldn't three trained men take down one crippled soldier? He strode to the outer door and heaved it open. The frigid air outside formed an ice blanket around his sweat-soaked skin. He eyed the ladder-like rungs to the side that would take him to the roof. Carefully he hoisted his body up onto the first rung with his good arm, then proceeded to climb to the top of the car.

The blast of wind knocked him backward before he grabbed at a wooden runner that ran lengthwise along the rooftop. He rose cautiously and steadied his booted feet against the icy surface. The night sky was clear and black, and he was glad to have the moonlight.

There was no sign of his men. By the time he made his way to the middle of the train, Hermann wondered if his soldiers had been left to die alongside the tracks. He stared out at the barren countryside rushing past him, deafened by the grinding of the train's wheels. The fierce wind, laced with caustic smoke from the locomotive, tried to push him back.

He'd barely taken another step when he slammed facedown against the snowy deck. Pain exploded in his brain, obliterating any thought except that he'd been shot from behind.

He thought he might be dying. His lower body felt numbed, even warm, despite the glacial wind buffeting his head and shoulders. Soon, he wouldn't feel anything . . .

He wasn't shot. The realization dawned as he tried to straighten and found half of his body had fallen through the rotten boards of the train's roof. The warmth against his legs was body heat—from the hundreds of Jews crammed in the cattle car below.

Hermann swore under his breath as he pushed himself from the hole, his shoulder screaming from the pain. He continued forward for a distance of ten more cars, moving crab-like along the slippery roof while keeping most of his weight on his right arm. He finally spied a lone figure on the roof, two cars ahead. "Wehrmacht," he growled, recognizing the tall, broad-shouldered silhouette.

Despite his injuries, Hermann smiled. He'd found his quarry.

Hadassah's eyes fluttered open to behold darkness. The air was stifling and reeked of urine and sweat. Feet shuffled around her head. She heard children crying, felt the rocking floor beneath her. A train?

She tried to rise, but something pinned her down. Her head throbbed with pain. She'd been unconscious. The guard . . .

She brushed her hands across her torso. The heavy weight— a child sprawled against her chest. She touched the baby-soft cheek, felt a thumb wedged securely between the child's lips.

Anna? She felt a moment's panic. No . . . no, the little girl from the ghetto—

The rest of Hadassah's memory came back in a rush. Joseph!

Help me. She wasn't certain she'd spoken aloud until the pressure against her chest eased as hands pulled the child off of her. Again she tried to sit up, closing her eyes and holding her head until the pounding lessened.

"I need to stand." This time she heard her own voice. Hands again reached out, this time grasping under her arms to raise her to her feet.

The air above the floor was noticeably cooler, and the stench lessened, too. Hadassah fought dizziness, but there was no danger of falling. A wall of bodies surrounded her.

"Is this the first car?" she called out, hoping for an answer. Human flesh pressed in on her from all sides, pushing her back and forth as the train rocked along its tracks.

A masculine voice spoke up beside her, "No, we're somewhere in the middle."

Hadassah's heart sank. "Where are we?"

"I think we passed through a city about twenty minutes ago," the voice answered. "There were lights—they shone through the window grates. We picked up speed again and they faded. That was before the roof caved in."

Hadassah looked up and saw moonlight flooding through a hole that was half a meter wide, an opening large enough for a human.

"Someone fell through," the voice said, confirming her suspicion. "I know it was a Nazi because he kicked a woman in the head with his jackboots. It didn't take him long to pull himself up again."

Could it be Aric searching for her? The cattle car suddenly pitched as the train made a sharp bend in the track. The body in front of Hadassah slammed backward with the motion. She felt the sharp jab of an object against her midriff. Several objects . . .

Flares! They were still inside her jacket—and the only means to signal Lenny Buczak.

She had to get to Aric. Hadassah glanced in the direction of the car door. "Does anyone have a gun?" she shouted so as to be heard.

"If we did," said the same male voice beside her, "we'd have already blown the door open. As it is, we can hardly breathe."

Her gaze flew to the hole in the ceiling. "I need to get up there."

"Are you serious?"

"I have the flares!" she hissed at him. "Our contact won't switch the track unless we give him a signal."

When he didn't respond, Hadassah wanted to scream. She might be too late. They could be near Prerov by now. "Didn't you hear what I—?"

"You're the one, aren't you?"

The awe in his voice brought Hadassah up short. Then she heard the word *salvation*, and her temper exploded. "I'll be your death if I can't get to the front of this train in time!"

Whether he took her threat seriously or finally understood her explanation, the man, after a brief silence, said, "I will need another man. Avram!"

A moment later Hadassah felt herself lifted above the crowd by two strong pairs of hands. "Stand on our shoulders," said the familiar voice. Others reached out to steady her as she planted a foot alongside either man's head, then reached to grasp an edge of the gaping hole. Working to balance herself against the rocking motion of the train, she slowly rose to her full height while hands clamped like iron around both of her ankles.

"When you're ready, Avram and I will push you through," the voice called out.

Hadassah sensed all eyes upon her. Breathing inside the car seemed to stop. For an instant she was again that child of five standing on top of her uncle's stack of crates. She said a quick prayer that this time she wouldn't fall. "Now!" she called to them. They immediately gave her a boost, and she hoisted herself through the opening.

Icy wind beat at her like a fist. Hadassah grasped the rail that ran lengthwise along the train. She fought to hang on, her body sliding back and forth against the icy surface like a netted fish. Exhaustion quickly set in and her shoulders ached. Splinters pierced her flesh as she gripped the wood even harder. She needed Aric . . .

Hadassah managed to pull herself forward a few centimeters before the wind overpowered her. She rested against the deck for several seconds, breathing hard, her teeth chattering. "P-please, Lord. Y-you didn't bring me this f-far to f-fail, did you?" she called to the skies. "I c-can't do this alone . . ."

Somewhere deep inside she found a small reserve of strength. Rising onto her knees, she clutched the rail. Frigid gusts whipped at her face, tearing her eyes as she crawled toward the front of the car. Above, she saw the moon glowing full and white, and the first stars glittered like diamonds against a black velvety sky. *Help me make it, Lord*—

The train jogged sharply. Hadassah scrambled to stay anchored—then toppled backward when the slat broke away in her grasp. She screamed and clutched the piece of wood as her body plunged over the side.

Aric sat back on his knees and stared into the opening he'd hacked into the roof. The pickaxe he'd borrowed from the Pavlik brothers rested beside him.

After four boxcars, he still hadn't found Hadassah. He tried to reassure himself with the possibility she'd boarded one of the cars farther back by mistake.

Aric didn't want to consider anything else. Yet as he gripped the strapped handle of the pickaxe and slung it over his shoulder, he couldn't help feeling that the attack on them by three of his soldiers had something to do with his missing fiancée.

Someone at Theresienstadt must have known he was on this train. . . . Hermann? Had the captain, by some incredible stroke of fate, returned to the ghetto in time to see Aric board? If so, how did he notify the guards?

Did he have Hadassah?

Aric's blood ran cold at the possibility. He ground his teeth against a shout of rage and slowly crawled along the slick surface to the next car. He had to find her.

Removing the pickaxe from his shoulder, he tore another meter-sized hole into the roof. Lying on his stomach, he leaned into the hole. "Hadassah!" he yelled over the wind. But only groans—and the fetid stench of unwashed bodies—rose from the darkness below.

He called her name again.

"Help us!" a woman cried.

Not Hadassah. Aric closed his eyes. "Have . . . faith," he called back. But the words made him feel awkward and angry as he struggled to rise.

He made it as far as his knees when the pickaxe suddenly flew from his grasp, clattered across the slippery deck, and disappeared over the side.

Aric stared at the pair of jackboots directly in front of him.

"Faith is the wishful thinking of fools, Wehrmacht," a familiar voice said. "Dead fools."

44

The couriers . . . raced out, spurred on by the king's command. . . .

Esther 8:14

Shouldn't they be here by now?"

From the driver's seat, Sergeant Rand Grossman turned to growl at Lenny Buczak, as if the young man harbored some secret known only to the railroad.

Helen sighed. Rand could be formidable at times, and she knew he was as worried as she about the commandant and the others. Still, Lenny couldn't possibly know; none of them were even certain the dangerous plan would work.

She eyed the shivering young man who sat beside her in the back seat. He'd just endured a three-and-a-half-hour ride in the trunk of the Mercedes, poor dear. He reminded her of one of the frozen hens her father kept hung in the blockhouse on their farm during winters. Rand had stopped only one other time in their journey—at some out-of-the-way place to avoid detection so that Lenny could come inside and thaw.

As before, she began to briskly chafe his arms and wrists to return the blood flow. Lenny offered a grateful smile.

"Perhaps the Kommandant was stopped." Rand shot Helen

a pensive glance in the rearview mirror. His voice held an edge. "They could have taken him . . ."

She paused in her ministrations to frown at Lenny. She gave his arm a meaningful squeeze. Staring at her, he said, "They . . . should be along any time now, Herr Sergeant . . . ?"

Good boy. Helen nodded and smiled before continuing to knead his frozen fingers. No good would come of Rand's being upset. They must be patient—

"Then let's go."

Rand opened his car door and got out. Lenny turned to her. "But . . . it's a quarter kilometer through the snow to reach the lantern switch at the track," he whined. "And I'm still frozen . . ."

His passenger door suddenly opened. Helen saw Lenny take one look at Rand's steel hook—the sergeant's favorite ploy— before he slid across the leather seat and, with a groan, out into the calf-deep snow.

Determined not to be left behind, Helen reached across the front seat and turned off the car's ignition. Then she buttoned her coat and left the car.

"You should stay here where it's warm," Rand told her gruffly. Her response was to smile and link her arm through his.

Moonlight illuminated a copse of bare poplars and birch ahead. The railroad tracks were visible in the distance. Rand sighed. "All right." Then to Lenny, "After you." With another groan from the young Pole, they began trekking forward in the snow.

Captain Hermann aimed the Walther P38 with deadly accuracy. "Don't move unless you have a sudden urge to get off this train," he shouted over the wind.

Aric stared down the pistol barrel. He had to stall long enough to reach the Browning holstered beneath his own coat. "I'll go, Captain, as long as you join me."

Hermann laughed. "Ah, you'd like a little hand-to-hand combat then, Wehrmacht?"

Aric eyed the sling cradling Hermann's left arm. "I doubt you'd prove any more of a challenge than those three underlings you sent after me."

"Green boys," Hermann scoffed. "Like Koch and Brucker. I told those two hotheads they would fail. They had no idea who they were dealing with. But I've seen your decorations, Standartenführer. They don't issue those medals to cowards."

Aric hid his shock. Hermann had known beforehand of the murder plot against him and Hadassah? "Of course, you thought to take my place once I was gone."

"It did sound promising," Hermann admitted. "But then the Jew boy and your mistress got involved." He shrugged. "It doesn't matter now anyway. Himmler himself has promoted me to Kommandant of Theresienstadt."

"Congratulations. I'm sure he'll be . . . enlightened along with the Swiss when they arrive tomorrow."

"You mean the fires? My men are taking care of that now. I simply need to take care of you." The captain was yelling. He'd planted his feet apart to balance himself against the snow-streaked deck while the frigid wind plastered his clothes to his body. He raised the bandaged arm. "And since I can't brawl with you at the moment, I hope you'll appreciate my other skills."

The barrel of the Walther shifted slightly; Aric sensed the moment Hermann flipped off the safety. He had to take his enemy. Even now the city of Prerov drew close. If Lenny Buczak didn't receive their signal, the train would miss the turnoff—their only chance at freedom.

"How did you manage to board the train?"

"You think to stall, don't you? It won't work, although I am curious to know why you're on a train bound for Auschwitz. Did you plan to die along with your Jews?"

"If necessary," Aric said.

"Really? That Jewess *has* poisoned your thinking. Just look at you! One of Germany's greatest war heroes, reduced to a traitor to the Reich. Dressed in a lowly corporal's uniform and groveling at my feet." Hermann waved his pistol. "Now, I want you to lie flat against the deck. When I shoot you, I can't have you tumbling over the side. I need the body." When Aric didn't move, Hermann laughed. "You're to be my trophy stag, didn't you know? My next promotion. Now get down!"

Snagging Aric's helmet with the barrel of his pistol, Hermann sent it flying over the side. Then he shoved him against the snowy deck with a boot, pressing the nose of the gun against his scalp. "Say your prayers, Wehrmacht."

The hand of God reached down and saved her.

One moment she'd been hurtling toward death—in the next, Hadassah found herself dangling over the rushing tracks, gripped by the collar of her jacket.

"Grab the rungs!" shouted a male voice, the same man who, along with Avram, had helped to raise her onto the roof. Cheers rose inside the cattle car when she twisted and clutched the iron ladder that led up to the car's roof. For a few seconds she hovered there, catching her breath. She then leaned toward the grated window opening and kissed the outstretched hands that had done so much. God had given her a miracle in this man. "What's your name?" she yelled.

"Isak," he called back.

"I won't forget you, Isak."

"Please, just save us."

Abruptly the hands disappeared from the opening and he was gone.

Hadassah climbed the rungs to the snow-dusted roof, then checked to ensure the flares and flare pistol were still tucked beneath her jacket. They were safe, and the Bible was there, as well. She marveled that once again her life had been spared. Had God truly given her uncle the vision? Was she to save them all?

Isak thought so. So did the others. Such faith by so many couldn't be denied.

The flame of her conviction began burning brighter, warming her despite the cold that attacked her flesh. She had to reach the front of the train.

"Two trains now, and no signal," Rand grumbled. The trio huddled under a snow-covered spruce near the tracks. "I don't like it. Something must have happened."

Hitler, that's what happened, Helen thought, shoving her gloved hands deep into her coat pockets. Lenny said nothing—too busy trying to keep warm in his heavy jacket—so she nudged him with her shoulder. When he glanced at her, she gave him another frown.

"We must be patient. They will come," he said, frowning back at her.

Rand grunted, seemingly satisfied. Helen smiled. Lenny let out an exasperated breath that rose like mist in the frozen air.

He looked at Rand. "What will you do when this is all over, Herr Sergeant?"

"If we're successful, I'll take Helen to Switzerland. We'll go to Poland first—if that is still your wish—or you can come with us and ride in the trunk."

Lenny snorted. "I choose Poland, thank you very much."

The cold night air had turned heavy. The white that blanketed the ground buffered all sound beyond their breathing. Helen burrowed deeper into her woolen coat.

A pinpoint of light suddenly shone in the distance. Another train, Helen thought, unable to stop her shivering. *Dear Lord, please let this be the one. Let them be safe.*

"Was the general happy with his prize?"

One side of Aric's face ached with cold as he lay against the freezing deck. He wanted to know if Hermann had taken his beloved. He also needed more time.

As Hermann had suggested, Aric prayed—for Morty's presence. The man handled a machine gun like he was born to it. In the meantime, he had to try and reach his Browning.

"That fat man will get your woman soon enough, though I admit, I'll miss her. She's such a sweet morsel, even for a Jew."

Fury rose in Aric like smoke spewing from the locomotive's stack. He'd never forget the bruises on her cheek. "I'll kill you for touching her."

Hermann chuckled. "You're hardly in a position to do that right now." He jabbed the muzzle of the gun harder against Aric's head. "And why should you care? You gave her to me. You must have known what I had in store for her, especially after your party—"

Aric let out a roar and pushed himself to his knees. He didn't care if he died, so long as Hermann died with him.

He made a lunge for Hermann, but the captain had already regained his balance enough to step backward. Aric's boot caught against the small opening he'd made in the roof earlier. He fell hard against the deck.

"Back to where we started." Hermann pressed the pistol barrel against Aric's temple. "Good-bye, Kommandant."

Hadassah went still at the agonized groan. She'd advanced across nine more boxcars by crawling on her hands and knees, grasping at the brakeman's rungs at the end of each car to pull herself across the meter of empty space between them.

Lying flat, she strained to make out the tall man in a greatcoat standing at the center of the next car. Aric . . . or an SS guard? She edged forward, hugging the roof. In the likely event it *was* a soldier, how would she get past him unnoticed?

She'd reached the junction separating his car from hers when she saw a man lying at the soldier's feet. Then she saw the gun.

Fear paralyzed her . . . until the man's head moved. He was alive!

She reached across open space for the brakeman's rung and pulled herself onto the next car. Then she removed the flare pistol from her jacket and slammed a green flare into its barrel.

At the same time, the tall soldier bent to ram his weapon against the side of the fallen man's head. The face on the ground lifted a fraction. Hadassah recognized the beloved features, agony and frustration carved into lines around his mouth . . .

"Aric!" she screamed, and aimed the flare pistol at the soldier's back.

The frozen ground trembled as the third train rushed past them on the track. No green signal. "Herr Kommandant's plan has failed. We must return to Theresienstadt." Rand was the first to rise from their burrow in the snow.

"Please, Herr Sergeant, we must wait awhile longer! She *will* save them."

"That's just Jewish nonsense. Captain Hermann has probably returned to camp. I must be there to aid Herr Kommandant."

Lenny shot Helen a desperate look, and she immediately understood. If they returned to the ghetto, this young man would likely die. And if he stayed here in this frozen wasteland, he wouldn't fare any better.

She gave him an encouraging nod. "Have you no faith in Herr Kommandant?" he said to Rand, and then looked shocked at his own boldness.

"You dare question my loyalty to him?"

Lenny pursed his lips. She saw him glance again at the steel hook, then back at her. Helen gave him another encouraging sign. "Then why not wait . . . at least awhile longer?" he said. "Maybe they got a late start. Or maybe . . ."

His voice trailed off as Rand hunkered back down into the snow. "We wait another fifteen minutes. Then we go."

Helen reached to squeeze Lenny's shoulder. He nodded at her. Quickly she withdrew her rosary and began to pray.

~ 45 ~

Esther said, "The adversary and enemy is this vile Haman."

Esther 7:6

"A ric!"

Hermann heard the scream and jerked around. Flames exploded at his throat. The force of the fireball knocked him backward, despite the fierce wind. Stunned by pain and confusion, he stared at the woman who had defeated him. He tried crawling toward her, but then another burning pain seized him—this time in his back. Then another. And another.

His vision dimmed as every cell in his body shifted, creating a weightlessness he'd never felt before. Even with his labored breathing, he imagined he could fly on the cusp of the icy wind, beyond himself, beyond pain. A shiver rattled his body. He felt so cold . . .

Aric lay on his stomach, gripping his pistol after unloading three rounds into Hermann's back. The captain's body dropped and rolled like a felled tree—then slammed into Hadassah, who was hovering at the edge of open space between the cars.

They both disappeared.

"NO!" Aric cried. He scrambled on his knees toward her.

She was clutching at a single support near the bottom of the car. Hermann's corpse—doubled in half and wedged into the small space—pressed against her.

Aric could imagine her fear when he saw her pale fingers gripping the rung. "Hold on, Hadassah!" he shouted, and reached down with his free hand to pull Hermann's body away from her.

Hadassah caught Aric's movement and ducked as Hermann's body plummeted past her. The corpse skidded against the side of the train, flouncing like a wild puppet on strings, before dropping beneath the bone-crushing motion of the train's wheels.

In the next instant she felt herself jerked upward by the front of her jacket.

"Are you hurt?" Aric demanded once he'd hauled her onto the roof of the train. His worried gaze traveled her length before he grabbed her frozen hands and tucked them inside his coat. "You're freezing."

"I'm f-fine," she insisted through chattering teeth.

"Honestly, Hadassah, I thought I'd lost you."

The torment in his voice pierced her heart. She slid her arms around his waist, and they clung together, exhausted. "What about you?" Hadassah would forever be haunted by the image of Hermann's pistol pressed against Aric's head. "I thought I might be too late . . ."

"But you weren't." He gave her a reassuring squeeze. "We're both alive."

"Only by a miracle."

"Yes." He smiled at her. "God seems to be on our side."

He placed a tender kiss on her lips, and Hadassah melted against him, her heart overflowing with love and gratitude. *Thank you for keeping him safe.*

"Come! We must hurry." He shoved to his feet, hauling her with him.

Hadassah remembered the flares. "Do we have enough time?" she asked.

"We'll find out." He glanced toward the front of the train. "Walk in front of me, and careful of the ice. Stay along the center of the car."

They made steady progress toward the forward half of the tender car. Once they arrived, she and Aric crouched out of the wind and peered beyond the tracks. Prerov's lights faded, leaving only a star-filled sky and the Ceaseless White. Would they make it in time?

Hadassah handed Aric the flare pistol and remaining three flares.

"Let's hope our friends are waiting for us." Aric stood with feet braced apart and shot the first Very flare. Hadassah watched it soar into the sky, burning iridescent green against the black night. He fired a second, then a third. Each flare soared higher, like the fireworks display she and her uncle once enjoyed during Mannheim's annual *Oktoberfest*.

The train gradually slowed. A signal light shone a few kilometers ahead. Hadassah held her breath and prayed that Rand and Helen had succeeded in smuggling Lenny through Czechoslovakia, and that they now waited ahead for the signal. And that the railroad switch operated properly so their train would not continue on its deadly path north to Auschwitz—

The signal light changed color. Aric let out a triumphant shout as the train veered to the right—away from Auschwitz. Hadassah released her breath and whispered into the night sky, "We are your people, Lord, and you are with us."

Once again the train sped up, moving south now. Aric tossed the flare pistol over the side and dropped down beside her. He pointed toward the bordering tree line.

Two human shapes stood near the track; a third moved up beside them. The moonlight revealed three hands waving silent good wishes.

Hadassah returned the offering, stretching her arms wide in an unspoken embrace. A smile battled her constricted throat. "Do you think we'll ever see them again?"

"We can hope."

But she knew with the war still raging and their safety at risk, it would be next to impossible. Yet the three had become such a crucial part of her life. "Good-bye, dear friends," she called out. "Godspeed."

"He'll take care of them," Aric said, and she found his assurance comforting. "Now let's get inside. There's still plenty to do before we reach the border."

46

Meanwhile, the remainder of the Jews who were in the king's provinces also assembled to protect themselves. . . .

Esther 9:16

THURSDAY, MARCH 9, 1944

General Feldman shifted uneasily against the back seat once his motorcade reached the gates of Theresienstadt. The place seemed oddly quiet; he'd left clear instructions to be met with a full complement of soldiers in parade dress, as well as a marching band.

Only three guards in standard uniform stood at the gate.

Something was wrong. As his shiny black Daimler passed through the entrance amid salutes, Feldman wished he could turn back the three staff cars behind him. If there was a problem, he would prefer the SS-Reichsführer, Eichmann, the Swiss Red Cross, and most especially the reporters from both countries wait until he quietly took care of the matter.

He peered out the car's window, scanning the ghetto. Where was Hermann, and why was he not here to greet them?

Anger replaced his disquiet as the car halted in front of the

Marktplatz. He disembarked without waiting for his driver. The cobblestone square was deserted.

He gazed toward the park where brightly painted park benches sat empty. Feldman scowled. Why weren't the prisoners outside and playing their parts? His anxiety conspired with the sausage he'd eaten at breakfast to drill a hole into his stomach. As the others parked and began exiting their cars, he cast around a swift, desperate glance, trying to anticipate their initial reaction.

His breathing faltered at the sight of the charred façades that only yesterday were the newly constructed storefronts of der Führer's "model ghetto." It looked as if war had broken out inside the fortressed walls. Several SS guards approached him and saluted, but the fear on their pale faces made the ache in his gut rise to his chest.

"Where is your captain?" Feldman glared into the vaguely familiar face of a tall young man, the highest ranking in the lot, a mere corporal. "Where are the prisoners?"

Overwhelmed by the situation, Corporal Sonntag opened and closed his mouth several times. Nothing came out.

"Answer me!"

"He's . . . Herr Captain left on the train for Auschwitz, Herr General," the corporal blurted, shaken from his stupor. "I believe he follows Herr Kommandant."

"What is this? Why was I not told?"

The heat of the general's anger burned him like a brand. The porcine face had turned scarlet while a whitish ring formed at his pinched mouth. Sonntag desperately wished to be elsewhere. "Herr Kommandant escaped. He . . . he . . . there are no officers here." His shoulders slumped. "We are only enlisted men, awaiting orders."

Muttering a string of expletives, some of which Sonntag had never heard before, the general darted a nervous glance over the corporal's right shoulder. Sonntag had already seen the men—

390

two decorated Nazi officials, four civilians wearing Red Cross bands, and about a dozen newspaper people. He could hear the camera bulbs popping off as reporters began taking photographs of the ghetto.

"Where are the Jews?" the general ground out. "Get them out here at once!"

Beads of sweat broke out on Sonntag's forehead. "There is another problem, Herr General—"

But the general wasn't listening. "With luck we can still pull this off. We'll tell the Swiss and the reporters that the fire was accidental . . ." He paused, glaring at Sonntag. "Well, Corporal? Get moving!"

"I'm afraid it's too late, Herr General." Sonntag stared past the general toward the compound. He craned his neck to glimpse the horrified faces of the civilians behind him. His knees began to shake.

"What do you mean 'too late'?" The general shoved hard at his shoulder. "Explain!"

"He means we . . . are already here," a frail voice said at his back.

The general spun around.

Leo Molski stood at the head of a motley tribe of hundreds that followed in his wake. Supporting his thin weight with a wooden stick he'd scrounged from the leftover construction materials, he paused to take in the crowd posing like statues before him.

Several reporters who had been canvassing the ghetto paused in their picture taking to gape openly at them. A few meters away, General Feldman stood transfixed beside a whey-faced corporal, his fleshy features contorted into a comic twist of fury and fear.

Behind them, a pair of Nazi officers posed in full-dress regalia. Likely they were the Jew Killers, Eichmann and Himmler. They stood perfectly still, and Leo felt rather than saw their cold-blooded contempt. But the four men beside them—men bearing the mark of the Red Cross—were not so cautious with their reactions. Leo saw their aversion, then their indignation.

Finally their outrage.

He turned to his people and tried to imagine what these men were seeing—a pathetic group of thin, hollow-faced creatures dressed in rags. Many wore soiled bandages, and some were so weak they had to be carried. Others limped or crawled into the ghetto's square.

Leo's skin heated with shame. They were indeed a grotesque lot. He had no doubt they would all die when this was over—and cruelly, as the murderers burned off their anger at being the brunt of such a joke.

The responsibility made Leo afraid. Not for himself—he'd been prepared to give his life in order to spare another, to let the world know the truth. But what right did he have to influence these others?

"You always did worry too much, Leo," Erna Brenner said beside him.

Leo gazed at the middle-aged woman who read his thoughts. He tried to imagine the loveliness that once blossomed beneath a face now worn from too much hunger and exposure.

"Our hearts are free now," she whispered. "We've made our decision. Even the Nazis can't take that away from us. And God knows we do a good thing." She patted his arm. "So we shall die a good death."

Again, Leo turned to the bedraggled faces of his followers. Determination lit the many pairs of eyes long weakened from suffering, and tightened the mouths long empty of joy.

A tide of conviction washed away the last dregs of his fear. "Gentlemen," Leo cried to the men of the Red Cross, spreading his thin arms wide. "Welcome to *Paradies*!"

47

*The king said to Queen Esther . . . "Now what is
your petition? It will be given you. . . ."*

Esther 9:12

The white-capped peaks of the Nizke Tatry loomed so close
that Hadassah imagined she could touch them. The train
plodded along the northern rim of mountains, the sun shedding
its watery morning rays against a world grown hushed beneath
a blanket of white.

Crouched in the snug space ahead of the tender and out of
the wind, she burrowed deeper into her blanket and enjoyed the
solitude. Joseph slept soundly inside the engine compartment.
Though she was pleased by his quick recovery, Hadassah still
felt pity for those crammed inside the cattle cars.

At least they were breathing fresh air now. Aric had kept
watch during the night, then ordered a halt at dawn before they
entered the mountains. As he scoured the train for any remaining soldiers, Morty and Yaakov released the bars on each car
so the doors could be opened wide.

A few decided to leave when the train stopped. Aric had
warned against it; they were still in occupied German territory. But the people could not be dissuaded, and Hadassah had

watched them as they disappeared into the mists of the forest. She prayed they would find safe haven before the harsh cold—or the Nazis—killed them.

Snow-laden branches hugged the outer edges of the track, while beyond lay an endless stretch of white hills, stark but for intermittent clusters of spruce and pine. She gazed at the cold open space, harsh enough to burn the eyes. And free . . .

Liberation. Because of Aric, it was within their grasp. Yet the gesture did not come without a price. His life was also in danger.

"Keep scowling like that and you'll freeze your lower lip."

Hadassah turned to her beloved. Aric swung down from the open door of the engine car to sit beside her. "Shall I warm it for you?" He kissed her before she could answer.

No longer in uniform, he appeared more like one of the prisoners. It didn't ease her concern. "I was remembering how Captain Hermann nearly killed you. I don't think I was ever so afraid."

"I was an idiot, letting his words make me so crazed."

"I told you, he lied."

His finger grazed the bruise at her cheek. "He still hurt you." The words seemed torn from his chest. "I'm so sorry, love. I didn't protect you. I can never forgive myself for that."

"I fought back, Aric. These bruises are proof. I consider them worthwhile, knowing my other choice. In time they'll heal."

When he looked as if to object, she pressed a finger to his lips. "It's over. He's dead."

Aric took her hand and lightly kissed her palm. "Most fortunate for him. I was an only child. I never learned how to share."

Hadassah smiled. "Neither did I." Her amusement faded as she said, "I was also thinking about Lvov. When the train arrives, we'll be safe. But you . . ." She paused to look out at the continual rush of white hills. "If the Russians discover you're a German soldier, they'll kill you, won't they?"

"Here. You'll catch cold." He ignored her question and instead fished a knitted cap from inside his jacket.

"Answer me."

He sighed. "Before we even reach that city, we must first cross the Polish border into the Ukraine. I'd imagine by now that General Feldman, the Reichsführer, and Adolf Eichmann realize our train never made it to Auschwitz. They'll have started an investigation. After they study all possible routes, they'll notify each border authority to watch for us.

"So before you start fretting over my life, beloved, worry about your own . . . and everyone else's." He tugged the cap over her short curls. "Now, do you suppose there's room under that blanket for one more?"

Hadassah pulled back the covers, and Aric slipped beneath the warmth. He felt for her hand. "What's this?" he asked, retrieving the Bible from her lap.

"I'm beginning to think it's my faith," she said, surprised at the wonder in her voice. "Each time I believe it's gone, it returns to me."

He gave her a puzzled smile before he opened the Bible to the bookmarked page. Recognition flashed across his face as he removed the snapshot. "Where did you get this?"

"It was hidden inside your mother's music box. I . . . kept it to remind me of you. I was going to give it back . . ." Her voice trailed off, seeing his expression soften. "She was a woman much loved, wasn't she?"

"Yes. And so are you," he said, leaning over to kiss her. He slipped the photograph back inside the book. "Keep it safe for me." He grinned. "Now you hold my past . . . and my future."

Before he closed the Bible, he glanced at the open page. "Romans, chapter five. Do you know it well?"

When Hadassah shook her head, he said, "Before she died, my mother often read to me from this passage. 'We also rejoice in our sufferings, because we know that suffering produces perseverance; perseverance, character; and character, hope.'"

Closing the Bible, Aric locked eyes with her. "'And hope does not disappoint,'" he finished, then gave her back the book. "I think she tried to prepare me for what was to come. And I did have hope, at least for a time. But then my father . . . and the war . . ." He shook his head.

Hadassah understood his pain. Last night, as they sat in this same place, each had unburdened a bit of the past to the other. "I don't pretend to know God's ways," she admitted. "For a long time I was angry with Him. I felt He'd abandoned me—all Jews—when He allowed our destruction by the Nazis.

"But then I began to see little miracles happen—in the care you showed Joseph, Helen, and Sergeant Grossman, and when you improved the food for my people in the ghetto. I started to wonder if there must be a purpose for my being in that house." She smiled. "That's when I fell in love with the man who lived there."

He smiled back. "And I was lost . . . until Dachau. I believe now that God wanted me to find you."

Hadassah pressed a hand to his cheek. "He did. There is a story about us, Aric."

"Another fairy tale?" he asked wryly.

"More like Jewish tradition," she said. "On the sixth day, God created the first man and woman as conjoined twins. Husband and wife began as one—before He separated the two, forming Eve from Adam's side. We Jews believe that at birth, each body contains a portion of one soul, and upon marriage the two parts unite again as one. Our *Talmud* teaches that forty days before a male child is conceived, a voice from heaven announces whose daughter he will marry. Our word for this heavenly match is *bashert*. It means 'destiny.'" She took his hand and placed it over her heart. "You, beloved, are mine."

Clearly stunned, Aric pulled her into his arms and kissed her deeply. Hadassah could sense how much her declaration had moved him. When they parted, unexpected tears filled her eyes. "I can't lose you again. Even in the face of my belief, I fear what's to come."

"We have to trust, my love." Aric held her close. "In the past, we both gave up on God. Now we must stay the course. We need to have faith in His purpose even if we don't understand, and despite what may occur. Did you think, weeks ago, that this moment would be possible?"

When she smiled and shook her head, he winked at her and said, "There you have it. The only other option is to jump off this moving train."

He reached inside his jacket and withdrew a single pearl. Hadassah recognized the lustrous gem—part of the necklace he'd once given her. "While you keep the photograph, I have this to remind me of you," he said softly. "You are *my* destiny, Hadassah, and my shelter against the world." He pocketed the pearl and smiled. "We'll trade when we reach Lvov."

48

*The king's edict granted the Jews . . . the right to
assemble and protect themselves. . . .*

Esther 8:11

Are we ready?" Aric asked.

Every man in the engine room nodded. The train had
begun the final leg of its journey across the ridge of the Carpath-
ian Mountains. Soon it would descend into the Polish town of
Krosno, where Przemysl, and the Polish/Ukrainian border, lay
only a few miles beyond.

Yaakov checked the safety on his submachine gun. "The last
time we stopped, I walked back to each car, Herr Kommandant. Every man, woman, and child is armed and waiting. They
have guns, rocks, sticks, and those who don't"—he eyed Aric
soberly—"have their teeth, fists, and God's will to live."

Aric nodded, then turned to the taller of the two Pavliks.
"How quickly can you stop this train?"

Karel glanced at his brother, who was stoking the firebox
with coal. "Depends on how fast we are going. Even at this slow
rate—thirty kilometers up into the mountains—we would need
a kilometer of track to stop safely."

"The Wehrmacht have no doubt set up some sort of blockade at the border," Aric said. "Before we left Theresienstadt, I received reports of heavy air bombing in this area over the past two months. There's every chance the tracks have been blown out. We may have to stop, or at least slow down enough that you can brake at the last possible moment."

He surveyed the men around the compartment. "This also makes us vulnerable to attack," he warned. "Best case is that the tracks are good and we can simply charge past any negligible blockade the Germans might have planned. Worst case is that our train will be forced to stop, and we'll have to fight for our lives. Those who manage by some miracle to survive can then march toward Lvov, staying close to the forest until they reach Russian territory."

Aric turned to the Pavlik brothers. "I advise you to stay on the train. If we fail, you can tell them I held you at gunpoint. If we beat them, you're welcome to join us."

They both nodded. Aric walked to the engine room door. Outside, Hadassah and the boy huddled out of sight in the cramped space of the tender.

God willing, she would be his wife, and the boy he would raise as his own. Would he make a good father? Aric forced a deep breath and refused to succumb to his greatest fear, that he wouldn't live long enough to find out.

"Old man." He turned to Morty, his voice low, urgent. "If I don't make it . . ."

"Yaakov and I will make certain she and the boy escape." Morty's eyes held compassion, along with a soldier's understanding. Aric felt grateful he didn't have to speak the words. He wished now that he and Hadassah had been able to marry before . . .

"You're probably wishing you were off on your honeymoon right about now," Yaakov said, reading his thoughts. "Never fear, Herr Kommandant. I predict that in a few days, you'll be rid of us old men and off to some romantic place with your beautiful bride. Call me a fool if it isn't so." He gave Aric an emphatic nod.

"I'd call you a fool in any case, Yaakov," Morty interjected. "But for their sake, at least, we can hope you're smarter than you look."

A dead pause fell over the room. Then all three Czechs burst into laughter.

∽ 49 ∽

The Jews would be ready on that day to avenge themselves on their enemies.

Esther 8:13

Outside the train, cold gusts blew across the mountains as icy rain fell in sheets. With the doors to each boxcar open, men, women, and children took turns soaking up the elements. The air, clean and pure and free of the ghetto's stench, served to heighten their feeling of expectation. Freedom was the seed that, once considered far beyond their reach, now blossomed into plausible reality.

Aric gazed out at them from the windowless opening in the engineer's compartment, then looked toward the ramparts of an old fortress looming into view, a red-and-white Nazi flag with the black Hakenkreuz blazing across its front. A cluster of soldiers stood on the tracks, armed with submachine guns. Between them was a battery cannon. Just beyond the soldiers, two lorries had been parked across the tracks. He turned to Morty. "It seems they've anticipated our arrival. Is it ready to fire?"

Morty nodded, ran a hand along the length of the Panzerfaust. An animal-like expression touched his features as he offered the tank gun to Aric.

"Keep the train moving, but slow enough to anticipate a stop,"

Aric ordered the Pavlik brothers. "If I'm successful, our path will be clear to continue eastward. If not, or if I end up taking out track along with the lorries, then we'll stand and fight."

Karel gave him a nod, pulling gently at the brake.

Aric went to his beloved. No doubt she was still unhappy that he'd taken Joseph back to the first car. Her fingers clenched and unclenched the grip on the Walther he'd given her for her own protection.

"Sure you can fire that?" he asked again.

"It's a lot like the flare pistol." But her sober expression and wide eyes told him she was frightened.

"Here, draw back the slide like this, then press the trigger." He took the pistol from her and demonstrated. "Leave the safety on until you're ready to fire." He returned the pistol to her. "Be careful." Gently he pressed his mouth to hers, ignoring his gnawing fear. He looked at Morty. "Remember what I said."

The old man glanced up from inspecting the submachine gun that Yaakov had just handed him. "It will be as you say, my son."

"Godspeed, everyone." Aric made for the door and, together with Morty and Yaakov, slipped out of the engineer's compartment and up to the locomotive's flat-top roof.

Once there, Aric knelt with the Panzerfaust balanced against his right shoulder. Sleet pounded their faces as Morty and Yaakov squatted on either side.

Without hesitating, Aric took aim at the lorries and fired. The impact threw him backward. If not for his two companions, he would have toppled over the side.

Both transport trucks exploded in a cloud of fire and smoke. Steel debris flew in every direction. One of the lorries' huge tires hurled a hundred meters into the air, then landed to bounce into the nearby woods.

Running soldiers had dropped for cover when the Panzerfaust hit its target. Appearing dazed, they struggled to their feet and fumbled for their weapons.

"Take cover!" Aric yelled. He raced behind Morty and Yaakov down into the tender. Tossing the spent weapon over the side, he climbed back along the outside rails of the locomotive. He remained there as the train crossed the border. Thankfully, not much debris littered the tracks. "Go!" he shouted to the Pavlik brothers. Miko hurriedly shoveled coal into the firebox.

No one saw the missing track until it was too late.

Less than a kilometer beyond the explosion, dead space stretched for several meters. The locomotive pressed forward and then lurched as it left the tracks. Tender and cattle cars followed, drifting downward along a slope toward the dense trees.

The train might have stayed upright except for the mud. Ukrainian mud, soggy and clinging, sucked at the heavy wheels like quicksand. The locomotive pitched at a precarious angle, and one car after another followed in its wake. Panic erupted as people jumped, fell, or stumbled over one another trying to escape from being trapped inside.

Hadassah clutched at the rail support of the engine room's inside door and listened to the terrified screams behind them. The huge iron box began to list like a sea-tossed ship.

"Hang on!" Karel Pavlik shouted, grabbing at a rung near the opposite door.

Hadassah waited, her heart racing with each passing second. One . . . two . . .

The mammoth beast finally groaned; metal plates stretched, twisting helpless against the impetus of its own weight. Like a grand horse having spent its last breath, the locomotive heaved onto its side, sliding down the hill another fifteen meters in the slick Ukrainian mud before it finally came to a stop.

Hadassah held on, swinging in the empty space like a human pendulum. Karel knelt down on the floor, now the opposite wall of the compartment, and reached for her. "Careful now." He held her legs and eased her onto her feet. "Let's get out of here. Miko . . . ?"

He turned to his brother and froze. Hadassah cried out when she saw Miko Pavlik lying at an unnatural angle against the floor. Eyes that once held kindness and laughter—life—now stared vacantly at them.

Karel Pavlik dropped to his knees beside his brother. A series of shots ricocheted off the locomotive. "We must go!" Hadassah urged. She retrieved the pistol from inside her jacket pocket, then tried to pull the engineer to his feet. He gave her a blank look. "He's with God now, Karel," she said. "Please, we have to get out of here!"

Fumbling for his pickaxe, Karel rose and followed her. Because the train rested at an angle, they were able to crawl underneath the side opening without having to risk being picked off by gunfire.

The rain had stopped, leaving only a sullen sky. Hadassah searched the throngs swarming across the muddy slope, hoping for a sign of Aric, Joseph, or Morty.

Nothing.

She peered toward the forest, dismayed to find the safety of trees still some distance away. Amidst the chaos, muffled cries rose to a fevered pitch from several overturned cars. Hadassah grabbed the front of Karel's jacket. "You must get them out!"

The Czech engineer surfaced from his well of grief. Giving a low shout, he dashed with his pickaxe to the first overturned car. He hacked away at the sides, and when at last the breach was wide enough, he moved to the next car while those in the first finished breaking away timbers and streamed from their death pens like fleeing ants.

German soldiers marched toward them. Machine-gun fire rent the air. Hadassah watched as thousands of her people stumbled in the mud, screaming and shouting in their panic to flee.

"Take a stand!" she cried at them.

But they ignored her. Several fights broke out, violence borne of blind fear and desperation.

"Salvation!" she shouted louder.

To her amazement, the clamor quieted. Many paused to stare at her, some with accusing faces, others with a kind of dazed bewilderment.

"Freiheit!" Her voice rang out. "You must fight for it!"

Still, no one reacted. Then gunfire shattered the silence, and Hadassah watched, horrified, as a dozen people crumpled lifeless into the mud.

"This is your chance!" she pleaded. "There are so many of you"—she pointed to the approaching troops—"and only a handful of soldiers!"

"*Purim!*"

A voice roared from the depths of the crowd. As the throng began to part, Hadassah's heart leaped at the sight of her uncle, knee-deep in mud and wielding a machine gun.

"Purim!" bellowed another from the outer fringes of the multitude.

"Purim!" cried a third, this time a woman's voice.

Instantly, thousands mired in the boggy slope took up the cry, a single word passed between them like a mantra, a *shibboleth* that alone could ensure their victory.

Their chant rose to greater heights as the German soldiers attacked. But this time when the machine guns opened fire, the ghetto people of Theresienstadt retaliated—with sticks, rocks, bricks, anything they could forage from the cold, muddy earth.

Hadassah spied Joseph struggling to extricate himself from a cluster of people, mostly women, showering bricks at a German soldier a few feet away. She ran to him, screaming his name as the affronted soldier aimed his gun into the crowd.

Joseph jerked his head toward her.

The soldier hesitated.

Hadassah rammed back the slide on her pistol. Flipping off the safety, she took aim and pulled the trigger. It didn't fire. Frantic, she kept squeezing at the pistol's mechanism. Nothing else mattered; she had to stop the smirking soldier from killing her little boy.

A single gunshot exploded from behind her. The soldier's smile faded to a look of astonishment, and then his body fell in a heap to the ground.

Joseph picked up the soldier's machine gun and ran toward her. He didn't look at her; he was staring at someone directly behind her. Fresh terror seized her. She grasped the pistol like a bludgeon and whirled to meet her attacker—

"Aric!" Hadassah sobbed as she threw her arms around him. Joseph reached them and offered up the machine gun.

"Why didn't you shoot?" Aric demanded as he hustled them away from the crowd of women.

"The trigger must be jammed." She handed over the pistol for his inspection. "I should have realized it right away, but I was so afraid for Joseph." She gazed lovingly at the boy. "You saved his life, Aric."

"You saved mine." He locked eyes with her a moment before he added, "Collect the children and take them into the shelter of trees. Stay low. You must work your way to the east. Lvov is only a few kilometers from here." He handed her his Browning. "Take Joseph with you. I'll join up with you shortly."

"Be careful!"

His answer was to seize her mouth in a quick, fierce kiss. "God go with you, my love." Then he strode into the violent fray that had gravitated down the slick slope for several meters.

Hadassah began gathering the children together. When she caught sight of Clara Brenner, she hailed her, and the pair of them along with Joseph soon had the youngsters moving toward the forest. Yaakov joined them, his machine gun poised for any sign of danger ahead. They made a slow trek around the fighting. The children stumbled every other step as their shoes caught and held in the quagmire of mud.

Having entrusted the two adults to lead the group, Hadassah

moved back among the children, righting those who fell and comforting the youngest, who whimpered from fear and the damp chill permeating their clothes.

Catching up the next toppling child, Hadassah realized she held the dark-haired little girl she'd met in the ghetto. The same child she'd carried to the train.

"Mama!"

The spindly arms squeezed her neck in a death grip. "It's all right, sweetheart, I've got you." Hadassah hoisted the little girl onto her hip before resuming her arduous trek beside the others. Every so often, she glanced back at the tumult, hoping to see the familiar faces of her uncle and Aric.

She was relieved when both finally sprinted forward to take up the rear of their party. Joseph moved back to trudge alongside her. "Are you all right?" she asked him.

The boy nodded, though his clumsy gait revealed his exhaustion. Only two days had passed since his brutal encounter with Hermann, and the train had afforded him little comfort. She reached to gently touch his cheek. "It's not much farther, kaddishel. Then we can rest."

He tipped his bruised face up to her. "When we reach the town, will we get to live there?"

"I think so." Her breathing labored beneath the weight of the child in her arms as she slogged through the mud.

"I mean," he said, staring at the ground, "when we get there . . . will you still be my mother?"

Hadassah paused to catch her breath. She shifted the little girl onto her other hip while a feeling of joy assuaged her fatigue. "I'll be your mother, Joseph, wherever we live."

His smile looked more like a sneer through battered lips. Hadassah caught his hand and they continued their trek. A silence passed between them before he asked, "Will he be my father?"

Hadassah shot him a glance. She hadn't actually thought about the fact that once she and Aric married, they would all be living together. Certainly Joseph's relationship with Aric was just as important as her own. "Would you like that?" she asked.

Again he inspected the ground, shuffling his feet through clods of wet dirt in his path. "I think he will make a good papa."

Hadassah blinked back tears. "I'm certain he'll be happy to hear it."

The shelter of thick pine stood only a few meters away. Hadassah scanned the group of children to ensure all were upright and making progress.

A burst of automatic fire sounded to the right. "Down!" Aric shouted. Immediately hundreds of terrified, squealing children and the handful of adults dropped into the mud.

Hadassah glimpsed the steel helmets of two German soldiers pressed into a hill north of the tree line. Armed with submachine guns, they sprayed bullets into the air just above their heads, keeping children and adults pinned to the earth.

Yaakov, Morty, and Aric returned fire, but the soldiers hidden on the slope had the advantage. They toyed with their prey; each time Hadassah or one of the others tried to rise, the guns let loose with another round of bullets.

She waited in the mud alongside Joseph and the little girl. The odor of decaying earth filled her nostrils and felt cold and wet against her cheek. Beyond the slope, the fighting had quieted. She wondered if her people were successful or if the Germans overtook them despite such greater numbers.

Hadassah didn't see Aric toss the grenade, but she heard its explosion. The two German soldiers flew through the air like circus tumblers. "Get moving!" Aric shouted.

Both she and Clara helped the children to their feet, then rushed toward the tree line. Yaakov covered the front while Aric and Morty took up the rear.

The group came upon the place where one of the Germans had landed after the blast. Though the soldier's body remained whole, he didn't move. As they trudged past him, Hadassah felt neither triumph nor enmity; only the certainty that he would now have to face God's justice.

No one saw his hand grope for the holstered pistol at his side, or raise his arm to sight in his retreating enemy.

Everyone crouched low at the first shot of gunfire behind them. Hadassah whirled to see the second round hit her beloved, knocking him to the ground. "Aric!"

Her scream set off a chain reaction as hundreds of youngsters responded in kind to the terror they as yet could not see. Morty finished off the soldier who had fired, and then Hadassah ran to Aric.

By the time she reached him, he'd struggled to his knees. The front of his jacket was covered in blood. "No, no, no . . . !" She dropped down beside him and caught his face in her palms. She saw for the first time his pale weariness and the grime and agony etched into his handsome face. "You must get up, beloved."

Tears blurred her vision as she struggled to lift one of his limp arms across her shoulders. "I'll help you, sweetheart. Just lean on me, we've got to make it to the trees. Aric, you said we had to get to the trees."

She was babbling, pulling on him to no avail. He was like trying to move a mountain. "Help me!" she cried, and her uncle and Yaakov hurried toward her.

Morty reached them first and grasped Aric's other arm.

"Nein," Aric managed to say. "It's not good." Green eyes, dark with pain, turned to her. "You must go, Hadassah. Finish this."

"I won't leave you!" Wild with grief, she became unreasonable. "You won't die!" she sobbed. "Please, beloved, you can't die!"

"Don't, Süsse," he said, his voice anguished. "Don't do this . . ."

Hadassah's breath sliced through her lungs as she pressed closer, breathing in his familiar scent, mingled now with the stench of blood and dank earth. When she'd managed to calm down, he sought her out for a kiss, one more tender than any she'd known.

"I love you," he whispered against her mouth. "Always . . ."

Fresh pain stabbed at her. "Aric—"

"You have to . . . save them." His breathing took effort as he turned to gaze at the hundreds of wide-eyed, grimy-faced children watching them. "They need you."

She pulled his face back to her. "I need you!"

Dark lashes fluttered against his cheeks, and his body leaned heavily against her. He brushed a bloodied hand across the side of her face before opening his eyes to her. His jaw clenched. "Get her . . . out of here."

"Aric!" She fought the strong hands dragging her back toward the forest, away from the man she loved. As if living a nightmare, she watched him sway slightly on his knees, then collapse face-first into the muddied earth.

Hadassah's world ceased to exist; she went limp in their arms.

"Daughter, get up!"

Morty's voice. Vague and disconnected, it was part of the same nightmare. She turned and gaped at him.

"We must hurry the children, Hadassah. Soldiers are coming!"

Children . . . Hadassah struggled to comprehend Morty's words, the urgency in them. She caught a glimpse of a dozen or so German soldiers circling to block their escape into the woods. Aric's voice seemed to permeate the damp air. *"You must go, Hadassah. Finish this. . . . They need you."*

A rapid burst of gunfire sprayed above their heads. Children squealed in terror behind her, and Hadassah swung around to see a small body crumple to the ground.

It was the little girl from the ghetto.

"Nooooo!" Hadassah screamed as she kicked and clawed at the arms holding her. She bellowed curses at Morty, at Yaakov, even at God, before she broke free and wrenched the machine gun from her surprised uncle's grasp.

"No more, do you hear me?" She rose to her feet and aimed the weapon at the wall of soldiers. "No more lambs!"

410

She squeezed the trigger, her body jerking backward with the impact of rapid shots. Hadassah kept firing, ignoring the whine of enemy bullets racing past her, unmoved by the sight of gray-uniformed men toppling into the mud like so much trampled grass.

Even after they all lay dead and her ammunition was spent, she kept pressing the trigger.

"Enough, child." Morty pried the weapon from her hands. "We need to go. Quickly."

Joseph ran up and clutched her tightly around the waist. Hadassah's anger faded at the sight of his frightened features. "It's all right." Her voice shook as she held him. "They can't hurt us anymore."

She helped to gather together the other children, all of whom had become eerily quiet. Hundreds of muddy, tear-streaked faces gaped at her with awe and apprehension.

Hadassah crouched beside the fallen little girl. She wished she'd known the child's name. "For you, Anna," she whispered, reaching to touch the dark, baby-soft curls.

Rising, she looked back at the place where Aric lay unmoving.

"Don't go back, daughter," Morty warned, reading her intent. "The past cannot help us now. Our only chance for life lies ahead with the future."

He was my future, Hadassah wanted to tell him. But she glanced at the helpless little faces around her and knew her uncle was right. "We *will* finish this," she said in a torn voice. "My beloved's death will not be wasted."

Taking Joseph by the hand, she marched the children through the cold Ukrainian slog, past fallen soldiers toward the safety of the forest. Toward the future and freedom.

She never once looked back.

50

Esther's decree confirmed . . . Purim, and it was written down in the records.

Esther 9:32

Lvov, City of Lions

*S*alvation—a word spoken reverently among the bedridden at St. Nicholas's hospital, and a reminder that the "Battle of Susa," as it was now called, had been declared an unprecedented victory for the Jews of Theresienstadt.

Even the Russians seemed pleased. The ghetto people had spared them the expense of precious munitions and troops to defeat the German forces at Przemysl. That Lvov until recently had struck its own fist of cruelty against the Jews didn't deter the conquering Red Army from opening its gates. The Reds provided food and medical attention, and cooperated with leaders like Morty Benjamin and Yaakov Kadlec to obtain temporary housing for the thousands of refugees.

Salvation. It was in that same breath they whispered *her* name. She who had fought for their cause. She whom God had chosen to lead them out of hell.

The prophecy had come true.

The days stretched into weeks, and the weeks into months, while the stories of her courage grew bolder with each retelling, her sacrifices greater. How she'd stood amidst a hailstorm of enemy gunfire and single-handedly destroyed an entire legion of German soldiers. How her fearlessness changed the course of battle and encouraged the Jews to defeat their enemy at Przemysl in one final, relentless blow. The wonder of her deeds spread far and wide, offering hope to those surviving the aftermath of battle, and strength to those who had yet to confront it.

None knew of her sorrow or comprehended the dark smudges beneath her eyes. The creases bracketing her soft mouth merely heightened her glory and attributed to her selflessness as she nursed them back to health, dressing their wounds and comforting their losses.

After all, *she* had saved them.

"You look like you need a rest." Clara Brenner drew up beside Hadassah and placed a hand on her shoulder. They both wore the sterile white uniform of a nurse's aide. "I think fresh air might do you good."

"I could use a little daylight," Hadassah admitted. "I feel as though I've been in a cave for the past week."

"That's because you *have* been in a cave," Clara said with a wave at their dismal surroundings.

The basement of Lvov's hospital had been converted into a makeshift ward to accommodate the enormous influx of wounded. To Hadassah, the place was a concrete tomb, complete with gloomy shadows outside the glare of naked lights, and a damp mustiness that mixed with carbolic to mask the stench of human sweat and blood. And its occupants were the winding-sheet that smothered Hadassah in praise she didn't want or deserve.

Two months had passed and still these people extolled her as some modern-day Moses delivering the Jews out of Egypt. They didn't know how she'd wanted to give up in those final moments, watching her beloved die . . .

"You haven't left this ward in days," Clara prodded. "Why not go upstairs to the terrace? Last time I looked, the sky was as clear blue as your eyes."

Blue . . . like Austria. The ache in Hadassah's heart hadn't dimmed. She tried smiling at Clara but managed only a nod. "I'll be back in an hour," she said.

"Take your time. You might find as I did that the fresh air heals what ails you better than any medicine." Compassion shone in Clara's eyes. She had also known great loss. A mother left behind . . .

Hadassah fled to the stairs leading up to the first floor.

Leaning against the wrought-iron rail of the terrace, Hadassah gazed out at the surrounding hills. The Ceaseless White was gone, and in its place, budding leaves of birch, hornbeam, and maple spread like a verdant mantle as far as the eye could see.

She breathed in the fresh air warmed by the sun, and for a few precious moments felt lifted from the weight of her grief. From her precipice she could see into the heart of the city below: cobbled streets amidst Baroque-style buildings, with tulips and daffodils and lilacs bursting into lavish color as basketfuls spilled from balconies, windowsills, and doorways. Pink bricks surrounded the large *Ploscha Rynok*, Lvov's market square, and blushed with a rosy golden hue in the afternoon light.

Yet beyond the picturesque town and green hills, the war still raged. Even the gentle cooing of pigeons, scrapping for morsels between cracks in the hospital's stone terrace, could not block out the distant howl of shellfire.

For now, though, it seemed vague to her. Like winter, little more than a memory, vanquished in the green of newly formed leaves, forgotten in the sunny warmth that kissed her skin.

Hadassah's nightmares had become worn and distant as well, as though years, and not months, had passed since her first glimpse of Dachau's barbed-wire fences; years, not months, since she'd stood naked and cold, clutching a child's hand while she waited to die. A lifetime since she'd been loved by a man so profoundly that he would surrender his life to save hers.

She reached inside the voluminous pocket of her nurse's apron to touch the cool surface of the Bible she still carried, where she continued to keep his precious photograph. *"You hold my past as well as my future."*

She choked back a sound that was half sob, half laughter. Surviving months of abuse, starvation, squalor, and afterward living among the enemy, she'd somehow managed to overcome impossible odds to save her people. Yet in the past two months she'd never felt more afraid or uncertain in her life. How could she face the future without Aric?

Hadassah closed her eyes and tipped her face toward the sun. She'd asked God this question many times since his death. Her heart still waited for an answer.

"Mama!"

Hadassah spun around to see Joseph at the doorway leading onto the terrace. The child worked like a soothing balm on her grief. His bruises and cuts had long ago healed, and she felt pleased at his easy adjustment to their new way of life. She only wished Aric could have been with them, especially in the years to come, to help guide this boy through the complexities of approaching adolescence and manhood.

Hadassah sighed. For now, he was still a child, hopping back and forth on the balls of his feet. His face broke into a grin. "You look ready to burst," she said, finding a smile for him.

"I have a surprise," he sang out, half running in her direction. When he stood before her, he said, "It's an engagement gift. One of the injured soldiers asked me to give it to you."

Hadassah flinched. Since their arrival at the hospital, her popularity had escalated—especially with the wounded. Several men had even asked for her hand in marriage. Though she probably should be flattered by their offers, it only exacerbated her pain. The only man she wanted to marry—the man who held the other part of her soul—was gone.

Blinking back tears, she crouched to his level. "Please, kaddishel, whatever it is, take it back." Her voice shook with emotion. "I don't want . . ."

She stopped speaking when Joseph held out his fist and opened it. Against his palm lay a single pearl.

The world began to spin. Hadassah, still crouched, grabbed for the boy to steady her balance. Then slowly she stood, and her heart felt wedged in her throat as she took the pearl from him. Images flashed through her mind . . . the indomitable soldier in black who first gazed up at her second-story window in Dachau . . . then a man, clad in brown sweater and slacks, his smile and green eyes full of warmth and mischief and the promise of a snowball fight. A pledge made to her while on his knees . . . a kiss on a train to seal their souls . . .

. . . a mud-streaked face, full of pain and anguish, kissing her for the very last time . . .

She stared at the pearl, afraid to look away for fear that if she did, the gem might vanish, along with her memories of him.

"Mama, he's here."

Hadassah looked up then—and spied a tall man watching her from the terrace doorway. His features were unrecognizable; the tanned face was extremely thin and lined with exhaustion, while his strange, homespun clothing fit loosely against his frame.

He pushed away from the doorjamb and moved in her direction. She noticed his limp.

"Hadassah," he called softly. Then he stopped and opened his arms.

"Aric!" Sobbing, she ran to him. Tears blurred her vision as she threw her arms around him and buried her face against his neck, reveling in his solid presence. Her body trembled as she breathed in his familiar scent of pine, spice, and Kaffee. Her beloved was alive!

His strong arms encircled her while his chin came to rest gently against the top of her head. Aric held her tightly, whispering soothing words to try and quiet her sobs. But when she finally looked up at him, Hadassah only cried harder.

"My love, please don't . . ." he said brokenly before he captured her mouth in a searing kiss that silenced her cries. She melted against him, meeting his passion with her own while the salt of their tears mingled together. It was as if a missing part of her had been found. The broken shards of their souls mended to become whole again.

"I thought I'd lost you forever," she whispered when their kiss ended.

"I thought so, too." His breathing labored as he leaned his forehead against hers. "But it seems God had other plans," he added with a smile in his voice.

She leaned back and searched his face. "Where have you been? How have you survived all this time?"

"Resistance fighters," he answered. "Apparently our arrival at Przemysl preempted their plans to attack. When they finally did show up to make prisoners of any remaining soldiers, they found me. Fortunately, several of our own who had fled to the woods came forward, so I was taken to a church in the village of Karpaty, in the Ukraine, where they brought in a doctor to patch me up. Afterward they hid me away with a crofter up in the foothills until I was strong enough to leave.

"Now I am here. For you, beloved." He kissed her again. "And our boy." He turned to extend his hand to Joseph, who hovered shyly several feet away. "Come here, son."

The child ran to them, his flushed face wreathed in a smile. Hadassah and Aric both pulled him into the circle of their embrace.

"Aric, what will happen now . . . to us?" Hadassah asked, trying to stem her sudden feeling of anxiousness. "Germany is losing the war. You'll be hunted down. Where will we go?"

"For now, we'll leave for Switzerland. Rand and Helen are waiting for us there." He paused. "After the war . . ."

He gave her a pensive look. "God has forgiven me, Hadassah, though I know I don't deserve it. He's gifted me with more than I ever dreamed—a chance to start over again, a new sense of hope, and the faith I thought I'd lost long ago." He smiled. "He gave me you." Then he reached down to tousle Joseph's hair. "And a son.

"But the world will still hold me accountable for taking part in Hitler's scheme," he continued. "Even now, when I think of the apathy I once held toward your people, it grieves me. If I'd had your courage, I could have done so much more. . . ." He let out a ragged breath. "When the war is over, I must face whatever justice metes out—"

"You won't face it alone, my son."

Hadassah turned to see her uncle approach, along with Yaakov Kadlec. "We will be there, too. We'll tell them of your actions and how you saved us all. I believe they will listen. After all"—her tatteh smiled—"God is on our side."

"Yes, He is," Hadassah said, and as she tucked the pearl into her apron pocket, she laid her palm against the miraculous Bible that held the photograph she would soon return to her beloved. The story of Elijah rose in her mind. "Whatever our future holds, Aric, God will be there to guide us," she said, gazing up at the man she loved. "We have only to listen."

A soft breeze arose at that moment, steady and sweet across the hills of Lvov. And Hadassah smiled, hearing His whisper.

Author's Note

Dear Reader,
    I hope you've enjoyed this story, a tale of redemption through faith and the power of God's love, and how the Jewish people struggled against their monsters and finally won the day.

Sadly, it's fiction. There was no "freedom train" to Przemysl. No Leo Molski to confront the Red Cross with true conditions in the ghetto. Only the suffering was real, the deprivation and hunger. I therefore feel honor-bound to the Jewish people and to all who suffered at the hands of Hitler's machinations to tell the truth as I understand it.

The transit camp of Theresienstadt—or Terezin, in what is now the Czech Republic—did actually exist. Founded in 1780 by Emperor Joseph II in honor of his mother, Empress Maria Theresa, the fortressed city was used by the Germans as a transit camp for Auschwitz from November 24, 1941, until its liberation on May 9, 1945.

The Nazis proclaimed Theresienstadt a "Paradiesghetto" and coerced 140,000[1] Jews from their homes. The new arrivals discovered not a resort city, as they had been promised, but a ghetto plagued by squalid, overcrowded living conditions, a lack of food and medicine, and much death and disease. Of those who entered this walled town between November 1941 and April 1945, over 90,000 were sent to their deaths in Auschwitz-Berkenau and other extermination camps.[2] Of those, 15,000 were children.[3] And of those who remained, 33,500 died in the ghetto.[4]

The last transport left the ghetto on October 28, 1944.[5] The terrible burden of filling the transports with the required number of victims was put upon the members of the Elder Council, the Jewish administrative body. With devilish baseness and cunning, the Nazis dictated the number of victims to be sent east, but placed the burden of selection on the Jews themselves, to select their own co-religionists, relatives, and friends. In the end, this unbearable responsibility destroyed the community leaders who were forced to make the selections.[6]

I have also taken the liberty of altering history's timeline to better suit my story purpose. Though the date of the Jewish celebration of Purim was Thursday, March 9, 1944, the all-important Red Cross visit didn't actually occur until June 23 of that same year. It came about because the Danish government was anxious to see for itself the conditions of the ghetto after 466 Danish Jews were sent there beginning on October 5, 1943. After sufficient pressure, the Nazis agreed and began their *Verschönerung*, or "beautification program," in late 1943 in preparation for the inspection. Because Theresienstadt housed so many prominent and well-known Jews—artists, musicians, and heroes of the First World War—the Nazis wanted to fool the world into thinking the Jews were being well treated.[7]

Unlike my fictional Red Cross delegation, who is not only surprised but enraged by the sight of Leo and his bedraggled followers, the real four-man Swiss-Danish team never encountered any such "unpresentables." After a six-hour orchestrated tour given by the SS, they left the ghetto satisfied that all was in good order. They were unaware that many old and sick patients—including the insane and those pretending to be—had already been sent east to be gassed, along with hundreds of raggedy and emaciated children. The fresh, new children brought in for the inspection were killed after the Red Cross gave the ghetto a clean bill of health.[8]

Wolkenbrand or "Firecloud" is a code name I borrowed from Heinrich Himmler's unsuccessful directive to annihilate the remaining prisoners at the concentration camp of Dachau prior to liberation.[9] At Theresienstadt near the end of the war, the real commandant, an Austrian, SS Colonel Karl Rahm, was similarly ordered by Adolf Eichmann to set up gas chambers and get rid of any remaining Jews before the Russians arrived.

The gas was delivered and one of the buildings set up as a gas chamber, but because Rahm feared being tried as a war criminal for such actions, he abandoned the directive and escaped just prior to the camp's liberation. He was captured after the war, and the Czech courts tried him and sentenced him to death. Meanwhile, the Russians found a raging typhus epidemic inside Theresienstadt, and although they did their best to help the sick inmates, many perished.[10]

There are other minor issues for which I've taken discretionary license. The fact that Terezin is quite a large city, while I attempted to give the ghetto a "small town" sense. The real commandant's headquarters were located inside the fortress near the Marktplatz; I chose to place Aric von Schmidt's home just outside the fortress to underscore his deliberate detachment from the Jews' plight. I gave my protagonist, Hadassah, a prisoner identification number from Dachau, tattooed on the inside of her left arm above the wrist. Yet despite the perception that all Holocaust prisoners were given tattoos, it was only those prisoners of Auschwitz after 1941 who were branded in this way.[11]

Finally, I offer my heartfelt apologies if I have omitted any other material discrepancies that would seem germane to this story. Suffice it to say, we must never forget the Holocaust and the millions who suffered and died at Hitler's hands, especially the children.

—KB

Notes

1. All numbers are approximate.

2. Chuck Feree, *Theresienstadt – Paradeisghetto*, www.jewishgen.org/forgottenCamps/Witnesses/TheresEng.html.

3. Jewish Virtual Library, *Terezin Concentration Camp – History & Overview*, www.jewishvirtuallibrary.org/jsource/Holocaust/terezin.html.

4. Theresienstadt History, *Famous Red Cross Visit to Theresienstadt*, www.scrapbookpages.com/CzechRepublic/Theresienstadt/TheresienstadtGhetto/History/RedCrossVisit.html.

5. Ibid.

6. Chuck Feree, *Theresienstadt – Paradeisghetto*.

7. *Famous Red Cross Visit to Theresienstadt*.

8. Chuck Feree, *Theresienstadt – Paradeisghetto*.

9. Michael Selzer, *Deliverance Day: The Last Hours at Dachau* (Philadelphia: Lippincott, 1978).

10. Chuck Feree, *Theresienstadt – Paradeisghetto*.

11. Jewish Virtual Library, *Tattoos*, www.jewishvirtuallibrary.org/jsource/Holocaust/Tattoos.html.

Glossary of Terms

German:

Achtung!: Attention!

Anschluss: Annexation of Austria into Nazi Germany, 1938; earlier attempts in 1933–34 failed.

Appell, Appellplatz: Roll call. Assembly ground in a concentration or extermination camp where prisoners muster.

Arbeit Macht Frei: "Work Makes You Free." Nazi slogan that marked the entrances into many of the concentration camps.

Blockführer, Blockführerin: SS rank, Block section leader, prisoner compound.

Das Schwarze Korps: *The Black Corps*, official newspaper of the Nazi SS during WWII.

Einsatzgruppen: SS-mobile task forces, usually for the purpose of "liquidation."

Endoslung: The Final Solution. Nazi plan to annihilate all Jewry in occupied Europe.

Ersatz: Replacement. In the ghetto, ingredients substituted for real coffee.

Hakenkreuz: Swastika. Nazi symbol.

HitlerJugend: Hitler Youth. Paramilitary organization comprised of girls and boys, 10–18 years.

Kleine Festung: Little Fortress. Small "punishment" garrison outside Theresienstadt.

Kristallnacht: "Night of Broken Glass." Nazis' destruction of Jewish neighborhoods, November 1938.

Lagerführer: Officer in charge of the prison compound.

Mischling: Crossbreed. Term used by Nazis for those with mixed Aryan and Jewish blood.

Paradiesghetto: "Paradise ghetto." Theresienstadt was given this euphemism so as to lure thousands of Jews.

Pflanzengarten: Botanical/vegetable garden.

Reichsführer-SS: Head of the SS, a position held only by Heinrich Himmler.

Reichsmark: German paper currency used from 1924–1948. Similar to the American dollar.

Sarah: Term Nazis used for Jewesses.

Schrank: Freestanding cupboard.

Schutzstaffel: SS/Waffen-SS. Political/military group created by Adolf Hitler and the Nazis.

Sonderkommandos: A detachment of SS that policed occupied territory.

Sturmabteilung: SA, "Brownshirts." Paramilitary group within the Nazi Party.

Wehrmacht: The German armed forces (Army, Navy, Air Force).

Jewish:

Adar: Last month of the Jewish ecclesiastical year.

Hanukkah: Jewish Festival of Lights.

Havdalah: Jewish ceremony that marks the end of Shabbat or festival.

Ketuvim: Third section of the Hebrew Bible.

Kiddush: Blessing and prayer recited over wine on the eve of Shabbat or festival.

Mogen Dovid: Star of David. Nazis required Jews to wear a gold star to identify their Jewry.

Nevi'im: Second section of the Hebrew Bible.

Rosh Hashanah: Jewish New Year.

Shabbat: Jewish Sabbath.

Shtetl: Small town or ghetto that is predominantly Jewish.

Sukkah: Booth or temporary hut used in Feast of Booths (Sukkot).

Tallit: Jewish prayer shawl.

Talmud: Jewish book of tradition, instruction, and law.

Tanakh: Hebrew Bible.

Torah: First five books of the Hebrew Scriptures. The Pentateuch of the Christian Bible.

Traif: Food that does not conform to Jewish dietary law. Forbidden.

Yarmulke: Prayer cap.

Discussion Questions

1. When *For Such a Time* opens, Stella finds herself held captive at the chalet of Aric's cousin in the German town of Dachau, not far from the concentration camp. After the war, many townspeople insisted they knew nothing of the Nazis' activities at the camp. What do you think? Were they truly unaware? Or did their guilt make them blind? Could we find this weakness of human nature in the injustices that surround us today—in our neighborhoods, our cities, our country?

2. Who was your favorite secondary character in the story? Why?

3. As Stella is taken to Aric's new post at Theresienstadt, she believes her people to be abandoned by God. Even now, the terrible inhumanity of the Holocaust remains incomprehensible; it is also difficult to reconcile with the will of a loving Father in heaven. If you were Stella, how would you come to terms with these events in your own faith? Do you think we can prevent the genocide still occurring in other parts of the world?

4. When Stella is directed by Captain Hermann to type up the train manifest for Auschwitz, she attempts to try and

save a few by omitting random names from the list. A small gesture, but one that requires courage. Consider your own character. To what lengths would you go to save someone's life? A child or another loved one? How about someone unknown to you?

5. Stella learns from Joseph that her uncle Morty is the sole Elder in the Judenrat and must decide who goes to Auschwitz. How would you cope in Morty's place?

6. Aric was originally an officer in the Wehrmacht, specifically the German Army. Because of his injuries, he was discharged and then approached by Himmler to take charge of the camp at Theresienstadt. Later at the banquet, Stella is shocked to hear him—having witnessed Heydrich's brutality at Babi Yar—disparage the Waffen-SS in front of his peers. Why then does he take the post of SS-Kommandant at Theresienstadt? Is he truly apathetic or does he feel he has no other choice? Is one better than the other?

7. When Aric learns of Wolkenbrand, his conscience begins to war with his sense of duty, especially when he considers what Stella will think of him. If the story events had not changed, do you believe he would have gone through with it or chosen some other option? What does it say about Aric's character that he has taken under his wing three persons, each of whom, like Aric, is damaged in some way?

8. The Bible finds its way into Stella's possession throughout the story, despite her repeated rejection. Finally, when she's desperate and struggling to justify sending her people on the last death train before the Red Cross arrives, the Bible reappears to her. As she reads the words of John 3:16, she finally understands the depth of God's love and knows what she must do. Can you share your own faith experience? Are you quick to accept the Bible's teaching, or is it more of a process for you?

9. At the end of the story, Aric reunites with Stella, and though he's helped save the lives of her people, he knows

Germany is losing the war and that he must eventually answer to the world for his part in Hitler's scheme. Morty assures him the Jewish people will speak out in his favor, but if the story were to continue, what do you imagine the eventual outcome might be?

10. Stella clings to her precious Bible throughout, and as she and Aric discuss the future, he is ready to reclaim his Christian faith. Do you think Aric and Stella's faith journeys will continue? Why or why not? In what ways can they both continue to grow?

11. What particular event or detail in the story surprised you the most?

Acknowledgments

Initially I had no idea that *For Such a Time*, from its conception until the final pages of editing, would be such a personal and spiritual journey for me. My "coming home" story. And no pilgrimage reaches its proper end without a guide—first and foremost, God, with His infinite wisdom and patience in finally convincing this wretched soul to follow the right path.

My family—my husband, John, who never stopped believing; my son, Johnny, whose precious "together time" I compromised more than once while typing away for hours; my mom, Marjorie, my brothers, Michael and Matthew, dear sisters-in-law, Debbie and Terri, and my extended clan, Bill, Carolyn, and Linda—their incredible love and support kept me going along the way, especially those times when the road seemed more full of ruts than not. And to my two darling nieces, my nephew, and my grandson—thank you for reminding me to see life through a child's eyes, that with wonder and imagination anything is possible.

My dear friends Bill McKenna, Bonnie Ballew, Dotty Sohl (rest in peace), Ramona Nelson, Sandi Hill, and Sheila McKenna—it was your honesty and generosity of time as proofreaders that helped me to polish this body of work. And Robert Rabe, for lending your expertise of German, all I can say is Danke!

To my sisterhood of writers and critique partners—Anjali Banerjee, Debbie Macomber, Elsa Watson, Janine Donoho, Krysteen Seelen, Lois Dyer, Patty Jough Haan, Rose Marie Harris, Susan Wiggs, Susan Plunkett, and Sheila Roberts—all of you, my invaluable comrades; I am humbled by your selfless contributions, and your endorsements are testament to an unwavering conviction that I would eventually reach my destination.

Finally, to Linda S. Glaz, Hartline agent extraordinaire, and to my wonderful editor, Raela Schoenherr, and all those at Bethany House—you helped to make this author's dream come true. I thank you all, most affectionately.

"We know that all things work together for good for those who love God, who are called according to his purpose" (Romans 8:28).

About the Author

A Florida girl who migrated to the Pacific Northwest, **Kate Breslin** was a bookseller for many years. Author of several travel articles, award-winning poet, and RWA Golden Heart finalist, Kate now writes inspiring stories about the healing power of God's love. *For Such a Time* is her first novel. She lives with her family in Seattle, Washington. Learn more at KateBreslin.com.

If you enjoyed *For Such a Time*, you may also like…

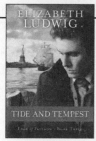
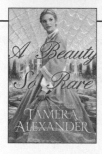

More Fiction You May Enjoy

When an abandoned child brings Nick Lovelace and Anne Tillerton together, is Nick prepared to risk his future plans for an unexpected chance at love?

Caught in the Middle by Regina Jennings
reginajennings.com

After three failed attempts, Everett Cline is not happy when yet another mail-order bride steps off the train—a woman he neither invited nor expected. But is she the wife he's been waiting for?

A Bride for Keeps by Melissa Jagears
melissajagears.com

Sadie is torn when she is offered the position of matron at the orphanage where she works. She loves her job, but she also loves her beau, Blaine—and tradition dictates she cannot have both.

A Home for My Heart by Anne Mateer
annemateer.com

MAY - - 2014

BETHANYHOUSE

Stay up-to-date on your favorite books and authors with our free e-newsletters. Sign up today at bethanyhouse.com.

Find us on Facebook. facebook.com/bethanyhousepublishers

Free exclusive resources for your book group! bethanyhouse.com/anopenbook

anopenbook